FORETOLD BY THUNDER

FORETOLD BY THUNDER

A Thriller

E. M. DAVEY

The Overlook Press
New York, NY

This edition first published in hardcover in the United States in 2016 by
The Overlook Press, Peter Mayer Publishers Inc.

141 Wooster Street
New York, NY 10012
www.overlookpress.com
For bulk and special sales please contact sales@overlookny.com,
or write us at the above address.

Cataloging-in-Publication Data is available from the Library of Congress

Typeset by Ray Davies

Manufactured in the United States of America

ISBN 978-1-4683-1296-6

2 4 6 8 10 9 7 5 3 1

For my parents

Contents

Fate

With domineering hand she moves the turning wheel,
Like currents in a treacherous bay swept to and fro.
Her ruthless will has just deposed once fearful kings,
While trustless still, from low she lifts a conquered head;
No cries of misery she hears, no tears she heeds,
But, steely hearted, laughs at groans her deeds have wrung.
Such is a game she plays, and so she tests her strength.
Of mighty power she makes parade, when one short hour,
Sees happiness from utter desolation grow.

Boethius, Roman scholar, 480-524 AD

Part One

Squall

It was by very accurately assessing their chances that the Romans conceived and carried out their plan to dominate the world.

Polybius, Roman historian, 200-118 BC

1

The journalist had been his last hope. But now there could be no salvation, for the thunderclouds were already gathering. Professor Roger Britton slammed down the phone and buried his head in his hands; but for the heaving of his lungs he was still.

The minute-hand of his clock moved onwards with a click.

Britton stared at it for precisely three seconds, before leaping to his feet and peering from the window. Black taxis inched along beside the Thames. A white Ford Transit which had been parked in a bus lane awoke and ambled away eastwards. The professor scrutinized the traffic: no green Renault Laguna, no silver Ford Focus, no gunmetal BMW. The list of cars he had to keep track of was increasing.

Was he going mad? He honestly didn't know.

Britton cancelled the morning's lectures, flinching at the protest. "Quite unavoidable," he insisted. "Last-minute preparations for the field trip."

The usual accusations ensued, but this time they were accompanied by threats of dismissal. Could he expect to find employment at another university as prestigious as King's College London? When had this become his life? Suddenly Britton realized his boss was no longer talking.

"Thank you," he said, in the hope she had been saying she understood. "I knew you'd understand."

He peeped into the common room. Florence Chung was working on her PhD, and he felt a stab of guilt. She had been a first-class assistant. No, more than that – a rock. And she was always willing to listen to his theories, although he kept the most outlandish close to his chest. He had neglected her thesis; she deserved better. But more important things were at hand.

He wondered if he would ever see her again.

"Professor?" Florence's eyes were wide. "Anything I can help with?"

Britton nodded rapidly, exhaling through both nostrils. "Yes please, Florence. I need some books. The Roman historians. Polybius, Livy, Tacitus, Cassius Dio. Anyone else? Ah yes ... you'd better bring Caesar too."

Florence glanced at the bookcase. "The first editions?"

Britton nodded grimly. Bugger them. Bugger them all.

What followed was a sight to make a Charing Cross bookseller weep. Chapters were torn free; cotton binding was ripped away; the room turned musty as dormant fibres took to the air. Britton's biro trembled as he circled words and underlined sentences. He was aware that his behaviour was demented, but he was past caring.

And it was important the journalist had everything.

Britton blinked twice – as though remembering something vital – and from his desk produced a slim paperback which he added to the pile of eviscerated pages. His fingers lingered on the cover before he remembered himself, urgency returning to his movements. Finally he bundled up the lot in brown paper and scribbled down an address.

The last thing Britton glimpsed before he departed was his wife, Wendy. The snap had been taken at a barbecue in Provence, before all this began. She looked happy. He pulled on his coat and rushed out.

A mature student was malingering on the staircase. Odd place to wait, now Britton thought of it, and he couldn't resist eye contact as he passed. His stomach slid instantly downward, adrenaline lancing through his thighs. He had seen this character before. Yesterday evening, in fact: *at a bus stop near his home in Enfield*. That snow-white spot in his hair was unmistakable. Coincidence? Britton fancied not.

Now Britton abandoned pretence and fled, taking the stairs three at a time, heart banging against his ribcage. Two students were coming in the other direction – female, attractive. He jinked past them, an improbable sight in bad tweed with his hair on end. Mirth echoed in his wake. When he reached the third floor he paused, listening as the laughter grew fainter.

It was penetrated by the patter of descending footsteps.

The philosophy department beckoned. Britton knew this place, he was familiar with the lecturers; yet today the department offered no sanctuary. Bored students flickered past his vision as he ran, package clasped to his chest and shoes squeaking on the carpet. The post trolley reared up before him like an iceberg. Britton hit it at full speed; letters and parcels flew across the corridor and a Trinidadian porter roared with indignation.

"Hey! Watch yourself, fool!"

The professor was apologizing and piling the packages back onto the trolley when the inspiration struck. He buried his own bundle with them, and in its place he swiped another, already franked and ready for dispatch.

The door behind him opened. It was the man from the bus stop. There could no longer be any doubt – the call to the journalist must have forced their hand. Britton was on his feet in an instant, offering the stranger a glimpse of brown paper in his arms. Then he was running for his life.

Hundreds of students were pouring out onto the Strand, and the professor found his way blocked by the throng.

"Oh God no," he whispered, glancing over his shoulder. "Please no ..."

They meant to kill him.

"You all right there, Professor?" Henry Buckingham was taking his course on ancient religion this year. Britton ignored the student, clawing his way into the press, feeling safer with every pace. He calculated his next move. If they grabbed him now the switch would be exposed. He needed to take the franked package off campus and get it posted – then they would chase the wrong parcel all the way to the sorting office.

There was a post-box on the Embankment.

A blast of winter air hit him in the face as he made it onto the street. A big trial was finishing at the Royal Courts of Justice and a phalanx of reporters rushed towards the famous arches. A blessing revealed itself: sightseers walking along the Thames, following their flag-waving leader like goslings behind a goose. Britton mingled with them, closing on the post-box. He was going to make it.

But wait ...

A BMW had emerged, a *gunmetal* BMW, crawling along the opposite side of the street. Britton felt a fresh convulsion of anxiety. The driver was plump and in his late thirties. Glasses, wavy brown hair. Was it that man who'd taken such an interest in him at the staff bar last week?

The shield of tourists parted. The professor slam-dunked the parcel into the post-box. At once the BMW zoomed away in a bark of highly-tuned engine.

Professor Britton considered his options. Temple was close by – he could take the Circle Line to South Kensington and dash for Heathrow. Then he would get the next flight to Istanbul, whatever the price.

Britton stopped dead. "Oh *shit!*"

Two German tourists gave the professor a wide berth, taken aback at the expletive from the mild figure. Britton didn't even notice. His mind shot back to the university, to his office, to the second drawer in his desk: where his passport still lay.

"Oh shit, shit, *shit!*"

There was a rumble overhead. The sky had turned overcast, a wash of grey that stretched from horizon to horizon. Directly above him the coming precipitation had been worked into a knot of black that twisted around itself in the sudden squall like the knuckles of a fist. Dark clouds streaked away to the north-west, their colour murderous. Tourists fumbled for umbrellas, but Britton was unmoved, staring into the heavens. A perplexed expression had come over his face – childlike, almost – and a pair of blueish lips mouthed something unheard. He followed the spoor of darker cloud to where it had emerged somewhere over Hampstead Heath. For several seconds he watched, as if seeking some hidden answer there. Then Professor Roger Britton was struck by lightning and killed instantly.

2

The historian's final telephone call had been to a reporter. Jake Wolsey was accustomed to fielding enquiries from the deranged, on whom newspapers seem to exert a magnetic pull – but his conversation with Roger Britton that morning stood out from a crowded field.

"I think I might have a story for you," the academic began.

Jake took a sip of coffee, brewed so strong it was masochistic. "Well fire away then, matey."

The news meeting was nigh and once again the reporter had nothing to bring to the table. He should be scrabbling for leads, not fobbing off some history wonk with a book to sell.

"I read your article today, Mr Wolsey."

Jake's gaze fell to that morning's paper – it lay open at page thirty-nine. His efforts had been subbed down to a measly hundred and fifty words, but at least they'd given him a byline for once.

"And I think I know why Winston Churchill was interested in the ancient Etruscans," Britton finished.

The journalist was paying attention now. He had thought it an intriguing tale, even if his editor disagreed. The genesis of the story was a single-line memo he'd spotted in a batch of newly-declassified Second World War documents. In darkest 1941, Churchill had scheduled a meeting with the head of MI6 on a topic described as '*the ancient Etruscan matter*'. And that was it: four little words, marooned by history, their explanation closed up and washed away by time. Jake's requests for elaboration from MI6 had been batted away – there would be no further disclosure. When his attempts to flesh out the story into a page lead had come to nothing it had gone in as a news-in-brief.

"Actually ...," and the professor paused, breath febrile on the receiver. "I think you may have stumbled across something rather big."

The reporter felt a tingle of editorial excitement in his stomach, though numbed by his hangover. "I'm listening."

In the next cubicle Thom Ellis pricked up his ears.

"Can we meet in person?" Britton asked. "I don't want to talk about it over the phone."

"Er, what? Why?"

"It's not safe."

Jake laughed. "What do you mean, not safe? We're talking ancient history here."

The journalist tucked long blond hair behind his ears and looked at his watch. This was starting to sound like a prank call.

"I can't," said Britton. "Sorry."

"At least give me a taster," said Jake. "We're fighting off the timewasters here."

He heard the 'glock' of an Adam's apple rising and falling as the professor mulled it over.

"Very well," Britton said at last. "How much do you know about the ancient Etruscans?"

"Only what I've mugged up on since I got hold of the file. They were the precursors to the Romans – a hill people who lived in modern-day Tuscany. At the height of their powers around, oh, 600 BC or something. Then they got swallowed up by the Roman Empire and the rest is, well, history."

"And what do you know of their religion?"

Jake leaned back in his chair to consider the question. He had a strong jaw and high cheekbones, but it was a lived-in face

– dark bags hung under his eyes and the arc of his spine was a chiropractor's despair.

"I haven't got the foggiest. I'm guessing they worshipped bearded, bonking, Brian Blessed types?" Jake's accent was rather posh, but his voice had a warm timbre.

"I suggest you do some more reading then," Britton replied. "Because it was to discuss religion that Mr Churchill met with his counterpart at MI6. Of that I am certain."

Jake's decision was made. "Look mate, thanks for your time," he said. "But I'm not sure it's one for us."

Protestations surged from the receiver. Then, with a click, Britton was gone.

"Nutter alert?" Ellis's eyes were alive with mockery.

Jake nodded. "Sad really. He was calling about my Churchill story this morning. You read it?"

"Not yet, not yet," muttered the big Mancunian, shuffling the newspaper. "Was just getting to it actually ..."

Jake massaged his eyelids with fingertips that trembled slightly. None of the staff bothered reading his work anymore – not since he'd been biffed downwards in the last reshuffle.

"No bother," he said. "The gist of it is that when Churchill should've been working out how to clobber Hitler he was wasting his time chin-wagging with MI6 about some ancient civilization."

Ellis's head moved from side to side as he weighed up the story. "Not a bad little story I suppose," he mused. "What's our man's take?"

"He wouldn't tell me on the phone," Jake said. "Not safe," he added with heavy irony.

Ellis rocked with laughter. "Man, that's a good one. Did I ever tell you about the guy who used to ring me up claiming the local council had installed listening devices in his flat? He thought they were targeting him because he'd appealed a parking ticket."

Jake ignored him. "The worry is this guy claimed to be a

professor at King's College London – that's a damn good university. And he thinks his phone's tapped because he wants to discuss ancient history. Poor bloke."

"Hey, that might be a decent line for you," said Ellis. "If this guy's well-known and coming out with stuff like that? It could be a giggle. What number did he ring from?"

Jake brought up the university's website. "Well, the call came from King's all right. And Britton exists."

There was a mugshot of the professor in the university's directory of experts. He was balding with a strip of auburn hair, a weak chin and a complexion mottled with patches of raspberry. It was not an appealing face. The professor had a number of books and papers in print, although the credits dried up about three years before.

Jake knew the feeling.

"There you go then," said Ellis. "That's a good yarn – top historian is paranoid nutcase. You need to keep your eyes open, pal."

"I don't know," muttered Jake. "It's just not me. Hounding some poor sod who's lost his marbles? I'll leave that for the red-tops."

Ellis shook his head. "You soft bastard. Well, don't come moaning to me that you don't bring in scoops anymore. You can't make an omelette without ..."

He was cut off by the phone ringing.

"Oh Christ," said Jake. "It's him."

"Let me handle it," said Ellis, mischief on his face.

But before he could answer Jake snatched up the receiver. "I'm sorry, Professor Britton, I'm afraid my mind's made up."

"I'll level with you, Mr Wolsey," Britton interrupted. "I think I'm being followed. I need your help, I really need your help."

Jake shielded the mouthpiece from his colleague. "Can I make a suggestion – have you considered discussing this with your GP?"

"You don't understand," shouted Britton. "You're just like all the others. Why won't anyone listen to me?"

On the other side of London someone was listening to them.

3

As the last traces of Professor Britton were being brushed from the Embankment that evening, Jake found himself in The Dolphin, King's Cross. The tremble in his fingers was gone and his pool cue glided over the fulcrum of thumb and forefinger. He blew a strand of hair from his brow and his brown eyes narrowed; the background fug of drinkers seemed to withdraw, belonging to a different place. Jake's life had become fuzzy and confused, like a lens knocked out of focus – only here on the pool table did it make sense. He released the shot with the crack of a sniper rifle and the black was assassinated.

They say skill at snooker is a sign of a misspent youth; reflecting on his adolescence, Jake could concur. He was clever but scatter-brained and only after muddling through university had he soared in ambition. That was before the booze had dragged him down again. Thirty-something, and he still hadn't grasped the vicious circle that linked falling achievement with rising intake of units. Jake took a double swig from his pint, the level falling by a clear inch.

"So what's this job then?" Luke McDonagh was a freelancer with a lazy eye whose freckled head reminded Jake of some kind of bean. He was also one of the best diggers in the business.

"An intriguing one, this," said Jake, handing the researcher his article. "Winston Churchill discussing classics with the Secret Service at the height of the war. I just don't know what to make of it."

"It's an oddity all right," said McDonagh. "What on earth's gone on there?"

"Lord knows. I've already whacked the Freedom of Information request in, but that'll take weeks to come back."

"Waste of time," said McDonagh. "If it's related to national security they can bat it back without explanation. They don't have to give you the information and they don't have to tell you why."

Jake smiled gloomily and took another gulp of lager.

"I'm thinking a forensic audit at the National Records Office in Kew," said McDonagh. "Let's find a linked document – cabinet minutes, other declassified files. Paperwork like this doesn't exist in isolation." He spun the black ball inside the triangle. "Do I get a bonus when it makes a front-page splash?"

"Ha ha, very funny."

McDonagh retrieved his cue, slapping the *London Evening Standard* on the table. Jake's pint was halfway to his lips when he saw the front page.

He let go of the glass.

The pint plummeted downward before exploding on the carpet in a foamy starburst.

McDonagh's trousers were soaked. "What the hell?"

"The paper," Jake croaked. "It's him."

The headline screamed: "*Lightning horror on the Thames.*"

Alongside the professor's photograph was an image of the strike itself, obtained from a nearby CCTV camera. The lightning bolt lanced to earth from the north-west, a jagged line of white in a sea of grey.

McDonagh peered at the mugshot. "You knew that guy?"

"Not really," said Jake. "He's some nutter – sorry – some bloke who rang me this morning. About this story, actually. He wanted to meet. But I gave him short shrift, I'm afraid. He wasn't well in the head. And now he's been struck by lightning, for Christ's sake."

The article's tone was grave, but as McDonagh read he struggled to keep the smile from his voice. "The professor had written several acclaimed papers on the ancient belief in interpreting the future through omens such as *lightning bolts.*"

4

Jenny Frobisher was four floors underneath MI6's Vauxhall headquarters and consequently, she calculated, actually *below* the Thames. She was also fuming – getting pulled off a case halfway through was a bloody nuisance. She had been tracking the Nottingham cell for the last eighteen months, and along with her colleagues in MI5 she'd linked the plotters to Lahore, northern Pakistan. This was not Al Qaida 'inspired' terrorism; it was the real deal. During the investigation Jenny could count the number of dinner parties she'd attended on one hand. But she was not a woman who let socializing get in the way of her job, nor did she mind as her circle of friends dwindled with each let-down, usually by telephone from some windswept northern service station. Even the collapse of her engagement hadn't distracted her. And now she'd been pulled from the case, the decision as abrupt as it was unexplained.

Jenny wore a charcoal skirt cut below the knee paired with an anonymous jacket. From the latter she produced a mirror to check her make-up. The face that stared back would have been attractive were it not so severely arranged. She wore her blonde hair in a neat bob and her pale blue eyes shone with intelligence.

There were two of them waiting to brief her: a silver-haired woman in early middle age and a man in his late thirties who looked flabby and slightly soft. Jenny had never laid eyes on either of them before. A copy of the *Guardian* lay on the man's desk and she glanced at the headline of the page at which it was open:

Britain's military power waning, says thinktank.

The man beckoned her to sit.

"Jenny, I take it? Apologies for hauling you off your job. Realize it's a pain in the arse." For a large man his voice was high and he struck her as rather effeminate. "This is Evelyn Parr," he said. The ladies exchanged nods. "And I'm Charlie. Charlie Waits."

Jenny had heard of him; only now did she see how wide of the mark her first appraisal was. The pupils observing her from behind tortoiseshell glasses were cold and his mouth was a small hard line. A knot of blood vessels had burst in the white of his left eye, an ugly sight. She needed to be more on her game to work for Charlie Waits.

Waits was a mythical figure within The Firm. He had stopped two IRA plots in their tracks by the age of twenty-five, before moving on to counter-espionage. There he'd done battle with his Chinese and Saudi counterparts, and seen more than one ambassador hauled into Whitehall for a dressing-down. Finally, aged twenty-seven or so, he'd vanished from the coalface – 'gone upstairs', it was widely assumed.

"Drink?" Waits's smile was drowned in the pads of his jowls.

Jenny glanced at her watch – it was 11.40 a.m. Was this some kind of test?

"No, thanks."

"Evelyn?"

The woman shook her head.

"Then I hope neither of you mind if I have a quick peg?"

They assented and Waits produced a bottle of Glenfarclas eighteen-year-old single malt. Jenny watched him half-fill a tumbler with the straw-coloured medicine. What decade was this? But Waits's fingers held the glass with the implacable grip of a glacier.

"We're asking you to work on a rather special brief," he said, sliding a file across the table. "There's a journalist we want you to monitor."

Jenny waited for him to continue, but Waits set down his drink and brought the tips of his fingers together. "That's all there is to it."

"What's the background? What's the case?"

"For now that's unimportant," said Waits. "I daresay if you stay on this beat you will, necessarily, learn more. We shall deal with the implications of that as and when they arise. It may be this journalist's nothing to worry about, in which case the problem goes away. So for now, be a sport and tell us what he's up to."

Parr spoke for the first time. "We want to know what stories he's working on, who he's talking to, that sort of thing."

"But we do want to know – *everything*." Waits ran a hand through his wavy brown hair, the handiwork of an expensive gentlemen's barber in Pimlico. "Leave out nothing whatsoever, no matter how daft it may seem."

Jenny pursed her lips as she digested the brief. "Fine. What's the level of intrusion?"

Waits waved a hand. "My dear, you can do whatever you like." The offhandedness in his voice was that of an elderly thespian. "You'll have a healthy war-chest. If you need more funds, just ask."

"So what's the journalist's specialism? Security?"

"Actually, he's a 'historical correspondent'."

Her brain whirred. "Some sort of declassified file issue then?"

Charlie's eyebrows shot up. "Perceptive, isn't she?"

"With respect, it could hardly have been anything else," she said. "Apart from declassified files it's a fluffy newsbeat, I should think. Can you tell me more about the journalist?"

Now Parr took over. "Jake Wolsey. Age thirty-three. Made the broadsheets eight years ago and before that with the local press. Our contact on the paper says he was a real high flyer when he arrived. The editor of the day took a shine to him – reckoned he had the 'gift of the journalistic eye', whatever that means. He lacks organization and ruthlessness, but rose on the back of being able to spot a story from nothing. Seeing things other people miss."

"A rather dangerous characteristic," observed Waits, a gleam in his eye.

"But he's been going backwards," said Parr. "Our man there reckons he's a drinker – in the last few years he's more or less stopped delivering the goods. That's why they shunted him to his current position."

"Personal life?" Jenny asked. "Foibles?"

"No relationships to speak of," said Parr. "Our contact thinks possibly gay. He used to go surfing in Cornwall a lot, but that seems to have petered out. An only child. His parents are still together – they live in Bath. The father's a retired actuary and his mother was a headmistress."

"Deputy headmistress," corrected Waits. "Now, I know I don't need to tell you this, but you're working on as high a grade of secrecy as MI6's lawyers have had the wit to enshrine in the English language. So do be discreet."

"Of course."

Waits's eyes darted from her, as though he were about to impart something distasteful. "By the way, this brief doesn't go to Reader Number One."

Jenny was shocked. Reader Number One was The Queen; every state secret crossed her desk.

"We're attaching three other watchers vetted to a similar grade," said Waits. "They'll be under your wing. You're in charge."

Jenny nodded, a touch of pink showing in her cheeks. "I'm really honoured, sir."

"Not sir," he scolded. "Charlie." He pronounced his own name delicately.

"Thanks, Charlie."

"One last thing." The spymaster's face was sympathetic. "I understand your mother isn't well?"

Jenny flinched – Mum had got her preliminary diagnosis only yesterday. How did they know these things?

"This job has the potential to become very – how shall I put it – *involving*," Waits said. "And before you sign on the dotted line, as it were, I just want to make sure you're ready to commit, regardless of any ... emotional difficulties that might lie around the corner."

The man was blandly enquiring whether she'd break stride in the event of her own mother's death. His detachment was staggering and very impressive. But Jenny wasn't able to keep the waver from her voice when she said, "The work comes first, Charlie, that goes without saying."

"Wonderful." Waits drained the last of his whisky and offered her a clammy handshake. "We'll be in touch."

As the lift sent Jenny purring up to ground level, one refrain looped through her mind. *What have I let myself in for?*

*

"So what do you think?" asked Parr once she'd departed. "The right choice? Or a little too curious?"

"Oh, definitely the right choice," replied Waits. "One does need a smattering of curiosity in this line of work. And have you seen her psychometric results? Her scores for loyalty and discretion are both off the scale."

"In any case, she's nothing we can't handle," said Parr with a private smile.

"Well, quite," said Waits. "Now, where shall we lunch?"

5

It was a quiet day for deaths, and the obituaries editor was happy to reserve Jake a few column inches if nobody important "popped their clogs". He felt guilty for not meeting Britton, who was survived by a wife; perhaps a write-up of his achievements would offer her some comfort. And visiting the university would be a good excuse to get out of the office. Jake needed the fresh air – he and McDonagh had made quite a night of it in the end.

The Embankment was teeming with barristers heading for

the Square Mile. Jake pictured period houses in Islington, a glass of red wine with supper, the cork back in the bottle – their clarity of mind seemed effortless. A post-box interrupted his thoughts. Jake had seen it in yesterday's *Standard*, and with a shiver he realized he was standing at the exact spot where Britton had lost his life. There was no chalk outline, no scorch-marks on the pavement; commuters hurried past as if the tragedy had never been. A Second World War sloop was moored at the riverside, the HQS *Wellington*. These days it was used for private functions, and a cook in chequered trousers was having a smoke on deck.

The reporter produced a notepad and trotted up the gangplank. "Did you see what happened yesterday?"

The cook smiled and shook his head. "Sorry, English no good."

Jake mimed a thunderbolt from above, flinging both hands towards the riverbank and making a plosive noise with his lips. "Lightning! Did you see?"

Enlightenment transformed the man's face. "Ah! Yes! Yes! But I no see. My manager, he see."

The ship's steward arrived, a south London gent with a silver barnet and a face like a toffee apple. "How can I help you sir?"

"I gather you saw the lightning strike?"

The steward nodded. "Awful business. I was checking this character" – he glanced at the chef – "had washed the deck, when I heard a load of tourists coming down the Embankment. The bloke who died was in the middle of the group, so I was staring right at him when it happened."

The steward was lost in the recollection, eyes milky. Jake used the hiatus to catch up on his quotes in shorthand.

"It looked as if he was rushing to make the Royal Mail collection," the steward continued. "He posts his letter, glances up and then he's hit by lightning, just like that. It was like a bomb going off – never known anything like it. I saw green for hours. Well of course, all the tourists were screaming and running to help the poor gentleman, but I could see it was useless. Half his head was missing, blown clean away."

Jake winced, but he kept writing.

"And that was it, really. The police came, ambulance, the works. We all knew he was dead of course – but I guess they have to do their box-ticking."

"Right, thanks for that. And is there anything you'd like to add? Anything I've missed out?"

It was the best bit of advice Jake got at journalism school: at the end of every interview, do not fail to ask the 'final question'. There might be something extraordinary the interviewee wants to get off their chest, the difference between a throwaway story and a front-page splash. But they're too nervous, or the right moment hasn't arrived.

The steward frowned. "Well ... there was something that struck me as a bit rum. When the emergency services are cleaning up the mess and so on a Royal Mail van turns up. The postman ducks under the police tape and empties the post-box, merry as could be. The coppers had a quick word, but then they let just him get on with it. It was about midday by then – normal collection times are 10 a.m. and 4 p.m. I guess the morning postie was running late and wouldn't allow death itself to get in his way. It seemed a bit disrespectful, like. You may be interested, you may not. But it might make a line or two?"

6

The dean of classics spoke about the debt the university owed Britton, his contribution to the discipline, yada yada yada. There was no anecdote, no sense of the man, and the don detected Jake's unease.

"Why not interview Britton's PhD student?" she suggested. "She accompanied him on a few digs. She'll be much better placed to flesh out the personality of the man than me."

But if Jake was expecting some dowdy old thing sniffling into her tea he was mistaken. The moment they were introduced – in Britton's very office – his heart juddered. *Why did she have to be beautiful?*

A string of failed relationships followed by a prolonged drought had left Jake incapable of conversation with attractive women. He forgot the basics, like whether you were supposed to hold someone's eye when speaking to them – and if so, for how long? The hotter the girl the more acute the problem, until he couldn't look them in the face at all. And so it was with Florence Chung. Oh Christ, he thought. *Ooooh Christ*.

She was third-generation Chinese, with a flawless complexion (always a turn-on) and a delicate, ethereal beauty. Her eyes were big and brown and on seeing him she smirked, revealing naughty incisors. Jake wondered what her legs were like and knew he would never sleep with her.

"I hear you want to talk to me about Roger?" Florence blinked and on cue her eyes were damp.

Jake stumbled over the condolences; when he grasped for his notepad the tremble in his fingers had returned.

"What was Professor Britton like?" he asked. "As a person."

"He was passionate about his work," she said. "And I mean truly passionate. It's just one of those things you say about dead people isn't it?" She laughed softly. "But with Roger it was the gospel truth. He *lived* for the period."

"Which was ancient religion?"

"Right. But he specialized in the Etruscans. We broke the earth all over Italy and made some important discoveries. It was his dream to piece together the entire *Disciplina Etrusca*."

"Sorry, the what? Can you spell that?"

She obliged. "It was the holy text of the Etruscans."

"Why are the Etruscans so important? If we want this obit to get a decent showing I need to really sell his achievements."

"They were a fascinating culture," she replied. "The first home-grown civilization on the Italian peninsula. The Etruscan dialect is unrelated to any other known language – it's as alien to Indo-European as the Kalahari click language. And they were the go-to people when it came to matters spiritual. If you wanted your fortune told in the ancient world, you'd find an Etruscan."

Jake chanced eye contact. "As it happens I wrote a story about the Etruscans earlier in the week. About a meeting set up in World War Two, by ..."

"By Winston Churchill!" she cried. "I read it. Very weird. I'd love to know more about all that."

Jake could feel her studying him – it no longer felt like an office in mourning.

"So then," he said to break the moment. "Tell me more about Etruscan religion."

"It was a different kettle of fish to Graeco-Roman theology," she said. "A bit ... darker, somehow."

"What do you mean by that?"

"Well, Greek and Roman Gods were all humanoid figures, running around sleeping with each other and getting plastered on nectar. But the earliest Etruscan Gods were formless, manifesting themselves in the air itself – closer to the modern idea of God, perhaps."

"How is that darker?"

"Because the Etruscans gave themselves over to their Gods completely – they dominated man's every activity. The Etruscan religion was pure subordination. In that respect I suppose it was nearer to Islam. 'Submission', as Islam translates to."

"I wouldn't exactly call Islam a 'dark' religion," said Jake.

"No, me neither," she snapped. "That's not what I meant. Anyway, Etruscan religion took submission to a different level. The Etruscans had a real dread of all these dark forces swimming around them. Man was a complete non-entity – he was under the thumb, his fate utterly in the Gods' hands."

"Sounds like a barrel of laughs."

Florence ignored him. "Etruscan religion was all about

attempting to divine the will of these dark forces by various means. Like examining livers of sheep, observing the flights of birds, or studying bolts of ..." she sighed.

"Lightning," Jake finished.

7

"Hence the irony."

It was a mistake. Tears sprang back into Florence's eyes at the comment and she stared out at the Embankment. Jake noticed the curve of her neck.

"I'm sorry," he said. "I shouldn't have gone there."

Florence sniffed. "It's just ... the other students are *laughing* about it, like this is some kind of joke. 'He didn't see that one coming,' and so on. Can you believe it?"

Jake sought a change of subject. "Tell me more about this ..." He flipped through his notepad for the two words that were not encoded in shorthand. "*Disciplina Etrusca*."

At once Florence was composed. "The story goes that some farmer was ploughing a field when he unearthed a live child," she said. "He was a young boy, but wizened as an elderly man. This kid was called Tages, and he revealed the *Disciplina Etrusca* to the farmer. It was essentially a rulebook concerning the relationship between the Gods and human beings. A precise guide to divining the will of the divinities, and ergo the fates of men. Along with Judaism, Etruscan religion is the only *revealed* religion of the ancient Mediterranean. In other words, God dictated the holy text to man word for word."

"And Roger was trying to, what, track down a copy of this *Disciplina* thing?"

"He was piecing it together bit by bit. No one will ever find a complete copy. Etruscan religion was considered heretical by the early Christians – all its sacred texts were destroyed. No

Etruscan literature survives, no history. Virtually everything we know is from inscriptions on graves. Here ..."

Florence slid an inscription across the dead man's desk. It looked slightly like Greek – but runic and primitive, a barbarian script.

"Of all the inscriptions yet discovered, just eight are more than a hundred words long," she said. "Three of those eight were found by Roger and me."

The Hollywood smile revealed itself.

"What did you discover?" asked Jake. This was good material.

"The *Disciplina Etrusca* was split into three books," she replied. "The first was the *Libri Haruspicini*, which dealt with examining livers. The second was about rituals – the proper ceremonies to carry out when founding cities and so on. But everything we discovered was from book three – the *Libri Fulgurales*."

Book of Thunder.

*

"Together we found two new passages," said Florence. "One in Rome, the other at a dig near Naples. We were supposed to be going to Istanbul next week to look for another segment."

That perfect lower lip wobbled. Jake risked a glance at it: a cherry-red sack, barely a fingertip long. He had the mad impulse to put his hand over hers, but of course he did not. The moment drew out and became uncomfortable.

"I have to ask this," the journalist said eventually. "I get the feeling Roger was – troubled, somehow. Am I right?"

Florence looked at Jake with vulnerable eyes. "You wouldn't write anything bad about him?"

"Strictly for background."

"You promise?"

"I flatter myself that I'm a proper journalist," he said. "I am not in the habit of lying to people."

Florence nodded and blinked. "Roger was depressed. He'd

lost credibility. He'd got a bit too tangled up in all the old beliefs. It happens to academics sometimes, when they've spent a lifetime living their subject. Roger was never overt about it, but he would make pointed comments every now and then to the effect that some aspects of Etruscan religion were worth taking seriously. That was enough to shoot his reputation. Then about six months ago he began getting seriously withdrawn. Paranoid, even."

"Why?"

Florence put her hands up. "I don't know, ok?"

After a pause, Jake said, "Right, that's probably enough material. I'm so sorry for disturbing you when everything's still so fresh."

"It's fine."

A statuette of a robed man wearing a cap shaped like an inverted funnel stood on the bookshelf.

"Who's that guy?" asked Jake. "He looks hilarious."

"He belongs in a museum really," said Florence. "But you wouldn't think he was funny if you were an Etruscan. In any way. He's a *fulguriator*. A lightning priest."

Jake studied the figurine. The orientalized eyes and eerie smile were a far cry from the realism of Roman sculpture and he saw then how the Etruscans were worlds apart from their contemporaries: China to the West.

"I'd be fascinated if you get anything more on that Churchill stuff," said Florence. "It was nice meeting you, Jake."

Unexpectedly she squeezed his hand; Wolsey felt an alarming flare of blood in his loins.

How can you be an archaeologist?

"Florence ..." A giddy moment. "Can I have your number?"

The smile departed her face.

"Just in case I find anything else out about the Churchill stuff," Jake backtracked, feeling his face turn beetroot. It was time to go.

"Of course you can," said Florence, sweetness again.

On the other side of London someone was breaking into Jake's flat.

8

It always made Jenny Frobisher smile to see Hollywood's depiction of a Secret Service incident room. There would be banks of glowing monitors, agents roaming around some 3D-rendered desert, satellites being repositioned at a moment's notice. The reality was somewhat different, Jenny thought, as she looked about her base of operations. Four computers, four telephones, whiteboard, kettle. The only impressive thing was the view of the Thames. She could make out a guide pointing up at them from the deck of a tourist ferry as he honed his James Bond spiel.

Jenny considered her team. There was Alexander Guilherme – a small, shrewd man whose parents were Sri Lankan émigrés. He was very London, very street; she knew from his file that in the Eighties he'd hung out with New Romantic bands and used cocaine. Paradoxically, MI6 valued such people. By confessing drug use or sadomasochism at the first opportunity, an agent became impossible to blackmail. At that moment Guilherme was in Battersea, dressed in workman's overalls and removing a window pane from Jake Wolsey's back door.

Sat in front of her was Jess Medcalf of Belfast: feisty, foul-mouthed and flame-haired. Like Guilherme, Medcalf was a party animal, but she was tough too. Her records revealed that as an eighteen-year-old she had beaten up two Catholic teenagers (both male) who'd attempted to assault her. Medcalf's crime had been wearing a Rangers shirt. One of her attackers ended up in hospital.

The third of Jenny's team was Edwin de Clerk, a computer boffin back from secondment at GCHQ's listening post in Cheltenham. He was pale and lank-haired, but a gifted triathlete. De Clerk was also a genius. They had trained together in Gosport; then as now amorous interest radiated from him shyly.

"Ok, folks," Jenny began. "For as long as this job continues, we work twelve-hour shifts. Edwin's the computer geek, so he'll be based here."

"It's true," de Clerk admitted. "I am a geek. That's why I love this job – I get to be surrounded by people just as geeky as me, all pulling together for a common purpose."

Jenny felt his eyes linger and averted her gaze. After the travesty of her engagement she had forsworn relationships altogether, at least for the foreseeable future. She had the sense men found her attractive and she would use this to her advantage if the job demanded. But romancing a colleague? Not a chance.

"That means the rest of us will have to take turns keeping tabs on the journalist," she finished. "One by day and one by night, while the third agent rests."

"Nice of you to join in with all the sneaking about," said Jess Medcalf.

"Nothing hacks me off like the boss being cosy and tucked up in bed while I'm up all hours," said Jenny. "Besides, I don't know why, but the powers that be have given us way less manpower than we need for a watch like this. We all need to muck in."

"I've already got a tap on his personal mobile and landline," said de Clerk. "The work phone's not far off."

"Just how hard are we going on this dude?" asked Medcalf. "Like, are we tapping his fecking parents?"

"Yes," said Jenny. "Good thought."

"And bugging their house?"

"No. Actually ... actually, yes. We'll see if we can spare Alexander to get down there tomorrow. Edwin, how close are we to his emails?"

De Clerk was frowning. "I've already got the Gmail account,

but the paper's security is tougher than most. Give me a couple more minutes."

"Good stuff. Alexander's putting ears in his flat, and he's got a little moped – a sky-blue Vespa. We'll get a tracker on that too."

Medcalf made furious notes.

"One more thing," said Jenny. "This is basic stuff, but I want you to all make sure your passports aren't out of date. Wolsey travels at short notice. His last ports of entry were Paris, Marrakech and Warsaw."

De Clerk stopped typing. "Jenny, do you have even a clue what this is all about?"

She smiled. "Edwin, as of this moment I haven't the faintest idea."

Jenny's phone bleeped; her smile tightened. Another text from Dad.

9

Where to begin the obituary? Going in on the lightning strike would be crass, but Jake had to start somewhere and Florence had given him a wealth of material to choose from. The plink of an arriving email interrupted his cogitations. It was a response from the Cabinet Office. His Freedom of Information request had been rejected. Already. That was weird – usually they prevaricated for weeks. Jake swept aside the sea of press releases and business cards that covered his desk and a tower of new post capsized under the wash. There was a package from King's College London.

Britton.

Jake turned the parcel around in his hands – it crinkled to the touch and when he opened it he was assailed by the whiff of old paper. This was normally a pleasant perfume, but now the odour only heightened his unease. He turned the package upside down and a bundle of pages spilled out.

Dear Mr Wolsey,
I hope you won't find this overdramatic, but I want to entrust this to you. If anything untoward happens to me, I hope you will have the decency to give it your full attention.
Respectfully yours,
Roger Britton

Jake's mouth was dry.

Well ... there was something that struck me as a bit rum.

An idea came to him and he called the Royal Mail.

"I'm doing a survey on collection times," he said. "You've got a letterbox on the Embankment, just west of Blackfriars Bridge. It was supposed to be emptied at 10 a.m. yesterday. Could you confirm whether that happened on time?"

"Right ..." Suspicion seeped from the press officer's voice. "Let me find out – we'll call you back."

As Jake waited, his gaze settled on a page of *The Histories* by Polybius, a Roman historian who lived in the second century BC. Britton had quadruple-underlined a paragraph.

The Romans succeeded in less than 53 years in bringing under their rule almost the entire inhabited world. It was an achievement without parallel in human history.

Jake frowned, rummaging through the pile. Another Polybius quotation caught his eye, this one on the defeat of Hannibal by the Roman general Scipio Africanus. Britton had marked it with a star.

Scipio made the men under his command more sanguine and more ready to face perilous enterprises by instilling into them the belief his projects were divinely inspired.

This was off the hook. Madness.

Amid the mass of pages lay a single paperback – *Life of Constantine*, written in the fourth century AD by Eusebius, a Roman historian and a Christian. It was the only unmarked item. Jake was still examining the book when the press officer phoned back.

"I can confirm that post-box postcode WC2 2PR was emptied at 10.06 a.m. yesterday," he said. "That's well within our targets."

Jake digested the information. "How can you be so sure of the time?"

"We record the progress of our vans through sat-navs. The collection was spot on – you won't be twisting this into a negative story I trust?"

Jake ignored the question. "When was the next collection made?"

There was a clicking of buttons. "Ten past four in the afternoon."

That was four hours after the boat steward had seen what purported to be a Royal Mail van empty the post-box a dozen paces from Britton's cooling body. Jake felt a little ill as he replaced the receiver. It was unreal. Plus it made no sense. When he ran a hand through his mane his hair felt claggy – he'd overslept that morning and had no time to shower.

On impulse he dialled Florence Chung.

"Hello, who is this please?"

Saints preserve us, he was actually speaking to her.

"It's Jake," he managed, regretting not having planned what to say. "We met earlier."

"Oh. You."

"Listen. There's been a development. Can we catch up?"

There was another pause. Then she said, "No, sorry. I'm flying out to Turkey this evening – the field trip's going ahead."

"I received a package in the post today from Roger Britton."

"Really?" Florence's whole voice had changed. "What was in it?"

"Pages, lots of pages – torn out of old hardbacks by the looks of it. He's underlined a few sentences. And one whole book – *Life of Constantine* by Eusebius."

"What else? Anything about Istanbul?"

Jake shuffled the pile. Bingo! "Yes – there's a diagram of the Agya Sophia here too."

The cathedral had been built in the city by Romans fifteen hundred years ago – it still stood.

"I have to see this diagram."

"Well ... let me come with you then."

Bemusement morphed into laughter. "I don't think so. Look Jake –"

"I can cover your dig," he interrupted, thinking fast. "Britton's death is the perfect peg."

"Peg? Excuse me?"

He bit his lip. "Sorry. Sorry. 'Peg' was insensitive."

"Why are you even interested in this?"

Jake could almost hear Florence's eyes narrowing. His thoughts crystallized. Freak occurrence of lightning aside, he was onto something here – and it centred on Britton. This sort of lead came along rarely; if he made something of it perhaps he could turn things around at the paper. He should stick close to Florence. Their presence in Istanbul might draw out more information.

"Hello?" She sounded impatient.

"It'll make a cracking feature," Jake blustered. "And great publicity for the university too. Besides, do you want me to share Britton's package with you or not?"

She sighed. "Fine, you can come. It doesn't look like I have any choice, does it? But you'll need to clear it with our media centre first."

The reporter was grinning like a loon as he put the phone down. Things were moving again. To Istanbul! To

Constantinople, as it once was! To the city founded by the Emperor Constantine, the ruler who had made Christianity the state religion of Rome. The crossroads of Europe and Asia.

His eyes were drawn back to that innocuous white book.

10

Jake scooped up the bundle and half-ran to see his news editor. More grim news for Europe raced across the overhead tickers: recovery flat-lining, stock markets in freefall, debt marching upward. China had just posted eight per cent growth, a performance any Western premier would kill for.

Niall Heston was perched at the end of the newsdesk. He was thin with a high forehead, wispy hair and an aquiline nose, like a hunting falcon in a suit. Heston was the link between reporters and the editor-in-chief. The big boss decided on the front-page splash, whether to run something legally hazardous and so on, while Heston kept him updated with the best prospects. In theory he knew what every reporter was working on and which exclusives would hit the streets in three days' time. It was the most enervating role in the newspaper.

"Aha! Scoop Wolsey! What crackers have you got in store for us today?" Heston's Aberdeen lilt oozed sarcasm – he had his favourites and Jake was not among them.

"I think I'm onto something good this time," said Jake.

Heston shot his underling a look. "Should I be calling David back from The Ivy?"

Jake forced a laugh.

"Go on then, what have you got for me?"

Jake rattled through the events of the last twenty-four hours: the unhinged professor, the mysterious postal run and now Britton's package.

Heston tapped his lips with his forefingers. "What are you saying then, Jake? There's some kind of conspiracy surrounding this professor and the forces of darkness have contrived to call down a *lightning strike* on his head?"

"Well, obviously the lightning strike's just coincidence."

"Right, good, glad we've got that cleared up. It's reassuring to know my highly-paid reporters aren't living entirely in cloud-cuckoo-land. So what exactly *have* we got? What have we got that's concrete, that I can run?"

"We've got a professor saying he's being followed."

"A *mad* professor," Heston interjected.

"And a day later he winds up dead."

"Killed by a freak of nature," said Heston. "A lightning strike for fuck's sake, witnessed by dozens of tourists."

"And we've got this phoney postal van making a collection at completely the wrong time."

"Bloody Royal Mail lying bastards covering their own arses," said Heston. "What's the likelier explanation – bullshitting postman is late for delivery, or some grand conspiracy to steal a package from a discredited academic who you've already admitted had lost the plot, big time?"

"What about the note?" Jake pleaded. "Britton writes an 'if anything happens to me' letter and a day later he's dead. Doesn't that strike you as strange? It's like ... it's like Princess Di telling people she thought MI5 were arranging an accident for her."

Heston burst out laughing. "Oh man, I can't believe you even *said* that. You just played the Diana Card! Right, definitely not a story."

Jake loathed this man.

"Why are you even telling me all this?" Heston continued. "What do you want to do with this so-called 'information' you've collected?"

"Britton's assistant is off to Istanbul to carry on his work."

"Ah, you fancy a nice wee jolly, is that it?" Heston sighed through his nose.

"We've got exclusive access," said Jake.

"Well, I suppose it might make a decent colour piece," Heston muttered. "But forget all this conspiracy shit, ok?"

"Fine."

"One more thing. Remind me when your contract expires?"

Jake felt a sickening in his gut. "This September ... why?"

"Just bear that date in mind, eh? If you're going to be burning more of my money on this caper I want some seriously shit-hot copy. Do I make myself clear? Seriously shit-hot."

Jake nodded.

"Are you sure you want to go? Do you understand what I'm getting at? If you want to change your mind, now's the time."

This was it – one of those moments on which pivots a career, a life.

"I'm sure."

"Very well then. The die is cast."

Jake felt giddy as he walked from the newsdesk. Strange decision.

The die is cast.

As Caesar said when he crossed the Rubicon.

11

Mum's hands had acquired a translucence of late. The skin reminded Jenny of cling film – it was silky, detached from the flesh. She found it difficult to reconcile this timid creature with the person who was once her mother. The woman who had bought her into the world without a bit of fuss was huddled in bed and peeping from the sheets.

With an effort Margaret remembered something. "How's Marc?"

"Mum, I told you already. We split up."

"Oh ... that's a shame. Sorry, I've got a memory like a sieve nowadays."

They had this conversation every visit and Jenny knew what was coming.

"He seemed like such a nice man," said Margaret, sticking to the script. "You were getting married, weren't you? Or were you?"

"We were. Until he dumped me."

For a moment some of the old fire returned to her mother's eyes. "The bastard. Well, it's his loss."

She slurred the 'ss' in loss.

Jenny had been taken aside when she arrived at Hammersmith Hospital.

"There's still no definitive diagnosis," said Dr Bryant. "But we're ninety-nine per cent sure it's genetic. Degenerative, too. It resembles early stage Huntington's – clumsiness, forgetfulness, a loss of balance. But the tests show it's *not* Huntington's, and we just don't know what it is. I'm afraid that leaves Margaret slightly in the lurch."

"Do you know what's causing the symptoms?"

"Her nerve cells are wasting." Dr Bryant moved gracefully and he had an aura of poise. "If it carries on we can expect further worsening in memory and speech. You might have noticed she's developed a slight slur in the last few days."

Jenny closed her eyes.

"I'm sorry," he said. "I simply can't imagine how upsetting all this must be."

Her eyes shot open. "I'm fine," she said. "What happens now?"

"Well, we continue to monitor her and do tests. The chances are someone else has had this before. It's just a question of finding them and then we can design a treatment programme."

"What's her prognosis? And please, do be blunt with me."

"It's difficult to say," admitted Dr Bryant. "If it follows the pattern of Huntington's we can expect deterioration on all fronts. Eventually breathing's affected. Then ..." his voice tapered off. "Heart function."

Jenny's eyelids closed again; this time the doctor kept his mouth shut.

"Is she unhappy?" she said.

"She gets distressed sometimes. But you must be thankful she recognizes you. Her long-term memory seems to be holding up – but it's definitely worth prompting it when you can. And she's still cracking jokes. That's a good sign."

Jenny willed herself to see the positive. "She was a formidable woman, you know."

The doctor had smiled at that. "I'm quite sure."

*

"Do you remember how you were always trying to get me interested in art when I was a little girl?" Jenny tried. "But all I wanted to do was play cops and robbers."

Margaret smiled gratefully, as if slipping into a hot bath. "Of course, dear," she said. "But you would only be the cop. You only wanted to be one of the goodies."

Jenny felt a weight press on her larynx.

"I miss ..." said Margaret. "I miss ..."

"Miss what, Mum?"

"I miss my kitchen."

Jenny laughed, spluttering as two emotions collided in her throat. The threat of tears dissipated. Silly cow, she scolded herself.

"Always wanted to be one of the goodies, you did," murmured her mother.

Jenny's phone buzzed – it was Alexander Guilherme.

"I'm at Heathrow," he said, the statement corroborated by a flight announcement in the background. "You need to get here right now – Wolsey's on the move."

"Oh *sugar*."

"He's booked onto the next BA flight to Istanbul. I've got us both a seat."

"See you there."

Her mother stirred. "Trouble, love?"

"Oh, work stuff. I'm really sorry, Mum, but I have to go, something's come up. Dad's coming in tomorrow."

"That'll be nice," said Margaret. "But don't let him put himself out on my account."

Jenny kissed her on the cheek, pausing to inhale; the scent was part of her own body.

"Mum, listen to me for a moment – this is important."

Margaret looked bewildered. "What is it, love?"

"We're going to take you back to your kitchen soon, no matter what. I promise."

As Jenny departed a thought occurred to her and she sought out Dr Bryant.

"You said this disease may be hereditary. That means I might be carrying it, right?"

The doctor looked evasive. "It's possible."

"What are the odds? If it was Huntington's, say."

"Not great," he admitted. "For Huntington's it's fifty-fifty."

Jenny blanched. "Is there a test?"

She had to know.

"Miss Frobisher, we haven't even worked out what your mother's fighting yet."

As Jenny sat on the Heathrow Express that evening she had things on her mind.

12

"There's something utterly vulgar about flying sober," said Jake, downing the dregs of his glass. "Whereas the gin and tonic harks back to the golden age of travel."

Despite herself, Florence laughed. She had made it clear a Heathrow chain pub was beneath her, but when it came to matters alcohol Jake would not be gainsaid. As he headed to the bar to buy more drinks, Florence realized she was making eye contact with a slight Chinese man. She turned away.

Jake watched her pore over Britton's package as he waited to be served. She wore hiking boots and a fleece top with no make-up, and her hair was pinned up in carefree fashion with a wooden chopstick-type thing. His heart screeched with desire.

The reporter set drinks on the table. "I've been going through the bundle chronologically," he said. "Britton was completely obsessed with lightning. For example, he underlined a bit about Hostilius, the second king of Rome, who was supposedly killed by a lightning bolt for rejecting the Gods. I didn't know Rome even *had* kings."

"Oh, it did, way back when," said Florence. "Actually, when Rome was a backwater it was ruled by Etruscan monarchs for a while. Then the revolution came."

Jake extracted a page from the bundle. "Here's another quote he's underlined, from Pliny this time. Etruscan lands were supposedly laid waste by some character called Olta – and hey presto, Olta got bumped off by lightning too."

Florence waved a hand. "Like I told you, Britton lost the plot. Anyway, death by lightning from the Gods is one of the oldest and most worn-out archetypes imaginable."

"I know, I know," said Jake. "It's just a coincidence given –"

Florence silenced him with a look and began examining the

plan of the Agya Sophia. The profusion of domes and buttresses resembled the blueprint of some extraterrestrial microchip.

"Is this the only diagram he left you?" she asked.

"Afraid so."

"God, he was a suspicious sod. He's made almost no notes on the diagram at all – I've got nothing to go on." Florence sipped her cocktail, gagged and spat into a tissue. "What the hell is *that* doing in there?"

He laughed. "It's only a blackberry."

"I'm very allergic," she replied, pushing away her glass.

Jake had an eye on the discarded drink as he asked, "What are you actually looking for out there?"

"A brontoscopic calendar. It gave a prediction in the event of lightning on each day of the year. The longest passage of the Book of Thunder yet discovered is a brontoscopic calendar." She passed him a translation. "Pick a day at random."

"June 16th," read Jake. " 'If it should thunder, it threatens not only dearth of food but war, while a prosperous man shall disappear from public life.' But surely it thunders somewhere every day of the year?"

"This calendar only applies for northern Italy," said Florence. "If you bought into this stuff, a unique calendar would be needed for each location."

Jake produced a notepad. "Do you mind? This is good background."

Florence assented. "There are plenty of theories about why the Etruscans went in for lightning prophecy in such a big way," she said. "The beginning of Etruscan religion coincided with a period of increased activity from the sun, which affected the earth's electrical field. That meant worse weather, more rainfall – and some spectacular storms."

Jake scanned through the calendar. "There's loads about farming here. Crops, animals, diseases ..."

"Understandably," said Florence. "The Etruscans were totally dependant on the land and the seasons, so they obsessed over a good harvest. But there's geopolitics too. Listen to the 12th of March: 'If it thunders a powerful man in politics will be overthrown. On his behalf battles will be waged.'"

Jake chuckled. "Beware the Ides of March! I wonder, was lightning spotted in Tuscany before Julius Caesar's assassination?"

"I hadn't thought of that – and Caesar is said to have ignored the warning of an Etruscan soothsayer before he was killed."

Jake wasn't listening. "Fascinating document," he said. "What's the Istanbul connection?"

"The text that survives was written there in 600 AD, when Constantinople was part of the Byzantine Empire. It was translated by a scribe called John the Lydian from a lost original. By then Etruscan civilization had been dead for centuries, but Britton was looking for John the Lydian's source material, the Etruscan master-document he translated into Byzantine Greek."

"If you already have this Byzantine translation, what's the point?"

"The Byzantine Empire was fanatically Christian," said Florence. "By sixth-century standards John the Lydian's material was seriously risqué. Britton reasoned he may have watered down the original calendar, because this translation's very sparse. As a matter of fact, we know Etruscan thunder prophecies depended on much more than the date alone. They looked at the colour and shape of the lightning, whether it struck the ground, if it damaged anything – and crucially, where it originated. Lightning from the north-east was a favourable omen, but lightning from the north-west was very bad news."

"Why look in the Agya Sophia?" asked Jake.

"Britton thought John the Lydian's grave might be there somewhere. If the scribe had a penchant for the *Disciplina Etrusca*, perhaps a line or two was buried with him. But the Agya Sophia was the largest enclosed space on earth for a millennium. There are acres of wall, hundreds of chambers and vaults, and all Britton's left us is this" – she stirred the pile – "a load of nonsense about ancient Rome."

"What's the plan then?" asked Jake. "You can hardly start knocking down walls."

"Of course not, it's a reconnaissance mission. To damage the fabric, in Turkey? You don't want to even think about the bureaucracy. If we can work out where his tomb is hidden, then the paperwork begins."

Jake grimaced. Niall Heston would not consider the write-up of a gentle academic potter "shit-hot copy", and the chances of finding anything looked remote. Would he have a job this time next year? If so, his instinct that there was more to Britton's downfall than met the eye needed to be spot on.

"Did you ever think there might be a good reason why Britton was suspicious?" he ventured. "Just because you're paranoid doesn't mean they're not out to get you and all that."

Florence studied him. "Why do you ask?"

Jake handed her Britton's final note. "He thought something was going to happen to him."

"He was mad," she whispered. "Brilliant, but mad."

13

Istanbul in January can be an ugly city. Mass housing on the outskirts, rising from barren earth like dragon's teeth; the harbour mucky and whipped into scum; the cityscape bleak against iron-shod skies. Istanbullus hurried along in anoraks and scarves, carrying themselves with all the grace of Londoners in rush hour. Only the mosques relieved the eye. The minarets rose in thickets, like bulrushes, pointing out the heavens.

Florence had booked a hotel in the Sultanahmet district, where the cobbles and wooden houses were more to Jake's taste. And he was relieved to see alcohol on sale everywhere – perhaps the Laphroaig he'd bought in the airport was unnecessary. Better safe than sorry, though. He had been caught short in Islamic countries before.

Florence had barely talked on the flight, engrossing herself in Britton's legacy. But if anything was hidden there it had eluded her, and she had grown infuriated.

"Why the heck did he leave us *Life of Constantine*?" she muttered as they took the sea air on the little toe of the European continent. "Eusebius lived two hundred years before John the Lydian. And this of all of his works! Chapter after chapter about what a devout Christian the emperor was – you'd never guess Constantine murdered his own family."

Jake didn't reply. He had learned that the archaeologist had moods in which she was best handled like a poisonous flower: from a distance and with gloves on. Instead he gazed out to Asia Minor, once gifted to Rome in the will of a Greek king.

Work at the Agya Sophia began at 9 a.m. the next day. The neighbouring Blue Mosque is the more famous sight, but it was the Agya Sophia that filled Jake with awe. The Sophia's crowning glory is a dome some hundred feet wide – during construction many had said that it could never support itself. The clay-red leviathan fell away beneath the rim, arch upon balustrade upon buttress.

"A truc monument to devotion," said Jake. "I've never seen anything like it."

He glanced at Florence, expecting scorn – but she was smiling at him.

A representative from the Archaeological Museum of Istanbul gave the pair a tour. Dr Adnan Gul had an explosion of pewter hair, skin like a used teabag and a nicotine-yellow moustache. Jake warmed to him at once. They entered through the Portal of the Emperor, with its forty-foot doors of oak and iron. Within was the biggest room he had ever set foot in, hewn from marble of blue and volcanic pink.

The scale of the undertaking hit him in full.

*

Jenny peered over the balcony. The people below were like matchsticks, but she could identify Wolsey by his shock of blond hair. He stood with palms flat as if steadying himself, and his mouth was a dot of black.

Her radio crackled.

"Can you see him?" said Jess Medcalf. "Coming through the really big door."

"I've got him," she replied. "I take it that's Chung?"

"That's her," said Medcalf. "I don't know if you can tell from up there, but man, she is a *hottie*."

Jenny's radio crackled again.

"We don't know who the third guy is," said Alexander Guilherme, who had attached himself to an Indian tour group. "A Turk, by the looks of it. They met outside – by appointment, I would say. It was all very formal."

Jenny's eyes went right, to where Medcalf was inspecting a brass chandelier strung from a hundred and twenty feet up. She smiled. They were a good team. But so they needed to be. Jenny felt another surge of adrenaline at what they were about to do.

14

It was the journalist's departure for Istanbul that had precipitated the decision. Charlie Waits had collected his thoughts and announced: "Oh, all right then. Let's get him."

The spymaster's voice was effete without being fey – Jenny found him rather frightening.

"Run along to the embassy in Istanbul," he continued. "We'll send a bag for you by dip-post. Pick it up and do what needs to be done."

Waits's next pronouncement was lost to Jenny. Her handler's voice was level as he hung up and said to the wall: "Fuck and shit and damn and balls."

The Foreign Office could send everything except radioactive material by diplomatic bag – no doubt cocaine was a frequent flyer. Yet the spymaster's gift was deadlier than Peruvian powder, and Jenny felt a chill in her bladder as she opened the Samsonite briefcase. Nestled within were three 8.5mm pistols, made from toughened porcelain to evade metal detectors. Lying alongside were the silencers, fat as leeches. There was another brick of Turkish lira, and then the *pièce de résistance*. Jenny couldn't help but smile. MI6 still did things with a flourish. The case contained two umbrellas with tips that could fire a capsule into the human body from close range using compressed gas. It was with such a device the Bulgarian Secret Service had assassinated a dissident on Waterloo Bridge in 1978 – the ricin took four days to kill him. She turned one of the umbrellas around in her hands. Black, masculine, expensive-looking. The canvas of the second umbrella was a printed ladybird. An old trick, that. Introduce one memorable detail and it's all the witnesses can recall – they would describe Medcalf's ladybird umbrella, but not her above average height nor her blue-green eyes.

And now the device was to be used.

A crowd eavesdropped on the old Turk as he pontificated on a carved pavilion that stood in the centre of the basilica. Medcalf loitered nearby, a splodge of scarlet protruding from her coat pocket. Jenny watched Jake rush to pick up a mitten that had been tossed from a pushchair by a toddler. He gave it to the child's mother – she hadn't noticed the garment being cast away and her gratitude was obvious. Jenny closed her eyes, opened them again.

"Jenny?" Guilherme was the spotter. "This is as good an opportunity as we'll get."

The single word nearly caught in her throat. "Go."

Far below her Medcalf broke away from the chandelier and

began closing on the pavilion. Jake and Florence had their backs to the agent, unaware of her approach.

But wait ... two Indian women were accosting Medcalf. Was it innocent? Jenny breathed again as the tourists handed her a camera and deployed their photograph faces. The Ulsterwoman snapped away, the umbrella tucked under one arm as she rearranged the tourists into different poses. What a pro. But the moment was lost: Jake's guide was pulling them away from the pavilion, shepherding them toward the upper galleries.

Then it all went wrong.

It's how these things always unravel – the unexpected, something no amount of planning can account for. To Jenny's horror one of the tourists broke from her friend's embrace and *gave Jake the camera.* The journalist turned, gormless, eager to help. And (God in heaven!) the woman threw an arm around Medcalf to include her in the photo. There was no escape – refusing to be in it would make her face ten times more memorable to the journo. Jake corralled the three into the viewfinder and hit the shutter release. Jenny was one down.

What on earth will I tell Charlie?

The tourists wandered off arm-in-arm, inspecting the photos. Medcalf peeled away in the opposite direction, making eye contact with Jenny as she passed below the balcony. Her expression was grim.

Something alerted Jenny to the movement of her other agent.

Guilherme had broken free of his tour group and was homing in on the targets. Jake and Florence drifted toward the main staircase, where sightseers were pressing to get in. It would be tightly packed in there. Guilherme was two feet behind the journalist as they passed through the archway, the black umbrella swinging from his wrist. Suddenly he gripped it like a dagger – Jenny realized her heart was racing.

*

The atmosphere in the staircase was claustrophobic. Tourists were all around Jake and he had to moderate his pace. Then several things happened in quick succession. He heard a yell of "Pickpocket!"; a Chinese tourist lunged towards him; he felt a stab of pain in the buttock. The pickpocket was away at a sprint, but Jake was left with the impression of a lean South Asian in his forties.

"He want your wallet," the Chinese tourist said. "I stop him."

"Thanks," Jake replied. He rubbed his backside and turned to Florence. "I think something just stung me."

15

When Jake and Florence arrived at the Agya Sophia the next morning, a curious thing happened. He emptied his pockets, but the metal detector went off anyway. The guard pulled him aside to scan him with the wand and as the device passed over his waist it bleeped.

"Empty pockets please," he said.

"They are empty," Jake insisted, turning them inside out.

The guard yawned and wanded him a second time; it bleeped again.

"Arms up, sir."

Jake could smell coffee and stale tobacco as he was patted down. He winced as the guard brushed his buttock – it was still sore from the insect bite and antihistamine had not helped. Finally the guard waved them through.

But it was not an insect that had stung Jake, nor was it a designer poison that would shut down his heart and leave no trace. For deep within his behind nestled a homing device. The transmissions were picked up by the British Embassy, encrypted and beamed into space; a nanosecond later they were received by SIS's satellite on the 57th Parallel, dissected into ten thousand slivers and fired down to Vauxhall Cross.

As Edwin de Clerk watched the magenta dot awake from its arrest and enter the precinct of the Agya Sophia, one corner of his mouth rose in a smirk.

*

Jake and Florence began with a sweep of the basilica's floor, examining the many engravings spread across it. The passage of tourists had worn most inscriptions down to a trace, but Florence said this was a blessing in disguise. If they had been readable John the Lydian's tomb could have been found decades ago; as it was, a sarcophagus might remain undiscovered. The journalist and the archaeologist fell into a routine. Florence was fluent in Greek, in which most of the carvings were written – but Latin was everywhere too, and Jake found his A Level classics returned quickly.

On the third day he found a flagstone by the altar engraved with the name 'John'. A second and third word followed, each worn to near-nothing. Florence's cheeks were flushed as she took high resolution photographs, using a series of filters to winkle out the original inscription. But there was to be a disappointment. It was not 'John *the*', but 'John *of*', and the final word revealed itself to be 'Nicomedia', a small Byzantine town.

The task became tedious. It was literally a fingertip search – every inch of the Agya Sophia had to be caressed in case touch detected what the eye had missed. Florence rose at 6 a.m. each morning, shaming Jake out of bed and working until the janitors threw them out at nightfall. And with each fruitless day Jake's anxiety rose. You didn't get a job on Fleet Street without knowing how to turn a sow's ear into a silk purse, but they'd found nothing whatsoever. Where would the words come from?

Florence was the silver lining. Jake had put her down as

a beautiful but unassailable bitch, yet as the days passed she thawed. Maybe it was the fact that he was mucking in with the hunt – or perhaps his love of history was shining through. Jake didn't care either way. The archaeologist's beauty was no longer a fearful thing, and at times he was coherent in her presence.

He learned about her background over grilled sardines in a blue-collar restaurant. Inside it was warm and pleasant and they wiped condensation from the windows to watch smokers fishing in the Bosphorus. Florence's parents lived in Richmond – her dad was a dentist who owned four practices, while her mum "lunched prodigiously". Florence had read law at Oxford, and her choice of profession had caused a hell of a stink.

"Archaeologists make even journalists look well-heeled," she said. "It's not a career a Chinese father has in mind for his only child."

"You look like you do ok for yourself," Jake observed with a nod to her wrist. Perched on that elegant slip of flesh was a watch by Tiffany.

"It was a present," Florence shot back.

But by the end of the week gloom was descending. They had found nothing of interest and Jake's hope of 'drawing out' some conspiracy looked naïve in the extreme.

"What's wrong?" Florence asked as they explored Sultanahmet one evening. "You seem quiet."

The whole story spilled out. How he would be sacked if he didn't pull off a 'spectacular', how he'd lost his way a long time ago, how he couldn't find the energy to cut it at the highest level. Yet neither could he rid himself of the suspicion he had special gifts: a good brain and the ability to 'stumble upon' stories other reporters missed. Jake felt wretched for wasting his talents. But still he didn't give the job his all, and the lethargy only increased with each setback. He stopped short of acknowledging that the consumption of eighty units a week contributed to the vicious circle. Florence listened with understanding and Jake realized he was close to falling in love with her; already he was dangerously in lust.

"Maybe it would help if you weren't so scruffy," she said, ruffling his hair in a way that made his balls shrink. "When was the last time you shaved?"

They were passing a barber's shop and before Jake could complain Florence pulled him inside. The elderly barber blinked rapidly as he worked, lending him something of the appearance of a mole rat. Florence shrieked with delight when he lit a paraffin-covered gauze to blow fireballs into Jake's ears. If only he could bring himself to make a move. *If only*.

That evening they visited the Cagaloglu Hammam, an Ottoman bathhouse once frequented by Florence Nightingale. Perhaps steam would ease joints stiff after hours knelt on marble. When he saw her wearing only a towel it was like being kicked in the heart. But the baths were segregated.

"Oooh," Florence whined. "I hoped we'd get to go in together."

Jake lay on hot stone and stared at the ceiling through patches of transparency in the mist. The only sound was the metronomic drip of water echoing off marble, and as dreams gambolled through his mind he had the feeling of being removed from time. He no longer cared if Heston fired him. He would become an archaeologist. This would be their life: wining and dining their way through the world's most electrifying cities, uncovering the glory of the past. Paranoid professors and lightning strikes could not have been further from his mind.

Then the whole imagined edifice came crumbling down around him.

16

"What have Tintin and Lara Croft been up to then?" Charlie Waits chuckled at his own joke. "Our intrepid reporter and his new squeeze doing anything I should know about?"

"She's not his squeeze," said Jenny. "I should know. We've got their bedrooms bugged."

"Well, not yet perhaps. In any case I think it's time we had a chat face to face, if you can indulge me."

"Of course." Jenny took the phone from her ear to check the time on the screen. "If I get the next flight I could be at Vauxhall for eight."

"Actually, I'm outside right now."

She ran to the window and there he was, wearing chinos and a pale pink shirt open at the collar. A cashmere sweater was slung over his shoulders – he seemed not to feel the cold.

Waits waved at her. "Shall we promenade?"

Medcalf looked up from her novel. "No fecking way ... Charlie's *outside*?"

Jenny nodded grimly.

"What is he, a ghoul or something?" The Ulsterwoman returned to her reading, shaking her head.

Jenny laughed. "I admit there's a whiff of brimstone about the man ..."

Jenny liked her agent. The pair had begun keeping each other company in their hotel rooms in the snatched moments of downtime, chatting or playing backgammon. It reminded her of university days, and Jenny was surprised to note a wistfulness for lost friendships.

Waits led her to the Grand Bazaar; he wanted to buy a carpet for his landing. The mass of stalls dealt in Ottomanesque tat for the most part, but there was the odd antique shop where one might find something decent. Out of season the stallholders were desperate for custom, yet at a glance from Waits they shied back, scenting the sulphur. The spymaster had been sitting at their last meeting and Jenny was surprised to see how short he was. But still he projected that haughty ease a certain breed of Englishman possesses in spades.

"Shall we talk about what happened in the Agya Sophia?" he enquired.

"Yes, let's," replied Jenny, bracing herself for a reprimand. MI6 didn't like things getting fraught, regardless of whose fault it was.

"Never mind about the photograph," said Waits, swatting away an imaginary fly. "Accidents happen."

"Thanks, Charlie, I appreciate that."

"I'm more concerned about this other fellow, the one who got involved on the staircase. Chinese chap." He stopped to peer at a rug. "What are your thoughts? An innocent bystander?"

"Alexander Guilherme thought he was clean," she replied. "Said he didn't seem the type. For a start he was very overweight ..."

Jenny caught herself too late. A glint of anger stirred in Charlie's eyes – perhaps her handler was conscious of his own ample figure.

"Nice one, that," he said, adjusting his glasses to peer at a rug. "Nineteenth-century Hereke, if I'm not much mistaken."

Jenny knew not to apologize. Contrition would only highlight Waits's loss of control.

"Alexander says if the Chinese guy was working for someone else then he was a damn good actor," she said, turning to look the spymaster in the face. "Was he working for someone else?"

"I don't know, why should I know?" Waits's chin quivered from left to right. "We've got absolutely no evidence anyone else is keeping an eye on him."

"Evidence is not suspicion. Is there suspicion?"

His smile fell away like rock cleaved from the cliff face.

"We've absolutely no evidence anyone else is keeping an eye on Wolsey but ourselves," he repeated. "Well then – how about tea?"

Damn the man, Jenny thought as they sat at a small café. Waits chose his words with the care of a Queen's Counsel barrister; the same judiciousness was now being applied to the cake-stand. She watched in distaste as he selected four large baklava, oozing with syrup.

"It would help if I knew *why* we're watching him," she said. "I could concentrate our resources better. There would be less chance of us missing something important."

"It's for your own good that you don't know, my dear, it really is." Waits inserted a pastry into his mouth. "You'll just have to trust me on that."

"Your interest in the Chinese tourist suggests it's to do with Chung's project," said Jenny mischievously. "With what they're up to in the Agya Sophia."

Her handler's eyes twinkled. "Maybe yes, maybe no."

Waits gobbled down the rest of his baklava, dabbing up the last traces of pistachio with his fingers. He was a most fastidious eater.

17

Jake felt nicely sozzled despite the modest intake. Only four beers that evening, yet there was a warmth inside him, a pleasant glow behind his eyes. For once he decided to halt the drinking there and turn in for the night. He paused at the landing, pleased with this little display of willpower. A storm was roiling over the Bosphorus – it was dry on the European side of the city, but curtains of rain swirled out to sea like the sides of some grand jellyfish. The mass of Asia was silhouetted by the regular crack of lightning, a black hump against the photo-flash white.

Someone was on the balcony.

A solitary figure, still and slow-breathing, as if meditating. Or preparing for action. Jake sought the amber cone of a smoker. But in Istanbul you could light up indoors.

He was breaking in.

The journalist's pulse quickened as his thoughts turned to Britton. For days he'd barely contemplated the man – but now he was overwhelmed afresh by all the suspicions he'd had in London. Yet he also saw the idiocy of his strategy. For if people were really following Britton, what the blazes did he intend to do when he encountered them? He was as much of a fighter as he was a lover.

Then a thunderbolt illuminated the balcony, and to his astonishment he saw it was Florence, staring up into the clouds.

Jake stepped onto the balcony. "Crazy, isn't it?"

Florence jumped. "Jesus!" She relaxed, leaned against the wall. "You scared me, Jake. Anyway, what's crazy?"

"That people once believed you could read the future in random discharges of electricity."

Florence gave a half-laugh and looked up again. The sky was overcast, but forked lightning crackled across the underside of the cloud, like the boughs of some electrified oak tree. Or a brain, now Jake thought of it. The cloud-mass was exactly like a glowing brain, the lightning its network of blood vessels.

"I thought you went to bed hours ago," he said.

"I did, but I couldn't sleep. What have you been doing?"

"I vanquished the barman on the pool table. And then I went through Britton's notes again."

Lightning scored the atmosphere once more, almost violet this time.

"Find anything interesting?"

"Britton underlines a lot about Rome's expansion," he said. "How one minor town suddenly starts beating up all its neighbours, and within three-quarters of a century it rules all Italy."

"Rome's domination of the Mediterranean in microcosm."

The wind was despicable and Jake hugged his arms around his chest; he noticed Florence wasn't wearing a coat. "You must be freezing. Want my jacket?"

Yet there were no goose bumps on her neck.

"Your chivalry's impeccable, sir," she said. "But I'm fine. Come on, let's go inside. The best of the lightning's over."

They sat on a sofa to watch the storm approach until raindrops rattled the windowpanes and the sky was lost behind rivulets of water.

"What else caught your eye in Britton's notes?" asked Florence.

Jake retrieved the pages he'd been studying. "Britton emphasises how the Romans neglected religion in the last century of the Republic," he said. "And how that was also a time of great turmoil for Rome."

Florence nodded. "Spartacus and the slave revolt for a start. And it didn't end there – the entire century was marked by unrest. All these super-powerful senators were striving to be top dog, often by force. The old checks and balances on democracy were lost. I make it seven civil wars in a century, culminating in Antony and Cleopatra and all that."

"Ah, the star-crossed lovers," said Jake. "Who end up getting clobbered by Julius Caesar's nephew Octavian, if memory serves."

"So there *is* a reason you're historical correspondent." Florence smiled at him.

"After he triumphed over Antony and Cleopatra, he did away with democracy, invented the post of emperor and consigned the Republic to the dustbin." Jake was showing off now. "And the Romans actually welcomed it – a bit like Germany embracing Hitler in the 1930s. Anything for a bit of peace and quiet."

"Good analogy," said Florence, moving closer. "Under both leaders the cult of personality flourished. And just as Hitler became 'der Führer', Octavian was renamed 'Augustus', as a mark of the Roman people's respect. Augustus brought back all the old religious rites that had been neglected in the previous century, Etruscan augury chief among them. Even Augustus's tomb was in the shape of an Etruscan burial mound. By the end of his life Augustus was considered a living God – he was the greatest emperor of them all. No wonder a month is still named after him."

"Odd you should mention the change of title," said Jake. "Because Britton is constantly underlining stuff about the 'Augustus' thing. How it literally means –"

"Augur," she finished.

Thunder echoed over Istanbul once more.

18

"Well, it's easy to see what the poor guy was trying to imply," said Jake. "In the dying days of the Republic, the religion which had turned Rome into a superpower was neglected. Chaos ensued. But under Augustus and the emperors who followed, augury was embraced once again. Rome was reborn."

"Then came the period known as the High Empire," Florence interrupted. "The peak of power and achievement."

Jake weighed the papers in his hands and sighed. "Do you get the feeling that, rather than a clue to the location of the brontoscopic calendar, I am in fact holding the prima facie evidence of one man's descent into insanity?"

A moment passed. "I guess that's about the size of it."

Jake was suddenly aware of her physical proximity, how alone they were in the lobby. She inched towards him again until their upper arms were touching. Then without warning her head flopped onto his shoulder. Jake's upper body went rigid. There was a tingling in his stomach. Was she upset about Britton? *Or making a move*?

They sat like that for a full minute as the rain pummelled down. Jake did nothing. He was aware of his own breathing, the rise and fall of his chest, raising and lowering Florence's lovely head. *All you have to do is kiss her.* The realization pounded through Jake's brain, yet he dared not move. Her breathing was getting lighter – he could barely hear it now, his neck was getting stiff.

Florence stirred. "You're sure you've shown me all Roger's notes? Absolutely everything?"

"Of course. I gave you the lot at the airport."

Her eyes were wide open. "Really? If you forgot to show me something before, just tell me, Jake. I won't be annoyed with you. I promise."

She nuzzled his neck.

"Florence, I wouldn't hold anything back from you."

"No, I suppose you wouldn't."

She closed her eyes again, but the sleep seemed to have gone out of her. She wasn't leaning into him as much. Her core was tensing, supporting itself.

"I have to go to bed," she said.

And with that she was gone.

Jake stormed into his room. The alcohol high had turned sour and full of anger and he leaned on clenched fists, staring into the mirror.

All you had to do was kiss her.

All you had to do was kiss her and she was yours.

Jake retrieved the Laphroaig. He had barely touched it since arriving, but now he poured himself a treble, grimacing as he swallowed it in a gulp.

Why, why, *why* was he like this? What an affliction it was – the cruellest of all, or so it felt then. It meant more than lack of sex: it spelled lifelong loneliness. Jake poured another treble, necking it again. That was better. At least he could rely on the booze, a true friend in need. He was going to get roaring drunk. Again came the clink of glass, the gurgle of whisky. Jake raised his tumbler for the third time, the liquid shimmering invitingly in the glass. But he didn't drink. His gaze had fallen on the small corner of white that protruded from his suitcase.

Eusebius.

Jake put down the glass and picked up the book. Florence had only warmed when his passion for history had revealed itself. And oh, how she had cooled earlier when he'd failed to provide her with anything new. He had to make the breakthrough.

Jake sat up straight – for once in his life he wasn't going to respond to a setback by getting hammered. He poured the dram back inside the bottle and stared at *Life of Constantine*, willing the text to yield its secrets. This was the only complete book Britton had given them – it had to hold the key.

As Jake read something clicked in his brain.

The human mind amazed him. Where did a thought come from? How could the consciousness produce something tangible from thin air, like energy created from nothing? But the idea was in his head now, it wouldn't go away. And each new chapter only reinforced his theory. A fierce joy surged through his veins as he put the whisky back in his suitcase and went to wake Florence.

19

"Not now," said Florence. "I'm tired and trying to go to sleep, leave me alone."

Jake's jaw clenched. *You had your chance and you blew it, matey.* Then again, did he ever really have a chance? Florence's voice said it all – it was full of *assumption* he would comply. But still the thrill of discovery was in him and he would not be fobbed off.

"I think I've cracked it," he said. "I think I know why Britton left us a book by Eusebius!"

There was a pause. "All right, I'm coming," she said.

"Well then?" Florence began once they had returned to the lobby. "What have you got me out of bed for?"

"Tell me what you know about Constantine's conversion to Christianity," said Jake.

She decided to humour him. "It was a battlefield conversion. Supposedly Constantine saw a crucifix in the sky and ordered his men to paint it on their shields. He defeated his pagan rival and Roman Christianity was born."

"Correct. Now read Eusebius's account."

Jake skimmed through *Life of Constantine* and handed her the book.

> *About the time of the midday sun, Constantine saw with his own eyes a cross-shape formed from light and a text attached which said, 'By This Conquer'. Amazement at the spectacle seized him.*

"Uh-huh," said Florence. "'By This Conquer' is one of the most famous lines of antiquity. What's your point?"

"It occurred to me Eusebius could also have been talking about the Book of Thunder."

Florence narrowed her eyes. "What do you mean?"

"Eusebius doesn't write that Constantine saw a 'Christian cross' in the sky, or a 'crucifix' – that would be the obvious thing to say. Instead he calls it 'a cross-shape formed from light'. Odd way to put it, don't you think?"

"Your point is?"

"He could just as easily be describing forked lightning."

Florence had one hand on her hip.

"Then Eusebius adds, 'with a *text* attached,'" Jake continued. "A text attached to a cross of light in the sky that gave prowess in battle. What does that sound like to you?"

"Enlighten me."

"I think Eusebius was writing about the *Disciplina Etrusca* – but disguising it as a Christian treatise."

"I don't buy it," said Florence. "At all."

"I wouldn't expect you to from that passage alone," said Jake. "But it's a theme running through all three books of the biography." He passed her the volume. "Read from Book One."

Florence sighed again, but did as he asked.

Today our thought stands helpless, longing to express some of the conventional things.

"Eusebius is writing just after paganism was abandoned," said Jake. "It's like he's pining for the old religion."

Our thought reaches to the vault of heaven. It pictures God, stripped of all mortal and earthly attire and brilliant in a flashing cloak of light.

"Not exactly the stereotypical image of God," said Jake. "No flowing beard, no long white robes. And the reader's left with something that sounds pretty close to sheet lightning."

"Eusebius's idea of the Christian God would've been totally different to the stereotype you or I have," Florence retorted. "He lived one thousand seven hundred years ago."

Jake took the paperback. "Just look at Book Two then – the part where Eusebius is describing the fate of a pretender to the throne named Licinius."

But he did not elude the Great All-Seeing Eye. Just when he hoped his life was safe he was struck down by a fiery shaft, his whole body consumed with the fire of divine vengeance so his appearance became unrecognizable. Dry, skeletonized bones were all that was left of him.

"But that could've been written about –"

"I know. Roger Britton."

"You're making the same mistake as before, though," said

Florence. "You're assuming that because lightning's mentioned it must have some special significance. But I keep telling you, lightning imagery is shot through all ancient religion, like, I don't know, like letters in a stick of rock. They were fascinated by it."

"Just look at Book One then," Jake pressed.

Bright beams of the light of the true religion brought shining days to those who before had sat in darkness and the shadow of death.

"Bright beams?" he said. "The true religion? Come on!" Florence shook her head. "Still not convinced." "And there's this bit, also from Book Two."

About this time a supernatural appearance was observed. This appearance was seen through the agency of a divine and superior power, and it was a vision which foreshadowed what was shortly coming to pass.

"That does sound like Etruscan religion," Florence admitted. "But Eusebius created the entire discipline of church history – you're asking me to believe the classical historian most associated with Christianity was a secret pagan. It's too much."

"Eusebius spent a lifetime working on religious scripts," said Jake. "He of anyone would've known how scripture could be encoded with hidden meanings."

"Great classicists have studied this text," said Florence shot back. "Scholars have pulled apart every line. You expect me to believe a *journalist* could spot something the entire discipline has missed?"

"Why else would Roger have left us this book?"

"He was going mad. I'm starting to wonder if you are too."

"There's something else."

"Oh is there? Let's get it over with then, so I can go back to bed."

"Eusebius was suspected of being a secret pagan in his own lifetime."

That threw her. "He was?"

"It's in the introduction," he replied, handing her the book.

> *Suspicions were raised after Eusebius survived persecution of the Christians carried out by Diocletian, one of the last pagan emperors. And how had Eusebius borne himself during this season of peril? A quarter of a century later a grave charge was brought against him affecting his conduct during the persecution. The bishop of Heraclea addressed him: 'Tell me then, wast thou not with me in prison during the persecution? And I lost an eye for the truth, but thou, as we see, hast received no injury in any part of thy body. Neither hast thou suffered martyrdom, but remained alive with no mutilation. How wast thou released from prison, unless it be that thou didst promise to those who put upon us the pressure of persecution to do that which is unlawful?'*

Florence read the passage, read it again. Jake noticed that spots of red had formed high up on each of her cheeks.

> *Many scholars are highly sceptical of the content of* Life of Constantine. *Eusebius's integrity has often attacked by academics. J. Burckhardt wrote, 'Eusebius utterly falsified Constantine's likeness'.*

"The Emperor Diocletian's retinue passed through Eusebius's home town when he was younger," Jake said. "They might have met. Perhaps Diocletian saw in Eusebius a man on the inside of Christianity, an ally against a dangerous and growing sect. Then along comes Constantine, who does away with the old order completely."

"Eusebius waited until Constantine's death to write *Life*

of Constantine," Florence whispered. "And Constantine's successors were committed to the new faith of Christianity – it was a time of religious dogma, the burning of books."

"If Eusebius was a closet pagan, if he was bent on preserving the Etruscan texts ... he'd have needed to be crafty."

Florence was deep in thought. "Could it be?" she said at last. "Could it be that Eusebius hid the Book of Thunder for future generations? That he crafted *Life of Constantine* as a map?"

"To safeguard it until the fad of Christianity passed."

"Only it didn't pass." Florence's eyes glinted at the machinations of the ancient scholar. "By This Conquer," she repeated.

20

Jenny was taking her morning jog when she saw the woman who should not have been there. To her left sprawled the Topkapi Palace, where the Ottoman sultans had kept their harem. To her right was a vignette of modern Istanbul: kebab houses, massage parlours, internet café. In the last was Medcalf.

The Ulsterwoman had her back to the street, hair bundled into a woolly hat. But one incendiary lock gave her away. Jenny slowed, jogging on the spot. Something was not right here. Her agent had been keeping tabs on Jake all night, she should be asleep – yet there she was, hunched before a screen and tapping away. Jenny slipped into the café and padded toward her agent through a soup of noise. Teenage gamers competed to be heard over Lebanese pop music, but even so Medcalf's senses were too acute for Jenny. Maybe it was a reflection on the screen; perhaps she simply sensed Jenny's presence. All the best agents possess a degree of instinct and intuition that is difficult to explain. But at the last moment Medcalf whipped around to face her superior.

"Oh, it's you."

Jenny smiled; steel was in her eyes. "Not asleep already?"

"I needed to send some emails to the family." Medcalf maximized her Gmail account until it filled the screen.

"What were you looking at just now?"

"Nothing."

"Yes, you were. What was it?"

"Nothing important."

Jenny wasn't smiling any more. "Stand back from the computer, please."

"It's private."

"Let me see what you were doing."

Medcalf's face pulsed scarlet. "You don't have the authority."

"Oh, I do."

Still Medcalf would not budge.

"Let me have a look or I'll have Edwin look up everything you've been doing remotely," said Jenny. "And I'd need to notify Charlie Waits about such a step."

As Medcalf's resistance wilted Jenny took the chair, her back very straight as she viewed the browser history. But as she clicked from page to page she blenched.

"I think you and I need to have a little talk," she said.

*

The first website was an *Encyclopaedia Britannica* article on Etruscan religion:

> *The calling of diviner-priest was seen by the ancient Etruscans as sacred; his concern was for the very destiny of his people.*

Then a dictionary website, open at the word 'haruspex':

> *A priest who practised divination, esp. by examining the entrails of animals. From the Latin hira (gut) + specere (to look).*

And the Wikipedia entry for '*Disciplina Etrusca*':

There is evidence a significant portion of Etruscan literature was systematically burned by early Christians in the fourth century. Arnobius, a Christian convert, wrote in 300 AD that 'Etruria is the originator and mother of all superstition'. Parts of Etruscan religion do indeed seem perverse to the modern mindset. Among the behaviours forbidden by the text was the consumption of blackberries, which were seen as a cursed fruit ...

21

Jake and Florence stayed up all night, scouring Eusebius for a reference to landmarks from Constantine's time. The Agya Sophia was built two hundred years too late – it could be discounted. The journalist's leap of intuition came just before dawn.

"Are there any statues of Constantine in Istanbul?" he asked.

Florence looked up from the tourist maps splayed across the table. "Why?"

"This chapter's entitled, 'Of the statue of Constantine holding a cross – *and its inscription*.'"

"No statue still stands," she said. "But there used to be one on Constantine's Column and that exists – just about."

Jake handed her *Life of Constantine*. "Read from here."

Constantine set up this great trophy of victory over his enemies in the midst of the imperial city, ordering it to be engraved in indelible characters that the sign was the preservative of the Roman Empire.

"By this sign, conquer," he said. "It's the same theme. Eusebius couldn't be more explicit – he says here 'the sign' saved the empire. If his account of the battlefield conversion was meant to be read two ways – with lightning as the true 'sign' – then here he's directly telling us the real saviour of the Roman Empire was the *Disciplina Etrusca*. And he's saying that it must be written with 'indelible characters', never to be forgotten."

"If it's written in indelible characters ..."

"... then maybe they're still to be found, where Constantine's statue once stood. And read the next bit."

> *Constantine ordered the following inscription to be engraved on the column in Latin. 'By virtue of this sign, I have set at liberty the Roman people and restored them to their ancient greatness and splendour.'*

"Eusebius is harking back to Rome's former glory," said Jake. "Remember, by Eusebius's time the empire had lurched from disaster to catastrophe for generations. It had just come through the 'Third Century Crisis' – there had been nothing but plague and rebellion for fifty years. The time of Augustus or Hadrian was like a lost golden age in comparison."

Florence's nostrils flared. "So Eusebius is saying this cross of light in the sky can restore that splendour."

Jake picked up the book. "'And all the inhabitants of the city,'" he read, "'seemed to *enjoy the rays of a purer light*.'"

*

"Seen better days, hasn't it?" said Jake as they stood beneath the column later that morning.

A fire in the eighteenth century had left the monument resembling a condemned building. The blackened drums were pinned together with metal, and scaffolding ran from top to bottom. Jake was on a hangover and four hours' sleep; his confidence had vanished and last night's breakthrough was the imagining of a drunk. Was this hulk about to save his career? It looked doubtful.

Florence's request for assistance had been granted instantly – Dr Gul brought a team of archaeologists with him this time, and expensive equipment was made available. Jake found it baffling. The Turkish authorities had a reputation for being awkward, but they were bending over backwards to help.

The archaeologists used an RM-15 resistance meter to fire electricity through the column. Stone is a bad conductor, but a compartment inside would be damp – electricity would pass through easily and thus reveal it. When the scan was complete Dr Gul led them to his vehicle, a yellow Citroen 2CV van that seemed to complement his persona. He laid the RM-15 in the boot and connected it to a laptop, which clicked and whirred as the data came through. The top of the column materialized on the monitor, grey against an obsidian background. Then it juddered up the screen to reveal solid stone. The column jerked upward once more.

Stone again.

As the computer worked its way through thirty-five images of nothingness, Jake despaired. What would he do when his contract ended? He could always become a press officer. It wouldn't be too hard finding work at a local council and the money was ok. But God, how depressing. What a crap job to confess to at dinner parties. Jake reckoned having a cool profession was worth at least £20,000 per annum. And when it came to women it was the only string to his bow.

Jake was considering the lot of a landscape gardener when it happened. There was a stir among the archaeologists, like the awakening of leaves before inclement weather. Dr Gul turned from the computer and clasped his hands together; his nose had abandoned its ashtray hue for the colour of stewed plum.

"A chamber," he hissed. "*There is a chamber underneath the column.*"

22

Jenny had it out with her agent by the Blue Mosque. The cascade of domes was reflected misty-grey in the surface of a pond as children chased a spinning top around the water.

"Do I need to replace you, then?" she began.

Medcalf flushed with worry. "What the hell? No, of course you don't need to replace me. Why would you do that?"

"Because I'm not sure I trust you anymore. What were you playing at back there?"

"Look, I was curious, ok? Aren't you? I mean, this is the weirdest job I've ever been on. Why would MI6 give a toss about the ancient Etruscans?"

Oh, Jenny was curious all right – the intrigue was hot in her throat. A commotion interrupted her thoughts. Two tourists were attempting to purchase the spinning top and the children had become little businessmen, faces earnest as they haggled up the price.

"I don't like it when members of my team hide things from me," said Jenny. "Alarm bells start ringing."

Medcalf's head shrank into her shoulders. "I was embarrassed, ok? Because this operation is clearly fecking mental, right? I thought you'd laugh if you knew I was actually reading up on the history. It would be like ..." she sought an analogy. "It would be like us investigating a spate of crop circles and me spending my time off logging on to UFO fansites."

"Nevertheless, this cock-and-bull story about emailing your family – I just can't have it. Lies are our stock in trade. If we aren't able to trust each other then we're lost."

A deal had been struck with the urchins and a fistful of lira was produced; the leader of the pack wound the string around his toy like a curator handling a Fabergé egg.

"I don't think you can continue on this job," said Jenny quietly. "Yes, I'm intrigued, and off the record I agree this whole project is totally whacko and Charlie must be mad wasting our time on it. But my opinions are irrelevant. You can see how worked up he is about the whole thing. My handling must be above reproach."

"*Please.*" Tears were in Medcalf's eyes. "It was a moment of madness. If you send me home it'll go on my file forever."

"I need total integrity from my agents. I'm sorry."

Medcalf began sobbing. "I'm such a messed-up bitch. Like to think I'm the hard case, huh? Well, look at me now. I didn't cry at my own dad's funeral, but screw up my career and I'm blubbing like a schoolgirl."

Jenny could make out every detail of the mosque in the pond; a fish broached the surface and the reflection shimmered away like a lost belief.

"I know how you feel," she said at last. "It does it to you, this job. You forget what's important. Friends, family."

"At least you've still *got* a job. I might as well ask for my P45 with fibs on my record. They'll bump me right down to the post-room." Medcalf laughed. "Massive black mark against my name and it happens on the most ridiculous operation ever."

Jenny knew she should do what needed to be done. Get rid, get someone else in and move on. If she wanted to be in Charlie Waits's shoes one day she had to be ruthless in these situations. But something Medcalf said had got to her – that bit about not shedding a tear at her father's funeral, yet weeping for her job. It had opened a window onto a life of ambition.

As Jenny watched the mosque reform itself she thought of her mum, trapped in that ward and staring at oblivion. She thought of her friends, giving up on her one by one. And she thought of her engagement.

"I never even see you," Marc had shouted in that final row. "All you care about is your wretched job."

More damning still: "*You're just no fun.*"

The pond had regained its mirror surface.

"I'm not going to send you back," she said.

An important decision.

"Thank you so much," Medcalf gushed. "You're a friend, a real friend."

"I hope so. I could probably do with one too, you know."

Medcalf was beaming. "I tell you what, when this job's over let's go on the lash in London, just me and you. Come on, you'll enjoy pretending you've got a life. Ministry of Sound perhaps, somewhere with decent house music."

It was hardly Jenny's scene, but it had been years since she'd had such an offer. And Medcalf's enthusiasm was infectious.

"Sure," she said, grinning too. "Why the hell not?"

Before the Ulsterwoman could reply Jenny's phone began ringing.

"I think you'll want to see this," Guilherme began.

"See what?"

"They've found something."

23

Being kissed by Florence was like getting punched in the face.

"You did it!" she shrieked, kissing him again. "You did it, Jake!"

"I did it," he repeated, touching his cheek in stupefaction.

The world was alive with possibility. Fleet Street, the *Disciplina Etrusca*, this stunning girl – all were his for the taking.

The chamber beneath the column gained definition as the computer did its work, a vault just big enough for a man to stoop in. The Turkish archaeologists were embracing and giving each other high fives.

"Don't you realize what we may have found?" Dr Gul said

between drags on his cigarette. “Don’t you know why they’re so excited?”

“Well, we do have an inkling,” said Jake.

“And do you think they will be down there? Will we really find them?”

“Find ‘them’? Wait a minute, find what?”

“The relics, of course.”

Jake looked blank.

“The relics St Helena brought back from the Holy Land.”

“I haven’t got the foggiest what you’re on about, mate.”

The academic finished his cigarette and lit another with the butt. “St Helena was the Emperor Constantine’s mother,” he said. “During a pilgrimage to Bethlehem she claimed to have discovered the true cross and various other, how you say, religious ‘bits and bobs’. Received wisdom is that they were kept in a shrine beneath the column. But maybe not, maybe they were foundation deposits. Buried *under* the column, to bless it.”

“What sort of ‘bits and bobs’?” asked Florence, who seemed less than thrilled with the revelation.

“The crosses used to crucify the thieves who died alongside Christ. An ointment jar used by Mary Magdalene to wash Christ’s feet. And the baskets that carried the bread and fish he fed to the five thousand.”

“Blimey,” said Jake, thinking about headlines and bylines.

“If only we could excavate right away!” Dr Gul wrung his hands. “It’ll be months before we get the paperwork approved. I can’t bear it.”

But as it happened the dig began the very next morning.

*

Journalists swarmed, Heston had dispatched a photographer at short notice and a helicopter hovered overhead. Girders had been thrown up around the column to prevent subsidence as workmen excavated a tunnel towards the chamber at a forty-five degree incline. Amid the furore nobody noticed the interest of a distant blonde picking at a ball of candy floss.

"But how did you get permission so fast?" Jake asked.

"Let's just say King's College has close ties with the Turkish authorities," Florence snapped. She had been livid after Jake filed copy, accusing him of creating a media circus which had imperilled the hunt. That it was his job to do so had not occurred to her.

"You must've bribed them, right?" tried Jake. "Off the record."

Florence's voice softened. "Off the record?"

"I promise."

"Ok. Off the record then, no, we didn't bribe them." She shot him a smile and stalked off.

*

At noon the diggers hit granite. They filed the mortar from around one of the blocks and jemmied it halfway from the wall. The moment was on hand.

"The honour of being first inside should be yours," Dr Gul told Florence, shepherding her to the tunnel.

All three donned masks and crawled in. In the first few feet of the tunnel the detritus of modernity protruded from the mud – pipes, cable, lumps of concrete. But soon this vanished, leaving only the odd twist of porcelain or rusted iron.

"We have reached the chamber," said the old academic.

Jake heard stone grind on stone as the boulder was removed. Blood throbbed in his eardrums as he contemplated what a discovery would mean for him. His knuckles were white against the mud. There was a hiss of escaping gas, a grunt as the block was heaved aside, the click of a torch.

Florence spoke at last.

"Empty," she said. "The chamber is completely empty."

24

Niall Heston's wrath was biblical. "Do you have any idea how stupid we look right now?" he shouted. "All up and down Fleet Street they must be pissing themselves laughing."

"I wasn't to know," pleaded Jake, glancing around the café they'd taken refuge in.

"Wasn't to know? Wasn't to fucking know? You wouldn't have thought that reading your copy yesterday. The way you were going on you'd have thought Noah's bloody Ark was hidden down there. Have you ever heard of something called 'tone'? You're the man on the ground, Jake, you're supposed to come to a level-headed judgement and appraise our readers accordingly. Not get carried away playing Indiana Jones and get us all wound up about an empty bloody room."

Jake held his head in his hands as the rant crashed about him, telephone vibrating under the assault. He could picture Heston's forehead at that moment: puce, veins pulsing.

"You know where your story went? Front page."

Jake was agog. "What, you *led* on the dig?"

"Of course we didn't lead on it. My Christ, you really do have the news sense of an anchovy. The column was our front-page picture. With the caption, 'Could the lost relics of the crucifixion be buried here?' Exclusive stamped all over it. God, we look like tits today."

"I'm sorry," said Jake in a small voice.

Heston sighed. "Right. When were you due back?"

"Next Monday."

"Next Monday my arse. I'm pulling the plug. Day after tomorrow you're here in London, understood? And then we'll see whether you can atone for your sins, my lord."

With that he was gone.

"That went well," muttered Jake, his head bowed.

"In hindsight, there was never going to be anything there," said Florence.

"So good of you to let me know."

"The column was erected in Constantine's own lifetime," she went on. "But *Life of Constantine* was written after the emperor's death."

"But I'm sure my thesis is correct," Jake said into a fist. "With Constantine gone Eusebius would've had a free hand to embellish accounts of the emperor's reign with his own hidden messages. And his references to lightning and prophecy are too frequent to be coincidence. We were looking in the wrong place."

"I'm not persuaded."

"There are passages I haven't even shown you yet," said Jake, flicking through *Life of Constantine*. "Tell me this one isn't about the Book of Thunder."

Others were caught organizing conspiracies against him, God disclosing the plots by supernatural signs. Divine visions were displayed to him and provided him with foreknowledge of future events.

"Wow," said Florence.

"And there's a ditty in Book Four." said Jake. "What does this sound like to you?"

By keeping the divine faith, I am made a partaker of the light of truth. Guided by the light of truth, I advance in the knowledge of the divine faith.

"Ok, ok," she said. "You've made your point. But even if Eusebius did hide something in Istanbul, what chance do we have of finding it? Roman Constantinople is six feet under." Jake glimpsed sudden fear in her eyes. "I can't return empty-handed, it's not an option."

"Don't you ever think about anyone else? What about me? If we don't find anything in the next twenty-four hours I'm finished as a journalist. I'll be back on the local press before you can shout 'planning application'. I've already been ordered back to London to face the Gorgon."

"They might not sack you," she ventured. "You weren't to know ..." her voice trailed off. "Jake? Jake? What's wrong?"

But the reporter was far away. "Gorgon," he repeated. "*Gorgon*."

"I don't understand. What is it, Jake?"

The journalist snatched up *Life of Constantine* and flicked through the pages. "Something just occurred to me. Here it is – in Book Two. One of Constantine's rivals is warning his soldiers not to attack the emperor's sign."

> *Knowing what divine and secret energy lay within the trophy by which Constantine's army had learned to conquer, he urged his officers not to even let their eyes rest upon it. Its power was terrible, it was hostile, and they ought to avoid battle with it. They advanced to the attack with lifeless statues as their defence.*

"The 'divine and secret power' is the Book of Thunder," said Jake. "But doesn't that bit about 'not allowing their eyes to rest on the terrible power' remind you of the Gorgon? Medusa turned everyone who looked at her to stone. Or 'lifeless statues' as Eusebius puts it."

"Is there a Gorgon in Roman Istanbul?"

"There most definitely is." Jake reached for the *Rough Guide*; a snake-haired head glared at them from its pages.

Florence looked up the location where the sculpture was to be found. "It's hard to believe something so prosaic as an underground water cistern could be fascinating," she read. "But combine Roman engineering with contemporary lighting and you get one of the city's most impressive remains."

"What do you think? Possibility?"

"It's subtle," Florence admitted. "But if your theory's correct Eusebius would have needed to be discreet. His life would have depended on it."

She read for a few moments longer and put down the book. "Wait – no, this can't be it. The reservoir was built two centuries after Eusebius lived."

But Jake took the *Rough Guide* back, an enigmatic smile playing on his lips.

"The ceiling of the cistern is supported by three hundred and thirty-six columns," he read. "But the two Medusa heads supporting columns in the south-west corner are *clearly relics from a far older building*."

25

The cobbles were daubed a streetlight yellow when they arrived at the cistern. Florence collared the janitor as he locked up for the night; as money changed hands Jake glimpsed a wedge of hundred-dollar bills in her purse. Still in thrall to the bank of mum and dad, then.

The lights were already off, so the janitor loaned them a torch. Then the pair descended into what felt like the stronghold of some dwarvish king. Lines of columns stretched before them, silent as pine trees. Arched ceilings were visible fifty feet above, and a whiskered catfish broke the surface of the subterranean reservoir before darting off into the murk.

"It was only rediscovered by Europeans in the sixteenth century," whispered Jake. "Some French guy saw locals selling freshwater fish and asked where they caught them. He was taken here."

It felt right to whisper; the only other sound was the distant drip of water echoing through the vaults. A gangway led to the south-west corner of the cistern and the shadows lurched forward as they walked across it, a forest of stone come to life.

The twin Gorgons stared into the underworld. One head was on its side and the other upside-down, reinforcing the strangeness of their presence here. Yet the nearest of the pair was not a classic representation of Medusa. There were no snakes for her hair and the face was too masculine. It looked more like ...

"Alexander the Great." Florence voiced Jake's thoughts: the head before them could have been the great Macedonian, his tresses trailing in the wind of battle.

"But why?" she asked.

Jake fumbled in his backpack for *Life of Constantine*.

"There's a passage about Alexander in here," he said. "Book One, verse seven."

Torchlight illuminated the page.

Alexander overthrew countless tribes of diverse nations. He waded through blood, a man like a thunderbolt. But Emperor Constantine began his reign at the time of life where the Macedonian ended it. He even pushed his conquests to the Ethiopians, illuminating the ends of the whole earth with beams of light of the true religion.

"A man like a thunderbolt," Jake repeated. "Beams of light of the true religion. If there's anything to be found then it has to be here. Eusebius mentions Medusa and Alexander the Great individually – and he alludes to the Book of Thunder both times. Then here they are, side by side."

Splashes interrupted him as Florence entered the water up to her knees. Her torchlight danced off the coins cast in by tourists, and a goldfish zigzagged away in fright.

"Eusebius said the divine and secret power lies *within* the saving trophy," she said. "Perhaps there's some kind of compartment."

Jake admired her at that moment – Florence might be tricky, but she wasn't afraid of getting stuck in. Yet the Gorgon refused to yield. He crashed into the water alongside her, gasping at the cold.

"I don't think there's anything inside Alexander either," he said, probing the head with his fingers. "Unless ..."

He paused mid-sentence. There was an algae-filled groove below the waterline.

Jake kneaded it with the tip of his finger, clearing the indentation of slime until it joined another notch, then another.

"There's some kind of mark down here."

"There's one here too," said Florence, feeling below the surface of the Gorgon.

She swept the water from the base of the head; Jake glimpsed symbols on the rock before the waters closed.

"Shut your eyes, I've got an idea." Florence grinned at him. "Just trust me."

Jake couldn't resist peeping; he copped a glimpse of bare back and screwed his eyelids shut again.

"Ok, you can look now," said Florence.

She had her coat on again. But in her hand she held the shirt she'd been wearing – and in the other was a crayon they had made rubbings with in the Agya Sophia. Florence dunked the shirt under the surface, clamping it over the first character and thrashing the crayon backwards and forwards. Then she retrieved the dripping garment and dangled it in the torchlight.

"My God," whispered Jake.

Even with his scant knowledge of the period there could be no doubt. The single character imprinted onto the shirt was not of the Roman alphabet. Nor was it Greek, nor Arabic, nor any of the other languages one might expect in that part of the world.

They were looking at ancient Etruscan.

26

Little filaments of light seemed to dart in the centre of Florence's pupils and her face was contorted in triumph; the sinews stood out in her neck. Jake had never seen her like this before.

"Do you realize what we've done?" she hissed. "Do you realize what this is? A new inscription. A genuinely new inscription."

She began pumping at the wall with her crayon, panting with the exertion. Soon the shirt was covered in the horny script and the rubbing began to inch down both sleeves.

"We've still got to check Alexander," she said. "Can you check the janitor will keep this place open?"

Jake picked his way back through the cistern, sodden but exhilarated, only the light of his phone to guide him. When he got back he would have a noggin of Scotch to warm himself up properly. And then he would write one heck of a feature. Heston could put that in his pipe and smoke it.

A shape flitted across the walkway, stopping Jake dead. But the glow of his phone was lost in the blackness, and when he willed his eyes to make sense of the gloom his vision swam with imaginary blotches.

"*Merhab*?" he said. "Hello?"

Silence.

"Is someone there?" he shouted.

The salutation bounced off all four sides of the cistern. It was answered by nothingness, save for the drips all around him and the far-off splashes of Florence at work. Jake laughed. The dark was playing tricks on him.

*

On the other side of the column Jess Medcalf clung to the masonry, her cheek pressed to stone. After an eternity the journalist moved on. When his footsteps had receded to silence she breathed again, oxygen rushing into her bloodstream. Finally she peeped from around the column. In the distance Medcalf could make out the cobalt flicker of the journalist's phone, a fairy dancing through the hall of the mountain king. She stole in the other direction. It was pitch black as she closed on the archaeologist – Florence's back was to the agent and her breath misted the air. The archaeologist stood to unveil a dripping shirt, strange writing imprinted upon it.

Then something unexpected happened.

Florence glanced in the direction of the exit and, satisfied she was alone, produced a rock hammer. She raked the sharp end back and forth along the masonry, grunting as she worked. Occasionally the tool broke the surface – Medcalf could hear steel bite into water-corrupted rock – then she darted to the second statue and repeated the vandalism. Soon the work of destruction was done. Florence tucked away her hammer, Jake returned and they were gone.

Medcalf flicked on her own torch and ran to the statue. Limestone dust floated on the water. The rock beneath the surface felt crude, and a chip of stone came away beneath her fingers. Whatever had been written there was no more.

*

Jenny was sleeping when the phone call came. Medcalf was cogent and concise as she relayed what had happened, and she was impressed at the Ulsterwoman's daring. If she hadn't risked entering the reservoir they might never have known of the inscription at all. When the call ended Jenny bit her lip; her phone hovered in the air. But there was nothing else for it.

"Our woman in Istanbul!" cried Waits. "To what do I owe the pleasure?"

Glasses tinkled in the background and Jenny heard the burble of genteel conversation.

"There's been a development," she said. "Thought you'd want to know right away."

"Very well, just give me a minute. I'm at Gormley's new show in the Tate. Private viewing." The noise faded into silence. "Right. What's going on?"

Waits was rapt as Jenny told him of the inscription. And as she described Florence's vandalism the silence magnified in intensity.

"Goodness gracious," he said at last. "Where's Jess now?"

"She's trying to catch up with them. They're both soaked – heading back to their hotel, I'd have thought."

"How soon can she be armed?"

"I beg your pardon?"

"I said how soon can she be she armed? You heard me the first time, so for pity's sake don't dick about."

Jenny was even more taken aback – Waits was never coarse. "It'll take a while," she managed.

"And where's Alexander Guilherme?"

"He's off duty, could be anywhere."

Waits exhaled sharply. "Right. Call him now and tell him to collect the guns I sent by dip-post."

"I beg your pardon?"

"When he and Jess get an opportunity I want that shirt collected from Wolsey and Chung. By force of arms if needs be."

"I beg your pardon?"

"I urge you not to say 'I beg your pardon' one more time."

Jenny recovered herself. "Those guns are for self-defence, the last resort. We aren't trained for that sort of thing. Get someone else in."

"That could take an hour," barked Waits. Then in a murmur, almost to himself: "Nobody expected they'd actually *find* anything."

"Who could you get in an hour? Are there others here? If so the least you could do is tell me – call it operational courtesy."

There was a pause. Then Waits said: "Oh, all the major embassies have a few smooth operators I can call on in absolute emergencies. E Squadron personnel – that's SAS or SBS types to you and me." He spoke like an office worker confessing to a stash of aspirin.

"Then bloody well call them," said Jenny. "Don't make my team carry out work we're not supposed to do."

Waits weighed it up. "Maybe you're right. Let me have a think about it. But don't let Wolsey and Chung out of your sight in the meantime. If they try to enter a hotel, a taxi – whatever – you move and you get that rubbing by whatever means necessary." He cleared his throat. "Consider that a direct order of Her Majesty's government."

27

Another storm was brewing as they made for the hotel; the clouds roiled overhead as if the heavens themselves had turned restless. The few Istanbullus on the streets scurried past with collars upturned.

"There's something I don't get," said Florence as they paced beside the Byzantine city wall. "The cistern was built in 532 AD. That's two centuries after Eusebius wrote *Life of Constantine*. How did he know Alexander and Medusa would be there?"

"You're forgetting something," said Jake. "John the Lydian – Britton knew he was involved in this somehow."

"Of course." Florence was clear-eyed. "The scholar who translated the Etruscan calendar into Byzantine Greek. *He* was alive in 532."

"Perhaps John the Lydian was a closet pagan too," said Jake. "Maybe he cracked Eusebius's code, just like we did."

By keeping the divine faith, I am made a partaker of the light of truth. Guided by the light of truth, I advance in the knowledge of the divine faith.

"But Britton was wrong about one thing," he continued. "John the Lydian's legacy wasn't hidden in the Agya Sophia at all. It was *underneath* Constantinople."

"John the Lydian was a bureaucrat as well as a scholar," Florence said. "In his day he was a powerful man – he could have seen to it that the statues remained in place when the cistern was enlarged."

"For all we knew he moved them into the reservoir from somewhere else entirely," said Jake. "But whoever installed them, it was a masterstroke. The water-level kept the inscriptions secret for the best part of two millennia."

"I only wish Roger had been there to see it."

Jake sought a distraction. This was his moment of triumph – if he was ever going to sleep with her it would be that very evening. He didn't want her getting weepy.

"What did the inscription actually say?" he asked.

At once Florence's mentor was forgotten. "It's the most complete Etruscan writing I've ever found," she said. "Sensational, in fact. And definitely from the Book of Thunder. It's an incantation to *dii consentes*. The pitiless ones. They were Gods of fate, the advisers of Tin, the Etruscans' supreme deity."

Florence produced the shirt and began gleefully reading by the streetlight. On her tongue the extinct language sounded almost feral; it gave Jake the shivers. She was interrupted by the crack of thunder over the European mainland to the north-west, and lightning licked the underside of the clouds like a forked tongue. It was answered immediately by the stirring of the breeze, as though the wind was gearing itself up to meet the challenge of its brother element.

"Let's get back to the hotel," she said, quickening her pace. "It's looking ugly up there."

"It's only two blocks away," said Jake. "If the heavens open we can sprint."

Florence's reply was to seize him by the lapels of his coat and haul him into an alcove in the city wall. For a horrifying moment Jake thought she was pouncing on him.

Any second now we'll be kissing.

But the kiss never came.

"What's wrong?" said Jake. "What is it?"

The archaeologist silenced him with a finger to the lips. Her eyes darted in the direction of their hotel.

"Be quiet," she mouthed.

Jake pressed himself into the shadows, all the old suspicions returning in force.

I'll level with you, Mr Wolsey. I think I'm being followed.

Together they skulked in the darkness; time passed and despite himself Jake began shivering in the chill.

"I'm sorry," whispered Florence. "I don't know what came over me. I suddenly felt so ... so paranoid."

For a moment Jake thought she was going to cry.

"Let's get you back," he said, leading her out of the alcove. "You need a hot bath. And we've earned a stiff drink."

"What must you think of me?" she said when they were within sight of the hotel. "I lost the plot back there."

"Forget about it. It's been a mad few days. And –"

Jake broke off mid-sentence. Two pedestrians on the other side of the street had abandoned their natural trajectory to make a beeline for them. *They were wearing masks.* Jake's heart-rate doubled and the glut of adrenaline made him want to gag. Next there were guns in their hands.

The crack of a whip: it seemed to burst from the air itself.

The shorter gunman staggered. A hand went to his neck. He began clucking. Then he ripped off his mask, and with astonishment Jake saw it wasn't a he at all – it was the flame-haired tourist whose picture he'd taken at the Agya Sophia. The woman's eyes were rolling in her head and she dropped her pistol with a clatter.

"I can't breathe," she rasped. "*I can't breathe ...*"

At first Jake couldn't work out what was happening. But two heartbeats later bubbles began foaming through her fingers. Then she let go of her neck and the blood squirted in a four-foot arc, as if the cork had been popped from a shaken bottle of champagne. There was a second crack as another bullet scythed the air. It hit the woman between the eyes and her skull was evacuated in a cloud of red. Instantly the strangulated gasps ceased and Jess Medcalf collapsed to the ground with the rag-doll swiftness of the newly-dead.

28

During the agent's death throes the protagonists had been powerless to look away. But when that red dot appeared on her forehead like a magical bhindi everything changed. Her accomplice reacted first, diving left as another bullet sliced through the night. There was no gunshot – merely a crack as the projectile broke the speed of sound right by them. Even in the chaos of the moment Jake realized the assassin must have a silencer. The bullet missed the plunging figure and a cobble erupted in a puff of shards. The stranger hit the ground in a roll, but he was instantly on his feet, running fast and low, jinking as bullets whizzed through space on either side of him. Three times the assailant fired his sniper rifle. Twice his aim was foiled by the turns. But the third bullet caught the gunman as he rounded the corner; Jake heard the crunch of lead into bone and sinew and the man's shoulder turned inside out like a juiced grapefruit. Somehow he stayed on his feet until he disappeared around the shoulder of the building.

Rain lashed against Jake's face as he ran. He gritted his teeth against the deluge, Florence's grip bony on his wrist.

Behind them Medcalf's body was inert: black became sepia as her lifeblood was washed beneath the streets of Istanbul. A Mercedes M Class roared into view and slowed, sniffing at the corpse, a man with a gun in the passenger seat. To the journalist's right a narrow set of steps wound its way between two nineteenth-century apartment blocks. He pulled Florence into the defile.

"The train station's this way," he said. "If we make it we can lose them in the crowds."

They rushed through the alleyway. Cracked plaster and graffiti; empty cooking-oil drums; a white cat fleeing before their onrush with its ears flat. The four-by-four slowed, hovering at the top of the steps, and for a moment Jake and the front seat passenger looked into each other's eyes: he was ginger-haired and square-jawed, with hulking shoulders. An understanding passed between the pair and then the car tore away, the sound of its engine growing quieter – only to grow in volume again. That was when Jake realized.

The lane doubles back below us.

The Mercedes rounded the hairpin bend to their left as they made it out of the defile. On the far side of the street another stairway beckoned. It was a race. Already the car was a blur – gaining speed, hunched forward on its wheels. If they didn't reach the next alleyway they would be run down like dogs. And it was going to the wire.

He wasn't going to get there. He wasn't going to get there.

He wasn't –

The car missed Jake by a hand's width. Displaced air buffeted him and he stumbled down the steps. The engine note fell away as it raced for the next bend, looking to intercept them below for a second time. Jake clambered to his feet. They had thirty seconds to clear this alleyway and burst across the main road for the safety of the train station. But Florence hauled him back out of the alleyway and pointed up the hill. "That way," she shouted.

The walls of the Topkapi Palace formed a black hulk against a sky that still flickered with lightning.

"It'll be closed for sure," Jake gasped.

Tyres screeched as the Mercedes reached the end of the alleyway they had been about to run down. A block away they heard car doors slam, a frantic three-point turn. Gunmen were coming up the stairway and the Mercedes would be back. There was no time to argue. Two pale arcs illuminated the street as the car rounded the corner. The driver gunned his engine, a bull stamping before the charge. Then the Mercedes shot from the starting blocks, hitting thirty, forty, fifty miles an hour. Jake's feet crashed through the puddles and his shadow was thrown up in duplicate on the road, a pair of fleeing figures that converged as the vehicle neared. The hill was steep and his breath was ragged. He felt himself surrender.

He had never known love.

Energy flooded back into Jake's bloodstream, his adrenal glands spurred into overdrive. Only this time the surge of hormones didn't diminish him. His strides became powerful and he pulled ahead of Florence, dragging her along. Now their shadows flickered on the ramparts. He saw a gate; it stood open. It was man against machine, muscle and sinew versus metal and precision engineering. The hunger for survival beside the instinct to kill.

The engine note rose to a scream.

29

Rubber squealed on the wet cobbles. If the driver hit them at terminal velocity the four-by-four would only be able to stop with the aid of Ottoman masonry. Rain became steam on the car's bonnet as it skidded to a halt. Men fumbled with door handles and Jake recognized the barracuda profile of a silenced

Heckler and Koch machine pistol. The gunmen opened fire; at once the ramparts became a blizzard of stone chips. Jake pulled Florence through the gateway into a small courtyard. Neither had been hit.

Inside grass glistened underfoot and a cherry tree spread its boughs low to the earth. Jake could see a row of ornate pavilions on the far side of the garden.

"Hey! You no allow now!"

Workers were everywhere – it appeared the annual deep clean was under way.

"Is closed mister! Mister, is closed!"

Now the gunmen were in the courtyard too, scanning for targets – but cleaners scattered in every direction and the killers were impeded by a screen of humanity. Jake and Florence made it into a double-domed room, a golden dais in one corner. This was the entrance to the Sultan's harem: a gilded prison where wives once poisoned children in a bid for the succession. They kept on running. The second room bore murals of fruit on every wall. The third was a chamber of blue and white tiles, praises to Allah fluttering across the wall like kites' tails. The rooms blended into each other as the pair headed deeper into the labyrinth. But the flight was uncontrolled and Jake lost his orientation.

He stopped running. "I don't know which way is out."

Left, right, straight ahead – from then on they chose the directions at random. Somewhere within the maze an alarm began to wail – and before Jake knew it they were looking at fruit murals again.

Florence was wild-eyed. "We're back where we started."

Jake led her into the mirrored throne room of the Ottoman Sultans. A marble colonnade skirted the chamber; a chandelier dangled like a glassy plum; the ivory throne was strewn with cushions.

Two gunmen walked in.

*

The MP5 is capable of firing nine hundred rounds a minute. That gave the men who now confronted Jake and Florence the firepower of three Second World War battalions. The machine pistols swivelled in parallel as they fired, tracking Jake and Florence's dash. The throne room disintegrated around the fleeing pair: mirrors smashed, ivory splintered, clumps of stuffing were propelled through the air. The structural integrity of the pavilion was shot through and the structure sagged to the ground. Somehow they cheated the devastation. Florence was sobbing – out of breath, out of ideas, mucus trailing from one nostril. Jake steered her into a chamber where they could hide. It was pitch black in there.

A motion sensor switched on the lights.

They were in a Turkish bath with walls of marble, modesty screens intersecting the room. Jake sensed movement and he grabbed Florence by the neck, pulling her for the cover of a marble bathtub as the gunman fired a burst from his machine pistol. At once the bathroom was full of zings and cracks as the bullets ricocheted off the bath, the ceiling, the walls, bouncing around the enclosure in geometric angles. Jake tried to cover Florence's body with his own as a bullet whipped past his cheekbone, warming the skin; another slammed into the floor by his foot. At last the rounds pummelled away their kinetic energy. The maelstrom ended.

Jake could hear what sounded like a seal slapping its flippers on the floor. He peered around the modesty screen. He winced. One bullet had travelled from bathtub to ceiling before revisiting itself upon the gunman – the flattened blob of metal had entered his kneecap from above and opened out a tennis ball-sized crater where it exited. His shinbone was barely attached. Snapped nerves trailed like vermicelli and the hapless man squirmed on the floor, mouth opening and shutting noiselessly.

"Oh my God," said Florence.

"This way," said Jake.

He felt himself take control. A new feeling. And a good one. Now their flight was ordered as they headed through the complex. There were no more encounters – perhaps the others were tending to their accomplice before he bled to death. Jake and Florence stepped onto a patio on the north side of the palace to see Europe and Asia splayed before them. Night-time Istanbul was sprinkled across the hills like mulched stars against the sky, a million-dollar view.

They dropped the small distance from patio to grass and sprinted through Gulhane Park to the perimeter walls, sirens closing in. The grounds were wooded and a few cleaners fled through the trees. Jake and Florence mingled with them, sneaking through the northern gate as the first police cars rounded the corner.

"What now?" Jake tried to take Florence's arm, but she pulled from his embrace.

"We can't go back to the hotel," she said. "Let's cross to Asia."

The Kadikoy ferry terminal was nearby.

Once they were on board Florence went to clean herself up. Jake watched the Topkapi Palace diminish as the ferry buffeted across the channel. The park had come alive, like a termite hill ransacked by children; police cars prowled through the darkness. Only then did he reflect on what he had come through that night. Only then did he consider what he was mixed up in. Only then did he weep with fear and relief, the salt water on his cheeks mingling with the saltiness of the breeze and his sobs lost amid the slap of waves on the hull. Abruptly the tears ceased. He would try not to cry again. He was strong, he knew that now. And he was alive. The storm had blown itself out and a chink of moon winked at him through the clouds, a pale eye keeping up its watch on the affairs of men.

Part Two

Tempest

To be ignorant of what occurred before you were born is to remain always a child.

Cicero, Roman orator, 106-43 BC

30

Jake awoke to find himself lying on grass – a moment of confusion. Further down the slope a campfire made a smudge against the night and as he watched a swarm of embers took wing like disturbed fireflies. There were voices around the flames; he sensed electricity in the air. Suddenly it made sense: he was at Glastonbury. Jake felt a rush of gladness and ran to join in.

Only this wasn't Glastonbury, he saw that now. There was no dance music, no hiss and rush as balloons inflated with laughing gas. He couldn't place the language being spoken around the fire. Yet it was familiar somehow. A spurt of flame illuminated thatched huts. Geese pecked in the dirt. *What was this place*?

A young woman beckoned him to sit. She was flaxen-haired and pretty, but there was something primeval about her face – the flat cheekbones, the heavy brow. She handed him a hollow ostrich egg and produced a jug of silver. The lines of the vessel were timeless, it could have been purchased from a Chelsea designer. But then he saw the archaic touch: a ram's head where handle joined rim. The red wine she poured him tasted tannic and astringent.

An old man wearing robes of red and yellow tartan approached the flames – his palms were open to the skies and he wore a hat shaped like an inverted funnel. Jake had seen one of these caps in Britton's office, on a statue that belonged in a museum.

Now he knew where he was. This was Etruria. It was a very long time ago. And he was looking at a *fulguriator*.

At first the lightning priest spoke softly. But there was a cadence to his voice, a rhythm. No, a *beat*, that better described it: a drumbeat that grew with intensity. The woman poured a slick of wine onto the fire, which sizzled in response. Next a goat was led forward. It seemed ignorant of its fate, willing even, and the priest seized it by the chin. Yet it didn't shock Jake when iron flashed in the flame, nor was he repulsed at the spilling of blood onto earth. The goat's legs surrendered, the animal pulled down by gravity to rejoin its mother element. Still the old man's words unfolded themselves, and the drumbeat of his tongue echoed about the hillside.

Jake could understand him.

He heard the priest invoke Tages, the child who had risen from beneath a plough to reveal the proper discourse between Gods and men. He felt the supplication to the pitiless *consentes*, advisers of the supreme Tin. He absorbed the appeal to *dii novensiles*, Tin's consorts, casters of lightning. And he trembled at the final entreaty to Tin himself, whom Eusebius had called the Great All-Seeing Eye.

At Tin's name the villagers cast themselves to earth. The clouds tumbled over each other, gathering their strength, and there was the rumble of thunder on the north-west horizon. At this a moaning arose on the hillside – the villagers pulled clods of grass from the earth, clawed at their cheeks. Still the priest continued his exhortation, still the drumbeat rose, and the thunder began to circle them in a dark halo. The beat was in Jake's ears, in his blood, it pounded through his heart and the air and the earth.

The lightning struck.

A rod of energy, smashing through the nearest hut, a column of light that lanced from the heavens to earth. For two seconds the beam held its form. It shrivelled eyes, blasted eardrums, the villagers' faces shone a ghastly white. Yet it was wondrous and no one could look away.

The chain of supercharged ions was broken. The hut burst into flames. The valley was quiet again, air filmy with heat. A few villagers whimpered; a baby started crying. A dog which had been pressed into the earth judged the time was right to flee and bolted down the hillside.

The *fulguriator* spoke once more, and at last Jake realized what he was witnessing. This was the foretelling of the end of the Etruscan kingdoms. This was the announcement of the always-appointed date, when the Etruscan age would cease, when the baton of power would be passed to a new and brighter people. This was the prophecy of the turning of the wheel.

And the war of civilizations would go on.

*

Jake awoke, gasping for breath. For the second time he was disorientated. Was he still asleep? A dream within a dream? He sat up to find himself on a sofa in a pay-by-the-hour hotel room. His belly was covered in sweat. A sleeping figure lay in the single bed, and slowly it came back to him. The inscription in the Roman Cistern. The woman with the ginger hair. He shook his head like a dog casting off water, trying to rid himself of the dream – the despair of its climax was all-pervasive. Something Florence had said about Etruscan faith came back to him.

A dark religion. Before the Gods man was a complete nonentity, his fate utterly in their hands.

Jake shook his head again – bewildered at the power of his own imagination – when his phone began to ring.

London calling.

31

No matter what happens in there, Jenny Frobisher told herself, remain calm. This is the supreme test of your professionalism. By all means let him know you're disgusted, tell him Jess Medcalf was your friend, show him you've got a good mind to go above his head if his answers aren't spectacular. But remain in control.

She was calm as the embassy guard passed her Hermes handbag through the X-ray machine. She was composed at reception. She was even unruffled when Waits himself appeared, cupping her right hand in both of his.

"Jenny. Thanks so much for coming."

Waits led her to a windowless room in the basement, so like the Vauxhall cell where she was first dragged into this insanity. A table, two chairs, a watercolour of Margate. There was a knock on the door. Evelyn Parr, Jenny guessed – but it opened to reveal an elderly woman with bottle-bronze hair who manoeuvred a trolley into the room.

"Tea or coffee, dears?"

"I'll have a tea, thank you." Jenny forced a smile.

"And you, sir?"

Waits didn't look up. "Coffee with cream."

Jenny stared at him; beneath the table her right knee began shaking uncontrollably. Waits met her gaze, blinked and settled on Margate. His mouth opened and closed – there was something so self-satisfied about the way his jowls settled. The tea lady was footling around with milk and a plate of bourbons. Jenny realized she was jabbing an index finger into her palm.

"There you are, dear."

The cup and saucer shook in Jenny's hands as she took them. "Thank you, that's lovely," she said.

The tea lady placed the biscuits in front of Waits and rotated out of the room, trolley jangling all the way. The door shut.

"You bastard!" Jenny screamed.

God that felt good. But Waits merely leaned back and folded one leg over the other; the little shit was imperturbable.

"You *knew* we were going into danger, but you sent us anyway."

Waits remained silent.

"You *knew* my team weren't trained for hot work, but you didn't care."

The spymaster smiled with irritation and flicked a forelock from his eyes.

"You sent us in blind and ignorant. And now a damn good agent is dead and another's injured and we've got a serious diplomatic incident on our hands."

Waits took a sip of coffee.

"And for what? For some ridiculous inscription? What the hell is going on here, Charlie?"

He had another sip of coffee.

"Say something!" she shrieked.

Waits gestured to her chair – it had been sent skittering across the room – and Jenny realized she was on her feet. She sat, and something about the action served to deflate her ire. She waited for him to talk.

"I want you to know that I don't hold that little outburst against you in the slightest," Waits began. "In fact I'd be worried if my agents didn't show any emotion when something awful, something *awful* like this has happened."

Jenny could feel heat pumping from her cheeks.

"But you must understand that we had absolutely no clue about what was going to happen," he said. "None whatsoever."

"Who were they?" she pleaded. "Who killed Jess?"

"They could be any number of people. We just don't know." Waits took a biscuit.

"What's this all about, Charlie? Why are we even here?"

Her handler didn't reply, and Jenny's temper rose once more.

"If you don't tell me I'll go as high up the chain of command as it takes," she said coldly. "Asking the same questions again, and again, and again."

"Do your job!" he screamed, gripping the table with both hands. "Do your job! Do your job! *Do your job*!"

Jenny had gone white.

"Do your job, Jennifer Frobisher," Waits commanded again in a voice now turned hoarse. "Do what Her Majesty's government pays you for, and remember the absolute and unfailing discretion we expect and for which you were selected for this assignment." He produced an orange handkerchief and dabbed at both temples.

"I will do my job," said Jenny. "But please, Charlie, I have to know what was worth Jess's life. Perhaps if you told me I would understand. Perhaps ... perhaps we didn't throw her away for nothing."

Waits fixed her with one eye, as if peering through a telescope. Then he produced a silver hipflask and swigged deeply, contemplating the nightmare this operation was becoming.

"We don't believe it's true, of course," he said at last. "We don't believe it works. But there are others who do. Britain's enemies. The feeling has always been that if we could obtain some of it – let them know we've got it – perhaps we could unsettle their decision making. Lead them into rash and unprofitable choices."

"Believe what's true? Believe what works?"

"What Jake and Florence have been looking for. The *Disciplina Etrusca*. The set of rules for the correct interaction between mortals and powers of a higher sphere." A whimsical smile settled on the spymaster's lips. "The power to predict the future, my dear."

32

The palace shooting broke on Agency France Presse shortly after midnight. By the morning it was world news; Jake's stay in Turkey was prolonged.

"I need you in Istanbul after all," Heston told him. "David wants to go big on it. We're sorting a graphic."

"Niall ... I was there."

"You get yourself down there and gather some colour. And give us a sidebar about the palace itself for a bit of context."

"Didn't you hear me? I was there. It was me they were after."

The news editor snorted. "Yeah, right." He paused. "Wait. Are you serious?"

"Yes, I am serious."

Heston digested it. "Jesus Christ, Jake. Are you ok? What the hell happened?"

"Two people with guns tried to rob us on the way back to our hotel. Then one of them got killed right before our eyes – she got shot in the neck and the head for Christ's sake."

"Wait a minute." Heston's voice had become tight. "Did you say *she*?"

"Yes, a redhead. Why?"

"The *Guardian*'s got an exclusive about an MI6 agent being shot dead. They can't or won't disclose the exact location, but they do say it was in the Mediterranean theatre. And they report two specific details. It was a she. And she was shot in the neck and the head."

Jake had turned haggard. "Well, it's got to be the same woman, right?"

"Almighty coincidence if not. Their source is unnamed. But it must be copper-bottomed, because they've plastered it all over the front page. It's causing a heck of a stir here. As far as anyone knows she's the first MI6 officer ever to have been killed by hostile action."

"Are MI6 confirming?"

"The death, yes. But the government's official position is to wander up and down whistling innocently." Heston exhaled. "We've got a hell of a story on our hands if her death's linked to what happened in the Topkapi. It'll be a proper shit-storm."

"I should've called last night," said Jake. "I wasn't thinking straight. I –"

"Not worried about that now," Heston cut in. "Just worried about what we're going to do with this stonking exclusive of yours. Tell me, Jake, what do you think is really going on here?"

"I reckon it's to do with this dig I've been covering. Earlier in the day we discovered an inscription. We copied it – and we were being held at gunpoint within the hour."

"Give me strength," Heston snapped. "Not this again. Biggest security story this newspaper's had all year and who's on the scene? Mr Forces of Darkness."

"Just hear me out." Jake noticed the assertiveness in his own voice. "I'm not trying to say this fortune-telling stuff actually works, of course not. But can we completely rule out that MI6 *thinks* that it works? Accept for the sake of argument that MI6 believes the Etruscans did have some sort of prophetic ability. At a stroke all the strange little things that have been happening make sense. Britton thinking he was being followed. That post-box being emptied at the wrong time. An MI6 agent trying to accost me and ending up being killed by God-knows-who. Then us being chased by men with sodding machine guns. All the pieces fall into place, Niall."

"Let's deal in facts, not theories." Heston's breath was hot on the receiver. "Fact one, an MI6 agent was shot dead and you may have witnessed it. Fact two, all she did was walk towards you – we don't actually know she was going to molest you in any way. Fact three, you were chased by gunmen. But they were probably just trying to eliminate eyewitnesses."

"What if the guys trying to kill us were MI6 too?"

"That's the single most libellous thing I've ever heard one of my reporters dream up and we'd both be in front of the High Court if even a whiff of it made it into print."

Jake was silenced.

"I'm not running any of this Etruscan stuff, Jake, I'm just not. But you're alive, that's the main thing." Heston mellowed. "And you did good. We'll lead the news agenda all week with this. Look, I'm going to get Marvin to put some calls in." Marvin Whyte was the security correspondent. "Hopefully he'll be able to get a steer from the Home Office, confirm the redhead and the dead spook are the same person."

"Then he'll take the story! Bloody hell, I could have died, Niall!"

"Ok, ok, your byline," said Heston. "I give you my word. But you need help standing it all up, and you don't have the contacts to do it. In the meantime I think you need to get your arse back here, for your own security. You can hardly go wandering around in Istanbul after what's happened. This is serious shit now, Jake. I don't want a reporter getting killed on my watch."

Jake picked up a newspaper on the way back to the hotel. The English-language *Hürriyet Daily News* had splashed on the Topkapi shootout. What else? He read the account with consternation. The story sprawled from pages one to five, yet there was no mention of a redhead killed at the scene. Whoever she was, her body had been removed. Then something else caught his eye and a jolt of fright ran through him, strong enough to produce nausea. In the bottom right-hand corner of page five was a photograph of Dr Adnan Gul; Jake read the story with growing fury.

A leading academic at the Archaeological Museum of Istanbul was found hanged this morning, police have revealed. Dr Adnan Gul was discovered by his cleaner at the small apartment where he lived alone in Sulukule, western Istanbul. Colleagues said he showed no prior signs of depression, and his apparent suicide came as a complete shock.

33

"They've killed Dr Gul," Jake shouted, throwing the broadsheet at Florence. "They've bloody gone and done him in."

The archaeologist put the inscription to one side – books on linguistics were already spread about the room. But as she read the article her head bowed.

"They were after Roger too," she whispered.

"Who are 'they', Florence? Is it MI6?"

"I think so, Jake. I'm frightened."

The word hung in the air.

"Maybe you should just ... let it go. History is important, but it's not worth dying for."

Florence's head shot up like that of a cobra. "Never," she spat. "Why should I? Why should I be cowed by them?"

Jake gaped. "Your eye, Florence. What's wrong with it?"

The archaeologist fumbled for a mirror. "Oh my goodness," she said.

A tangle of vessels had burst across her eyeball, leaving a bloody streak across the white – it looked vaguely bestial. Florence studied her reflection for a long time. Then she replaced the mirror without comment and returned to the inscription.

"What do you think these are all about, then?" she asked. "The Roman numerals at the end of the engraving."

"Who gives a damn? I've just told you Dr Gul has been murdered. Don't you care about that?"

"What is there to say?" she shot back. "Someone's killed him, that's the end of it. I've got a job to do."

Despite himself Jake peered at the shirt. Runic letters were scrawled across the material like the product of a disturbed mind – but the inscription concluded in four Roman numerals: *IV*, *VII*, *IV*, *XLI*.

"Four, seven," said Florence. "Followed by four, forty-one. What does it mean?"

Jake considered the problem. "Well, it's simple isn't it? Book Four, verse seven. And then Book Four, verse forty-one. Eusebius is telling us to read on."

Florence's mouth fell open. "You are *amazing*," she said, scrambling for the paperback and looking up the first passage. "It's entitled, 'Ambassadors from barbarous nations receive presents from the Emperor.'"

I have often stood near the imperial palace and observed an array of barbarians in attendance, bringing for Constantine their most precious gifts. There I have seen the distant Ethiopians, that widely divided race, from the most remote part of the world. They presented to the emperor those gifts which their own nation held in most esteem - crowns of gold, diadems set with precious stones, barbaric vestments embroidered with gold and flowers.

"What did Constantine give the Ethiopians in return?" Jake wondered. "The title says the barbarians received presents from the emperor too."

Florence frowned, reading the page several times over. "It doesn't actually mention his gift in the body of the text - only in the title."

"I can't see Eusebius omitting that detail by accident," said Jake. "It's almost as if he's trying to draw particular attention to the gift the Ethiopians received from Rome by not saying what it was. And we know what Eusebius thought Rome's most precious possession was. The gift he held in 'most esteem.'"

"It would have made sense to hide the Book of Thunder in Africa," admitted Florence. "There were ties of faith and diplomacy between Rome and Ethiopia, established trade routes. And it was the edge of the known world, far from the reach of Christian zealots. I don't know though. Making such a leap based on three little sentences? Really?"

"But there's another line about Ethiopia in *Life of Constantine*," said Jake. "Don't you remember? The bit about Alexander the Great - we read it in the cistern."

Florence sought the passage in a flurry of page-turning.

From among the Macedonians Alexander overthrew countless tribes of diverse nations. He waded through blood, a man like a thunderbolt. But Emperor Constantine began his reign at the time of life where the Macedonian ended it.

He even pushed his conquests to the Ethiopians, illuminating with beams of light of the true religion the ends of the whole earth.

"A man like a thunderbolt," she said.

"Beams of light," Jake replied. "The true religion."

Florence closed the book. "It's in Ethiopia. The *Disciplina Etrusca* is in Ethiopia."

There could be no doubt. Jake could almost sense the long-dead scholar chuckling at the solving of his puzzle – they were touching fingertips across the millennia.

"But Ethiopia's the size of France," said Florence. "And we don't have a clue where to look."

"Yes we do. The second passage indicated by the numerals." Jake sought it out. "Book Four, verse forty-one. Eusebius is describing the preparations before a sacred festival."

Others interpreted passages of scripture, and unfolded their hidden meaning, while those who were unequal to these efforts presented mystical service for the Church of God. I myself explained details of the imperial edifice and endeavoured to gather from the prophetic visions fitting illustrations of the symbols it displayed.

"Jesus," said Jake. "Not much to go on, is it?"

"We've got you, though." Florence looked him up and down. "You're our secret weapon, with your massive sexy brain. You see what other people miss. It's like you've got a third eye."

At that exact moment Jake ceased to find her attractive. She had been using him, leading him on whenever she needed to make use of his intellect. But he needed her knowledge of the period just as sorely.

"Florence," he said. "Can I ask you a question?"

There was something in Jake's voice that made her look up. "What is it?"

"When the Etruscans were at the height of their powers, did they assume their civilization was going to go on forever? Like, I don't know, like maybe some Americans do now? Or did they have an appreciation that the Etruscan world would end one day?"

"Why do you ask?"

"Oh, it was just a dream I had last night."

"Intriguing dream," she said, examining him. "Yes, as a matter of fact they did think their civilization would end. They believed it was limited to a timescale fixed by the Gods. Etruscan civilization was allotted a ten saeculum lifespan – that's equivalent to ten long lifetimes. And as it happens this proved remarkably accurate. An Etruscan haruspex called Volcatius saw a comet after Julius Caesar's assassination and announced the final saeculum."

"Caesar?" said Jake. "But he lived two centuries after the Etruscan kingdoms were overthrown."

"In Caesar's day there would still have been Etruscan nobles," said Florence. "Families who spoke Etruscan. Etruscan neighbourhoods. But fast forward a hundred years and no one speaks Etruscan anymore. Etruscan civilization ended bang on schedule."

"It's strange," said Jake. "I must've read about all this saeculum stuff when I was researching my article. But I'd completely forgotten about it until that dream. Amazing how something can linger in your subconscious like that."

Florence seemed not to have heard him. "There's something quite profound about such an understanding among an ancient people," she said. "Because it's true, isn't it? No nation lives forever, however mighty. Rome fell, Napoleon is history, the sun set on the British Empire."

"Thou know'st tis common." Jake was quoting Shakespeare and he stuck out his chin. "All that lives must die."

"Passing through nature to eternity," Florence finished, more seriously.

"And it's happening as we speak," he said. "Think of the movement of money from West to East. India and China are racing ahead, industrializing, trying to put a man on the moon. Soon Brazil and Mexico will be powerhouses too. And look at Europe, the sick man of the world. Drowning in debt, hugely uncompetitive, out of energy, out of ideas. We're being eclipsed."

"In our lifetime everything will change." Florence glanced at the inscription. "Asia awakens. We're living through the end of Western domination."

The dream returned to Jake then. Not the content – but its *feel*.

And the war of civilizations would go on.

34

Jenny was sitting outside the journalist's new hotel in a blue Fiat as the phone call came in. She groaned. Another hectoring from Charlie Waits, no doubt – the control-freakery emanating from that man's office knew no bounds. But when she looked at the caller ID it felt like a wet cloth had torn inside her chest.

It simply said: Home.

Jenny had visited her mother nightly during her time in Istanbul. Mum was always back to full health, but the dreams would typically be underscored by some prosaic difficulty she was facing. Last night it was a surprise birthday party for Dad. There were too many guests, not enough places for them all to hide.

"Daddy?"

"Jenny. Oh, Jen."

Her world tilted. "What's wrong? What's happened?"

"It's not the worst," he said quickly. "But I'm afraid your mother's very poorly. Her condition deteriorated overnight. Quite markedly."

Jenny said nothing, forcing him to continue.

"Just after midnight she went into convulsions," he said. "Then it was breathing difficulties. By the time I arrived she was hooked up to a machine to keep her lungs working."

"I can't believe this is happening, Dad."

Jenny forced herself not to cry. She hadn't since Marc had left her – and the memory of that breakdown still made her prickle with embarrassment. It finally came at the supermarket checkout, a full fortnight after he had dropped the bombshell. The weekly shop was so much cheaper without all his meat and booze in the trolley, and with only one person packing the damn items had come down the conveyor twice as fast as she could bag them. That was when it hit her she was alone – and possibly always would be.

Why was she thinking of this now?

"They've got her in an artificial coma," her father said. "So she's not in any pain, love."

Of course. Loneliness. When all this came to its logical conclusion the number of people on her side no matter what was down to one.

"Dad, do I need to come home right away? To see her."

"No, don't be silly." His voice was thick. "It's not come to that yet. The doctors say there's no imminent danger of ... the worst. She's peaceful for now."

"And is this a permanent state of affairs?"

"Oh love, we just don't know. But it looks bleak, darling. I'm so sorry."

To her own disgust Jenny's instinctive thought was for herself. A fear reflex, generated like the jerk of a leg struck below the kneecap.

What if I'm a carrier too?

For the second time that day she realized she was digging her fingernail into her palm.

"When will you be back, love? I know your work is really important and everything. But perhaps if you spoke to her while she's sleeping, like I've been doing – she'd know you were there."

Jenny could picture him at that moment: a balding, delicately featured man in late middle age. Slightly stooped, almost certainly wearing his dressing gown. He'd be in the armchair by the piano with a carafe of coffee, one hand on the cat perhaps, his forefinger tracing circles of worry on the top of her head. The dratted cat would be purring away without a care in the world.

"I'll be coming back soon, Dad," Jenny promised, hating herself.

When she hung up it felt as if the world was projected around her on screens and none of it was real.

Her phone buzzed: it was the transcript of Jake's latest conversation with his news editor. Amazingly, the journalists *still* weren't taking proper precautions on the phone. She pulled herself together. Duty calls. Jenny read the dispatch without interest at first. She had studied hundreds of Jake's communications by then, most trivial. But as she read this transcript she shifted in her seat.

What if the guys in the Mercedes weren't the ones who shot the agent? What if they were MI6 too?

At once her mind went to another conversation – when she'd pulled Waits out of his jolly to tell him of the discovery in the cistern.

Oh, all the major embassies have a couple of smooth operators I'm authorized to call on in absolute emergencies.

For the first time Jenny thought the unthinkable: maybe her handler was responsible for an attempt on the life of two British citizens. That still left the question of who killed Medcalf. She read on, and another line jumped out at her that rang so true her skin seemed to shrink around her body.

I'm not trying to say this fortune-telling stuff actually works. But can we completely rule out that MI6 thinks that it works?

Could Jenny rule out that Waits thought the Book of Thunder

was a functional instruction manual for predicting the future? Patently she could not. It was, now she considered it, only slightly less plausible than his line about wanting to unsettle Britain's enemies. Before she could develop the thought her phone rang again. It was de Clerk in Vauxhall.

"You're not gonna like this," he said. "Chung just paid for two tickets to Addis Ababa on her credit card. They're flying in three hours."

The cradle of humanity beckoned.

35

The visa desk at Bole International Airport was a glory of bureaucracy. Six elderly men wearing bobble hats brandished forms, each with his own stamp to be stamped or sticker to be stuck. The queue took an epoch and when Jake thought it was over they were sent back to the beginning so each actor in the farce could tick off the others' contribution. It was an infinite staircase of a border control, and Jake knew he would like this country.

His newspaper was on sale in an airport kiosk, and with a rush of excitement Jake saw he had the front-page byline – the first he'd had in three years. But his face darkened as he read the copy. The story he'd wanted to tell was that all this violence was down to an archaeological fixation at the top of MI6. But every mention of ancient history had been expunged. The top line was that the security services were in some way involved with the Topkapi shootout, with a female agent shot dead nearby. She was named as Jess Medcalf. The claims were attributed to 'sources close to MI6', and at the end it said *additional reporting by Marvin Whyte.*

Niall Heston had refused to sanction a trip to Ethiopia to pursue some "damn fool hunch" – and he had only relented to Jake's request for two weeks' immediate leave after a review of his personal security was carried out. The resulting risk assessment ran to seven pages. Jake wasn't dissuaded. This was the biggest story of his career; he was young and unattached – if ever there was a time for swashbuckling, dangerous journalism it was now.

They emerged from the airport, blinking at the magnificence of an African morning. Ethiopia is in the tropics, but Addis stands at twice the height of Ben Nevis. The altitude counters tropical sunshine, so it was pleasant beneath the sun but cool in the shade. The capital was comely by the standard of African cities, high-rises interspersed by greenery, with entire city blocks abandoned to baobabs and warka. Dome-shaped mountains ringed the metropolis and eagles patrolled above. Jake had anticipated the bedlam of a Mumbai or a Bangkok, yet there was little hassle, most people lolling in the shade. The shantytown parted to reveal agricultural land. Women wearing headdresses tilled the fields; a river choked with rubbish cut through the pastures, while cannabis plants nodded in the breeze.

Florence was nervous – "this is Africa" – so for a soft landing they checked into the Addis Hilton, a brutalist 1970s megalith. The embassies nearby were guarded by teenagers with AKs dressed in mismatched uniforms. But something was missing. There were no guards outside the big houses, no machinegun posts or razor wire. Addis was not Johannesburg.

Jake and Florence planned their next move in a restaurant. Ethiopia lay before them, a land of deserts and mountains so inhospitable it had taken Europeans two millennia to conquer it. For the twentieth time Florence studied the prose. But Eusebius's pointer was oblique to the point of uselessness.

Others interpreted passages of scripture, and unfolded their hidden meaning, while those who were unequal to these efforts presented mystical service for the Church of God. I myself explained details of the imperial edifice and endeavoured to gather from the prophetic visions fitting illustrations of the symbols it displayed.

"What does that even mean?" she asked.

"It definitely *sounds* relevant," said Jake. "Hidden meanings in scripture, prophetic visions and so on."

"But it's too dense to make any sense of it."

"That phrase, 'the imperial edifice,'" said Jake. "I haven't seen it anywhere else – it's a little odd. But trying to single out a site from those two words?"

Florence groaned. "We haven't a hope."

36

The only option was to investigate every historical site contemporaneous with Eusebius. But there were dozens to choose from: it looked like folly.

"What about this Lalibela place?" said Jake. The guidebook pictured churches carved by hand from the red rock. "It's a world heritage site, and the Ethiopians believe it was created by angels."

Florence wrinkled her nose. "Look, it dates from the twelfth century AD. Much too young."

Their food arrived, a spicy lamb stew served on a sour *injera* pancake. It was delicious and they used strips of *injera* to claw up the meat.

"The grog's pretty special too," said Jake. The national drink was *tej*, a honey wine served in glasses shaped like laboratory flasks.

A Dutchman at the next table overheard him. "What are you drinking that crap for?" He was tanned and thick-necked, with greying ringlets greased back over his head.

"When in Rome," said Jake.

"Each to their own, I suppose. You two here to work?"

Jake and Florence exchanged looks.

"Holiday," she said.

Their companion sneered. "Holiday? Why would anyone come to a dump like this for a holiday? Ach, I suppose the natives are sweet enough in a sort of childlike way. But their attempts at running a country are laughable, no?"

Jake's jaw clenched involuntarily. If this narrative continued he might say something he would regret.

"I like this country," he countered. "It defies expectation. If you believed what you read in the papers it would be some fly-blown hellhole."

"Oh, Ethiopia has lots of bits like that," said the man. "Take it from me. But it's all so unnecessary – they just don't make the best of what they've got here. I'm a consultant, and working with *these people* I don't know whether to laugh or cry."

Jake turned his back on the drinker.

"For sure, man," said their companion, riled now, spoiling for an argument. "I see lots of dancing and praying, but I don't see any actual schools being built. They're batshit mental, that's the problem – even the smart ones. Did you know for example that every Ethiopian believes the Ark of the Covenant is kept in this country?"

Jake turned to face him again.

"That's right." The Dutchman snorted with laughter. "They think King Solomon sent it here to the Queen of Sheba, of all people." He finished his beer and clicked his fingers at the waiter.

Florence had stopped picking at her food. "Where is it kept?"

"Some place called Axum, up in the far north. It's a nice fairytale I suppose. But there's a catch. Only one person alive has actually seen the Ark – this ancient monk guy who's the guardian. Every other Ethiopian has to take it on blind faith." He laughed again. "And there's another problem with the story.

This Axum place was built in the fourth century AD. But King Solomon lived, I dunno, a thousand years before that. Just think of it – all these Ethiopians worshipping some secret trophy which cannot possibly be the real thing." He gave up on the waiter. "Ah, forget it, they just lost a sale. Adios my friends. Happy travelling."

Florence and Jake met each other's eyes. Neither spoke; their food cooled slowly.

Eventually the reporter raised a glass. "I think that's what they call a break, old girl."

But even in that moment of euphoria the sadness of the country was bought home to them. Three barefooted children were eyeing up the food from a polite distance and Jake gestured to the unfinished pancake.

That was all it took.

Bang! The youngsters pounced with the fury of a great white, gobbling up the sustenance in fistfuls, each child afraid to slow down in case the others got an extra morsel. In seconds the feeding frenzy was over. The eldest snatched the last shred of *injera*, stuffing it into his mouth and gloating at the spasm of consumption, eyes like egg whites. Without a word they sprinted away. The display reminded Jake just where he was in the world; there was a lump in his throat.

"That was intense," he managed.

Florence rolled her eyes. "Disgusting behaviour," she said.

Jake didn't know how much longer he could put up with her.

37

Axum was in the northernmost tip of the country, a five-day journey by car, so they had no choice but to brave Air Ethiopia. The propeller-driven plane resembled a Lego toy. But once they were airborne air safety records were forgotten: this was true wilderness. The aircraft's shadow was a midge on the landscape as the Great Rift Valley slipped below them, a cleft lip on the world. It was there that ape became man. They scudded over a silvery lake the shape of a Christmas tree. How long since human foot had trod its banks? Next Jake saw a tombstone of rock the size of a tower block embedded in the earth, like a prehistoric henge cast down from space. Soon the ground faded from sight, cloaked in a pall of dust that made it impossible to tell where earth ended and the sky began.

To pass the time Jake retrieved Britton's notes. The century-old pages were now dog-eared, but he had given up hope of finding anything useful in them. If *Life of Constantine* was a map, then the bundle accompanying it was a testament to delusion.

"What are you doing?" Florence's voice became sharp on the 'do' and rose on the 'ing', turning the question into a challenge.

Jake ignored the hostility, immersing himself in the pages. Florence stared at the seat in front as he read, her head buffeted as the tiny aircraft skidded over the airstreams.

"I'll tell you what," he said, despite himself. "If you were willing to suspend disbelief, some of Britton's conclusions almost make sense. You can see why someone predisposed to mental illness would read something into this stuff."

"Such as?"

"Well, this for a start. In 217 AD the Colosseum gets hit by lightning. It's easy to imagine what a stir that must have made in a superstitious time. The Colosseum was built with treasure stolen during the sack of Jerusalem – it symbolized Roman power. The strike was seen as a warning. Within two decades Rome gets its first Christian emperor, Philip the Arab. Then *voilà*, lightning strikes the Colosseum again. It's like the sky was grumbling. And what happens next?"

"The Third Century Crisis," said Florence. "Plague. Barbarians at the gates. Civil war after civil war. The Emperor Valerian suffered the indignity of being captured by the Persians, something totally unheard of."

"It says here the Persian King used him as a living footstool. When he got bored of that he had Valerian flayed alive." Jake grinned. "Not ideal."

"There were sixteen emperors in as many years," Florence went on. "Gallienus and Aurelian spent their entire reigns rushing across the empire fighting fires. The Goths were hammering on the door at one frontier, Persians at the other. Athens got destroyed by barbarians – the very birthplace of western civilization."

"And in 283 the Emperor Carus was actually *killed* by lightning," Jake said. "While he was campaigning in Persia. To us, as much of a coincidence as Roger's death. But to Roger while he was alive? Or to ordinary Romans in the third century? More evidence that the skies were angry."

"Evidence the skies had been snubbed by Philip the Arab," said Florence. "Pagan Gods gave Rome a whole world. By taking the auspices the empire had become the greatest superpower ever known. Look how the Gods were repaid."

"And which emperor finally restores order?" asked Jake, handing her another page. "An emperor famous for his devotion to Paganism? An emperor who persecuted Christians without mercy?"

"Diocletian," Florence whispered.

Jake shivered. For an instant it had all felt real and his dream returned to him in a spasm: the end of the Etruscans, foretold by thunder.

"The Emperor Diocletian," Florence repeated. "Who we think *met* Eusebius, when he visited Palestine. The perfect moment to convince Eusebius to become his man on the inside."

"But why was Eusebius up for it? If Christians were willing to be martyred in the blood-pits of Rome, a few honeyed words from the emperor are hardly going to convince him to abandon his faith."

"Well, if Diocletian could show him that the *Disciplina Etrusca* actually worked ..."

Jake guffawed at that; the dream retreated.

"Nice one," he said. "You know, I almost admire Roger's intellect. Pulling the whole weird web together."

"Especially as first-hand sources for the Third Century Crisis are so rare," said Florence. "That so few manuscripts from the period survive tells its own story."

"It's just a shame Roger's version of history is a complete work of fiction, brilliantly embroidered though it may be. But even if you engage with his theory it makes no sense, any of it. If the Etruscans really could tell the future, ask yourself this. Why didn't their civilization dominate the world? And if Rome somehow stole that power from the Etruscans, why did they lose a single battle? Why are we not at this moment speaking Latin and wearing togas?"

38

Jake tried not to make a habit of disobeying Foreign Office guidelines, so he stepped out of Axum's matchbox airport with unease. They were close to the disputed zone between Ethiopia and Eritrea, where four backpackers had just been shot dead by bandits who had crossed the porous frontier. There was speculation that the killings were ordered by the Eritrean government; the Foreign Office was recommending against 'all but essential travel' to within ten kilometres of the border.

Axum was the home of the Ethiopian Orthodox Church. But this was no Vatican City. Lone camels clomped past shacks stained ruddy by the universal dust of Africa; there was a sense of the Wild West in the wind. A dozen obelisks shaped like stone electricity pylons dominated the town centre. Each stele was hewn from a single block of granite, circles and rectangles carved down the sides.

"The steles of the Axumite rulers." Florence's eyes shone. "Each one erected to the memory of a dead king."

"I've never even heard of the Axumites," Jake admitted.

"It's one of those civilizations which for some reason never permeated the public consciousness," she said. "But it was one of the four great kingdoms in its day. Rome, China, Persia, Axum. They were literate too. Ge'ez is still the language of the Ethiopian Church."

One of the steles had toppled in the distant past and the colossus had fractured into five blocks, each the size of a minibus. The shattered rock was warm to the touch. A lizard scuttled away in fright.

"That one would've stood higher than the tallest obelisk in Egypt," said Florence. "To this day nobody knows how they got it to stand vertical."

Jake channelled Shelley. "Ozymandias, king of kings. Look on my works and despair! Nothing remains."

"No nation lives forever," said Florence quietly. "All that lives must die."

Jake leaned against the broken monolith and gave her a loaded look. "The imperial edifice?"

"There's only one way to find out."

The sun had slouched low in the sky by the time they finished searching the stele field. Damp patches emanated from Jake's armpits and the dust had turned his hair strawberry-blond. But not a trace of Etruscan could be found.

"There's nothing here," said Florence.

"Then let's see what we came here to see." Jake grinned, his teeth white behind the mask of dirt. "The Ark of the Covenant."

*

All the wretchedness of humanity was awaiting them at Ethiopia's holiest site. There was a man with no nose, a boy with no hands or feet, an elderly woman with mushroom-like protrusions on her face. A suspension of sweat and decomposition was in the air – the smell of poverty – and culture shock hit Jake like a breezeblock to the head. It was like nothing he'd ever seen before. Not in Addis; not even in India. Beggars clawed at his arms as he muscled through the press and there were shouts of '*faranji*', foreigner. Jake looked at the ground, at the litter and the faeces. A phrase came to mind. *In tatters*. The worst of medieval London must have been like this. He offered the mushroom woman a banknote; her tongue glistened as she grasped for it and the general cry for money became more persistent. He batted a little hand away from his pocket as they made it to the gate.

Inside the compound the noise fell away: the desperate were not allowed in. The trees were ablaze with violet blossom and a vermilion bird threaded its song around the trunks. The late afternoon sun cast the world orange and the air was warm and still. An elderly monk wearing saffron robes and a fez leaned on his prayer stick, one foot dangling above the ground as he regarded them through cataract-ridden eyes. At first Jake wondered if the holy man could see them. But when the reporter held his hands together as if in prayer the monk's face contorted into a toothless smile. Then he mumbled something in Amharic and pointed at a man in a frayed suit who came skipping towards them.

The newcomer beamed, revealing huge gums. "I am guide."

The pair were led to a church with battlements and irregular walls. Little light penetrated the interior, which was imbued with the smell of parchment and desiccated wood.

"This place has to be a thousand years old if it's a day," said Florence.

Wooden panels cordoned off the inner sanctum, a mural of three bearded men spread across the screen: the Father, the Son and the Holy Spirit. The faces glowered at Jake as if sensing his intentions.

"The Ark is kept inside?" Florence's words bounced about

the basilica.

But the guide shook his head, taking her by the elbow and leading her back into the sunlight. "Ark is here, madam."

Jake had to laugh. The purported inheritance of Solomon and David had been stashed in a tiny modern chapel, lime green with an egg-shell blue pimple of a dome perched on top. The garden was a riot of nature; weeds proliferated and a column of termites snaked towards their mound.

"The Ark of the Covenant is kept *there*?" asked Florence.

The guide nodded, emotion welling in his eyes.

"It fits with Eusebius," said Jake. "The Axumite steles are the imperial edifice – and the Ark would always have been kept in a 'Church of God.'"

Florence glanced around. "Only these two old-timers here," she said. "Do we go for it?"

Jake stroked the stubble on his cheeks as he considered it. "I don't know. It feels wrong somehow – this is their sacred place."

"We're not going to steal anything," said Florence. "We'll take a few photos and do a rubbing. And anyway ... aren't you curious? We may even find ourselves looking at the Ark of the Covenant. The chest that contains the tablets on which the Ten Commandments were inscribed by God. Just think of it!"

Jake felt a welt of excitement. "Ok, ok," he said. "Of course we're going in there. But I'm not going to just leg it through the door. The old boys will raise hell. We need to be cuter than that. It's nearly full moon, right?"

Florence frowned. "Not sure – why do you ask?"

"I've just had a bit of an idea ..."

39

Jenny had been to "proper" Africa twice. In Nigeria she had bribed an informant in the Islamist group Boko Haram, and she had been briefly deployed to Somalia on account of the Al-Shabab insurgency. Ethiopia was an altogether more peaceful undertaking, and Jenny smiled as she took in the pace of the life from her hotel balcony. Dawn had brought a blanket of cloud to Axum; the rains were supposed to be months away and there was palpable excitement at a drink for the crops. For the first time in days she began to relax.

There was a knock on her door. Frank Davis was the replacement for Medcalf, whose body had just been released to her family in Belfast. Davis's face was handsome and hard with a suggestion of acne scarring, his hair steely-black but for a white pebble. Jenny could tell he was seasoned. That morning a hessian sack blowing down the street had briefly caught her attention. Davis had his back turned to the bag, but he'd noticed her eye-movement. He was facing the sack at once, one hand already in his jacket. Yet it was more of a drift than a jerk, a natural motion. The reflex had been entirely subconscious and he'd resumed conversation without missing a beat.

"I thought you should know they're up to something," Davis said. "Wolsey just told Chung they'll wait until 2 a.m. before going back to that chapel they were in earlier."

"Not your standard sightseeing hour, is it?"

Davis looked away, unsmiling. "Will you tell Charlie or shall I?"

There was something familiar in the way he pronounced her handler's name that troubled Jenny.

"Leave it to me," she said, reaching for her phone.

Waits clucked as he considered the development. "Are you sure they don't mean 2 a.m. by the Ethiopian clock? That would be a perfectly normal time to visit."

Trust him to be informed about the detail on the ground. Ethiopians count the hours from sunrise rather than midnight – so 2 a.m. by the Abyssinian reading of the hands was 8 a.m. to everyone else.

"They've been working by the European clock," said Jenny. "Don't worry, we'll be there. I'll let you know what happens right away."

Waits cleared his throat. "No, you won't, actually."

"I'm sorry?"

"I said, no, you won't. You're coming back to London."

Jenny's lips parted. "But I've only just got here."

"Unfortunately Angela wants you back on the Nottingham AQ case. Terrible nuisance, but it can't be helped."

He was lying, she was certain of it. Angela would be informed of her need for Jennifer Frobisher within the hour.

"You're in demand, my dear," Waits was cooing. "You should be flattered ..."

*

Waits hung up and inspected his telephone, as if the device itself displeased him.

"More problems?" said Evelyn Parr.

"Frobisher was the wrong choice," he said. "We misjudged her, I'm afraid. She's proved to have a few too many scruples. And she's thinking too much."

Parr ran a hand through silvery hair. "It's going to be tough for Frank and Alexander with her gone," she said. "And we're not getting anyone else involved. In all the years SIS have been across this there have never been more than three of us on the case. Now it's me, you, Frank of course – plus Jenny, Edwin and Alexander." She ticked the names off on her fingers; Medcalf was not enumerated. "I know they're all discreet, but really, Charlie, I'm getting jumpy."

"In all these years we've never had such a fluid situation," he said. "The moment Britton blabbed to Wolsey we had an unprecedented scenario on our hands. There was no choice but to widen the cabal." He sighed. "Anyway, tonight we put a stop to this charade. It's time to do what we should've done a long time ago."

"What we should've done a long time ago was bring Wolsey into the fold," said Parr. "Sign him up or pay him off. As it is we've got one agent dead, another so worked up she's unsafe and a stinking mess left behind in Istanbul. Plus there's an entirely new inscription out there in God-knows-who's hands. Because it's certainly not in ours."

"Frank will extract the Istanbul inscription tonight," said Waits in a reasonable voice. "By hook or by crook. And Alexander Guilherme's a good boy. I should think he's got the ruthless streak too, when it comes to it."

"I worry about Frobisher. She's not stable. Latest reports from the hospital are that her mother's on the way out too. What if she does something rash?"

"Oh, don't be so silly," said Waits. "She's proved a bit more, ah, passionate than we'd hoped. But she's a professional. Her record's intact, officially. She's got a whole career to lose."

*

Jenny's mind churned over the phone call. Her bag remained unpacked. Something she had *just told* Waits had precipitated this.

"You all right there?" Guilherme had returned from watching duties, one shoulder enlarged by the bandages under his jacket.

"They're sending me back to London."

"No!" His outrage was convincing. "Why?"

"Apparently I'm needed on another case."

Guilherme looked appropriately shocked. "I just want you to know, I think you've played a blinder on this operation, Jenny. I'll say as much to Charlie."

"Thanks." She hesitated. "Alexander?"

"Yes?"

"Is there anything you're not telling me?"

"What do you mean?"

"Is Charlie planning something tonight?"

There was a jolt. A widening of the eyes, though he recovered in a second.

"Not that I know about," he said, looking her straight in the eye.

"Right. Well ... I'd better get packing."

Jenny felt nauseous as she piled her possessions into a suitcase. Something evil was happening, she could sense it. Two faces came to her then. First Jess Medcalf, grinning through the streaked make-up.

When this job's over let's go on the lash. Just me and you.

The second was that of her mother.

Jenny remembered their last conversation. "Do you remember when I was a little girl?" she'd asked. "How you were always trying to get me interested in painting and art? But all I wanted to do was play cops and robbers."

Mum had smiled.

You only wanted to be one of the goodies ...

A third face came to her then: Wolsey. No, not 'Wolsey': Jake. Call him by his first name, for Christ's sake. She recalled him in the Agya Sophia. Taking the photos, rushing to return that mitten. At the time she'd thought the journalist gormless, but thinking back it was a kind gesture. Having followed him for three weeks she was sure of it. Jake was a good man.

The sports bag they'd collected from the Addis embassy was under the bed. From inside she selected three objects: a pair of night-vision goggles, an automatic pistol and a pinhead bug which could be subtly attached to a man's coat. After a moment's thought she replaced the gun. That was going too far. Then she went to say her goodbyes.

40

The old monk stirred in his bed. He had lived a long life, praise be, but the Lord was testing him in his dotage. It hurt when he moved nowadays, darts of agony pinging in his joints. And tonight they were playing up more than usual. There was only one thing for it: a slug of the sweet Gonder wine that was his only indulgence. The monk grinned and licked his lips.

Then he forgot about the wine.

The window of the chapel was illuminated. But this was no torchlight – there was something unsullied about the luminosity. The holy man strained to make sense of the vision; curse it, the world grew more blurred with every day. An American woman had told him there was something growing on his eyes that could be fixed by doctors. Yet the cure would cost more than he received as alms in five years, and besides, he knew the truth. He had been given a trial of faith, and this he would overcome. Even as the monk watched, the evanescence faded. He heaved himself up with a prayer stick, chuckling at his own senility.

Yet this was no figment of his imagination. The radiance was back, stronger this time, the window dappled with falling starlight. The holy man glanced at the holy of holies and began a series of obeisances – bowing and crossing himself, lifting one leg, murmuring in Ge'ez. Then he hobbled to the door of the chapel and peered outside. The light enveloped his eyes completely, cascading down upon him in waves. It occurred to him that he had died. Or, praise be, it was a miracle.

The eyes of the blind shall be opened.

The ears of the deaf shall be unstopped.

The starlight dissipated and with disappointment the monk realized the world was still filmy, as if impure glass separated him from the night. Then he saw the patch of light hovering between his feet. But when he looked at it the light zoomed off across the dirt, eddying away towards the ancient church. The holy man cried out, dropping his prayer stick and hobbling after it. The beam reached the church, rose up the walls, came to rest on the Messiah himself. Blood dripped from Christ's feet, oozed from the wound in his side, trickled from both hands. The monk threw himself to earth.

Stigmata.

In that moment the aged one knew true beauty.

*

The moon seemed bigger up here in the mountains and the air was thin, with fewer particles to adulterate its glow. Jake and Florence had mirrors angled to the lunar surface, and the distillation of moonlight they had brewed converged on the statue in a nimbus of white. The monk was in ecstasies, pressing his forehead into the earth, jabbering in that arcane language. By Jake's side lay two empty bottles: wine that had become the blood of Christ. The journalist left Florence to maintain the illuminations and stole towards the chapel.

It was a dreamlike moment, dashing up the overgrown path and heaving the door aside to enter the forbidden place. The room was clogged with the holy man's personal effects – rags, empty wine bottles, a dozen prayer sticks leaning against the wall. Jake felt a shadow of guilt. They had played a shabby trick on an old man.

The chapel was bisected by a wooden wall, diabolic imagery swarming across it. A purple devil whipped a naked man strung up by his hands; another demon led a white-clad figure into the desert by the chin. The angels above were winged heads with Afro-style hair, peeping down at the hellions in their frozen dance. A velvet curtain hung over a door in the partition, and Jake paused to compose himself. Through that wooden screen might lie the Book of Thunder, guarded for more than a thousand years. Or the Ark of the Covenant, though it was insane to think it.

As Jake squeezed through the aperture his throat tightened. A stone chest stood in the middle of the chamber.

41

Jake was not a religious man, but the enormity of what he was looking at affected him more than he had anticipated. He took two steps towards the chest – and the wonder evaporated. The chest was inscribed in Ge'ez, and the stylized angels were identical to those in the murals outside. The Ark was a medieval fraud. But when Jake heaved open the lid he saw gold. There were emerald-studded crucifixes, bejewelled goblets, a gold-handled scimitar and an umbrella of purple felt with gold brocade worked across it. The artefacts sat on a sea of coinage sourced from across the breadth of the Old World. Jake recognized a Tudor sovereign of Henry VII – these went for £25,000 at Sotheby's. This was the treasure of the House of Selassie, dumped here with one senile monk standing guard. It boggled the mind. Jake scoured the hoard for Etruscan, vainly seeking a foreign character amid the Ge'ez inscribed upon the chest. He was too engrossed to hear the far-off peal of thunder.

Nor did he hear the door open.

The guardian was back inside the chapel; Jake registered him too late. The holy man flew at the journalist with astonishing speed, smiting him across the face with a prayer stick. Jake's lips exploded. He heard a tooth splinter. In his panic he had become wedged in the doorway, and as he struggled the monk seized another prayer stick, taking aim again. The old man's arthritis was forgotten – every muscle from his deltoid to his dorsi was working towards destruction. Jake took the second blow on his forehead with a crack that made the room shudder. But mercy had deserted the monk. He was filled only with righteous fury at this infidel who had dared gaze upon the Ark. The holy man reached for a brass crucifix, sending it zinging across the chapel like a Frisbee. The projectile struck Jake's temple and a flap of skin fell open. Florence appeared in the antechamber and the monk flew at her like a bat, sinking his teeth into her throat.

"Get him off me!" she shrieked. "Please get him off me!"

But the monk's rage had imparted him a wiry strength, and Florence was unable to claw him away. The holy man had clenched his jaw shut, tendons protruding from his neck. Jake used the hiatus in his assault to wriggle free of the door. He crossed the room in two strides and plucked the monk off Florence – the old man was light as a wishbone. The monk's legs pedalled the air as Jake held him by the armpits and he clawed at the journalist's face.

"Let's get out of here," he shouted.

"But what are we going to do with him?"

Jake's answer was to bundle the old man through the wooden screen, slam the door shut and wedge it with a prayer stick. At once a beating arose from the holy of holies, accompanied by a litany of curses.

"Where the hell were you?" Jake roared, spitting out blood. His shirt was a mass of scarlet and it looked as if a Doberman had been at his face.

"I got distracted."

"Distracted? By what?"

"I just got distracted, that's all. Did you find anything?"

"Nothing at all."

Florence's face was a mask of frustration as they exited the chapel. Another crack of lightning illuminated the compound and the rain began to fall.

42

Jenny jerked the night-vision binoculars away and blinked in agony. The fifth-generation model was unavailable to the public, but the lightning had overloaded the device in a stream of ions. One moment her footage depicted Florence emerging from the chapel, a new streak of burst blood vessels in her eye; the next a pitching sea of rubble and a gallop of night sky.

Jenny had accepted her orders and set off for Addis Ababa by Jeep that morning. But she had no intention of returning to the capital, and after fifteen miles she found a track striking out across the countryside. She drove in a grand circle around Axum, nosing between valleys and precipices before approaching the town from the north. The Jeep was deposited in a ravine, and then she scaled one of the peaks overlooking Axum. She chose a spot from which she could monitor Frank Davis's hotel, Jake's guesthouse and the church compound in a single sweep of night-vision goggles. If Waits was about to do something shameful it would be broadcast to the world. Once Jenny was in position she tuned in to the bug she'd attached to Guilherme's jacket. It wasn't long before she had heard a conversation that chilled her.

"We'll wait until they've moved on the church." It was apparent from Davis's languid tone that he'd assumed command. "We'll take whatever they find there, and we'll get the Istanbul inscription too."

"What if they won't hand over the Istanbul inscription? The bastards might've hidden it." Guilherme had assumed a tone of machismo to impress his new boss – pathetic – but Jenny could also detect nervousness. Last time he had tried his hand at hot work this man had taken a bullet.

"Charlie's authorized WB," said Davis.

The bug picked up the noise of Guilherme opening and closing his mouth.

"WB? Really?"

"Yeah."

Jenny couldn't believe what she was hearing.

Waterboarding.

"But I ... I didn't think we used that."

"We don't." A low laugh. "Officially, anyway. But in the real world it's damn good at loosening tongues."

"You've done it before then, have you mate?"

"Not personally, but I sat in on a session a few years back in Morocco. It was a hell of a lot rarer than the media made out, but it did go on. Are you ok with all this?"

"Of course."

Jenny visualized Guilherme puffing up his chest. When he spoke again his voice had assumed a note of perverted curiosity, like a child about to tear the legs off a beetle.

"How do we go about it then, mate?"

"Piss easy," began Davis. "You get some restraining cords ..."

As he explained the mechanics of waterboarding – the tethering down, the muslin cloth over the face, the instant submission – Jenny's earliest memory popped into her to mind. Mum had dropped a load of eggs in Waitrose and burst into tears, an uncharacteristic display. Jenny had always assumed Mum must have had something else going on in her life at the time. Why had the recollection come to her now?

Suddenly she saw it: her first memory was of vulnerability.

Jenny tried to call Jake with her satellite phone. But she went straight to his voicemail – regular mobile phones couldn't get signal up here. And suddenly it was too late. Jake and Florence had set off for the compound; there was no time for her to get down the mountain. All she could do was record what happened on the hard drive of her goggles and ensure Waits paid for this outrage with his liberty.

*

That was how Jenny Frobisher came to be perched on an Ethiopian mountain in the rain, eyes stinging from the night-vision flash. Tears ran down her cheeks and she wiped them away with her sleeve, determined not to miss a second. Slowly her vision returned. To the naked eye the compound was a halo of bulbs around a black oval, but when she put the goggles to her eyes the scene was thrown into clarity. The two MI6 men were lurking outside the perimeter wall. Frank leaned against the masonry, the bulge of a firearm tucked into his jeans. Guilherme presented a less indolent spectacle as he paced up and down, eyes fixed on his GPS scanner.

Jenny panned right, the compound passing in a luminous smear of tree and rock. Jake and Florence were heading right into the trap. But a disagreement had broken out. Florence was tugging at his sleeve and urging him in the other direction; Jake was impervious to her appeals as he strode towards the waiting Landcruiser. Jenny swung the goggles left again. Her former colleagues were alert to Jake's movement. Davis's body was taut, a leopard scenting impala on the breeze.

All hell broke loose.

Florence was the catalyst for the violence, abandoning her protest and dashing for the far side of the compound. For now Davis and Guilherme remained in position, unaware of the archaeologist's flight. Then Jake sprinted after her and Guilherme detected the movement on his scanner, starting for the ladder. At once the far side of the street was alive with muzzle flashes, the pop of gunfire reaching Jenny a half-second later.

Guilherme was exposed. One bullet snapped his head to the side, tearing the jaw away. Two more hit him in the solar plexus, slamming him against the wall. Davis bounded towards the Toyota, running low and firing blind. The instant return of fire unsettled the shooters, buying him the dozen paces to his Toyota. He dived through the rear door – it had been left open for Jake – and a moment later the four-by-four was away in a screech of gravel. Tyres blew; glass shattered; the car's bodywork became a colander of bullet holes. Davis was hit in the upper arm and the vehicle jerked with the impact, beads of red smattered across the windscreen. He kept on driving.

Jake and Florence clambered out of the far side of the compound, heading for the mountains that encircled the town. Jenny focussed on her former colleague. Guilherme had slid down the wall to assume a foetal position, leaving a snail-track of gore on the masonry behind him. He was mutilated. A tongue dangled; a hand went to where his jaw had been. His fingers fluttered at the maw and went limp.

43

The scree was slippery in the wet, sliding downward with each step and sapping Jake's energy. Rain fell from Florence's hair in rivulets as she scrambled over boulders. The frozen rock numbed their fingers. When they were half-way to the top Jake paused, trying to plot a course up a mountain that grew only steeper.

"How did you know they would be waiting for us?" he panted.

"I had a bad feeling about it." Florence was gasping for breath too. "That's why I got distracted in the chapel. I ... I can't explain it better than that."

Beneath them flashing lights were winding into town. There was a body outside the compound and a crowd was gathering.

"That's twice," he said. "Everywhere we go people start bloody well killing each other. Who the hell are they?"

"Not now," said Florence. "Let's get over this peak and find somewhere to shelter – our body heat will stand out like a beacon here."

The path was impeded by rock-fall and they had to squeeze through gaps between the stone. At one point a boulder the size of a cottage blocked their way; it took ten minutes to retrace their steps. It was 3 a.m. when they reached the summit, to be blasted by a wind carried from the highlands, where ice and snow still lay. Florence collapsed beneath a mushroom-shaped rock protruding from the ridge. Jake slumped beside her, numbed by fatigue. She pressed into him, craving the body heat. Jake felt his eyelids droop ...

*

He launched himself off the ridge, using the buoyancy of the dream-flier to thrust up through the atmosphere, seeking out the boundary between earth and the void. Curiously, pine branches encircled the world. Jake pushed through, emerging from the Narnian wardrobe. Only it wasn't branches. It was his duvet. He laughed uproariously at the discovery. He had been scrabbling around in bed at his flat in Battersea, worrying his sheets downward.

Wait.

Something wasn't right.

He wasn't in Battersea, he hadn't been in England for ages. In that case where was he? Jake confronted the problem. London, Istanbul – where did they go next? Oh of course, Ethiopia. Addis Ababa – Axum – the Chapel of the Ark ...

Oh Jesus, I'm on the mountain.

Jake opened his eyes to find rain driving into him horizontally. He didn't know how long he'd been out – it could have been seconds or an hour. Florence's head lolled on her neck and she whimpered as he shook her awake.

"Wha ... what? What's going on?" She focused on him with difficulty. "Where are we?"

"Come on, we can't stay here." Jake's lips struggled to form the words. "We've got to keep moving."

As he hauled Florence up he thanked whatever recess of his subconscious had awoken him. They had come within an inch of death from exposure.

44

Jake guided Florence by the waist, the pair staggering along the ridge like competitors in a three-legged race. He prayed for a cave, a fissure, anywhere to provide shelter from the stream of frozen air. He'd never dreamed it could get so cold in Africa. They had no matches to light a fire, and he knew from far-off memories of Boy Scouts that rubbing sticks together was a waste of time.

"Down there!" shouted Florence.

On the far side of the mountain from Axum a flicker of yellow was visible through the rain.

"Well spotted," said Jake, with impressive understatement.

The pair skidded down the slope, frantic for warmth. As they lost altitude the harshness of the upper reaches gave way to grass that glittered with dew. The village was like the Africa of childhood imagination: circular huts, mud walls and grass roofs. Flaming torches had been dotted about to ward off baboon and hyena, and vegetable gardens had been planted between the hovels. Jake saw nothing that would have been out of place in prehistory.

There was an explosion of barks as six dogs shot from the enclosure – they were of one bloodline, wiry and long-haired with muzzles of black felt. The pack ran circles around Jake and Florence, howling in anger but unsure what to do. Children arrived next, shaven-headed tots in tartan shawls with knees too big for their legs. They were shocked to see *faranji*, and Jake was led by the hand into the largest hut.

The interior had been landscaped into an amphitheatre of mud benches around a fire; the smoke wafted out through vents in the thatch. Faces peered at the newcomers in the flickering light. The women had braided hair and wore dresses of yellow cloth, a cross tattooed on each forehead in green ink. One of them pointed at Florence and circled her face with an open palm, cooing to her neighbour. The archaeologist was unaware of their interest. She stared numbly into the flames, steam rising from her knees.

A woman in her twenties produced a shallow pan and a handful of red beans which she roasted in a little oil. She crushed them and placed the mulch inside a clay flask with some water. When she set it on the embers the smell of coffee began to fill the hut. As it came to the boil she lit a pinch of frankincense and the two aromas twirled around each other. Then she handed them cups of black coffee, hands darting back like a startled animal as each drink was received. Jake recognized this as an exquisite moment: backpackers spent a lifetime seeking this sort of cultural penetration. Their beds were strips of leather stretched across frames and he soon fell into a dreamless sleep.

But the night's events were not over.

Something else was to happen before daybreak, something strange and elemental. At the stillest moment of the night Jake awoke. The rain was over, although thunder could be heard to the north. The fire had collapsed in on itself leaving a triangle of embers. Snores echoed through the hut – but beside him there was silence.

Florence had gone.

After half an hour Jake surrendered to chivalry and went to check on her, creeping out of the hut. He saw her at once: storm-watching again. The violence of the weather system had moved towards the Eritrean border and the horizon crackled with energy as the clouds smashed into each other. That was when the lightning hit, arcing to earth far away in the north-east and holding its form for three seconds, like some crooked finger pointing from the heavens. Jake had never seen lightning like it.

Except ...

Except on a hillside in northern Italy, when the end of days was foretold by thunder. Florence was kneeling with the same reverence as those Etruscans of his imagination, fixated on the spot where the bolt had struck.

That was when it hit Jake.

Florence believes it too.

45

Niall Heston was wading through the two thousand emails which had arrived overnight. Had he known how much administration this job involved he might have reconsidered becoming news editor – sometimes it didn't feel like being a *real* journalist. And it was rare that he could get his teeth into a story. That said, £200K was a fair old whack. He must be in the top percentile of the profession. A door knock interrupted his reflections.

"Marvin! Come on in."

Marvin Whyte was a short South African with a magician's goatee who'd risen to be the best-connected security correspondent in the country. He was valuable to the newspaper and he knew it; the last salary negotiation had been a gladiatorial haggle worthy of an Arab merchant, complete with several pretend walkouts.

"You're going to like this, boss," Whyte began. "Jeez, you're going to like this. I just got tipped off that *another* MI6 agent has been killed abroad."

Heston started forward. "Who gave you the heads-up?"

The smile of a crocodile whose dinner is assured crept across the reporter's face. "The Foreign Secretary. We can quote him as a 'highly placed government source'. The minister is hopping mad – he's supposed to authorize all overseas interventions. Well, MI6 just went ahead and did whatever it is they wanted to do without asking. And it's ended in another fatality." Whyte paused, revelling in the scoop. "The minister dragged the chief of MI6 in for a bollocking, but apparently he denied all knowledge. So at best, we've got the head of MI6 losing control of his own organization. At worst – Jeez, Niall, I don't even know what it means at worst."

"Is the killing linked to Medcalf's death?" Despite her family's pleas for a private funeral, the church had been surrounded by a host of television cameras.

"The minister swears he doesn't know. I for one believe him."

"In Istanbul again?"

"No – Ethiopia, of all places."

Heston turned sickly. "Ethiopia?"

"Yep. Why?"

"Jake Wolsey's there. Against my better judgement I let him take a couple of week's holiday. But he was using it to stand up a hunch about what went down in Istanbul. Bit of a coincidence, no?" Heston exhaled, tapping his forehead with the tips of his fingers. "We need to get Jake on the phone as soon as possible. Check he's all right. Get him back here, discreetly. And I think we need to give some serious thought to all these wild theories he's been coming up with."

"What's going on here, boss?"

"I don't know for certain. But I'm beginning to suspect Jake might be onto something more sensational than anything this newspaper's had for a very long time indeed."

*

Two children were keeping watch when the sleeping journalist awoke and sneezed. The youngsters burst into giggles and fled.

Sunlight was streaming through the door of the hut, catching on particulate air; from outside came the rhythmic 'thunk, thunk, thunk' of cassava being smashed into powder with a staff. Jake's head was pounding too – it felt like he had nailed a bottle of gin. Yet confusingly, for the first time in months, he hadn't touched a drop. He yawned and his lips split open, the reason for his headache coming back to him at once. Gingerly he explored the gash across his temple. His hair was matted with blood. He needed a dentist. Then he stepped outside and thoughts of his injuries vanished.

The air was clear and he could see for fifty miles. The heavens above seemed huge, a blue dome to humble the skies of England. A cataclysmic landscape fell away beneath his feet: mountain, precipice, escarpment and plateau, each jousting to be highest. The abysses beneath their feet boiled with foliage, mysterious places where waterfalls flowed.

The woman who had made coffee for them gestured for Jake to sit. She had a bowl of water and began dabbing at his forehead, cajoling him in her high voice.

"*Amesegenallo*," said Jake. 'Thank you' was one of the few words he had learned in Amharic. The woman was delighted to hear her own language and she set about her work with new tenderness.

When Florence ambled out of the hut to join them, Jake did a double take.

"Your eye!" he exclaimed. "It's happened again."

Another twist of blood vessels had burst to the left of the pupil; Florence caressed her eye socket with her fingertips as she studied her reflection.

"I'm sure it's nothing to worry about," Jake said. "People get them from time to time ..."

He was interrupted as the woman began jabbering in Amharic and pointing down the hillside, where an Ethiopian man in western clothes was approaching.

The newcomer questioned the woman in businesslike tones.

Then he said to Jake in English, "Bad place to get lost. You were lucky to find this village, I think. Big storm."

It transpired the newcomer was a health worker who made a circuit of remote villages treating basic ailments and advising on sanitation. He had been educated in Cairo and spoke English well. The medic put three stitches in Jake's temple and gave them both a shot of antibiotics.

After he had finished his ministrations Florence asked something troubling. "Are there any historical sites in this direction?"

She pointed to the north-east.

My God, thought Jake. She's every bit as dotty as Britton.

But to his astonishment the medic nodded. "Yes, yes ... you mean the Monastery of Debre Damo. That way, maybe fifty kilometres drive. It is more than one thousand five hundred years old."

"How do we get there?"

The man waggled his head. "Not possible. It's not safe, madam. Too close to the border."

"How close?"

"Maybe five, six kilometres from Eritrea, something like this."

"The Foreign Office advisory, remember?" muttered Jake. "We're not supposed to go anywhere near there."

"It's dangerous," the Ethiopian agreed. "Really. Last month Europeans shot by Eritrean bandits there. Very bad men, come to Ethiopia to make trouble."

But Florence merely stared at the horizon.

"I'm going," she said at last. "You stay here if you want, Jake – it's up to you."

Jake couldn't let her go into danger alone. In the throes of this obsession she would get herself killed and his conscience wouldn't allow it.

"If we did want to get there," he began, "how would we go about it?"

"A man two villages from here has a car," said the medic. "And he speaks English ok. He can take you, I think. But not cheap. Many dollars."

"I'll pay," said Florence. "We'll find something there, I'm sure of it."

Jake felt a weight in his stomach, as if a heavy stone was lodged there. He followed her eyes to the north-east.

46

The pickup truck bounded through a landscape of baked orange scrub, hemmed in by distant mountains. The earth had been carved into terraces, and in each field a figure could be discerned, bashing at the dirt with a hoe or wandering behind oxen. Most of them seemed to be children. Jake was flung into the air by a bump and he gasped, clinging to his seat.

The driver cackled. "Ethiopia road, is disco road!"

Berihun was a barrel-chested rogue with a snatch of dark beard; the feel of a hundred US dollars had him in high spirits. He stopped to check the map and the children seemed to generate out of the earth itself, tiny bodies dashing to meet them from every ridge. When Jake produced biscuits it became bedlam.

"*Faranji! Faranji! Faranji!,*" they cried. "You! You! You!"

"Like feeding ducks in the park," said Florence witheringly.

Jake ignored the comment. "Look at that one," he whispered.

A boy of three was sniffing at his biscuit; evidently he did not know what it was.

They passed a gang of Chinese labourers, hacking a road out of the desert. European statesmen had given up on the continent, but the Asian scramble for Africa continued apace.

"What do you think about that?" Jake asked Berihun. "Good thing or bad thing?"

The driver frowned. "I not like. Just pretend he wants to help us. China is new Mussolini in our Ethiopia." He remembered Florence and blushed. "Sorry madam."

"I'm not Chinese," she said. "I'm British."

The driver looked sceptical about the claim, but he let it go.

As they neared the badlands the villages thinned out, leaving only a sense of desolation until it was like driving across Mars. They passed a field of mortars, pointing north on their tripods; a dozen pieces of artillery; a column of teenagers in camouflage jogging alongside the track. Finally they reached the end of the line.

The outpost was fortified with sandbags and a heavy machine gun pointed towards Eritrea. A piece of string was strung across the track, the winning tape at the end of a marathon. A soldier sauntered over, chewing on a stick, and addressed the driver in rapid-fire Amharic.

"He says is not safe past here," Beriuhn translated. "If you want go further, you must buy permit. Is costing five hundred dollars."

"I have three hundred." Florence began counting out banknotes. "Will that cover the paperwork?"

The soldier eyed the cash.

"Three fifty, is ok," muttered Berihun.

"Didn't you hear what the man said?" said Jake. "It's too dangerous."

"He just wants money. This is Africa, remember?"

She handed over a wad of bills and the teenager lifted the piece of string. They were through.

"Madness," Jake groaned as they drove into no-man's-land. "Absolute madness."

Beyond the checkpoint it was deserted. Jake and Florence kept up a constant watch, expecting a Kalashnikov to start clattering away at any moment. Cacti assumed the form of desperados before betraying themselves with their scarecrow stiffness. It reminded Jake of swimming in Australia, that dread of a dark shape passing underneath. Even Berihun was tense.

Without warning he hit the brakes.

"What is it?" demanded Jake.

The engine chugged over.

"What?" repeated Florence.

But the driver was grinning. "It is the Monastery of Debre Damo."

A flat-topped mountain rose before them, a house brick dropped in the desert. A spire was discernible at the peak – but the cliffs appeared to be sheer.

"How do we get up there?" said Florence.

"Rope," the driver replied.

Now Jake saw it – a sliver of spaghetti dangling fifty feet from the summit, two monks lounging beneath it. He felt his stomach turn over in synch with the engine. And something else perturbed him, though at the same time his blood pulsed with irrational hope.

"This might be coincidence," he said. "Actually, it *must* be coincidence ..."

"What's coincidence?" said Florence. "Just spit it out, for God's sake. Why do you always have to dither so much?"

"Don't you remember? Eusebius, Book Four, Verse Forty-one. 'I myself explained details of the imperial edifice.' And look."

The cliff towered above them, bearded with trees at its summit.

"The edifice," said Jake. "And above it, a 'Church of God.'"

"It's not coincidence," Florence whispered, almost to herself. "*This is the place.*"

47

The rope consisted of leather strips tied together with granny knots, dangling from a dry-stone guardhouse far above. As Jake looked upwards the cliff seemed to topple towards him by degrees.

"Are we really going to trust our lives to this thing?" he said.

"Is good rope," said Berihun. "Very strong."

A monk grinned and yanked the line with both hands. It held.

"I'm not sure I can do this," said Jake, resting his palms against the rock. "I'm not a big fan of heights."

"You must," Florence replied.

"Why?"

She turned away. "Because I need you. I've needed you all along. Why else would I let you tag along this far? Ok, happy now? Has your ego been massaged enough?"

Jake looked up again, blowing air into both cheeks. "All right then. Let's do this."

The monk tied the rope around Florence's waist and whistled through his fingers. Instantly it became taut and she was plucked off the ground like a sprat on a hook. A minute later she disappeared through the door of the outhouse and the rope snaked back to earth. There was a sense of unreality as Jake was lifted clear of terra firma. He scrabbled at the rockface to keep steady, trying not to think about the rope snapping or the monks loosing their grip.

Just keep going. Just keep going.

As quickly as it began, the ordeal was over. Jake grasped for a handhold and hauled himself into the guardhouse – the doorstep was pebble-smooth. He found himself in a grotto cut into the cliff. An old man in combat fatigues slouched against the rock, AK cradled in his lap. The guard peered at Jake's hands, which were trembling like an Alzheimer's patient.

"You ok?" said Florence.

He gave her a shaky thumbs up. "Yep, home and dry."

Their ascent had been watched.

*

The Monastery of Debre Damo stood amid olive and cherry trees, and the scent of blossom hung in the air. It mingled with a smell Jake couldn't put his finger on – something herbaceous, a little wild. The church itself was a hunch of masonry held together by beams protruding from the walls at each end; a bell jangled listlessly in the breeze. A monk wearing white robes and a black fez glanced at them before returning to his Codex. The bible was hand-written, the saints' names inked in scarlet. The monk read each name aloud, raising a knuckle to his forehead. With each clank of the bell the relaxation flowed through him more deeply, and Jake felt his shoulders loosen. For a crazy moment he fantasized about staying here, to hell with the world and the *Disciplina Etrusca.*

"What are we waiting for?" said Florence. "Let's go inside."

"Just ... two minutes, ok?"

"Jake!" Her voice lashed at him like a whip. "Come on. We've got work to do."

The journalist abandoned his daydream and stepped into the cool of the church. The first room was plastered and painted with naive religious figures, and Florence set about them, examining each scene for a hidden meaning. A young monk produced a bible and showed Jake the pictures – only to become distracted by a line of scripture and begin mumbling it to himself, suddenly far away.

"There's nothing here," Florence hissed. "Let's go further in."

They stepped into a panelled room, the timber black with age; each panel bore a religious scene and a few letters in Ge'ez. They worked in silence, checking the walls methodically, Florence releasing the occasional 'humph'. But there was nothing to be found. Finally she said, "There's shit-all here."

The profanity jarred him in those surroundings, and Jake rolled his eyes to the ceiling.

"Holy fuck," he said.

"What?"

"Florence – look up."

The ceiling was swathed in Etruscan.

It was as if a night sky full of stars had revealed itself after weeks of cloud. The characters stretched from wall to wall, hundreds of them: this was twice the length of the Istanbul inscription. And at the far side two Roman numerals had been carved. Florence moaned, staggering slightly. Jake was oblivious to her. The world eddied around him. His mouth had fallen open and the little finger on his left hand trembled.

"It's real, isn't it?" he said.

48

Florence broke off from her vigil. "What's real?"

Insects crawled beneath Jake's skin and the room felt as if it were rotating; he fought to control his bladder. Again he heard the incantation from his dream, the beat of the drum. He tried to blink himself awake, like a patient told he has advanced cancer. But this was reality.

"The Book of Thunder," he managed. "*It works.*"

Dark shadows had formed under Florence's cheeks. "Why do you say that?"

"Because it's the only explanation," he said. "There are thousands of churches in Ethiopia, and we stumble on the very one where Eusebius hid the inscription? No. You knew it was here."

"A lucky guess." She tried to laugh.

"I saw you last night, Florence. Storm watching again. I saw the lightning – the bolt hit this exact spot, like ..." he struggled for an analogy. "Like a finger, pointing the way."

"Coincidence."

"No, no, *no!*" Jake was angry now. "It's too much."

He couldn't believe it. But he couldn't *not* believe it. Not on top of the death of Professor Britton, struck down by lightning. That, and the ebb and flow of Roman history: how it dovetailed with thunder from beginning to end. He thought of all those 'leaps of intuition' Florence had made. Her chanting in Istanbul and the instantaneous crack of thunder over the mainland. She had pulled him into an alcove. *I suddenly felt so paranoid.* Seconds later they walked into a trap. Florence had sensed what was coming, even if her prescience was fuzzy at the time.

Under that same turbulent sky she had pulled them into the Topkapi – on the one evening its doors stood open for cleaning.

And after the lightning in Axum she had insisted they flee from the chapel in the opposite direction from MI6. She knew there was trouble waiting for them: the skies had told her so.

Something else occurred to him. "You once said the Etruscans believed lightning from the north-east was a good omen," she said. "And lightning from the north-west a bad one."

Reluctantly she nodded. The room seemed to darken as Jake pictured the lightning that killed Britton. That CCTV image left no doubt: the bolt had come from the north-west. Jake made another geographical calculation. The thunder in Istanbul was over the European mainland – north-west again, auguring ill. And the portent that bought them here had pointed from the north-east.

It was as if the book wanted to be found.

Still the revelations came. "Your eyes," he whispered. "Every time you read a sign there were more burst blood vessels in your eyes. Every discovery we made, you were increasing your power."

Florence didn't deny it. In one epiphany each little strangeness of the last few weeks had resolved itself. And all he had learned about existence and the rules that govern nature was blown away – like Einstein standing over the rubble of a clockwork universe.

Pure subordination.

A dark religion.

The world had become creepy. Every object looked different: the rugs, the beams, the tapestries. Brought to this place by causation and chance? Or by the decisions of men? The runic letters seemed to sneer at the notion. For if actions could be read in the clouds before they happened, what of free will?

49

Now Jake understood this deadly race; now he appreciated MI6's scramble for every scrap of text; now he saw why desperate men were doing battle from Europe to Africa, why they were prepared to kill. The power to predict the future: it was the power to command the world.

"So you finally worked it out," said Florence. "Well done you."

"Does that mean you believe in their Gods?" Jake's mind reeled at what he was asking. "Are they real?"

"Nobody knows," she said. "There's a lot we don't understand about the universe. It's strange, strange beyond comprehension. Any quantum physicist can tell you that. All we know is it works."

"And what of Rome? Was Britton right?"

Florence gestured to the ceiling with open palm. "This is an incantation to *dii novensiles,* the casters of lightning," she said. "On these words titan legions marched. Kings and countries fell. On these words western civilization was forged."

"I don't believe it," said Jake, taking a step back. "It doesn't make sense. Come on, Florence, you're a historian. Think like one. If the Etruscans harnessed this power, how come Rome conquered them, not the other way round? Why was it Rome and not Etruria that spread across the globe?"

"You know why."

From somewhere two words rose to Jake's mind.

Ten saecula.

The Roman legions. The clank of armour; the blast of the

war horn; the destiny of so many souls. The violence, the glory. Blade on leather; blood on blade; the Roman eagle planted across the Mediterranean. Through all the smoke and chaos of the centuries the *Disciplina* had been their lodestar, guiding them on.

"We think Britton was spot on," said Florence. "And it cost him his life."

"Who is 'we'?"

She flinched.

"Who are you working for, Florence?"

The archaeologist closed her eyes and relaxed her shoulder blades. "I suppose you were always going to realize sooner or later. Too sharp for your own good, Jake Wolsey. Which means unfortunately – I must do this."

When Florence opened her eyes a pistol was in her hand. She aimed it at his forehead.

"Thanks for all your assistance, Jake," she sneered. "I couldn't have done it without you. And the above will be a big help. Trust me on that."

Jake couldn't take his eyes off the tiny hole wavering before him, nor comprehend the death about to whistle through it.

"This is it, then?" Again he fought to control his bladder. "You kill me in cold blood? Just like you killed Britton?"

"That wasn't me. Roger taught me everything. I would never ..." The pistol trembled. "I don't know how to ..."

"... how to call down lightning strikes?" Jake laughed, though his stomach caved inward. "Hostilius, slain for rejecting the Gods. Otto the Barbarian, struck down on the say-so of Etruscan priests. Emperor Carus, electrocuted on the plains of Persia. And finally it was the turn of Roger Britton."

"I didn't kill him."

Jake judged it the truth. "But that means ..."

"I know," she said. "It means someone else killed him. It means there are people out there who already know how to wield this science."

"Science? An odd choice of word, don't you think?"

"But that's what it is, Jake. Don't you see? A science they discovered how to tap into in 800 BC, a science we're only beginning to understand."

There was a noise of dismay to their left. Berihun stood in the doorway, head alternating between them like a spectator at a tennis match. Florence glanced at the intruder.

Jake charged.

50

The archaeologist had time to fire a single bullet. But the ferocity of Jake's advance took her by surprise and the shot went high and wide. Before she could fire again Jake was upon her in a dive and they crashed to the floor. Florence clawed at his face with one hand, raising the pistol with the other. Jake grabbed her wrist and held it easily, using his other arm to pin Florence as her legs thrashed beneath him. She fired again, but the bullet splintered through wooden panelling.

"Don't just stand there," Jake shouted at Berihun. "For God's sake do something."

The driver prised the gun from Florence's hand, casting it across the room. Still she squirmed in Jake's hold, her eyes feral. Then she saw it was hopeless and lay back.

"What are we going to do about this little situation then?" said Jake.

"*Wo bei ren jia gong ji. Kuai la ya. Kuai la!*"

He was taken aback. "What did you just say?"

The noise that gave her away was on the very edge of audibility: a little 'schhhh' sound, followed by a whisper of Mandarin. *It came from her collar.* Jake explored the material with his free hand – he felt two wires connecting to a solid blob. There was an imperfection in the seam. Jake tore the material apart, and a tiny transmitter fell into his hand.

"What's this then?"

Florence spat in his face.

"Classy." Jake wiped his cheek with his shoulder. "Very nice indeed."

"Please sir," said Berihun. "What is happening?"

Jake considered how to respond. Florence's accomplices had to be close. But perhaps with assistance they could be fended off – Debre Damo was a natural fortress. He recalled Berihun's suspicion of the work gang and inspiration struck.

"She's a Chinese spy," he said.

Florence's body stiffened. The reaction lasted less than a second, but it was enough to betray her.

"My God," Jake whispered in her ear. "Is that what you are, Florence? A Chinese spy? Have your guardian angels been following us all the way?"

Everywhere we go people start killing each other.

"You killed Jess Medcalf," said Jake. "Or your friends did. You strangled Dr Gul. It was your people back there in Axum."

"You're being ridiculous."

"The authorities in Istanbul," he pressed. "Bending over backwards to facilitate your every request. Under pressure from the embassy, I assume?"

"If I was working for the Chinese, why the hell would I allow you to tag along?"

"At first because I had Britton's notes. But later? You said it yourself. You needed me."

"Please sir," said Berihum. "What we do now?"

"Her friends are coming. I need your help."

"Then we must pull up rope."

Berihun dragged Florence to her feet and clasped her wrists behind her back. Before they left Jake photographed the ceiling; then he tucked Florence's gun into his jeans – like they do in the movies.

When they arrived at the guardhouse two monks were

already working the rope, feet braced against the doorstep and grunting. The cord was taut, skipping along the step with the pull of a pendulous weight. The elderly guard spoke to Berihun in Amharic.

"He says Chinese tourists already down there," warned the driver. "One coming up now."

Jake peered out. Swaying twenty feet below was a man wearing a sunhat and carrying a satchel. Five others watched him from the foot of the cliff, squinting into the light.

"They're here," he said quietly.

"Then we cutting rope," said Berihun.

If Florence's accomplices made it onto the plateau he knew they would be killed.

"Do it," said Jake.

Berihun relayed the order to the monks, who stopped pulling and entered into debate. The driver gestured to Florence, forming a pistol shape with his fingers; Jake produced her gun, and at corroboration of Berihun's tale the guard cut the cord and cast it over the edge. The rope pirouetted to the ground.

There were a few shouts between the Chinese team. Then the agent began to climb, gaining in confidence with each handhold. Beneath him three more men took to the rock, which was crisscrossed with fissures and natural grips. The guard removed the safety catch on his AK 47 and leaned out over the drop.

"No come up! Monastery closed! No come!"

The old man's head jerked backward and a splatter of gore hit the rock. He stayed on his feet for a few seconds, rotating on the spot. Then he crumpled down quickly, like a child playing musical chairs. A tunnel was bored through his head.

Berihun snatched up the AK. "They want fighting? Ethiopian man can have hot blood too!"

He edged to the doorway and unleashed a ragged burst, aiming vertically down. The response was impressive. Six snub-nosed MI6 assault rifles and a heavy machine gun opened fire on the guard house, bullets whistling into the masonry in a fury of snaps and splinters. Jake had been under fire before, but nothing like this – the volume of lead made them powerless to manoeuvre. He cringed into hard cover, face in the dirt. The climbers would be there in moments. There was nothing he could do to stop them.

Suddenly there was a noise like the end of the world, and the mountain seemed to cave in around him.

51

Frank Davis had watched the arrival of the Chinese tourists with concern. Several elements of their cover were lacking: they didn't have a guide, they weren't taking photographs and their bags were too large. Moreover, they were wary but comfortable – and this was bandit country. Hostile environment training was written over every movement. And then the shooting began.

Davis's GPS showed Jake was in the guardhouse. That meant he was pinned. Soon the Chinese would take the plateau along with anything they found up there – and this was not something Davis could allow. The agent smiled coldly as he unzipped his backpack and saw oiled metal inside. Before being recruited to MI6 as part of the so-called 'Increment' of ex-forces personnel, Davis had been an SAS sniper. In Afghanistan and Iraq he had come to take great pleasure in the game of ending other peoples' lives. Losing Guilherme was a setback, but at heart he was a lone wolf – it felt good to be operating by himself again. Now the only cock-ups to worry about were his own.

He loaded five rounds into the L115A3 Accuracy International sniper rifle and snapped its stock into position. Next he screwed in the weapon's noise suppressor, admiring the finesse of its thread as it turned. The British-made weapon was considered the finest sniper rifle in existence. In Afghanistan he'd made a kill at more than a kilometre with this puppy, sending the bullet high into the sky and watching as it plummeted to earth to decapitate its target. Now he was at a twentieth of that range: it would be a doddle.

The machine-gunner was positioned some distance from the others on the rooftop of a mud hut. He was using tracer fire to direct the bombardment, every fourth bullet laced with phosphorus, and it was strangely beautiful to watch the glowing bullets ricochet in all directions before the straight line of their travel became a curve with the tug of gravity. But tracer rounds were always a double-edged sword, as they betrayed the machine gun's exact location. Davis peered down the telescopic sight. The gunner's head bobbed above the lip of the hut every few seconds, distorted by the heat coming off the weapon. Davis didn't open fire. The Chinese deployment might be careless, but they were packing some serious firepower. Once he'd committed he had to be sure of killing every last one of the motherfuckers. A bit of shock and awe was in order. Davis smiled again as he retrieved an M79 grenade launcher. It resembled an oversized sawn-off shotgun, like something a cartoon character would carry. He broke the weapon and inserted a mini-artillery shell into the breech. Now he was ready.

Davis took a moment to become calm, breathing deeply, allowing himself to settle into what the British Army calls the 'Condor Moment'. The sensation is of soaring: watching the battlefield from upon high, a waking dream imbued with laser-like focus. Most soldiers experience it in combat, brought on by training, adrenaline and knowledge of the possibility of death.

One hell of a feeling.

Davis took aim with the blooper and pulled the trigger. The

projectile fizzed across the barren terrain at seventy-five metres a second, hitting the first climber between the shoulder blades as he reached for the guardhouse. The explosion propelled bits of the agent over a wide radius and a ball of fire rolled up the cliff, morphing from orange to red and then chemical black. His accomplices clung to the rock as the shockwave rushed down. Already Davis had the rifle pressed to his cheek. And he was firing repeatedly. The machine-gunner's skull vanished in a cloud of red. The second climber was shot in the neck, the third through his heart. One after the other they peeled away from the cliff, spinning through the air and hitting the ground with a 'thunk'. Davis's movements were languid as he selected the next target. He was mildly disturbed to find he had an erection.

*

The flight of the grenade shell was just visible in the air, like a rocket at a daytime fireworks display. Jenny traced the line of sparks to its point of origin. Even before she peered through her goggles she knew it would be Davis. For once in her life she didn't know what to do. This was not the MI6 she knew: the organization had spent decades trying to dispel the myth it was some sort of a paramilitary group, permitted to kill and maim at will. The MI6 of Ian Fleming was pure fiction, or so she had thought. Certainly in all her service she had never heard of lethal force being deployed by an officer – and now this carnage was unfolding before her eyes. Even as she watched, another coil of smoke shivered through the air. The grenade hit the Chinese Jeep, which was racked by a double conflagration. First the high explosive shell lifted it into the air. There followed a secondary blast as the petrol tank ignited, jerking the vehicle onto a new flight-path. The agents sheltering behind the car were riddled with shrapnel. The mangled Jeep crashed to earth. A pair of human torches fled across the sand; Davis finished them off with the sniper rifle. And with that the slaughter was over.

A pall of smoke and silence fell across the landscape.

Jenny let her head fall into her arms. Once again she heard her father urging her to consider a career in the City; her ex-fiancé's pleas for a family; Angela's orders to return to Nottingham. But this had all been her choice. She had made an appointment to be here.

Jenny couldn't have returned to work as though Axum never happened. She didn't want to be involved in a road accident or spontaneously decide to throw herself under a tube. As she saw it, the choice was stark: nail Charlie Waits to the wall or live in fear.

She could have posted Davis's boasts straight to *Newsnight*. Yet that wasn't sufficient. Waterboarding would enrage the left, but it was old hat and Waits might survive the scandal. All this death had been unleashed because of his fixation with the *Disciplina Etrusca*: that was what needed to be exposed. But if she began talking about Etruscan soothsayers they would paint her as deranged. She didn't have enough evidence – no journalist would give her the time of day.

Except one: Jake could be an ally.

Jenny glanced at her scanner. The reporter had survived the bombardment – the blue dot was on the move again, tracking across the plateau and away from the church. Davis must have spotted it too, for he broke from cover, dashing towards the cliff. He had abandoned the sniper rifle for an automatic pistol.

He's going to kill Jake too.

Jenny glanced in the direction of her four-by-four, hidden by a dip in the terrain. It was do or die time. She looked at the scanner, recoiled, looked at it again.

Jake had disappeared.

52

Plumes of dust erupted from the wall and the floor was a sea of geysers. Jake's head rang as if it had been smashed with a sledgehammer. His organs shook. His heartbeat was knocked out of synch. The guardhouse became illuminated as the fireball rose up past the doorway.

The explosion diminished: *BANG! Bang! Bang.*

It was replaced by a thrumming that seemed to emanate from Jake's very eardrums. When he asked Berihun if he was hurt he couldn't hear his own voice. He put his hands to his ears and inspected them, but there no blood. The driver's face was streaked with dirt, contorted into a pastiche of shock; his mouth could have accommodated a fist. The monks were spread-eagled against the rock. There was mud in Jake's mouth and he spat on the ground. But something had changed. They weren't under fire anymore. The battle had ended.

Jake stole to the doorway and peered out. Two climbers lay at the foot of the cliff, limbs broken at horrible angles. It was not immediately obvious what had become of the man who had nearly made it to the top. But then Jake spotted his head, a few scorched lumps of clothing. Something fired in his memory. *Florence!* She had vanished during the bombardment. Jake's hand went to her pistol, still tucked into his waistband.

He leaned into Berihun's ear. "How can we get out of here?"

The Ethiopian crossed to the other side of the room and spoke to the monks, who huddled in conference. The teenagers pointed fretfully across the plateau.

The huts around were abandoned, the church empty. In the space of ten minutes the community had become a ghost town. The monks led them to the far side of the mountaintop and began picking their way down a path that offered a three-foot leeway between the cliff and a terminal drop. The rock face was honeycombed with caves and a stench like rotting fish arose.

"This is monk graves," said Berihun.

Some caves had been blocked up, but others remained open. Inside one Jake saw a wooden coffin, in another a fibula, blackened fibres stretched across it. The first monk clambered into the sepulchral cavern.

"We're going *in there*?" said Jake.

"Yes, quickly," insisted the driver.

The stench of putrefaction inside was unbearable. There was something greasy about it, and Jake swallowed hard as vomit rose up his throat. Soon the fissure narrowed to a crack. He wriggled through to find himself in a hollowed out space. It was pitch black and he shivered. The air felt thick in his mouth; he could actually *taste* the decay.

When Berihun sparked a lighter Jake saw they weren't alone. Monks were dotted about the cave like a parliament of owls, staring down at him. Three bodies bound in cotton sheets lay on the cave floor.

"If is danger, monks are coming here," said Berihun. "Is secret place. You first white man coming here."

"*Amesegenallo*," Jake thanked them, touching his heart.

Heads nodded all around the cave.

"*Minimaydelem*," they murmured back. "*Ishee, ishee*."

"What now then?"

"We waiting," said Berihun. "We waiting long time."

Waiting, while killers combed the plateau. It was not an appealing thought. Jake sat on a rock and tried to meditate.

Ink. It was his mantra, learned years ago in a failed attempt to control his neuroses. *Ink*. He breathed in; he breathed out. That was better. From nowhere a measure of relaxation materialized. *Ink*. A thought bubbled up through the barrier. They would be searching the plateau. *Ink, Ink*. They would find it empty, they would know there was a hiding place. *Ink, Ink*,

Ink. They would look in the caves, they would be systematic. *Ink! Ink! Ink!*

Jake's eyes shot open. "I don't think we're safe here."

Meditation had never bloody worked.

53

Berihun inclined his head. "Why is not safe?" he said in a musical voice. "They not finding us. This is grave, *faranji* not like go in."

"You don't know these people. They are not normal *faranji*. They will come."

A discussion arose in the subterranean chamber, the replies of the monks bouncing from the walls of the cavern.

"They say cave goes far," said Berihun translated. "There is way out of mountain. But hard to find exit. And bad men still out there. Is better stay, I think."

Jake felt his gut swirling. The restlessness accumulated in his knees and calves until he wanted to kick out at the air. He switched on his phone and stumbled to his feet. "Which direction is it?"

Berihun pointed into the gloom.

"Will you come?"

"I am staying. You want, you go. No problem."

"Thank you, my friend. Goodbye."

Jake stumbled through the intestines of the mountain, brushing the ceiling with his fingertips. He forced himself through defiles, blundered into rock, dodged a cavity that yawned up beneath his feet. Just when the claustrophobia threatened to overwhelm him he saw a glow. As Jake got closer it brightened, morphing into a bar of yellow that burned the eyes. And then he was out, laughing with relief as tears streamed down his face. He fumbled his way to a boulder, wedging himself behind it until his eyes accustomed themselves to light.

Degree by degree he prised open his eyelids; finally he could see.

When Jake stepped out from the rock a man was standing there.

He looked tough. His features were chiselled and he stood at ease, one hand on his waist, the other behind his back. There was a white patch in his hair. Jake felt the world rushing around him. *This man has just killed six people.*

"Find anything up there, did you, fella?" The stranger spoke with a slight London accent. "Well? Chop-chop. I haven't got all day."

Frank Davis produced a pistol from behind his back and pointed it at Jake's face. His eyes were a flat grey, the colour of the Irish Sea, and with a lurch Jake realized these might be the final moments of his life.

"Yes, yes we did actually," said Jake. "A new inscription. Florence will have destroyed it – but I took photographs."

Davis's eyes widened. "Show me."

Florence's gun was still tucked into his belt.

Jake had never fired a gun – and this guy was MI6. What chance did he have? But what other choice was there? As Jake braced himself for the denouement a nasty thought occurred to him. Didn't guns have a safety catch? What if it was on? His fingers quivered, like those of a Wild West gunslinger.

Davis read it in a heartbeat.

"Put your hands up," he shouted.

Blown it.

Jake could feel Florence's pistol in the small of his back, hopelessly out of reach. He raised his hands and looked into the stranger's eyes, trying to connect with him.

It was like trying to connect with a drill-bit.

Suddenly Jake couldn't be bothered anymore. He looked at the rock behind his killer. How red was the stone, how beautiful. It was a pity he wouldn't experience more of this world – he rather loved it. But the thought was abstract. There was no more terror left in him.

"Enough of this," the stranger was saying.

Jake thought he heard a car coming around the mountain.

Davis took aim. "Night night."

A Toyota burst from the plateau. Jake saw a shock of blonde in the driving seat.

The assassin turned to face the approaching hazard. "What the fuck?"

Davis unloaded the entire magazine into the vehicle, the windscreen shattering in a mist of glass. But Jenny ducked below the steering wheel, protected by the bulk of the engine. The car hit Davis square on, chipping him over the bonnet and sending him cart-wheeling through the air. He crashed to earth twenty feet away, heaved himself up, abandoned the struggle, shuddered and was still.

Deliverance, again.

The Toyota skidded to a halt and the passenger door flew open.

"Mr Wolsey, I presume?"

Jake registered three things. First: the Stanley-Livingstone reference in an African wilderness. Second: that the woman looked vaguely familiar (it was as if he'd been to school with her or something).

Third: she was beautiful.

"Who are you?" he said.

"Just get in, will you?"

Jake clambered into the car.

"Jenny Frobisher." She offered him her hand. "It's a pleasure to meet you at last."

Instinctively Jake brushed his mane into a semblance of order. He was sweating and his breathing was shallow.

"That was a bloody close shave," he said. "I really thought I was a goner."

"You can thank me later. We've got plenty to talk about."

Jenny was aware of the irony. She'd spent a career running agents, turning sources, twisting their minds. Now she had been turned by Jake – and he hadn't even been aware of doing it. She hit the accelerator and the two renegades streaked away under a sky that was big and blue and full of hope.

Part Three

Maelstrom

And when we have won, who will ask us about the method?
Adolf Hitler, German dictator, 1889-1945 AD

54

February 7th

THE crisis engulfing MI6 threatens to spiral out of control with the revelation an experienced agent has "gone rogue" in Ethiopia.

The female operative last reported to superiors 24 hours ago after being ordered back to London, sources reveal. She is said to be disobeying orders after becoming disillusioned with an operation that has led to the death of two MI6 spies – the only officers publicly known to have died as a result of hostile action in the history of the organization. The first operative, 28-year-old Jessica Medcalf, was shot in Istanbul last month. The second officer – who is yet to be named – was killed in an apparent ambush in northern Ethiopia earlier in the week.

And astonishingly, this newspaper understands the operation in question may relate to an archaeological matter. Senior MI6 officers are said to believe discoveries in both Turkey and Ethiopia may be of importance to national security. In light of the latest revelations the Prime Minister has called an immediate meeting of the Joint Intelligence Committee. Number 10 is said to be apoplectic that MI6 has been active in both countries without Foreign Office authorization. The chief of MI6 denies complicity in the actions, leading to speculation that a cabal within the agency may be acting independently.

Meanwhile, diplomats in Ankara are attempting to placate the Turkish authorities, following suggestions that MI6 was involved in the gunfight at Istanbul's Topkapi Palace, witnessed by one of our journalists. The episode has severely shaken trust between the allies, with implications for Anglo-Turkish co-operation over the situation in Iraq and Syria, Iran's nuclear programme and in the continuing battle against Islamist terror plots at home.

Evelyn Parr folded the newspaper and placed it on the table. "It doesn't look good, does it?"

"No." Waits produced the Glenfarclas. "No, it does not."

"Do you know, I don't think I've ever come to your office and *not* seen you take a drink, no matter the time of day. What point are you trying to make exactly?"

Waits poured three fingers of Scotch and rotated the tumbler under his nose. "It's about control."

His grip remained steady on the glass.

"I don't see much evidence of control at the minute – in fact I'd say events have proved quite beyond our ability to keep a hold on." Her eyes returned to the headline. "Oh, for Christ's sake, I think I'd better have one of those too."

"As you like." There was a glug as Waits half-filled a second glass which he prodded across the table.

Parr took a sip. "God, I needed that."

A crooked smile passed the spymaster's face as he placed his spectacles on his nose and picked up the newspaper.

"What worries me is the lack of bylines," he said, voice muffled behind the pages. "Including leaders and comment pieces, I make it six articles on the topic in this edition, yet no one's owning up to writing them. It can only mean the reporters are scared. Of us, probably."

"Then there's this line about the 'archaeological matter,'" added Parr. "We know Wolsey's been sniffing around it, but our man on the paper said the editor wasn't taking his claims seriously. Well, he is now."

"They've left it vague," said Waits. "That suggests they don't trust Wolsey's journalism – or they haven't got the evidence. The cat's not out of the bag yet, my dear."

"If not now, it soon will be. The opposition wants a public inquiry. What the hell are we going to do?"

Waits banged his whisky glass down on the table. "We carry on going! To the bitter end, Evelyn. There's no choice now, don't you see that? If we get what we're looking for, if we show the PM that it works? *Of course* he'll hush it up. No man of power could resist. The whole affair will be swathed in red tape and the Official Secrets Act and nobody'll get near us. But first we need to lay our hands on the infernal thing."

"I wonder sometimes ..." Parr put her head in her hands and sighed. "All this bloodshed. And yet ..."

"And yet what?"

"And yet the end result is already preordained. No matter what we do."

"You know we can't think like that," snapped Waits. "It's circular. If we decide not to do whatever it takes to obtain the *Disciplina Etrusca*, that decision would be precisely *why* it's fated that we fail. A self-fulfilling prophecy, in other words."

Parr studied him, picking over each detail of the florid face that confronted her. "You're right," she said. "It's the only way."

"Think what our predecessors would've done. We're so *close* now, Evelyn – so close after all these years."

"Are we that close? We haven't added to our manuscript at all. And our only remaining asset's been hospitalized."

"Frank came round this morning – I just got off the phone to him. He's got a few cuts and bruises but he'll be ok."

"What did he say?"

"Well, there's good news and bad news," said Waits. "The bad news is that the driver who hit him was our very own Jenny 'off-the-scale loyalty' Frobisher."

"Good God," whispered Parr. "We're finished."

"Not at all," said Waits. "Not if we get the *Disciplina*. As I say, we'll be protected from upon high for ever and a day. I daresay even Reader Number One would approve. She's nothing if not a pragmatist."

"But how do we get it?"

"That's the good news," said Waits. "Before Frobisher came riding to the rescue, Wolsey told Frank he'd found a new inscription in the monastery. He photographed it. Begging for his life, you see. The inscription's been removed by our rivals, but if we catch Jake, we get the photos of the Debre Damo texts – and whatever he got in Istanbul to boot."

Parr nodded.

"Frank's a proud man," said Waits. "He won't appreciate having been bested by the likes of Frobisher. If I had to put money on it, I'd say our journalist friend and his new accomplice will not be around much longer."

"You do realize he's a borderline psychopath?" asked Parr. "Literally and clinically, I mean."

"Frank's propensity for violence has proved just the right side of useful."

"Do you know how many people he killed in Iraq?"

"It takes dangerous men to take on dangerous men," said Waits. "Given the stakes, I'd say it's rather comforting to have the certified most lethal man in the British Army at our disposal. Wouldn't you?"

"But he's one person," Parr pressed. "One guy against an unravelling situation and the full apparatus of Chinese state security. We don't have enough boots on the ground to compete – and we certainly can't bring anyone else into the fold."

"Well, you know what they say." Charlie poured himself another dram. "If you want a job done properly ..."

"What, you'll go out there yourself?"

Waits inclined his head, and Parr seemed to relax.

"Let me tell you a little story," he said. "It's 1942 and the Battle of El Alamein is raging. Rommel looks set to break through our lines. As you might expect, Cairo's in a bit of a flap – secret documents going up in smoke, the colonials fleeing, that sort of thing. And do you know what the British ambassador did?"

"What did he do?"

"He ordered the railings of the embassy to be repainted."

For the first time in the meeting Parr smiled.

"To *sangfroid*." Waits raised his glass.

"To *sangfroid*," Parr repeated.

55

The Monastery of Debre Damo receded into the distance, its secrets stolen at last. Jake leaned his temple against the window as the vehicle hurtled along the track. During the conflagration all he could think of was staying alive, but now he returned to what he had learned. The world was made anew: a dark and unsettling place. Could it be that his escape from the monastery was written? The arrival of this woman with seconds to spare pre-ordained? And if so by what? Or by whom? Jake wrapped his arms around his chest. He needed to be somewhere safe, somewhere he could make sense of it all. Without meaning to, he let out a groan. Jenny hit the brakes and the car skidded to a halt in a graceful slalom of dust.

"You ok?"

He sat up straight. "Yep. No problem."

"You sure?" Jenny looked him up and down. She needed this man.

"I'm trying to be stoic about all this," said Jake. "You know, all the people shooting each other and stuff. But it is rather a lot to take in, if I'm honest."

His voice sounded nicer in person, Jenny thought. Deeper. Posh, certainly, but not unacceptably so. She hit the accelerator.

Jake stole another look at her as they drove. Right away he had known she was the type who made him unsure whether to hold eye contact. He was grateful for the road ahead, demanding her attention. Jenny's brow was furrowed in concentration, her hair tied in a ponytail; she drove like a hurricane and at that instant a more impressive figure could not be imagined. She ordered a pint, Jake reckoned. That was a good thing, obviously. But Jesus, she was *way* out of his league.

"I've got a confession," said Jenny, catching him looking and pursing her lips in what might have been a smile.

"Go on."

"I know quite a lot about you."

"Really? Why?"

"I've been following you for three weeks now."

Jake's fingers went to the door-handle. "You're MI6?"

"Ex-MI6. I saved your life just now, remember? We're on the same side. And I wouldn't do that if I were you, we're doing fifty. It would flay the skin from your body."

"I don't know who to believe any more. How do I know this isn't a trick? For all I know you're trying to, you know ..." A soft laugh. "Bring me in quietly and all that."

"There are some ruthless people in the Security Services. Bad people, I know this now. But not even MI6 would run over its own agents to soften up a mark."

Jake relinquished the door handle.

"I'm trying to help you," she said. "I'm hoping you'll help me too. I just – I just need you to trust me, ok?"

"Never trust anyone who says trust me," he muttered, although strangely enough he did.

"I'll prove it to you."

There was a village approaching, a dozen mud-brick huts gathered around the single shop. A Maersk cargo container had been abandoned by the roadside long ago, and it gave Jake an inexplicable shiver to see that symbol of western commerce in such a setting, cast up by the tide of modern trade. He heard the clank of steel at some Baltic port, pictured huddled troubadours smoking away the night.

Jenny stopped at the shop – a tanker was parked up and the driver was decanting petrol into cartons while several men looked on. The store was an Aladdin's Cave of washing powder, asymmetric vegetables and tins of processed meat. There was Coca Cola too: they were back in civilization. Jenny leapt from the car and began conversing with the shopkeeper in Amharic.

The key was in the ignition. The engine was running.

Jake considered his options. A trust-building exercise? Or part of the ruse? Jake's thoughts circled as Jenny finished her transaction. Money was being handed over; he had five seconds to decide. But what if she was being straight with him?

Four seconds. Stealing her car? Three seconds. Marooning her here?

Two seconds.

He couldn't do it.

One.

The car door opened.

"Thanks for not driving off," she said.

Jake looked at his knees. "Don't be silly."

After a mile Jenny veered off the track without warning and killed the engine. The sun seared through the windscreen and with no air conditioning the temperature rose by the second.

"I need you to get into the back of the car with me," she said.

Ribbons of fear and desire twisted inside him. A single word came to mind: *honeytrap*.

With perfect synchronicity Jenny produced a bottle of *tej*.

"What is all this?" Jake looked bewildered.

"I need to do an operation on you. It may hurt. I thought you could use some anaesthetic – this is honey wine, their strongest brew."

"I told you, I'm fine. Not a scratch on me."

"No, you don't understand." A diamond-shaped blade was in her hand. "We put a bug in you. I need to get it out."

56

"You put a bug *in* me?"

Jenny's eyes were downcast.

"How?"

She shrugged. "It's in a capsule."

"I don't believe you."

"There isn't time to argue about this, Jake. As long as it's inside you they know where we are."

Jake opened the car door. "If you think I'm going to let a complete stranger cut me up on blind faith you're mad. Raving mad."

She showed him the scanner. A blue dot pulsed on a topographic image of their surroundings; he could even make out the Maersk container.

"The bug might be in your pocket for all I know," he said.

"Well it isn't."

Jake allowed himself proper eye contact for the first time. The desert light had turned her eyes cerulean, like those of a snow leopard.

"Think back to the Agya Sophia," she said. "Do you remember a feeling sharp pain in your ..." a smudge of rose touched each cheekbone. "In your backside?"

He frowned. "Actually, now you mention it I do remember that. It was really painful. How do you ..."

"Know about it? Because we did it. We fired a pellet containing a tracking device into your ..." she blushed again. "Into your arse."

Despite himself Jake laughed. "Good grief. You did, didn't you?"

Jenny laughed too. "Yeah, I'm afraid we did. Sorry about that. But we do need to get it out." She was serious again. "Otherwise

I leave you here. I can't have you drawing them to me."

"Ok then." He swallowed. "Let's get it over with."

The *tej* was unadulterated fire. Jake's eyes watered as he knocked it back and he gasped for breath. *God, it felt good though.* He hadn't touched a drop for days, and the booze always hit him with fresh loveliness after a hiatus. He took another swig, the alcohol high eddying through him, his mind foggy yet clear. It was only after the third swig that he remembered he shouldn't trust this woman. MI6 had to know his foibles. And here he was, getting smashed at her suggestion. Just one more gulp, he decided. God knows, his liver could handle it. Jake raised the bottle again – but before he could drink Jenny placed one hand on his wrist.

"Hey. Not too much." Her touch was cool on the skin. "You might need your wits about you later."

The journalist stumbled as he clambered onto the back seat. Wow – that stuff was seriously powerful. Had to be fifty-five per cent at least.

Nice.

Jenny was cleaning the knife with antiseptic. Jake was not a fan of operations and once this scenario would have been the cue for panic. But strangely, not now. The booze helped; yet perhaps there was more to it than that.

Without warning she jabbed the knife into his buttock. Jake yelled with fury and punched the door. The blade was a red hot poker, a centipede boring deep inside him with slashing mandibles.

"Hold still," she implored. "We're almost there."

Blood poured down the back of Jake's leg; his teeth were bared and he was close to passing out. "Get on with it!" he yelled.

Still Jenny probed and twisted, cut and pulled, until –

With a plop it was over. A pellet landed on the chair and Jenny began damming the wound with tissues which turned warm on her fingers before disintegrating.

"You don't think you've nicked an artery?" Jake gasped.

"Not a chance. There are no major arteries in that part of the body. In London the street kids slash each other's backsides when they want to send a warning. They know it can't end in a fatality."

"How reassuring."

After a few minutes the bleeding was staunched and Jenny bandaged him up.

"Well done," she said. "I realize that can't have been much fun."

Jake retrieved the pellet, his revulsion turning to astonishment. "Well, blow me down. Will you take a look at that?"

They returned to the village. Jenny got out of the car, and when she returned it was without the bug. "See that tanker over there? Sudanese licence plate. With any luck they'll be chasing shadows in an entirely different country by tomorrow."

"Very conniving."

"How are you doing? You look pale."

Jake pulled himself up, doing his best to look rugged. "Absolutely fine. Barely felt it."

She raised an eyebrow. "Oh *really*?"

He was about to respond when his work phone began bleeping. It was the first signal he'd had for days, and the emails came galloping in. Jake fished out the device, skimming through his inbox – Heston might have been in touch and he was down to the last bar of battery.

Subject: Roger Britton.

"What is it?" said Jenny. "You jumped."

"Hold on," said Jake. He didn't recognize the sender.

Dear Mr Wolsey,

My name is Dr Giuseppe Nesta. I am a scientist. I was in communication with Roger Britton before he was killed. There are some things I must tell you about his death. Can we meet?

Regards,

Dr G. Nesta.

When he saw the signature he jumped again.

Senior researcher, CERN
Large Hadron Collider, Geneva, Switzerland

Britton had been in touch with a theoretical physicist. Slowly the implications sank in.

"What is it?" said Jenny. "What's going on?"

"I'll tell you in a sec, just let me reply to this."

Jake fired an email back. When and where should they meet? Dr Nesta replied within seconds.

Don't come to LHC. We could meet in Rome in two days? I have friends there I can stay with.

It had been years since Jake had been to the city, so he suggested meeting at the first landmark that came into his head. Nesta agreed to be at the Spanish Steps by noon, wearing a red baseball cap for identification.

Rome: how apt it was. They were going back to where it all began.

57

With each mile of Davis's descent from the Ethiopian highlands the mercury rose. By the time he reached the plains of South Sudan it was hotter than anywhere he had ever been deployed – the open window of his car was like the door to a blast furnace and the sweat got in his eyes, impeding the drive. But he dared not use the air conditioning. He had only half a tank left, and there had been nowhere to fill up since the border. And he couldn't go fast enough to get a breeze through the window because the track was too bad. If you could call it a track, that was. An hour ago it had joined the bed of a long-dead stream, and the wheels jolted from boulder to stone. If he took it too fast he would bust an axle. Then he would be in a pickle.

The country he had left behind straddled two worlds, Africa and the Middle East, and the Ethiopian highlanders possessed a twist of Arabia about their features. But the world's newest nation was Black Africa proper and the people he passed gawped at him. He found the women very beautiful.

Reeds rose ten feet high on each side of the riverbed. He was driving into an African wilderness and he prayed the car would not break down. Then again, Davis mused, he had almost caught them. His concentration was furious as he picked his way along the obstacle course.

A heavy jolt sent agony through Davis's broken ribs and dislocated shoulder; his flank was a patchwork of black and greens where the Toyota had struck and he suspected internal bleeding, no matter what the doctors said. Davis's face became a scowl at the thought of what he'd do to Jenny when he caught up with them. Abruptly the expression melted into a grin.

The dot had stopped moving.

Jenny had parked in a small village a couple of kilometres upstream – it was the middle of butt-fuck nowhere with no ragtag local police to worry about. *Perfect.* A delicious shiver overcame Davis, the sensation a bull shark must feel as the white membranes roll back over its eyes. After a few minutes he turned off the riverbed and accelerated along a well-used trail. A hut flashed past, then two more, a woman with a basket of dung balanced on her head. There were farmers trying to sell their produce by the side of the track; nothing was on offer but tomatoes and red onions. With rising excitement Frank saw the dots converge on his display. He swept into a clearing between the huts, feeling for his pistol. He frowned – there was no sign of Frobisher's Toyota. The only vehicle was a petrol tanker, surrounded by a gaggle of villagers pouring fuel into drums. Davis leapt from the car, his pistol in one hand, the scanner in the other. He felt his heartbeat slow.

Condor time, baby.

A girl of about fourteen wearing only a pair of yellow shorts watched open-mouthed as Frank bounded across the ground. He rounded the vehicle. But there was no one to be seen. The scanner was adamant: Jake should be standing right in front of him. Realization flared. *How could he have been so stupid?*

A bundle of oily rags was wedged between the tank and the chassis. Already knowing what he would find, Davis unravelled the parcel. A metallic pellet gleamed in the sun. He hurled the device across the village, punching the tanker hard enough to cleave the skin from his knuckles. The empty cylinder boomed its reply.

Charlie Waits would not be a happy bunny. The race for the final inscription was on – but as with so much in the modern world, West was playing second fiddle to East.

58

"You idiot!" shouted Jenny. "You absolute idiot!"

"Why?" said Jake. "What did I do wrong?"

"I can't believe you emailed him. Don't you realize we read all your correspondence? Christ Jake, don't you read the *Guardian*? It's not exactly a big secret nowadays."

Jake's faced turned wan. "Oh yeah."

"Now they know exactly where you're supposed to be meeting him. They'll grab him for certain. That's if he is a real person, of course."

"It's no problem. We just email him again and tell him not to go there."

Jenny shook her head. "Honestly, Jake, it's a miracle you lasted this long. From now on every email you send him will be intercepted. MI6 won't let it through. Plus anything you receive from the scientist will actually be from them. If he exists he's going to the Spanish Steps now, no matter what."

With the help of Google they ascertained that Dr Nesta existed. He had been a leading light at the Massachusetts Institute of Technology before moving to Geneva, where he had worked with some leading quantum physicists. But there had been a fall from grace. A gossipy profile in the *New Scientist* revealed Nesta was attempting to detect elements of the supernatural using maths and quantum theory. The work had not been received well and his funding was to end. Jake felt queasy reading the article; he had a fair idea why the scientist and historian were in touch.

He didn't tell Jenny of his suspicions. Of course, he had filled her in on Eusebius and his *Life of Constantine* – but trying to convince her of the living reality of the technology? She'd think he was mad.

Jenny phoned the Large Hadron Collider, claiming to be a research student from Cambridge. The receptionist informed her Nesta had taken leave at short notice – he had just walked out of the building. She asked for his mobile number, to be told they were "not at liberty to divulge personal information". He wouldn't even pass on a message – Dr Nesta had said it was a family emergency and he specifically asked not to be contacted.

Jake put his head in his hands. "He's lost. Jesus, I've cost a man his life. And we haven't got a chance of stopping them. Because Nesta won't even be there, will he? They'll kill him as well, at their own convenience."

"You don't get it, do you?" she said. "You're still not thinking like us. Of course he'll be there."

Jake looked up. "What do you mean?"

"They know that I'll be telling you all this. Which means *they* know that *you* know Dr Nesta will be there, no matter what. That's why they won't change the rendezvous."

"I don't understand." Jake clenched his hair in his fists; it had been two days since he had showered and when he let go the strands remained vertical.

"They've analyzed your personality, Jake. They've

run psychological tests, studied your emails and phone conversations. So they know you'll probably try and get him out anyway. Because that's what you're like. And then of course they'll get you too."

"Well, we do have to go and get him," Jake blurted. "Of course we do."

He paused to consider what had just come out of his mouth.

Blimey. You're actually not a bad guy, Jake.

"We can't go to Italy," Jenny was saying. "Don't be an idiot. This is exactly what they want, I've just explained it all to you."

"They'll kill him though. Won't they?"

She was silent.

"And he was trying to help us."

"Jake, they'll grab us too. There's no way we can get him out of there. I'm sorry."

"So you'll let him be murdered."

It was Jenny's turn to put her head in her hands.

You only wanted to be one of the goodies.

She sighed. "Well ... I suppose we could go and have a look at the lie of the land."

Heston paid for the tickets without argument, and wired them a fighting fund of £25,000.

"Buy whatever you want, bribe whoever you want. Just get the story."

With a glorious rush Jake realized the newspaper was right behind him. He was the arrowhead at the tip of a vast editorial machine, the cutting-edge of British journalism, on a story that all Fleet Street was desperate to own. It was an exhilarating sensation.

"Lives lost in pursuit of the tooth fairy," his boss had crowed. "It's amazing stuff."

Heston thought they could bring down the government.

But Jake's decision to go to Italy was not wholly altruistic. Whatever Britton and Nesta had been talking about, he had to know.

It prompted the other thought which had been squatting in Jake's mind – that no matter what they did, the success or failure of this endeavour was already decided.

All the world's a stage, and all the men and women merely players.

59

Here was Vespasian, a soldier-emperor, grizzled and thick-set. And here was Marcus Aurelius; the philosopher's eyes were pools of reflection and a sadness played about his mouth. Then came Trajan, the great conqueror who had expanded the empire to its fullest extent. Once these eyes had stared in dismay at Asia itself, taking in a landmass that funnelled only outwards. Jake submitted to Trajan's glare and moved on. The heads fanned across the Palatine gallery like a wing of ghosts as he confronted each emperor in turn. Here was Commodus, who had shocked the world by fighting as a gladiator. Hercules reincarnated, or so he had claimed. He wore a lion-skin and his face pulsed with testosterone. And then Augustus, best of them all. A baleful gaze, that tilt of the head; he bordered on godliness.

Were you holding a secret?

Jake stared into eyes of stone, challenging them for answers.

The procession ended with Constantine, a macho figure with his proud nose. The features were rendered in the brutalist style of Soviet propaganda.

Did you change history more than we ever knew?

"Hello? Earth to Jake?" Jenny smiled at him.

"Sorry – off in my own little world."

After the museum they sat at a café overlooking the Pantheon, getting to know each other, trying to work out how the hell they could snatch Dr Nesta from the jaws of MI6.

"You drive a moped in London," said Jenny. "A sky-blue Vespa."

"Do you have any idea how unnerving it is for someone you've only just met to know everything about you?"

"I'm sorry," she said. "But it could be useful. Two wheels is the only way to get anywhere fast in this city."

"Yes, then," he sighed. "I do have a sky-blue Vespa."

"Are you an experienced rider?"

"Fairly."

"What about motorbikes – ever driven them?"

"Only on holiday," said Jake. "In Thailand and places. But I think I could handle one if it wasn't too much of a beast."

Jenny allowed herself an inner smile. He was a likeable guy. But he lacked confidence. He seemed afraid of eye contact, for a start. And he was definitely a drinker, Jake's colleague was spot on about that. Already he had polished off most of his beer, and only on noticing her coke was barely touched had he reigned back: a coachman in charge of untameable horses.

"You've met Frank," she said. "Not a nice bloke. But if we do try and get Dr Nesta out ..."

"What?"

She looked him up and down. "You need to be even more careful of this Charlie Waits chap, Jake. He might not look like much. But he's a scary, scary man."

"Tell me about him."

"The key to understanding Charlie is that at heart he's a patriot. He really does love Britain – he loves the Queen, the countryside, he loves the institutions. The National Trust, the BBC. God, he bloody *idolizes* Churchill. Nothing wrong with all that *per se*. But somewhere along the line he became completely obsessive in defence of what he sees as the national interest. To the point that the way he acts is frankly un-British ..."

A Coke and a beer came to thirteen euros. When Jake grumbled at the price the waitress's nostrils flared. "But this is Roma!" she cried. "This is the Pantheon!"

"All right, all right, point made."

After the waitress had gone, he showed Jenny the photographs of Debre Damo.

"Look at this," he said. "Etruscan characters are written all across the ceiling. And at the far side are two more Roman numerals. It's just like in the cistern. Eusebius is telling us which verse to look at next."

"Amazing," admitted Jenny with a shake of her head. "Just amazing."

"I've already looked up the chapter. It's from the end of the book – Eusebius's reflections on the Emperor Constantine after his death."

Jake passed her the battered volume.

Chapter LXVIII: An Allusion to the Phoenix.
We cannot compare Constantine with that bird of Egypt which dies, and rising from its own ashes soars aloft with new life. Rather he did resemble his saviour, who, as sown corn multiplied from a single grain, yielded abundant increase through the blessing of God. A coin was struck. On one side appeared the figure of our blessed prince, with the head veiled. The reverse exhibited him as a charioteer drawn by four horses, a hand stretched downward from above to receive him up to heaven.

Jenny handed him the book. "I'm not a historian. But it sounds like a pointer to Egypt to me. Would that make sense?"

"Egypt was part of the Roman Empire in Constantine's day," said Jake. "But whereabouts? Eusebius could be talking about anywhere from Alexandria to Aswan."

"What does it matter?" said Jenny. "We don't even need to find any more of the *Disciplina*, do we? It's now an academic exercise. You've already proved Eusebius stashed it all over the world. And you can show he wrote *Life of Constantine* to guide people to the inscriptions. All we'd achieve by looking for more passages is unnecessary danger. The only thing we should be concerned with is proving my old boss is psychotic enough to believe lightning prophecy actually works."

Once again Jake was unwilling to meet her eye.

60

The journalist peered from the doorway of the Church of the Holy Trinity. The Spanish Steps heaved with tourists. No sign of Davis, nor anyone fitting Jenny's description of her boss. But it would be easy to lose yourself in this crowd. The steps were overlooked by dozens of windows. Jenny reckoned they wouldn't shoot him; Waits needed Jake alive to extract the last two inscriptions. If she was wrong, it was from there he would be liquidated. Davis had to be watching. Once Jake stepped from the eaves of the church he was committed.

No sign of a red baseball cap. For some reason adrenaline always made the journalist need to urinate; a full bladder was one distraction he did not need. It was 11.45 a.m. They would already be in situ; there was no time to relieve himself. Jake took a step forward. The laughter of tourists was shrill in his ears as he moved from cover into danger. At any moment he expected his head to snap backward. Death would be instantaneous. He took another pace. Then another. Then another, until he was standing in plain view. The Baroque steps fell away beneath his feet, their width undulating elegantly. A memory entered Jake's head. His grandfather had been inordinately proud of having hopped all the way up the Spanish Steps as a young man. He smiled at the recollection, despite all the fearfulness of the moment. There was still no sign of a red baseball cap. At the bottom of the steps a Hispanic man with matted dreadlocks was fishing coins out of the fountain. His positioning was suspicious. Jake felt a bead of sweat escape his forehead and trickle down his temple. To his left was the house where, the journalist knew, John Keats had died of tuberculosis in the nineteenth century.

Would I were steadfast as thou art ...

Red baseball cap, at the bottom of the steps. It looked daft on the head of the elderly man who was waving at him. At first the pensioner took the stairs hesitantly – but he gained in confidence as he ascended and when he reached Jake he handed him the cap with a courtly flourish.

"I believe this is yours."

Davis to his left, Waits to his right, both of them closing in. The spymaster drew a pistol. There was a bulge in Davis's coat. *How did they get so close?*

The old man's eyes skittered between them and his voice was tremulous. "What is this?"

"Hands up please, sir," said Waits, blowing a forelock from his glasses. "If you would."

"And you," Davis growled.

The journalist lunged for the cover of a lamppost, which sprouted from its sizeable marble base a few steps down. Before Davis could retrieve his pistol he was behind the block: where the Suzuki scrambler he had hired that morning stood, engine running. Jake's vision shimmered as he got a leg over the bike. He pulled the throttle too hard. At once the Suzuki leapt forward, front wheel rearing up into the air. Davis dived for the vehicle, catching the rail behind the pillion seat with his free hand. He was jerked clear of the stairway and for two seconds both of them were airborne, the gunman clinging to the furious machine. The bike landed a half a dozen steps down, unbalanced, leaning at forty-five degrees. Rubber met marble with a shriek and a puff of smoke; then the back tyre gripped and the bike flung itself into the air again, clearing another six steps with the second bound. It landed with a bump that re-dislocated Davis's shoulder. Somehow the assassin held on. Jake had control of the bike now and he zigzagged down the steps, face jiggling with each bump – as though the flesh was disconnected from the skull. Tourists parted before the onrush of the machine, dropping cameras and tripping over each other in their haste. Still Davis clung on, lashed left and right behind the Suzuki like a human tail. An elderly balloon-seller juddered closer, frozen in shock. Instinctively Jake jerked the machine to the left. Their shoulders kissed and the pensioner let go of his balloons, arms wind-milling the air. Jake fought to steady the Suzuki, the marble fountain rushing to meet him. He wasn't wearing a helmet: the impact would pulp his brains. At the last moment he threw the bike into a slide across the piazza that stripped the skin from his thigh. This was too much for Davis and he let go, slithering across the pavement as if in fast forward and crumpling into a heap. The bike spun on its side in the opposite direction and came to a halt. Terror gave Jake strength as he heaved it onto two wheels and kick-started the engine, pinning the machine between his thighs like a cowboy on a mustang. He yanked the throttle and the bike launched itself forward again, his cheeks sucked back with the g-force. Davis was already up and firing, but lack of control made the Suzuki's turns erratic and his shots were wide. The gunman limped into the path of an oncoming scooter; menaced the rider with his pistol; dragged him off the moped by the neck; threw him to ground. Waits had vanished, the elderly prisoner with him.

The Hispanic guy seemed to be talking to himself.

61

The Via dei Condotti is Rome's most exclusive shopping street: straight, narrow and clogged with pedestrians at this hour. A pregnant mother in a puffer jacket shrieked at Jake as he jinked through. "*Bastaaa!*"

The yell distracted him and when he looked up there was a middle-aged woman wearing Jackie O sunglasses directly in his path, shopping bags fanned out over her left arm. Jake snatched at the brakes and the machine squealed back to stationary with centimetres to spare.

"I'm sorry," he said.

Designer shopping bags quivered in the rubber smoke.

"*Scusate signora,*" he tried.

But the woman wasn't looking at him any more. She was looking *beyond* him. Jake turned to see Davis bearing down at speed, shoppers scattering before the stolen scooter. The journalist accelerated off. One by one the labels flashed past: Prada, Dior, Gucci, Bulgari. The motorbike was twice as powerful as Davis's scooter, but in the crowds any advantage was lost. The Suzuki cornered heavily at slow speeds, threatening to tumble over. And the scooter was in its element, threading a path through the shoppers, sailing over the feet of an elderly Roma gypsy who was begging in the road. This was another advantage the assassin held: he just didn't care who got hurt. They burst free of the crowds, like jet planes clearing thick stratocumulus, the odd straggler darting to safety. In Jake's wing mirror he saw the vibrating image of Davis, levelling his pistol, horribly close now, preparing to fire. There was an alleyway coming up and Jake wrenched the handlebars to the right, sending the bike into a sideways skid that sucked the blood to one side of his body. He came to a halt facing up the passage – a manoeuvre only terror could produce. The alleyway was devoid of people; he hit sixty in two seconds. Davis had become a distant figure in Jake's mirrors by the time he emerged into the passage behind him. The journalist pulled a left, to be rewarded with another empty alleyway. This was better. The cityscape was playing to his motorbike's strengths now. And he was mastering the bike, learning to lean with it as he cornered. Davis appeared behind him again as he reached the end of the second alleyway; the gap had expanded to fifty metres. One more stretch like that and he would have lost him, he'd round the corner before Davis came into sight. There was another turning coming up. Jake took this one at speed.

He had the momentary impression of stalls rushing towards him.

The motorbike went straight into a postcard stand, which flipped up into the sky like a juggler's club. Jake's face was smarting, but somehow he kept the bike on its wheels, a confetti of cards fluttering down onto the cobbles in his wake. The street market sold books and art and Jake was forced to slow as he wound through the punters. Now Davis was in the alleyway too; instead of slowing down he sped up. The market became a blizzard of paper as the killer bulldozed his way along. An artist was painting a caricature of two Danish girls and Davis tore through the easel, shearing the canvas in half. Ahead of Jake stood the Church of San Carlo Corso, a pedestrian walkway leading past the chapel. He tore along the pavement; bounced down some steps; rounded a corner; ran straight into a film crew. A model dived out of Jake's way, stumbling into a camera which crashed to the ground. A lighting rig came down after it; bulbs shattered in a blinding flash. Jake weaved around the lunge of a corpulent director and raced away once more. In his rear-view mirror he could make out the paint splattered across Davis's face as his scooter emerged into the walkway. The director rushed into the path of the oncoming vehicle, hopping from one foot to the other in paroxysms of rage. Davis went right through him, like a prince dispatching riffraff at a medieval joust.

Jake emerged into a park dominated by a windowless cylinder of brickwork, three storeys high and two hundred feet wide. The monument was topped by a conical hillock, cypress trees dotted about the summit. Jake accelerated across the grass towards it.

Two men holding hands wandered into his path.

For the second time in that deranged chase he was forced to ditch the bike. He felt no pain as he slammed sideways into the earth, grazing his cheek and expelling the air from his lungs. He manhandled the Suzuki onto two wheels, swung his leg over the machine, fired it up again. A policeman appeared in front of Jake then, yelling and drawing his gun; behind him Davis's moped buzzed into the park. The only option was to race down a shallow set of steps and into the ditch that circled the monument.

Davis pursued him, and for a mad few seconds they chased each other around the cylinder of masonry, doing laps of the ditch. But Jake's tyres were better suited to the terrain and he pulled away, the brickwork sliding across his rear-view mirrors until the assassin could no longer be seen. Seconds later Davis appeared in front of him. The spy was hunched forward on his moped as the grass sprayed up from its rear wheel, unaware he was about to be lapped. Jake swerved out of the ditch before Davis could spot him. The steps acted as a ramp, launching the Suzuki through the air in front of the astonished policeman.

By the time Davis worked out what had happened, Jake was out of the park. Neither man ever knew that they had been doing laps of the Mausoleum of Augustus. Jake came out by the Tiber: here at last was a stretch of open road, and he put a kilometre behind him in thirty seconds. There was still no sign of Davis, and Jake punched the air. It had been easily the most exhilarating two minutes of his life.

62

Jenny Frobisher checked her watch for the fifth time in ten minutes. It was 11:45 a.m.: fifteen minutes until the rendezvous. She took a sip of espresso and screwed up her eyes. For her plan to work a scary amount of things had to go right.

First, she had to be correct in her calculation that they would be facing a team of two – three at the outside, if Evelyn Parr was in Italy too. But she was certain Waits wouldn't bring more agents on board – not with all the murder left behind them in which any newcomer was not complicit. There was always the awful possibility that he would deploy some E-Squadron personnel.

Oh, all the major embassies have a few smooth operators I can call on ...

But after what went down in Istanbul, Jenny thought it unlikely. That had been a rapidly-developing situation, whereas the spymaster had had days to prepare for this snatch. And Waits was arrogant – he would like to think he could handle it himself. Jake's life now depended on this.

Secondly, Jenny needed to find an unwitting accomplice who resembled Dr Nesta. They had agonized over the ethics of this detail, but she was adamant the individual would be unharmed. Killing a civilian would create more loose ends than it tied off; Waits would scare him and let him go.

Third: Jake had to be as good on two wheels as he evidently thought he was (though he didn't voice this minor pride).

Getting the bike in position without alarm bells ringing had been an issue, but they found the solution. The Suzuki was brand new, and Jenny had approached the tourist police, asking to do a photo-shoot on the steps. She'd been told paperwork was required; heavy flirtation somehow negated the need for it. The motorbike had been there since 5 a.m., with a little boy paid to polish it; every now and then the officers sauntered up to the kid and asked him when the attractive English lady would return. Jenny reckoned it looked natural enough.

Finally, the timings had to be perfect. For public transport reasons Jenny thought it likely Dr Nesta would approach from the east, at the bottom of the Spanish Steps. So she positioned herself at the back of a café overlooking the piazza, ready to pounce on him.

Jenny told the decoy that she was the fiancée of a long-haired blond man who would shortly be arriving at the top of the steps. Her lover didn't even know she was in Rome; Jenny had bought him this red cap on the day of their engagement. Would the gentleman be kind enough to hand it to him, point her out in the café and pass on a message of *amore*? It was a story no Italian could resist.

At noon it would be all systems go. Without question, MI6 were already in position. All in all, she was reasonably confident in her plan. Similar swoops had worked in the past, although admittedly nothing with so many variables. If Dr Nesta arrived late it would be dicey; if he was early it would be a catastrophe. Jenny didn't even want to think about the possibility of a third watcher remaining behind once Jake succeeded in diverting Davis and Waits was occupied with his prisoner.

Suddenly it was time.

There was Jake, stepping into the open, walking like a man on a tightrope. Off went the decoy, taking the steps if he was walking down the aisle: a silly smile plastered over his face. To Jenny's eyes the whole thing looked ridiculously contrived – Waits couldn't possibly go for it. But he did.

Then Jake was tearing down the staircase on the scrambler, Davis dragged behind him, the Italian being led away by Waits as tourists fled in all directions. Amid the mayhem a man wearing a red cap approached the piazza from the east, as she had calculated he would. Dr Giuseppe Nesta observed the scene for a few seconds before throwing his headwear on the ground and fleeing. Jenny sprinted after the scientist, slipped a disposable phone into his pocket, and it was done.

63

The journalist found it gratifying to see how many other clichés of spy-craft were reality. Jenny's counter-surveillance routines were copious. She doubled back on herself, crisscrossed the street, changed bus and Metro routes exhaustively. And she insisted it was safest to meet Dr Nesta in public, where there was less chance of being eavesdropped on and more avenues of escape. On the clean phone line they agreed to meet in the old Roman forum, where they could blend in with the tourists.

Jake tried to make a joke of it: "Should we ask him if the fishing in Leningrad is good this time of year?"

Jenny ignored him. He could detect a sense of humour lurking somewhere beneath the surface, but it was as if it had been hermetically sealed from the world.

They met the physicist under the shoulder of the Colosseum. For a statement of raw power the stadium retained considerable elegance in its columns and arches, yet it was brutally functional too. Jake pointed out the numerals marked over gates that once admitted the mob: Roman crowd control.

Dr Nesta was elderly and pigeon-toed with round spectacles that seemed to exaggerate his eyes. He reminded Jake of a puffin come down from the colony to share its secrets, and looking at his shuffling walk an almost motherly sensation welled in the journalist.

"I hope when I have told you what I must, you will not think me too mad," Dr Nesta began. "So. What do you already know of Roger's work?"

Jake filled him in as they promenaded through the political

heart of ancient Rome. He spoke of the trail set by Eusebius; the new inscriptions; the desperation of the men and women who hunted them. With each revelation Dr Nesta's eyes widened until it seemed he was more eye than man. Jake left out one detail: that he believed in the same thing as Britton. Jenny had to see the proof of that for herself.

Dr Nesta stopped under a triumphal arch erected to honour Constantine after his victory following the vision. "By this sign conquer," he said grandly. "But it was not by any Christian sign that Rome mastered the world." Instinctively Dr Nesta crossed himself. "Roger was killed because he realized that what my ancestors believed was ... it was true."

Jake saw the twist of a smile pass over Jenny's features.

"Well, you have not run away." Dr Nesta clasped his hands together. "That is a good start. Now I can show you the mathematics and the science to prove it."

"Dr Nesta," began Jenny. "You said you had information about Roger Britton."

"Signora," he interrupted, "I can tell you now that they called down a lightning strike on his head!"

She regarded him with pity.

"You don't believe me, of course. Why would you? But *he* knows it's true." Dr Nesta wheeled to face Jake. "I can see it in his face."

Jake made no reply.

"Let us proceed this way," said Dr Nesta, gesturing onward. "And I shall give you the science."

They wandered into the Forum itself. This was where Cicero made his prosecutions and defences, where his head would end up on a stake; where Mark Antony delivered the funerary oration to Julius Caesar. And where before all that, Etruscan kings had drained the swamps and thrown up shrines to their forgotten Gods. The temples were reduced to white fingers, rising from the ground to point out the lost greatness of Rome.

"I was engaged in the hunt for the Holy Grail of modern

physics," Dr Nesta said. "The Grand Unified Theory. You are scientifically minded I assume?"

Jake looked awkward.

"I did physics at A Level," Jenny offered. "And I'm half-decent at maths."

"Then please interrupt if I start patronizing you," said Dr Nesta. "You are aware, I am sure, that the two great breakthroughs in physics of the last century – Einstein's theory of relativity and quantum mechanics – cannot both be correct. They contradict each other. The search for the theory that marries the two has cost vast fortunes without success."

Jenny nodded. The Large Hadron Collider – a tunnel under the Swiss border through which particles were fired at almost the speed of light – had devoured two billion euros in construction alone.

"My attempt to solve this problem led me to develop a new theory, one that combines quantum physics and relativity. It was this that led me to Professor Britton. Or, should I say, led Professor Britton to me."

A group of Portuguese schoolchildren clattered past – all braces, puffer jackets, perfect skin. Once the hubbub subsided Dr Nesta continued, "Relativity applies to things on a big scale. Snooker balls, planets, us. But a different set of rules seems to apply at a quantum level. That is to say, to tiny things – neutrons, electrons and so on. Mathematicians have always assumed Einstein's theory of relativity was correct, so they have always tried to redefine quantum theory to fit with Einstein. I took the other approach." He raised an eyebrow. "I threw relativity out of the window, signora."

"So Einstein was wrong then?" said Jenny.

"You are cynical, of course," said Dr Nesta. "So are my colleagues. They cannot accept it. Their brains are inured to new concepts. But I tell you, relativity is a false religion. Einstein himself admitted it. When he was an elderly man he told a friend his work would not stand the test of time. Perhaps he'd got it wrong after all."

"How does this relate to the Etruscans?" asked Jake.

"I'm getting to that. Please bear with me." Dr Nesta's expression was both smile and grimace. "Under my theory there is no curved space-time. There is no constant speed of light. All of Einstein's findings I refute. There are simply two types of energy – a positive energy and a negative energy. Like the Yin and Yang in the old eastern philosophies."

Something in this was beginning to make Jenny uneasy.

"This idea is not new, of course," he went on. "But it was discarded because it did not fit with relativity. Of course, now we have forsaken Einstein this does not cause a problem. Indeed, we can strike out his other great fallacy – the belief that it is impossible to create energy out of nothing."

There was a moment's silence. Then Jenny said, "How?"

"The answer is in the way these energies *collide*," said Dr Nesta, his voice husky, as if whispering state secrets. "For centuries the maxim has been accepted that energy can neither be destroyed nor created, that it can only change form. But as I will illustrate, if positive and negative energy exist side by side, this maxim should read that energy *can only be destroyed or created in equal amounts*."

Jenny stared into the sun. An aircraft buzzed across its surface, no more than a floater on the fiery retina. Humble star, minor outpost of the Milky Way, still blazing out light and heat as it had for billions of years before her birth. She frowned. Energy from nothing? *Could it be?*

64

Florence Chung leaned her forehead against the window of the private jet and stared at Rome. The hills of Lazio had given way to the city itself: sprawling and confused, the Tiber slithering through it. St Peter's rose above the cityscape like a Baroque wedding cake, and – a heart in mouth moment – there was the Colosseum. It was stunted by comparison with modern Rome. Yet it seemed dogged somehow, unwilling to erode under the bombardment of time. Finally they were over the Forum; Florence had visited Rome often and still the sight of it humbled her.

Another roar of "Happy Birthday to you!" interrupted her cogitations.

Florence glared at her compatriots. What was officially a Chinese trade delegation had departed Addis that morning, but her team had played the part of a Shanghai business trip too well in that they were all roaring drunk. Florence had always felt superior to the China-born, and now she was reminded why. The middle class was desperate to emulate westerners; for the men that meant Anglo-Saxon feats of drinking. The result was this bilious little jamboree.

"Happy Birthday to you!"

She snorted. It was nobody's birthday – the game was for everyone to charge their glasses until at some unknowable moment they downed their drinks and sang a verse.

Florence closed her ears to the carousing and recited the incantations to herself again. First, the paean to *dii consentes*, the pitiless, advisers of the supreme God Tin. Istanbul would always be special to her – it was the place where she'd first managed to tune into the frequency. Then from Ethiopia had come the incantation to *dii novensiles*, casters of lightning. An extra *je ne sais quoi* had coursed through her veins since then – like mercury or liquid iron, white heat ... Florence couldn't explain it, but that inscription had done something *biological* to her. Her period hadn't come for one thing. It was a worry, but never mind – with each discovery she had gained in potency. A glow emanated from her lower body at the thought and she wriggled in her seat, suddenly aroused. What was still to be found? It could only be an incantation to those numinous powers closest to the Great All-Seeing Eye, *dii superiores*, who advised Tin on when to throw the most dreaded thunderbolt of all: that of destruction.

Florence's prescience was burgeoning; indeed it was on her reading of the portents that they had travelled to Italy. But the final weapon in her armoury was missing – the ability to do to others what had been done to Roger Britton. The last inscription would be the key to it all, and without it her augury would forever be vague.

She had to have it.

"Happy Birthday to you!"

Florence scowled at the party. Then she leaned back, succumbing to her memories. Like so many spies, her initial motivation on joining a secret service had been the thrill of it all. Despite her advantages in life she'd always lacked confidence in her intellect. She had a decent enough brain; she could learn by rote and through sheer hard graft she had made it to Oxbridge. Yet Florence felt self-conscious around people with real intelligence: the ability to *make connections*. People like Jake. So Gods, what a buzz it was to be headhunted by the land of her forefathers, to play her part in making China the most powerful nation on earth. And at this, the dawn of China's millennium. Her peers may have been hoovered up by the chambers of the Square Mile, but Florence was part of something bigger. Something with the seductive scent of danger about it – and plenty of cash on offer too.

Then they had told her to become an archaeologist.

She smirked to recall how bitter she was at the start, scraping away in the dirt with a trowel while her friends sashayed through the Old Bailey. But then she began to understand what her paymasters had in mind for her, and a third motivation crept in alongside the excitement and the money. The most insidious vice of all: power.

With her growing capabilities, the lust for it had elbowed lesser foibles aside. She bit her lip, aroused once again. Soon she had slipped into the realm of daydream, indulging herself with thoughts of how far she could go and what she might become. Were her handlers mentoring others to be *fulguriatores*? If not, and if she acquired the next inscription – why, then the People's Republic of China would be in thrall to Florence Chung, rather than the other way around. Energy radiated through her at the thought, a crackle that began in her cranium and ran down her nervous system, through her bone marrow, the organs in her abdomen. It was an unnerving sensation. But an exciting one.

The fantasy was interrupted by her ears popping; they were coming in to land. The sensation reminded her she was still human, composed of flesh and bone.

No Augustus yet.

65

"So you're saying energy *can* be created from nothing?" Jake felt like a chimpanzee subjected to a discourse on Voltaire.

"Exactly so!" snapped Dr Nesta.

"How?" asked Jenny, her eyes slants of doubt.

"Imagine, if you will, two snooker balls colliding," he said. "We expect them to move off away from each other in predictable, geometric angles."

Jake nodded. Now the scientist was talking his language.

"But there is no overall change in the amount of energy in existence after balls have struck. One ball has transferred some of its energy to another, causing it to move off. The rest is bled away into the air and the felt of the table until the balls both lose momentum and stop."

"I'm with you," said Jake.

"Now imagine one of the balls is an atom. But instead of carrying positive energy, it carries negative energy. In this scenario, after they collide *both balls will move off in the same direction*."

"Negative energy?" said Jenny.

Jake rubbed his scalp. "This is making my head hurt."

"Yes, negative energy," said Dr Nesta. "Negative mass. The so-called 'exotic matter'. It exists only hypothetically – although some of its effects have been produced in the laboratory."

"Explain please," said Jenny.

"Very well. Ask yourself, can space contain *less* than nothing? Common sense dismisses the idea. You would think that if you removed every atom from a space the least it could contain is a vacuum. Strangely, this is not the case. Under quantum theory, space *can* contain less than nothing. Which means the energy density – the energy-per-unit volume – can in fact be less than zero. This is negative energy. Now let us return to your colliding snooker balls moving off in the same direction."

"Yes, let's," said Jake.

"The point is that under the influence of exotic matter, for this strange double sideways motion to take place, both balls *must* have gained energy – because there is a net *increase* in momentum. And this additional energy must have come from somewhere. It's like a ..." The scientist was lost suddenly. "It is like a *breeding* of the energies."

"How is this relevant?" asked Jenny.

"Because we have shown it must be possible for energy to be created from nothing. And collisions have been going on between tiny particles in space since the beginning of time. My theory is that in the wake of each collision, each breeding, a *filament* of energy is left. The universe is strewn with them. I believe these filaments of energy are what holds the universe together and keeps it expanding, what stops it from collapsing in on itself due to the pull of gravity. You will be aware of the hunt for the Higgs Boson? The so-called God particle? Here it is."

Jenny had gone pale. "Filaments stopping the universe from collapsing in on itself? That's like ... that's like the *ether*."

The concept of the 'ether' – a background medium which

allowed gravity and light to be transmitted – had been around since Newton before being debunked by twentieth-century physicists.

Dr Nesta's eyes flashed. "But that is exactly what it is! A background medium spread throughout the entire universe. I tell you, I have seen it with my own eyes. I have seen it in my laboratory."

"But how does this relate to the Etruscans?" Jake repeated, hoping to pull the conversation back to a world he could comprehend.

The Italian leaned forward. "Because in the course of my research I made a great leap, even if I say so myself. I found that this ether behaves like a super-fluid, similar to liquid helium. That is to say it is frictionless, yet it permits the flow of waves through the filaments almost instantaneously. These waves are spikes of intense energy, like the ripples on a pond."

Jenny's anxiety cranked up a notch. They were standing beneath the Temple of Saturn; the eight remaining columns formed a gate of marble, enclosing the sky.

"Thus we have a three-dimensional grid structure of energy which fills the entire universe," said the scientist. "Through which ripples of energy can be transmitted almost instantly. To what does this bear an uncanny resemblance, you might ask?"

Jake looked blank, though he too felt a growing disquiet.

"Why, the network of neurones that makes up the *human brain*."

*

"Are you trying to say you proved the existence of God?" Jenny asked, once she had recovered her poise.

"God is a strong word," said Dr Nesta. "It is more a kind of intelligent background medium, all around us. Energy travels down this network of filaments faster than the speed of light – like thoughts transmitted through the human mind."

"I don't believe you," said Jenny.

Jake knew differently.

He couldn't pretend to understand the physics. Yet what this man proposed gave structure to the insanity of what he had already observed; a measure of rationality had returned to what seemed by its very nature irrational. The world made a modicum of sense again.

"We are looking at a huge interconnecting system of switches," said Dr Nesta, a fleck of foam at each corner of his mouth. "A system that developed the characteristics of consciousness and intelligence. A celestial supercomputer, if you will."

"This is science fiction," said Jenny. "How could random filaments of energy develop consciousness? The idea is absurd."

"Respectfully, signora, you are not thinking on a quantum level," Nesta replied. "It is true that large objects tend towards disorder. For example, if you knock a plate off a table it shatters into thousands of pieces. You don't see shards of broken china leaping from the floor and reforming themselves. But at the level of the quark and the electron quite the opposite is true. Particles tend to *order themselves.* And here we have a googolplex of filaments, a matrix the size of the universe and thirteen billion years of development. The emergence of sentience was a certainty." Nesta paused, kneading thumb and index finger together, as if assessing the fineness of an invisible fabric. "Imagine the power of calculation of a computer the size of every particle in existence," he continued. "To such a consciousness, determining the future paths of molecules and the decisions of men is like adding two and two. This is a game it plays. And so it tests its strength." The scientist's tongue started from his mouth, licking each globule of foam clear. "It was this network my ancestors learned how to tap into, long ago."

"We're wasting our time," said Jenny.

"Einstein himself said the religion of the future will be a

cosmic religion," the scientist said, urgent now. "It will avoid dogma and theology. And what better way for such a network to communicate its will than a bolt of lightning? The intelligence speaks to us in its own element."

Jake gazed at a patch of long grass. Poppies picked their way through chunks of column and statuary and Dr Nesta followed his eyes to a sandaled foot, broken off at the heel.

"Do you not realize that, biologically, the whole human body is an electrical system?" he said. "Everything you see, feel or think is electricity. Every impulse and desire is carried through your body in ions. Energy flows through us, just as it flows through the universe. It makes us who we are. It is the language of the stars." He looked up at the Temple of Saturn. "Of the Gods."

66

"I'm not sure how much more of this I can listen to," said Jenny. "It's not helping us."

Jake pretended not to hear her. "Let's say for the sake of argument you're right," he said. "How could the Etruscans have stumbled on this network when mainstream science" – on seeing the doctor's glare he backtracked – "when all the rest of science missed it?"

"This is a matter wherein Roger's research correlated with mine so precisely that I became convinced we had found symptoms of the same phenomenon. Are you familiar with Etruscan religion?"

"I'm not," said Jenny.

"Let me fill you in then," replied Dr Nesta. "A child prophet named Tages was said to have dictated the Etruscan holy text to man."

"He was unearthed under a plough," said Jake. "It was one of the only 'revealed' religions of the ancient world."

"Correct. Very good. But did you know that in 1982 a grave thought to be that of Tages himself was discovered here in Italy?"

Jake was caught off guard. "No way."

"Indeed yes. At a place called Pian di Civita, an hour's drive north from here."

"How did they know it was Tages's grave?"

"It dated from about 800 BC," said Dr Nesta. "That coincides exactly with the beginning of Etruscan religion. And inside was the skeleton of a boy who was obviously revered."

"So he was a prince of some description," suggested Jenny.

"There was evidence of child sacrifice," said Nesta. "For several generations after the boy was laid to rest, infants were killed and buried in the vicinity of his skeleton. This is unique for Etruscan burials."

A cold breeze stirred, whispering through the Temple of Saturn.

"The bones also showed evidence of frequent periods of famine," Nesta continued. "If you accept this was Tages, it would explain the *Disciplina Etrusca*'s preoccupation with agriculture, predicting whether the crops would fail."

Jake recalled the brontoscopic calendar.

If it should thunder it threatens dearth of food.

"More fascinating still, the child's skull showed he'd had a cranial haemorrhage – it is likely he suffered from severe epilepsy. That could have led to ..."

"Hallucinations," interrupted Jake. "Visions, like Joan of Arc had."

Dr Nesta nodded. "But Roger and I go further. We posit that this brain damage attuned the child to this background medium. He tapped into the grid, taught others to communicate with it. The incantations he set down in the *Disciplina Etrusca* ... how can I put this? *Flattered* the network. It was compelled to listen."

"Carry on," said Jake in a guarded voice. "What happened after Tages died?"

Jenny glanced at him.

"The Etruscans shielded their secret," said Dr Nesta. "And for a time they were top dog in the western Mediterranean. But Rome stole it away. Whether by espionage or raid we can never know. But overnight the town's fortunes changed forever. Then the conquest of Italy began. And as Rome rose, so Etruscan civilization fell. Roger even went so far as to suggest the exact year of the theft – 390 BC, when barbarians from Gaul sacked Rome. It was the last time the city would be overrun for nine centuries. Roger hypothesized that such a crushing defeat led Rome to try to mimic their Etruscan neighbours' success. To covet what they possessed." Dr Nesta lowered his voice. "In 390 BC the smooth flow of history was interrupted, like a ... like a needle knocked from a record. Within a hundred and twenty years Romans had conquered Italy. The world was next. Only the theft of the *Disciplina* could explain it. Could explain this." He indicated the Forum with a sweep of the arm. "This was the centre of an empire spanning from Spain to Syria, from Scotland to the Sahara Desert. Ask yourself – in a pre-industrial age, could such a feat of conquest and administration be possible without help?"

"It pains me to engage with this fantasy," said Jenny. "But if your theory's correct, why didn't the Etruscans take over the world?"

"Because, signora, the Etruscans were by their nature pessimists. Every surviving inscription portrays a fatalistic race, a people who had long believed their civilization would end after its anointed *ten saecula*."

Jake felt a crackle of gloom on hearing the words.

"For them the *Disciplina Etrusca* led only to a self-fulfilling prophecy of defeat and decline," Nesta continued. "But in the hands of the Romans, a people with ambition and confidence? It became a golden circle of conquest. The skies would have predicted triumph after triumph."

"But Rome suffered defeats," Jake shot back. "Long after you claim they obtained the *Disciplina*. When Hannibal crossed the Alps with his elephants it took the Romans completely by surprise – Carthage nearly destroyed Rome forever."

"Do not underestimate human arrogance," said Dr Nesta. "The Roman senators may not have believed such a feat was possible, they may have ignored the warnings. Or perhaps the soothsayers were afraid to reveal what the omens were telling them."

"But Hannibal ravaged the Romans for twenty years. If they could predict the future, how do you explain the defeat at Cannae? Why did they lose a single battle?"

"Perhaps the clouds predicted only losses," said Dr Nesta. "And what preceded the final defeat of Hannibal? A great increase in devoutness in Rome. Religious rites were observed with especial rigour. For the first time in centuries slaves were sacrificed. The network was appeased – Hannibal met his Waterloo."

"What stopped Rome then?" said Jenny. "Why doesn't the empire live on?"

"That we know," Jake blurted out.

There was a moment's silence. Then Jenny said, "It almost sounds like you believe it yourself, Jake."

"Don't be so silly."

"Go on then, what were you going to say?"

"He was going to say that Constantine ordered the destruction of the *Disciplina Etrusca*," Dr Nesta replied. "He trusted to Christianity instead. It was a poor decision. And again, history is our prime witness. Consider the greatest historian of them all, your Edward Gibbon. The *Decline and Fall of the Roman Empire* blames only Christianity for what befell the empire." Again Dr Nesta crossed himself.

"Gibbon merely argued that with Jesus as a rival figurehead to the emperor, Rome lost cohesiveness," said Jake. "And without the figure of a divine Caesar to hold the empire together, it fell apart."

"Gibbon identified the symptoms, but he misidentified the cause. Do you think the ancients would have kept on about this science for a thousand years if it didn't work? What modern arrogance! It's as Roger always said. There is this public misconception that ancient people were not fully evolved – cavemen grunt, modern humans think and our ancestors were somewhere in between. But the human who emerges from ancient literature is the *same species as us*. You see, the people who the ancient texts portray were every bit like us. They loved and lost. They planned for the future. They lied and schemed and were afraid of disease. Indisputably the classical world contained true genius, and yet still Rome clung to augury. Ask yourself why?" He grimaced. "For centuries Rome was governed as badly as ... as Italy today, for instance. The emperors were mad, the civil wars were unending, the society was a stew of corruption. And yet for all its flaws Rome always seemed to prevail. What *edge* did it have?"

"If what you're saying is true," Jenny pressed, "then why isn't thunder prophecy the central theme of Roman literature?"

Dr Nesta laughed. "First, because there was something very *un-Roman* about it – relying on superstition for success. The Romans liked to pretend everything they achieved was through hard work and endeavour, not some stolen secret. And if you had the edge on your rivals, wouldn't you keep it to yourselves?"

"The Romans made a big show of taking the omens," Jake observed.

"And yet it was examining livers and interpreting the flight of birds that were central to public ceremony," said Dr Nesta. "If you knew the future was encoded in bolts of lightning, how clever to celebrate such ludicrous, such silly techniques."

The group had meandered to the Temple of the Vestal Virgins, the priestesses charged with keeping the sacred flame of Rome alight. All that remained was a circular row of columns; it reminded Jake of a classical folly in the grounds of some Victorian mill-owner.

"And these were the women who kept the secret for so long," said Dr Nesta. "Every Roman knew the Vestal Virgins were fundamental to the security of Rome – but not *why*. A dire power is best kept by a secretive group. Who controlled the Vestal Virgins controlled the fate of Rome. For they were keepers of the *sacred flame*."

"Power in the hands of women?" Jenny snorted. "I thought we were second-class citizens."

"Roger had a theory that females were more capable of interpreting the omens than men," said Dr Nesta. "More perceptive, more open to the frequency. It was not for nothing the Etruscans gave their women a degree of freedom that scandalized the ancient world."

Jake thought of Florence.

"Enough of this." Jenny's eyes glittered. "We met you at considerable risk, hoping for information about Roger. Stuff that would stand up in a court of law. Have you got anything useful to tell us? Anything at all?"

The scientist grimaced again. "Beyond what I have already said? No. But they killed him, signora. You must believe what I say."

"With a lightning bolt?" Jenny laughed. "Even if that was possible, why would they get him like that? It's so blatant."

"I believe you have the phrase in English," said Dr Nesta. "Hiding in plain sight."

*

"That's what you get when you bring together a pseudo-scientist and a disturbed historian," Jenny growled as they returned to the hotel. "And we risked everything to meet him. I should have my bloody head examined."

"Perhaps there was a grain of truth in what he was saying about the grave of Tages," muttered Jake. "All that stuff about the haemorrhage. It was interesting, at least. And it wouldn't be the first time in history somebody with a brain defect was hailed as saviour."

Jenny gripped his wrist.

"What?" asked Jake. "What is it?"

"Grain ... saviour ..."

"I don't follow," he said.

"I think I've just worked out where Eusebius's final hiding place is."

67

That night Jake lay awake, listening to the ambient noise of Italian lives floating through his window. Almost midnight, and children were still out playing. The journalist padded to the window and watched them thwack a football against a wall. A mother emerged from her apartment to shepherd the kids inside and a teenager ambled to his scooter, scorching away downhill. In the window opposite Jake could see a television flickering, half of a man wearing a vest with a beer in his hand. This was still a happy city – despite the Eurozone meltdown, despite all the difficulties Italy faced.

How much Roman blood pumped through their veins? Jake had once read that most Italians have a splice of Arabian in their DNA, testament to the millions of Middle Eastern people sucked into ancient Rome as economic migrants or as slaves. That revelation had been seized on by twentieth-century eugenicists to explain the fall of Rome; yet now Jake found himself drawn towards an equally outlandish conclusion.

Why had this people lost the reins of power? It was the most important question in history, and especially for the West.

What would Augustus make of Italy today? Bankrupt; globally irrelevant; derided for lack of organization and, by Roman standards, worse: for lack of grit. Italy had been superseded by states that were also in the process of being superseded, and Augustus would think the Italians flowery and fey. Cultured, yes, but still to be sneered at. As Rome once sneered at the flowery Greeks.

Jake rinsed out his cafetière and watched the suds swirl anticlockwise around the basin. Was the dance of each dot preordained? How could any intelligence keep track of so many multitudes? Anyway, wasn't that what the rules of physics were for: controlling the path of earth and the planets and each of these thousands of dots in their ballet? But how were the laws of physics chosen? And if you knew those laws, if you had a big enough calculator ...

Jake rested his head on the sink – you could go mad thinking about this stuff. He wondered whether Jenny was asleep, smiled to think of her lying a few feet away in the neighbouring room. Then he stopped smiling and raised his eyebrows, impressed anew at her leap of intuition.

Chapter LXVIII: An Allusion to the Phoenix.
We cannot compare Constantine with that bird of Egypt which dies, and rising from its own ashes soars aloft with new life. Rather he did resemble his saviour, who, as sown corn multiplied from a single grain, yielded abundant increase through the blessing of God. A coin was struck. On one side appeared the figure of our blessed prince, with the head veiled. The reverse exhibited him as a charioteer drawn by four horses, a hand stretched downward from above to receive him up to heaven.

Was it not, Jenny had suggested, about Tages? A saviour who had himself risen from the ground? Did a charioteer with four horses not allude to the plough that had disturbed him?

Sown corn multiplied from a single grain.

And Eusebius described a hand stretching downward to pull

the saviour up to heaven – as a ploughman had yanked Tages from the ground. The more Jake considered it, the more it made sense. Eusebius hid the final inscription in the most fitting place of all: the tomb of the child who had taught humans the proper discourse between Gods and men.

Jake could not sleep. His mind whirred over the day and with dismay he realized he believed every word Dr Nesta had said. The scientist's theories explained not only everything that had happened during the last few weeks, but history itself. Something *had* happened in 800 BC. The Book of Thunder *had* been appropriated by Rome. And with that advantage, a provincial town had become a superpower. And the results were all around him still – in law, in language, in literature and democracy, in aesthetics and architecture, a culture handed faithfully down to the modern age across twenty centuries. Not just in this city; not just on this continent; across the world. Jake saw then how – after a hiatus between the collapse of Rome and the Renaissance – western culture had become humanity's culture. Everywhere doing well, at least. Western transport, Western medicine, Western industry and banking and communications: the toolkit had been adopted wholesale almost as far you might travel.

Yet Europe was in trouble. America stagnated. Meanwhile China and India raced to catch up, a host of other nations on their heels. The rest of the world had identified what made the West great after the kick-start of the *Disciplina Etrusca*, and it had copied the lot.

Jake glanced at the minibar; he was never going to get to sleep at this rate. He crossed the room in three strides and flung open the fridge so that a corridor of light bathed the floor. With trembling hands he selected a miniature Scotch and fiddled off the lid.

*

When Jake slept at last he dreamed of it again. He was standing on a lunar landscape, staring into space, his arms flung behind him and fists clenched. A wave of luminosity crashed over him and he bathed in it: ions, particles, starlight, *energy*. The stream of light was running straight through him; he looked at his torso and realized that was made of light too.

The incantation, the drumbeat, that devil tongue.

With each verse the radiance grew in intensity until Jake was staggering through a world comprised only of light. And then he saw the light was in fact a grid of astonishing intricacy. He could stare at each passing electron and see how it linked to every other electron in existence: all pulsing and swelling, singing to one another. Suddenly he was far above, looking at the plane of the known universe from the outside. The grid swelled into a spike, as if a drop of water had landed in the celestial pond. The spike was stretching, getting taller and thinner, and Jake realized the universe had flipped upside down and he was looking up at it: a stalactite the size of billions of Milky Ways, reaching down to touch him. But it was losing the smooth curves of its form, becoming jagged. And the beat had changed too – it was no longer the bang of a drum. It had evolved into a different rhythm: tramp, tramp, tramp.

Jackboots.

Jake knew then this grid was not godly but capricious, it delighted in playing with the dreams of mortals to appease the boredom of its intelligence. Still the spike lengthened, became crooked, craning towards him.

Zap! Crack!

Lightning disgorged from its tip and blasted him through the forehead.

Jake awoke with a cry. His hand shot to his head. He was panting, shaking compulsively, his sheets were drenched in sweat. The darkness of the dream was like nothing he had ever known.

Jake stumbled out of bed and leaned on the windowsill. A strip of gold was spreading across the horizon. A new dawn. He knew then what he had to do – why he had been put upon this earth, no less.

He had to find the last inscription.

And destroy it.

68

Jake awoke filled with a determination he had only known during the golden years after university, when he had soared to that improbable job on Fleet Street. He had often since marvelled at his escape from the local press. That had been before he began drinking every day of course, but now he felt the same single-mindedness.

He was going to succeed.

Jenny reckoned they would be best advised to fly back to the UK to launch the media assault. But Jake convinced her it was worth a visit to the tomb as it was nearby, claiming another discovery would give the story more legs.

The Pian di Civita was once home to one of the foremost Etruscan city states, and there were plenty of references online to the 1982 dig. But to frustrate grave-robbers exact coordinates were withheld. The most they had to go on was the disclosure that the tomb was found in a "cavity on the hill". The expedition looked speculative, but at least there was a town nearby – perhaps the locals could point them in the right direction.

"Are you feeling all right?" asked Jenny once they hit open country. "You seem quiet."

"I'm fine," he said.

Jenny took her eyes off the road to study him, much as she had as they fled the Monastery of Debre Damo. "Sure?"

"Really. I had a bad dream and I didn't get much sleep after that."

"It's understandable," said Jenny, one hand resting on the steering wheel. "I'm scared too, you know."

For a few kilometres neither of them spoke and Jake stared out across the Mediterranean, sparkling in the early spring sun. Presently they wound into the hills; he knew this landscape from his dreams. Poppies had turned the fields matt-scarlet, like blood seeping into the land, and the mountains in the distance were parabolas of violet.

"Beautiful world," she muttered.

Jake glanced at Jenny, a fist in his stomach. Still the determination coursed through him, and he knew if he was to eradicate this accursed text from the face of the earth he might need her help. There was something he had to say – or at least try to say.

"This Charlie Waits of yours," he began. "He's one hundred and ten per cent convinced the *Disciplina Etrusca* is real, right?"

"Right."

"And so is the Chinese Secret Service."

"Uh-huh."

"These are intelligent people ..."

Jenny's eyes flicked to her passenger. "What are you getting at?"

"I just think perhaps we need to keep an open mind."

"You're not going mad on me are you?"

Jake saw amusement in the corner of her mouth and he forced a laugh. "No, I'm not a carrier of the defective Roger Britton gene yet."

A shadow moved across Jenny's face.

"What is it?" asked Jake. "Did I say something wrong?"

Jenny shook her head. "No, nothing at all."

They didn't talk at all after that, but the mood in the car had changed – as though the melancholy of his dream was contagious.

*

The defective gene.

Jenny hadn't received an update on her mother for days, but neither had she sought one. Clearly the worst had not happened – Dad would have been in touch. The guilt was still there though, the suspicion that she was a bad daughter. And there was something else. The notion had occurred on reflex when Jake said the word 'gene', yet that didn't lessen how daft she felt for even thinking it.

If the thing worked ... *she could find out whether she was a carrier too.*

Jenny sighed. She shouldn't be too hard on herself. She was under a lot of stress. But there was clearly something wrong with any job so involving that one could forget about a dying mother for days at a stretch.

Before you sign below the dotted line I want to make sure you're ready to commit, regardless of any ... emotional difficulties.

As the final miles peeled away Jenny made herself a promise. When she got through all this, she would realign her life. If the case had taught her anything, it was that people were more important than work.

The town was a hotchpotch of medieval houses, a lackadaisical air permeating cobbled streets. They bought bread, cheese and tomatoes from a small shop; Jenny watched with interest as Jake reached for a beer and then paused, hand wavering. Finally – some inner conflict resolved – he passed on.

At the checkout was a bespectacled girl in her twenties.

"*Ciao bella*," said Jake as they left.

The girl went red.

"Do you know what you just said?" asked Jenny.

"It's a polite way of saying goodbye."

"No it's not. You said 'Goodbye, gorgeous.'"

It was Jake's turn to blush. "Did I? Christ. How embarrassing. That's really not my style, I promise."

Jenny turned away, but Jake could tell she was grinning from the movement of the skin behind her neck.

Nobody had heard of Tages, let alone his grave. But they were pointed in the direction of the Pian di Civita at a shop selling chic and expensive kitchenware.

It was more in hope than expectation that they departed.

*

Maria Marcella returned to her window display. The spinster was proud of her little shop – to her mind it was certainly the most stylish in town, even if she rarely sold anything. She'd just found the spot for the Le Creuset when another group of tourists clattered in. Maria sighed and fixed her sales smile to her face.

But here's the strange thing.

They were asking directions to exactly the same place.

69

The Pian di Civita rose above the surrounding countryside, a desolate bar of land covered in swaying grasses. Jake's eyes narrowed as he scanned the hilltop for masonry, earthworks – anything that would indicate a tomb. But apart from the track there was no trace of man to be seen.

"What do you think?" asked Jenny as she scoured the landscape.

"I don't know. We're not going to find anything, are we?"

No sooner had Jake spoken than he saw it: a pimple rising from the uniform flatness of the summit. The sides were rounded as a Christmas pudding and masonry was scattered across the peak – it reminded Jake of a boutique hill fort. This was where a sickly child was laid to rest more than twenty-eight centuries ago; where Eusebius's trail came to an end.

Jake felt it in his bones.

They trekked across a field of sheep to reach the mount. Trees were dotted about the hillock and birdsong carried across the countryside.

Suddenly Jenny's hand was on his shoulder. "Over there – look!"

A wall had been built into the far side of the mound, but this was not the dry-stone boundary of an Italian shepherd. The wall was composed of half-ton boulders and in its centre was a small cave, wild grasses shivering before the entrance.

"The cavity," he whispered.

Jake manoeuvred himself into the fissure, scenting chalk and mushrooms, damp earth. The ancient builders had used a natural cave for the tomb, walling it in and piling earth on top to create a barrow. A narrow channel cut into the rock had once allowed libations to be poured into the tomb from outside, but otherwise the cavern was unfinished and unpainted. To Jake's relief there were no Roman numerals chiselled into the rock.

"Anything?" asked Jenny.

"It's the place all right. But there's nothing here."

Whatever it may once have contained had disappeared.

"We haven't been very clever, have we?" Jake said as he clambered out. "Did we really expect to find something a team of professional archaeologists missed?"

She shrugged.

"But d'you know what?"

"What?"

"Who cares?"

"I'm sorry?" Jenny replied.

Jake couldn't resist grinning. He had followed Eusebius to the end of his map and found nothing; the *Disciplina Etrusca* was no more.

"I said, who cares? It's a beautiful day. Look around you. What say for the next hour we forget all about MI6 and Charlie Waits and everything else. And have a picnic."

She felt a rush of warmth for him then; at that moment in her life it was exactly what she needed to hear.

People are more important than *work*.

They lay in the grass and ate. The bread was tough, the cheese spongy, but any food is delicious if consumed in the wilderness. And the tomatoes were divine. Jake drew in the air with its scent of leaf and grass and felt the first whisper of contentment in years. For a moment he thought he heard the note of a car engine carrying on the wind, but he let it go; now was not the time. It occurred to him that the countryside looked much as it must have when the first traders arrived from Greece and Carthage in search of iron ore.

"Isn't it amazing," he said between mouthfuls, "to think this was once the edge of the known world? When the first Greeks arrived it must have blown their minds. The people they found were wearing hides, not far removed from hunter-gathering. It would've been like visiting untouched tribes in the Amazon."

Jenny swung to look at him, face serious.

"What is it?" he said.

"Can you feel the spirits rising, Jake?"

He held her gaze, startled. Seconds passed; a crumb fell from his mouth.

The twitch at the corner of Jenny's mouth betrayed her. And knowing she was undone she roared with laughter. That set Jake off too, the pair of them howling at the madness of it all until tears ran down their cheeks.

When he stopped laughing she was looking right at him.

Right. At. Him.

Jake's chest fluttered, as if someone had released a handful of butterflies in his lungs. He opened his mouth, said half a word, blushed and turned away.

70

Jenny felt a rush of childish disappointment. The message was clear enough, but at least she knew where she stood. Anyway, what was she thinking? They were playing too dangerous a game for distractions. She blinked and swept the crumbs from her lap.

Jake snapped his fingers right under her nose.

She looked up at him, annoyed now. But Jake's eyes were wide and he cupped one hand by his ear. Then she heard it too: people speaking Mandarin, not far off. And the language barrier couldn't hide the identity of the hectoring female voice soaring above the rest.

It was Florence.

And she was getting closer.

"Quickly," Jake hissed, snatching up the remnants of food and bundling them into his shirt. "Down there."

They scrambled to the bottom of a shallow valley below the mound. The depression was choked with hawthorn bushes and they wriggled into the foliage.

"How did they know to come here?" whispered Jenny.

"Florence had the Ethiopian inscription too, remember."

But privately Jake doubted she could have deduced the meaning of Eusebius's gnomic prose.

She had been drawn here.

Twenty minutes passed before the Chinese team reached the conclusion that there was nothing to be found. Jake heard raised voices, glimpsed Florence's face through the screen of leaves. Her features were twisted in frustration. *How did I ever find that woman attractive?*

But instead of departing Florence sat and stared at the horizon, as if waiting for something. Her agents began to smoke and play cards. Jake and Jenny had no choice but to remain in the thicket – the slopes around them were too exposed to make a dash for it. After three hours he heard a powerful engine approach.

To his astonishment a JCB digger hoved into view.

*

The excavation took all night. By the small hours the temperature had fallen to single figures, but Florence's voice could still be heard, directing the dig. A veil of condensation fell, leaving Jake sodden. Yet he dared not move – the Chinese had erected powerful arc-lamps, turning night into day. Jenny clung to him for warmth, shivering without complaint, and he did his best to wrap her in his body. Cramp set in, then hunger and thirst; it felt as if the night would never end. Sleep came in fits and starts before Jake finally drifted out of consciousness at about 4 a.m.

He awoke to silence.

The world was cast that simmering blue which precedes sunrise, as if a projectionist had been challenged to brew up the sky. As Jake listened the dawn chorus picked up in a collage of cheeps and rasps. He peered through the foliage – they were alone.

Jake unfolded himself from Jenny and clambered from the bushes, groaning as he stretched; they had been lying there for more than twelve hours. The Iron Age mound had been clawed from existence. Earth and boulders lay strewn across the hillside, as if some giant mole had erupted from beneath it. For two thousand eight hundred years this place had defied the elements. Now it was destroyed forever, and even in his exhausted state Jake registered anger at the vandalism.

His phone began ringing.

"Hello? Who is this?"

"Jake, Luke McDonagh here – I got your new number from Niall."

The image of a freelancer with a lazy eye swam to mind. Jake hadn't thought about McDonagh for weeks; the man belonged to a previous life. When had they last met? Swiftly it came to him: The Dolphin, deepest King's Cross. Suddenly Jake was wide awake.

Winston Churchill.

1941.

The ancient Etruscan matter.

For weeks Jake's head had been full of thoughts of Rome. And with the constant fear of death, that dash across the globe, he had almost forgotten how it all began: a single-line memo from a batch of declassified documents. But good old McDonagh had been nosing away in the National Archives all the time.

"I think I've found something," he began. "Don't know what to make of it to be honest ..."

"Don't say anything else!" Jake interrupted. "Don't say anything at all."

Jenny was beside him, rubbing her eyes. "What's going on?"

"A contact on the phone," he mouthed. "It's related."

"Tell him to get out of wherever he is right now. Tell him he needs to lie low somewhere until we get back in touch, nowhere he normally frequents. For God's sake don't let him stay with a family member or anything."

"You hear that, Luke?"

"Yes. Jake –"

But before McDonagh could finish Jenny snatched the mobile and hung up. Instantly it began ringing again, but she dropped the call and turned off the phone.

"We need to get out of here," she said. "Right now."

*

In London Edwin de Clerk punched the air in triumph. "Yeah! Gotcha!"

With Jenny brushing away Jake's technological spoor,

de Clerk had changed tack: he had arranged a tap of every individual Jake had been in contact with over the last two months. Not even Jenny would suspect a fishing expedition on such an industrial scale. De Clerk had sat through countless hours of it by then. Journalistic patter; trips to Indian restaurants planned by people he would never meet; the seditious politics of the bridge club attended by Jake's mother. And now the breakthrough had come, just as de Clerk teetered on the edge of a nervous collapse through exhaustion. McDonagh was a trusted freelancer, so Jake's gatekeeper at the newspaper had given him the newest mobile number right away. But either McDonagh had ignored Heston's order not to ring from his normal phone, or he had forgotten.

Mistake.

*

When they were back in Rome, Jake followed Jenny's precise instructions on how to make contact with McDonagh. First he bought two pay-as-you-go phones. Then he texted the freelancer, telling him to buy two disposable phones of his own. McDonagh sent Jake the number for just one of the devices, and Jake called that number on his first pay-as-you-go phone. With that line he asked McDonagh to read him the number of his *second* disposable mobile. This McDonagh did right away, before de Clerk had time to tap the conversation. Jake then rang this number with *his* mobile number two, and *voilà*: a clean line of communication had been established, de Clerk powerless to catch up.

"What's going on then, mate?" McDonagh began, fear in his voice now.

"Have you been following all this MI6 stuff in the papers, Luke?"

"Sort of – why?"

"It's related to the Churchill file, somehow."

"Oh, shit."

"You'll need to stay in a hotel tonight," said Jake. "Keep the receipts of any expenses, obviously we'll cover them. I'll be back in London tomorrow, then let's meet."

"Sure thing, oh my God, sure thing. Where?"

Jake thought fast. "Same place, same time. See you tomorrow, Luke."

*

The use of four phones to establish a safe line was cute, but immaterial. Because after the first call McDonagh had dithered for thirty minutes, unsure whether to take Jenny's order to get out seriously or not. And by the time he left his flat, Evelyn Parr was waiting outside.

71

The British had warned him not to return to the Large Hadron Collider. They told him to run away, to avoid crossing borders at all cost. Go to Naples maybe, go to Sicily, hide up in the Apennines for a while. Yet Dr Nesta had no choice. He was on the cusp of *measuring* the network's presence; his work would rewrite science and religion. Nobel Prize be damned: Nesta's name would be spoken of alongside those of Darwin, Newton, Galileo and Archimedes. Alongside that of Jesus.

But for the scientific community to accept such a paradigm shift the evidence had to be irreproachable – and he wasn't there yet. To prove it beyond argument he needed more time with the particle accelerator. But six other projects were sharing it and his funding ran out in a fortnight. With his current reputation he would never get his hands on the damn thing again. He had four remaining sessions in the tunnel, a little less than sixteen hours to prove the existence of a higher sphere of intelligence. *Ergo*, he had to return.

If Dr Nesta made it back to the complex he knew he would be safe. The collider was ultra-secure and there were sleeping quarters he could stay in until his experiments were complete. After that Cern would take care of him for evermore.

The train ride to Switzerland was intense. At Florence a white-haired British gentleman got on and asked him how long it might take to get to Geneva. Dr Nesta answered the foreigner and made a show of leaving for the dining car before getting off at the next stop. Rather than continue by rail he caught a taxi to Genoa Airport; change routes constantly, Jenny had said. He caught an Iberian Airways flight to Barcelona, waited in the Islamic prayer room for six hours, then returned to Switzerland via Hamburg. At such short notice the plane tickets cost hundreds of euros. A Chinese woman sat next to Dr Nesta on the final flight. And in the taxi rank at Geneva Airport there she was again, waiting in the queue four people behind him. The scientist felt his heart go into palpitations. But he was *certain* nobody followed him in the taxi, and he was quite alone as he passed the security checks at the LHC complex. He booked into his new quarters, briefly wept and then fell asleep.

*

But it was naïve of Dr Nesta to think he would be safe there. The British government had hundreds of millions of euros invested in the collider. The scientists were looking for dark matter, the secrets of the universe; there were fears a black hole might be created. *Of course* there were national security implications, *of course* MI6 took an interest. So it stood to reason they would have an agent inside. And Charlie Waits was at the third-highest grade of the organization, with access to almost its entire network.

It was a challenge for Travel Service to knock up the documentation, given the quick turnaround. But their handiwork had passed sterner security checks in the past. The documents went by Dip Post to Geneva, where they were picked up that evening. Back in London Edwin de Clerk pinpointed Dr Nesta's room from the comfort of his desk. He didn't know what the information would be used for, but at Vauxhall Cross that was normal.

By 1 a.m. Dr Nesta was asleep in an armchair, still wearing his suit, his unopened suitcase in the centre of the room.

The door slid open with a beep.

The scientist awoke, gasping with fright. "Who are you?"

Then Dr Nesta's eyes focused. He relaxed a little. It was a security guard, Cern ID pass dangling around his neck.

"*Bonsoir, mon ami*," said the guard. "*Ça va*?"

Instantly Dr Nesta was terrified. The stranger's accent was appalling. And he wore gloves.

"*Ça va*?" the guard repeated.

"*Oui, ça va bien*," managed Dr Nesta.

"*Très bien*," said the stranger. "*Très bien. Pardon, monsieur, parlez-vous Anglais?*"

Without warning Dr Nesta dived for the fire alarm. Davis was too quick for him. He grabbed the scientist by the collar of his jacket and unceremoniously dumped him back onto the sofa. Then he locked the door and sat on the bed facing Dr Nesta.

"I said, *parlez-vous fucking Anglais?*" Davis repeated.

"*Oui*," said Dr Nesta. "I mean yes, yes. I speak English well."

"Good. Then you and I are going to have a little drinky." From his bag Davis retrieved a bottle of Teacher's whisky and a cheap cognac. "What's your poison, fella?"

"I don't really drink."

Dr Nesta began trembling.

"Oh, don't be a party-pooper. I've come a long way to see you."

"Please, I don't want to."

"But I insist."

Davis laid a gun on the bedside table.

"In that case, I'll take the whisky." Now his lip was wobbling.

"Good choice. Horrible French muck, cognac."

The room came with equipped a mug and kettle and there was a water glass by the sink. Davis poured a dram into the latter and sipped it.

"Best of the budget whiskies, in my humble," he said. "Nice and smoky. Better than Bell's anyway – that stuff'll give you a blinding headache if you drink too much of it." He filled the mug to the brim and handed it to Dr Nesta. "Now, down the hatch."

"Please," said Dr Nesta.

Davis growled, revealing the fillings in his teeth. "I said, *drink it*."

Dr Nesta tasted the whisky.

"You're annoying me now," said Davis, screwing the silencer into his pistol and glancing at his watch. "I'm going to give you ninety seconds. If you haven't polished off that mug of whisky by then I will take it as an affront to my generosity. And I will not be a happy boy."

The corner of Davis's mouth twitched upward as Nesta gulped down the spirits, gagging, whisky dribbling down both cheeks.

Davis refilled the mug. "And another."

Dr Nesta seemed calmer after the second helping.

"Now then," said Davis, pressing record on his smart phone. "You're going to tell me all about your work, all about Roger Britton, and all about that little Italian rendezvous with Jake Wolsey and Jenny Frobisher."

They talked for hours. Davis had two singles; Dr Nesta consumed the rest of the bottle. When the whisky was finished the assassin opened the cognac, refilled the mug and sniffed at it suspiciously.

"See, what did I tell you? Disgusting French muck. Here, you try some."

Dr Nesta knew he had to try and please this man if he wanted to live. He raised the mug with both hands – like a chalice – and forced down a third of the liquid. At once he was violently sick and slumped to the floor, gasping; trails of vomit led from his mouth. The whole room was spinning, and when he looked right the speed of rotation increased. He was about to beg for mercy when he became aware that his tormentor had left the room.

The fire alarm was almost within reach.

Dr Nesta tried to stand up. He fell flat on his face. He attempted again. This time he made it to his feet, taking three steps towards the alarm. Suddenly Davis towered over him.

"Oh, no, you, *don't*," he hissed, slamming the scientist onto the floor in an impact that beat the air from his lungs.

Dr Nesta could hear water running in the bathroom.

"Don't kill me," he whispered, acknowledging for the first time that this was what must surely be coming. "Please, don't kill me, please don't do it."

Davis stripped Dr Nesta's lower half first, the scientist's corduroys turning inside out as they were pulled downward, catching on his ankles. A pathetic sight.

"It's time for you to have a good wash," Davis snarled. "Because you're a *dirty, little, boy*."

*

It was so unlike Dr Nesta, his colleagues agreed afterwards. He was a temperate man who nobody could recall drinking more than two small glasses of wine at supper. But he had been under a lot of stress lately – for a start that ludicrous project of his was headed for the buffers. It was the only explanation for him drinking a bottle and a half of spirits by himself. But what a tragic way to go, what a waste of a mind that once seemed to offer so much to physics. Drowning alone in the bath like that.

72

The Dolphin, King's Cross. It was in this pub that Jake's story had taken its first lurch towards the nightmarish with the news of Britton's death. He recalled it perfectly: the garish headline, a plummeting drink; astonishment that the professor he had just been speaking to was no more.

Well, here we are again.

Jake took in the fading chintz, the smell of old beer. A drunken city boy was singing folk songs to a pair of Dubliners. The pub was the same, but Jake's understanding of the universe had changed forever, and he felt a pang of longing for his old life. Luke McDonagh sat in the far corner, two pints and two whiskies already lined up in front of him.

"This is how you journalists roll, is it?" said Jenny. "And there was I thinking Fleet Street was grown up nowadays."

McDonagh reddened and a hand flitted to his fringe. Jake recognized the gesture: shame at the vice, panic at the approach of an attractive woman.

"Jenny and I are ... workmates," he said.

"A pleasure to meet you." McDonagh gestured at the drinks. "Tuck in."

"Just one of them for me," Jake mumbled, hand hovering before he settled on the pint.

Jenny ignored the display, evaluating the other drinkers. The old timers were definitely clean and the city boy looked innocent enough.

"Before I tell you what I've got," said McDonagh, "I want you to know I've put a lot of work into this whole project. Plus there's all this stress and upheaval, having to get out of my flat and so on."

"Luke, if you deliver the goods we'll really look after you," said Jake. "I promise you that."

"Great. Well then. I started off looking in the National Archive. I won't bore you with the techniques, but everything drew a blank. There's not a trace of the ancient Etruscans in the whole damn place. And then it hit me. I was doing it the wrong way around. Churchill was scheduling a meeting, remember? The answer was simple – check his wartime appointment diary."

"Of course," said Jake. "Why didn't I think of that?"

Throughout the war, Churchill's secretaries recorded his engagements on a stack of appointment cards. They had gone under the hammer at Christie's a couple of years back; Jake had covered the story.

"Churchill College Cambridge has a copy of the cards in its archive," said McDonagh. "I went up there last week, and sure enough, there it was."

McDonagh rummaged through his folder, producing a photocopied appointment card. The handwriting was impeccable.

20th September 1941.
1 p.m.: Head of Special Intelligence, 54 Broadway, St James's Park.
Prep – W.S.C. to read Dicks Report, 41 pages. Highly classified.

"W.S.C. is Winston Spencer Churchill," said Jake. "Obviously. But what's this 'Dicks Report' he's got to read?"

"That's where things get really interesting," said McDonagh. "Dr Henry Dicks was a British psychiatrist. His most famous patient was. Wait for it ... Rudolf Hess."

"Hess?" said Jenny. "As in Hess, Hitler's deputy? The Nazi who flew to Britain to try and make peace?" She recalled beetling eyebrows, a thick-set skull.

"That's him," said McDonagh. "In 1941 Germany found itself fighting the British, whom Hitler admired, and at peace with the USSR – which he wanted to annihilate. In short, he was fighting the wrong war. Hess was a bit ... a bit simple, and he dreamed up this crackpot plan to put the situation right. Without telling anyone what he was planning, he flew solo to Scotland, parachuted out of the plane and contacted a right-wing aristocrat who was thought to favour peace. He wanted to arrange a ceasefire that would give the Nazis a free hand to invade Russia. But when Hess landed he was arrested. He spent the rest of the war as a P.O.W. It was a big scandal in Germany."

"The Hess affair was one of the most mysterious episodes of the war," said Jake. "It's been the subject of conspiracy theories ever since."

The journalists both took a swig of beer; their whiskies had been neglected for fear of Jenny's disapproval, and they huddled together for comfort.

"Dicks carried out a series of interviews with Hess in June 1941," McDonagh finished. "He was trying understand the mindset of the Nazi leadership."

"But what does Hess have to do with 'the Etruscan matter?'" asked Jake.

"Ah. That I don't know."

"I take it this Dicks Report is still under lock and key?" asked Jenny.

"Actually, no," said McDonagh, fishing once more in his folder. "Photocopies of Dicks's notebook are in the Wellcome Library in Euston for anyone to inspect. It's of medical interest."

Jake studied the cover page. The handwriting was a doctor's scrawl, but it was legible enough.

Points for study.

** Sexual delinquency confessed.*

** Superstitions: amulets.*

** War guilt. Atrocities and reprisals: ranges from sadistic*

participation, approval, detachment, disassociation (washing hands of it) to mild/violent disapproval.
** Latent needs: Aggression (hate, sadism), exhibitionism, heterosexuality, omnipotence – "magic control of objects."*

Jenny peered at the list. "He sounds like quite the character."

"Yep," said McDonagh, "a proper wrong 'un and no mistake."

Jake started forward – the name 'Mark Anthony' was written at the bottom of the page without explanation. "What's this all about?"

"Again, no idea. There's no further mention of him in the entire report." He laughed. "Or Cleopatra, for that matter."

Jake began reading the psychiatrist's notes, which were copious.

2nd June. The first impression is of a schizoid psychopath. Compared to the photos in the press, the face is that of some tormented beast – the face is bestial, ape or wolf. At one time, it might have been quite charming – it is now hounded and haunted by this blasted German Satanism. The gaol-bird or chronically unemployed, failure-in-life look is there.

"Well, whatever the Etruscan connection there's no denying it's a scintillating read," said Jake.

There is a tremendous feeling of stone-walling. This is not on the level of the man who does not wish to give himself away – it is withdrawn-ness. He is not rude, he is detached. He barely smiles at jokes, he will not volunteer anything, he appears uninterested. He is a good specimen of the rudderless nothing who is only alive in reflected group energy. At times he evidently gets acute paranoid fears of the poisoner or secret enemy.

"It gets better," said McDonagh, taking the report and

turning a few pages. "Read the entry for the fourth of June."

He is in a state of apprehension which varies only in degree. Surveillance, gently as it is done, deprives him of sleep. He is, I suppose, constantly on guard against assassination – the slightest noise in the guarding suites, or the orderly officer creeping into his room to see whether he is alright, wakes him. I am too unfamiliar with the personalities which rule in Germany to say whether this is the normal attitude of the Nazi leaders, or whether this man has an additional personal paranoia system. The expression of his eyes is perhaps the most significant – hunted, unhappy, wolf-like, and also shifty.

"And this one," said McDonagh.

7th June. He is not even equal in knowledge of culture or world affairs to his mess mates. And he is the third man in The Reich. Miserable, pricked balloon, dramatizing himself as the saviour hero.

"He sounds like a man on the edge," said Jenny.

"Not a bad analysis," said McDonagh. "Pretty spot on, actually. Because shortly after that entry was written Hess tried to commit suicide by throwing himself over a balcony."

*

De Clerk frowned as he studied his monitor. He had taken control of Camden Town Hall's network of CCTV cameras with ease – it was just a question of finding one in the right place to peer into The Dolphin. Suddenly he had it. He zoomed in to see pints on the table. Whisky too, by the looks of it, and a wad of paper being handed from person to person.

"Three of them," de Clerk said into his mouthpiece. "Looking at documents."

"What sort of documents?" asked Waits.

"No idea, the resolution's not high enough."

"Ok then. Frank and I are almost in position. Keep a good eye out – once they're on the move we'll nab all three of them."

73

"Hess was definitely mad," said McDonagh. "Even the Nazis thought so – it's amazing he climbed so high. He was a member of the Thule Society, a German occult group. And he consulted horoscopes religiously. Here, read this bit."

He passed Jake the report.

> *15th July. I have little cause to revise my opinion either of the nature of his personality, the mental trouble from which he is suffering, or the causes which led to the appearance of his abnormal mental state, culminating in attempted suicide. Yet, important changes have taken place in his attitude since then. I should like to comment upon them. A short while after his attempted suicide, his delusional fears of being poisoned began to disappear. By July ninth, after frank discussion of his symptoms, he admitted his mental state had been a psychosis. He is at present in a much saner and more cheerful frame of mind. One is bound to emphasize again his obvious limitations. His mental processes are primitive, and his philosophical outlook is that of a superstitious fatalist, derived from the murky levels of German hero-fantasy and national self-adulation.*

Jake turned to the final page. Dicks had concluded:

He has to accept the source of his fears in his own fantasy, and he perhaps could be brought to acknowledge that it was a reasonable fantasy to have for one who has been in a regime of unprecedented persecution and secret conspiracy.

Jake tamped the pages into a pile and set them on the table. Something was nagging at him. Granted Dr Dicks was a psychiatrist; but Hess wasn't the first person they had certified insane in the last few weeks. Roger Britton, Charlie Waits, Florence Chung, Giuseppe Nesta: each of them had been written off as a lunatic. Jake suspected they were all as sane as he. The journalist drained his pint and stared at the dram.

"There isn't a mention of the Etruscans in this entire document," Jenny was saying. "It's not very helpful. If anything, it just raises more questions."

"You haven't noticed then," said McDonagh. "Thought you were supposed to be top journalists?"

Jake's looked up. "Noticed what?"

"The note in Churchill's diary said the report was forty-one pages long. But there are only thirty-seven pages here."

"Which means ..."

"Which means four pages have been removed," said Jenny.

"Exactly," McDonagh replied. "And it's obvious which ones."

"It is?"

"It is indeed. There's an entry every few days in June, but then nothing in the run-up to July's suicide attempt. No description of the crisis coming to a head, nor even the night Hess threw himself over the banister. Not a sausage until July fifteenth, when he starts making his recovery."

"Then who removed the four pages?" said Jake. "Where are they now?"

"Well, I should have thought that's perfectly obvious."

Jake waited for him to speak.

"Oh – perhaps I forgot to tell you where Dicks carried out

his interviews?"

"Go on."

"After Hess was arrested he was held at a local farm. Then they locked him in the Tower of London for a couple of weeks, the last prisoner ever held there, incidentally. Finally he went to a detached house in Surrey called Mytchett Place – That's where Dicks carried out his interviews. Mytchett Place was a safe house run by MI6."

There was an intake of breath.

"Given that Churchill was meeting the chief of the Special Intelligence Service, I'd say MI6 look a good shout for the page removal," McDonagh finished. "Wouldn't you?"

Under the table Jenny gripped Jake's knee. Jake grabbed one of the whiskies and downed it in one.

It all came down to four pages from a psychiatrist's notebook. Four pages to explain how Rudolf Hess was the link between MI6 and the Etruscans. Four pages to reveal how the whole fractured jigsaw fitted together. Four pages that would turn history upside down.

*

The door of the pub swung open and three figures emerged onto de Clerk's monitor. "They're on the move," he observed calmly.

There was a handshake between Jenny and McDonagh, another between the journalists. Then the freelancer was off, pacing towards Bloomsbury at speed.

"The group's splitting up now," said de Clerk. "Frobisher and Wolsey are heading east – they've got the documents. Advise who to follow?"

"Keep on those two," said Waits. "Evelyn's on the other chap's tail, we'll pick him up later. Is the coast clear?"

De Clerk rotated the camera. The Dolphin was on a backstreet behind King's Cross proper. One side of the road was red-brick Victorian tenements; the residents, well-heeled nowadays, would be at work. The other side was bordered by the Town Hall, but the building faced the opposite direction, the rear used only for deliveries. The street was empty – they wouldn't get a cleaner chance than this.

"Coast's clear," said de Clerk.

The targets were making for a passage that cut past the Town Hall to join Euston Road, where a discreet snatch would be impossible. It was one of the busiest arteries in London.

"You've got thirty seconds," he warned.

*

"We need those missing pages," Jake was saying.

Jenny laughed. "Do you have *any idea* how difficult getting them out of MI6 would be? We'd have more chance raiding 10 Downing Street."

They were twenty paces from the passage when Jake heard the bark of an engine nearby. Boy racers, probably. There was an estate a few blocks away.

"Aren't MI6 files stored digitally?" he said. "We wouldn't have to get the physical document."

That car was getting closer; a white Ford Transit clattered towards them from the other end of the street.

"Even if it was stored digitally, which is far from certain, you'd need a hacker with some serious skills," said Jenny. "Nothing short of a genius, actually."

A gunmetal BMW rounded the corner. There were ten paces to go before they made it to the passageway. Beyond it Jake glimpsed Euston Road, billowing with traffic fumes.

"We might have a bit of a problem finding one of those at short notice," he said. "Geniuses don't grow on trees."

There were five paces to go when it hit Jenny. *Did she dare?*

Three paces, two paces, no paces.

74

"Hold it, hold it ..." de Clerk stared at his monitor. "School trip incoming ..."

A class of primary school children in red sweatshirts had appeared on the Euston Road side of the passage; two teachers herded the group in and at once the cut-through was full of bobbing heads. De Clerk watched Jake pause at the entrance, letting the children pass. But his warning had come too late to abort the swoop. First he saw Davis's van enter the shot, then the sleeker form of his boss's BMW. The car swept gaily past the school trip and was away down the street.

"Damn," said Davis. "Damn, damn, fuck, damn."

"Language please, Frank," said Waits. "Circle around and let's try again. Edwin, keep on them, would you?"

*

Jake glanced at the car as it shot by. He had been mistaken: it wasn't a boy racer at all. It was a top-of-the-range BMW, going too fast for him to see the driver. A Korean boy glanced up at the journalist as he pushed past – toothy grin, the devil's own eyebrows – and Jake chuckled, fighting the urge to ruffle the kid's hair. He had always identified with the naughty ones. They squeezed through the passageway and out onto Euston Road, where the traffic was gridlocked, as always. King's Cross Tube Station was on the other side of the street. And the flat where they were staying was a couple of miles away; it belonged to a university friend who was holidaying in France.

"Come on, let's stroll," said Jake. "I could do with the walk."

*

De Clerk used a camera owned by Network Rail to track the pair past the station, but they went out of shot as they crossed from Camden into the neighbouring borough of Islington. De Clerk's fingers were a blur as he brought up a camera used by local police to keep tabs on drunkards and prostitutes. Then he had them again. They were turning onto Caledonian Road, a residential street striking northwards through the borough.

"They're heading up the Cally Road towards Regent's Canal," said de Clerk. "Just passed a Tesco Metro on the left. There aren't many pedestrians about further up the street. Reckon you might have another chance if you get there asap." He pronounced the abbreviation as a single word.

"On our way," replied Waits. "Just tackling the one-way system. Blue lights on now I think, Frank ..."

Jenny was deep in thought as they passed a row of neglected period properties. The frontages were caked in soot and the paint flaked away, as if the terrace was afflicted by some dreadful skin complaint.

"I don't know how you'd feel about this," she said. "But I do know a guy who could tackle MI6's firewalls. A genius, as it happens – literally."

"Oh?"

"There's only one problem. He's MI6 too."

"Well, it's a bit academic then, eh?"

"The thing is ..." Jenny bit her lip. "I always got the impression he kind of – *liked* me, if you know what I mean."

"What are you suggesting?" Jake laughed. "You seduce him into helping us?"

An elderly woman hobbled by pushing a pram full of shopping, a remnant of Cockney Islington. She was overtaken by a shaven-headed Hare Krisha devotee in orange robes, and Jenny waited for them to pass.

"I wouldn't exactly 'seduce' him," she said. "That's not the right word. But if he's susceptible to my charms – it might give us an 'in.'"

"Well, you *could* try that I suppose ..."

Jenny glanced at Jake. Was that a flush of jealousy she spied on his cheeks? She smiled to herself, and not unkindly.

*

Waits made it through the one-way system to emerge at the southern end of Caledonian Road. Jake and Jenny were half a mile away, ambling towards the canal bridge.

"Frank, my boy ..." The spymaster's voice was terse, like someone who knows vast erotic pleasure might be on the cards. "Where are you now, Frank?"

"Still circling round," Davis replied through gritted teeth. "Heading north, running parallel to you. I should come out ahead of the targets in forty-five seconds."

"Faster please, if you'd be so kind."

The request was answered by the roar of Davis's engine, a cacophony of horns.

*

Jenny's suggestion was not a palatable one. Jake recalled Tages's tomb, that picnic where for one short hour they'd been able to forget about everything going on around them. It had only been a look from her – and he was inept at interpreting the signals of the fairer sex. Yet he could have sworn something was there, something so unlike Florence's avaricious advances.

Missed opportunities, always the missed opportunities.

"I'm not going to sleep with him, for God's sake," said Jenny. "But it might give me a persuasive edge. Make him hear me out at least. I don't deny it's a high risk strategy."

Jake considered his time in Istanbul. Florence had led him on something chronic when she thought he was holding back Britton's notes. And when the archaeologist's wiles were at their height he'd have told her his innermost secrets and regrets.

"How would it work?" he said.

"First we'd need to arrange the bump."

"What's a 'bump'?"

There was a lull in the traffic as they crossed the canal bridge. The flat was in sight.

A Ford Transit pulled into the road ahead.

75

The van accelerated, blue lights flickering in its windscreen, airborne as it hit a speed bump. Jake heard the wail of pistons and the squeal of a turbocharger behind him; he turned to see that same BMW approaching at sixty miles per hour. Then he recognized the driver. There was nowhere to go, so they waited on the canal bridge like lemons as the claws of the pincer slid shut. The vehicles skidded to a halt in unison, penning them in against the barrier.

"My old dears," cried Waits, manoeuvring himself from the car with the grace of a sugar plum fairy. "Welcome back."

Davis grinned at Jake and raised his eyebrows. "Third time lucky, eh, fella?"

The journalist peered over the bridge. It was a cold day and the surface of the water had an oily sheen to it.

"Jennifer Frobisher, as I live and breathe," said the spymaster, clapping his hands together. "Tut, tut, tut."

"Charlie," she managed, and her voice was a rasp of fear. "I – I'm sorry, Charlie. I never meant ..."

"And Mr Wolsey," Waits interrupted, fixing Jake with piggy black eyes. "We didn't get the chance to do formal introductions in Rome."

Davis opened the slide door of the Transit; the interior was panelled in steel and Jake shivered suddenly.

"What are you waiting for?" Davis gestured to the van with the barrel of a gun. "In you get, then."

By way of reply Jenny popped her backside onto the railing of the bridge and perched there for a moment. Then she toppled over backwards into space.

For several seconds the three men looked at each other, unable to comprehend what had happened. Jake heard it first: the shout of annoyance, a chugging noise that emanated from under the bridge. Suddenly he understood. He threw himself over the edge too, tumbling into the narrowboat's back cab as it cleared the crossing. The skipper was sent sprawling into the boat, his breath hot on Jake's face as the pair disentangled themselves.

"Just what the hell do you two think you're playing at?"

It was too late for the gunmen to jump, so they dashed for the tow path. The narrowboat ploughed on at three knots and Davis jogged alongside, weighing up the distance, preparing to leap.

"Take out the engine," Waits ordered.

At once the air was full of gunshots, pummelling through the rear of the boat until black smoke began pouring from the engine. Jake scrambled into the cabin where Jenny cowered from the bombardment, white-faced and panting. A log stove cracked and tinkled.

"What now?" shouted Jake.

"Don't ask me."

The chug of the engine had ceased but the boat's momentum carried it on, and with no one at the tiller it veered to port, away from the towpath. Feet turned to inches; Jake realized what was about to happen moments before it did. The narrowboat crashed into the mooring with a boom, throwing Jenny onto her hands and knees. Every bulb in the boat flickered and sparks flew up the hull as it screeched along the concrete. The vessel came grinding to a halt. The smell of diesel filled the cabin. Davis's crosshairs tracked back and forth across the portholes, straining for a glimpse of person.

He felt a touch on his forearm.

"I think you'd better put the gun away," said Waits.

"Why?" Davis panted. "I can wade ..."

Waits pointed at the glass-and-steel building under which the narrowboat had come to rest. Smartly-dressed people gathered at the windows, fumbling for mobiles.

"That's the offices of the *Guardian*," he said. "I suggest we make ourselves scarce before they find someone with a decent camera ..."

Jake watched their pursuers turn and flee. At first he couldn't work it out. But then a man with a notepad dashed along the bank and he realized where they were. He began to laugh.

*

As he strode through Hackney that evening Luke McDonagh was smiling. It had been a scary couple of days, but he felt safe enough. Nobody would really hurt them, not with a national newspaper on their side. And earlier Jake had paid him £2,500 – not bad, for what had been much less work than he'd let on. That explained his presence in east London. He was about to pick up an ounce of 'skunk' cannabis, and then he would stay up all night indulging the second of his vices: an online fantasy computer game. This single job would allow him to withdraw from the real world into his infinitely-preferable other life for several weeks.

Footsteps interrupted McDonagh's thoughts, approaching him from behind. The journalist glanced about, cursing his dealer's nocturnal hours – he needed to watch his back around here, especially with a hundred and fifty pounds in his pocket. But when he saw the man who was following him he relaxed. The guy looked sporty and respectable; a PE teacher, perhaps. The patch of snow-white in the stranger's hair shone orange in the streetlight. McDonagh's thoughts returned to the night of gaming that lay ahead.

A cord was around his throat.

The journalist's hands went to the garrotte, but his fingers were flabby and he couldn't get any purchase. The cord tightened. He tried to shout but no air would come out. The cord tightened. Tightened again. McDonagh sank to his knees, eyes bulging. The cord tightened. Not a word had been said. The cord tightened again and now McDonagh felt a knee between his shoulder blades. He blacked out for a few seconds, then he was back in the road. The cord tightened once more and suddenly he saw whorls of red and blue, a kaleidoscope of colour brought to the boil.

He realized he was dying.

The last thing that went through Luke McDonagh's mind was some abstract thought about the online game: it was like he'd been downloaded into it. Before his eyes the graphics became a million points of light, each linked to all the others by fronds of energy, the web shimmering all around him in a final display of phantasmagorical beauty.

Then there was only darkness.

*

Davis hauled the corpse up from the pavement and heaved a dead arm over his shoulder, as if McDonagh was a drunk and he the Good Samaritan. He glanced at the watch on the stiff's wrist. It would take half an hour to get to Epping Forest at this time; there was a shovel in the back of the van. He was doing it the old fashioned way. The East End way.

He dumped his load in the vehicle and slid the door shut, the satiated smile of the hyena that has just dined spread across his face. One by one he was eliminating every tie between MI6 and the *Disciplina Etrusca*. He would finish up with the journalist and that beautiful bitch Frobisher. Then when the PM realized what the *Disciplina* could do he would be untouchable. There would be a bonus; perhaps he could retire. Then again, maybe not. Not while he was having such *fun* at the office.

76

Pace, pace, pace, pace. The paving slabs flew beneath de Clerk's feet as he ratcheted up the tempo, smiling as his legs took the burn. He emerged by the Oval Cricket Ground. It was dawn and the sky behind the stadium was fractured into lilac and blue, like torn strips of paper pasted across the heavens. At this hour a few chancers lurked by the stadium, but they left the runner alone. Six miles so far, and he had barely broken a sweat.

There wasn't much in de Clerk's life apart from work and computers, but he did have his fitness. It took discipline to shoehorn a jog into a twenty-hour working day; yet as he ran the spook felt a relaxation sleep could not achieve. His flat was nearby and it would be a short stroll to Vauxhall for his shift.

A scream interrupted his trance.

De Clerk paused, jogging on the spot. And there it was again, echoing from a nearby cul-de-sac. The shady characters had moved on; the council estate was impassive; the only witnesses were the seagulls, circling the Kennington gasworks.

"Help me! Please! *Somebody*!"

De Clerk was wearing running shorts. His phone was in the flat. He had to deal with this alone. He rounded the corner in a spurt of acceleration – to find himself in a row of graffiti-strewn lockups. There were no streetlights, but through the gloaming de Clerk could make out two men pinning a woman against a garage door. They were diminutive, teenagers perhaps. Youths stabbed each other on a daily basis in London; this was dangerous. But he had to do something.

"Leave her alone," he shouted.

The assailants turned and de Clerk saw they were not teenagers, but Chinese guys in their thirties, tattooed and wiry and mean.

Oh, flip.

But when de Clerk looked at their victim his jaw dropped: it was Jenny Frobisher.

"Edwin? Edwin! What are you doing here?"

One of her assailants stepped forward. "You. Go!"

De Clerk knew enough about the Etruscan operation to recognize this for what it was: a Chinese snatch squad.

"Please ..." begged Jenny. "Help me, Edwin."

His heart twanged to see her, but rather she was in a British jail than a prisoner of the Chinese Embassy. Jenny was a tough cookie, but de Clerk doubted she could withstand torture. She had gone rogue and it was his duty to bring her in.

"Go," the man commanded a second time. A dagger was in his hand; the blade shone dully in the immature light.

De Clerk stood his ground. *This was it.*

All those years of training and now it was really happening. He cut a nerdy figure with his pale skin and wispy hair, a bulbous head that somehow recalled a clove of garlic. But he was very fit. And like many MI6 officers he'd been trained in close combat – krav maga, the Israeli system. There were two of them, and they had a chance.

The violence, when it came, was swift and invigorating.

Both men advanced on de Clerk, daggers extended. Jenny saw her chance and charged one of the knifemen, leaping on his back and grabbing him by the throat. The pair went to ground, grappling for the blade – now de Clerk could fight one attacker alone. He had to defeat his opponent before Jenny was overpowered, before it was two on one again.

The pair circled each other testily. The knifeman held his weapon pointing downwards, thumb on the hilt, jabbing out like a stinging insect. De Clerk assumed his knife stance. He stood sideways on, one elbow raised to protect the face and eyes, the other arm covering his exposed armpit, gateway to the chest. At each thrust of the blade de Clerk leaped backward; the evasions riled the knifeman and he hissed and spat. Suddenly he lunged for de Clerk's throat with a downward motion, as if wielding an ice pick. It was the opening the spy had been waiting for. He sidestepped and grabbed the knifeman by the wrist. In the same movement he swung his left arm into his opponent's jaw, hard, using the outside-lower forearm where the bone is shaped like the shaft of a hammer. He grabbed the knifeman by the hair, pulling his head in a downward arc. Then he kneed him in the face.

Now De Clerk had him by the hair with one hand, by the wrist with his other – like he was riding a Harley Davidson. The arm with the knife was turned inside out, elbow skyward. His attacker was bent double, dazed, facing the ground. The move had gone exactly as it did in training and de Clerk experienced an instant of wonder that krav maga worked in real life. He let go of the man's head and struck him just above the elbow, where the nerves are exposed. Again he used the bone of the forearm, clenching his fist to increase the power. It must have been agony – but still the knifeman clung on to his weapon. De Clerk began to pull the man's wrist upward, applying pressure on the spot above the elbow. He was the stronger man, he could feel it; the knifeman was yielding, yelping in pain. He increased the pressure. Much more of this and the arm would break at the elbow.

Bang!

De Clerk saw points of light that vanished when he tried to focus on them. He had been hooked in the jaw. Somehow he kept the knife locked. The points of light dissipated. His attacker tried another hook. De Clerk blocked, just about. Another hook, another block. It was stalemate.

The pair rotated on the spot like Siamese twins at the tango, the blade trembling in its vice.

De Clerk saw how he could win.

He had to outman his opponent, use his superior strength and size. He leaned into the arm-lock, straining every sinew to it, his opponent's wrist bent to breaking point.

"Aaaaah," said the knifeman. "Aaaaah ...."

The dagger tinkled across the tarmac. The Chinese agent tore himself from de Clerk's lock, diving after the weapon. His fingers closed on the hilt. But he had misjudged the distance between them; de Clerk was closing in fast. The knifeman's head turned and there was panic in his eyes as he realized he was about to be kicked in the face. De Clerk gave it everything. The knifeman was knocked into oblivion, flying flat on his back with his lips twitching. The second agent prepared to charge. Jenny was slumped behind him. De Clerk seized the abandoned blade, and for the second time he danced that wary dance.

I'm going to have to kill this man.

The realization flooded through de Clerk's brain, drowning out the cold morning air and the cries of the seagulls above. The only thing left was the face of his foe – bobbing up and down, isolated in his vision, as though a high aperture lens had blurred the world around it.

There was movement behind the knifeman.

Jenny was on her feet – bloodied but closing on her intended victim with alacrity – and before he could react she brought a brick down on his head with a dismal crack. The agent's eyes rolled back into his skull, he fell to the ground and was still.

"There may be more of them," Jenny gasped. "We need to get off the street."

"My place," de Clerk said. "It's round the next corner. We can shelter there while we" – and the realization he had to detain her throbbed in his head – "while we work out what to do."

They dashed up the path of his flat, de Clerk fumbled a key into the lock and the door closed behind them, shutting out the pale blue world and all the imagined enemies flitting through it.

*

For the men de Clerk fought weren't Chinese agents. They were the managers of the Camden martial arts club where Jenny studied wing chun. When she offered them a grand each for their assistance they were happy to play along with her deception. Jenny knew de Clerk was a jogger, she knew where he lived, and she knew he was a creature of routine. She had staked out his house until she learned his route and then chosen a spot for the theatrics. One of the people loitering by The Oval had been Jake, on the phone to Jenny to tell her when to scream. The daggers were blunt. And the two martial artists could control the ebb and flow of a fight as if turning a tap. For authenticity de Clerk got a blow to the head, but they had let him triumph, as a kitten overpowers a human hand. Jenny felt a touch of professional pride at her chicanery as she was led into de Clerk's flat.

'The bump' had gone perfectly.

77

The key to socially engineering people is to get them on your side. Make them like you, and if they can help you they might, even when it flies against reason. With de Clerk that battle was half-won before it began. But Jenny was up against years of training and role-play. That was why the bump was necessary: his 'saving' her had nurtured the fertility of the emotional ground exponentially.

Jenny could see how effective it had been as de Clerk bumbled around his kitchen, looking for something to occupy himself with. Like a sommelier of human sentiment she identified his emotions. Longing, protectiveness, and ... now, what was that last essence? Pride, perhaps. Yes, that was it: vanity at this newfound machismo. The wave of emotion she had unleashed broke against the walls of training and duty.

"I know what you're thinking," she said. "And I won't try and talk you out of it – you've got to do what you've got to do. But before I start running can we call a truce for a few minutes. My nose ..."

Blood dripped from one nostril. Jenny was glad of the injury – it added a layer of realism to the bump.

"I won't do anything for now," said de Clerk, scrambling for kitchen roll. "I promise. Let's catch our breath."

"Thanks," she replied, meeting his eyes a heartbeat longer than was decent.

Jenny glanced around the flat. The only traces of his personality were a stack of running magazines, a computer and a shelf of books on maths and computer science.

"Cup of tea?" he asked lamely.

"Thanks," she said. "I could probably do with one."

De Clerk's hands shook as he prepared the brew and his breath tapered through his lips. He poured himself some milk and took half the glass in two gulps. She could turn this man. She was sure of it.

"Why did you go rogue?" said de Clerk. "You leave me no choice, Jenny. I've got to take you to Charlie. I've got to." He looked at her face, then the floor. "But I want you to know it will hurt me. Very deeply, in fact."

In a world of secrets and lies the best way to make someone do your will is to be honest with them – one of the crowning ironies of espionage. Win their trust, make them want to help, then tell the truth. So that is what Jenny did.

She described her disillusionment with the operation; how she had realized Jake was a good man; why she thought Waits was working not for the good of Britain, but his own maniac delusions of power. As Jenny spoke she saw de Clerk's heart and his head do battle. In the pacing, in the fingers that wrung around each other, in the glass of milk that lay half-drunk, condensation running down its sides.

"You say all this," muttered de Clerk. "And it's convincing, I'll admit. But you don't have any actual *proof*, do you?"

The whole gamble relied on her judgement that de Clerk was a 'clever-stupid' person. Jenny's grandfather had taught her there were three types of people in the world. Stupid-stupid –

well, they weren't much good for anything. Clever-clever – that was her, even if she admitted it herself. And clever-stupid, like Jake. In her experience, geniuses were prone to the latter state: brilliant, but fundamentally lacking in judgement. A Churchill, a van Gogh. If de Clerk was clever-clever they were in trouble.

Jake was outside, eavesdropping via the open phone line in her pocket. Who would win in a fight between these two men? Jenny didn't want to find out – she cared for them both. It was time to play the trump card.

When she reached into her pocket de Clerk jumped.

"It's ok, Edwin," she said. "I haven't got a weapon."

"Sorry. I'm feeling a bit jumpy. It's been a crazy morning."

"I understand," said Jenny, a pen drive in her fingers. "Can I plug this into your PC?"

Jenny studied de Clerk's reaction as the recording began to play. Davis and Guilherme filled the screen, larging it in an Ethiopian hotel room; those boasts about waterboarding were no more palatable with the passing of time.

"I don't believe it," de Clerk whispered. "I thought all this stopped years ago. And they planned to do it to a *British journalist?*"

But when the carnage at Debre Damo played out he was speechless.

"Why haven't you sent this to the newspapers?" de Clerk said when it was over.

"It's enough to send Frank down," Jenny admitted. "But Charlie's not implicated. Frank would say he was acting alone – and then it would be my word against theirs. You know Charlie's standing in the Firm. There would be only one winner in that tussle. And you can see how they deal with their enemies. The only way is forward. Gather more evidence, blow the whole scandal out into the open."

De Clerk staggered to the kitchen table and sat down, cradling his head in his hands. For a time there was silence. Then without looking up he said, "I'm not going to turn you in,

Jenny. Of course I'm not."

She walked over to de Clerk and placed her hand on his shoulder. "Thank you, Edwin."

De Clerk put his hand on hers. Then he sharply withdrew it, glancing up at her. "What were you even doing here at this time in the morning?"

Jenny stared out of the window, in the direction of the Thames. "When they caught me I was on the way to Vauxhall Cross," she said. "I wanted to scope out which guards they had on, in case there was any chance of getting in."

"But why?"

"Because there's something in there that might solve this," she said. "Something that might put them away – if only we could get to it."

A thought occurred to de Clerk and his face brightened. "Well, I still work there, don't I?"

Clever-stupid.

78

The council of war was held in a chain coffee shop at Victoria Station.

On the agenda: ascertaining whether one of the most top secret documents possessed by Her Majesty's Government could be liberated.

To be in attendance: Jake Wolsey, Jenny Frobisher, Niall Heston, Edwin de Clerk.

Jake had dissuaded Heston from inviting Marvin Whyte. Heston trusted his security correspondent, but every newspaper on Fleet Street had staff run by MI6 officers and it was easy to imagine him being fed scoops from Vauxhall Cross in return for information. The smaller the circle, the safer they would be. And Jake had an ulterior motive. If this story stood up he would become one of the highest profile journalists in the country. He would be damned if Whyte was to share in *la gloire*.

It was patently unsafe to meet at the newspaper, which was bound to be under surveillance. Their homes and cars would be compromised too. But a coffee shop in one of Britain's busiest stations provided both anonymity and intimacy.

Heston had not arrived yet.

"Passports," Jenny said.

"What do you mean, passports?" Jake replied. "I haven't bought mine with me, you never said I'd need it."

"No, not *your* passport. That won't get you very far if this thing goes wrong and we need to get out of the country. We'll need new identities, three each. That goes for you too, Edwin."

"I know, I know," said de Clerk, shaking his head. He turned to Jake. "Travel Service can run the documents off pretty quickly for us. They have to do it all the time – it doesn't even need to be sanctioned at a high level. Once they've fixed them up I can alter our database. They'll be real passports with real microchips – but MI6 will have forgotten how they were made. You'll need to create your legends of course."

"Legends?"

"Your new identities," he replied simply. "Names, dates of birth, how many dependants, stamps in each passport – the backstory generally."

"We'll have to take new photographs," said Jenny. "Dress up a bit." She grinned. "You can have a bit of fun with this stuff."

Heston arrived at the table, the collar of his leather jacket turned up. Jake thought he looked flushed.

"Sorry I'm late," began Heston. "Got delayed by a security alert at the Tower of London. This might amuse you actually. There were rumours of a bomb at first. But it transpires one of the turrets got struck by lightning."

Jenny laughed. "There is no escape!"

Jake made no comment.

"Tell me then," said Heston. "This file you're after. Can it be done?"

The MI6 agents exchanged looks.

"Edwin knows more about the official secrets side of things," said Jenny.

Heston's gull eyes studied de Clerk. Then he opened his palm and gave a half-wave, as if to say: speak.

"Seeing as we've been talking about the Tower of London," de Clerk began, "let me put it like this. I think it would be considerably easier to steal the Crown Jewels."

Jake winced, sipped his coffee and winced again. He'd ordered an Americano with an extra double shot – it tasted of crude oil. "Perhaps you could explain the hurdles we'd need to cross?" he said. "Hypothetically speaking."

"That would be a start," said Heston.

"The first difficulty is that this document will almost certainly only be stored on paper," said de Clerk. "To give you an example, the FSB – that's the modern-day KGB – are a paper-only organization. It makes Russia a hundred times harder to spy on. You can't hack your way in. You have to physically get what you want in your hand. In the UK paper is also used for the most highly-guarded documents. The ones classified at a level *above* top secret."

"There is such a thing?" said Heston.

"You bet. Second problem. There's a chance this document is kept at Gosport – it's an old fort on the south coast. MI6 mainly use it for training, but there's a sizeable archive there too."

"Surely it can't be more protected than Vauxhall Cross?" asked Heston.

De Clerk took a sip of his own coffee, something weird involving cinnamon and soya milk. "Just as impenetrable," he said. "The public can't get within two miles. Actually, for our purposes it's worse. I'd need an excuse to visit and an official request from my manager. You can't just wander into these places without good reason, even at DV level."

"What's DV?"

"Developed vetting," said Jenny. "That's the level Edwin and I are at. Sorry, the level I *was* at."

"They ask if you've ever taken drugs," said de Clerk. "If you watch porn, whether you masturbate and if so how often. The idea is that you tell them the lot – then there's nothing left to be blackmailed with."

And this was the organization they were attempting to penetrate.

"Edwin would need an excuse to even leave the office," said Jenny. "Since the Gareth Williams case they've been pretty hot on that."

Williams had done the same job as de Clerk until he was found naked and dead, zipped up in a hold-all; the disclosure that he'd been missing a week before MI6 raised the alarm had led to some uncomfortable questions.

"I don't think it would be in Gosport," said Jenny. "Not knowing Charlie. He'd want to keep it close."

"The third problem is discovering the name of the file," de Clerk. "Actually, that's the biggest hurdle of all. The Dicks Report won't be mentioned in the file name, and these archives aren't the sort of place you can go rummaging around in – you're admitted to inspect a single file, and you need the exact title. Without that it would be like finding a needle in several hundred haystacks."

"What's the naming convention?" asked Jake.

"There's a nine digit reference number and then a date," said de Clerk. "The date we know – 20th September 1941. Next comes the level of secrecy. I'd guess this report is 'belt3', which means for your eyes only, paper only. Unless there are even higher levels of secrecy I haven't heard of, which I can't rule out."

There were groans around the table. Jake watched Heston tap his lips with his index fingers, looking from face to face as the task became more daunting.

He's not going to go for it.

They could always go it alone, of course – but having a national newspaper behind them offered a frisson of extra security. If they got caught, other journalists who knew where they were could be something to bargain with. And if Heston was involved throughout he would be more likely to publish whatever they found.

"Finally there's a codeword," said de Clerk. "That's the real kicker. The rest I can work around, but if we can't get the codeword we can't find the file, it's that simple."

"What sort of codeword?" asked Jake.

"They choose a word at random. It could be anything – armchair, ratatouille, shuttlecock, whatever. But it'll be totally unconnected to the subject matter."

"Then how do we find it?" asked Heston.

"We don't," said de Clerk. "That's the point. In this case only two people will know it, Charlie and Evelyn. Hence why the system is impervious."

"Saints wept," he replied.

"And if we could obtain the file name?" asked Jake.

"We'd still need authorization from Charlie to access the file."

"And what *then*?" said the editor.

"If Charlie's permission could be faked, someone – me I guess – would have to physically go and get the file. In theory once you've got all the authorizations that part's easy."

"You could do it, Ed."

Jenny squeezed his hand; Jake sickened at the contact.

"If only we could get that far," she finished.

"That's a big if," sighed de Clerk. "It's impossible, isn't it? Surely."

The contradiction came from an unexpected quarter.

79

"No." Heston sat very straight and his tiny eyes examined each of them in turn. "No, it's not impossible – few things are, when you put your mind to them. And we have several advantages. First off, we have a person on the inside, which gives us a massive edge. And that person is a computer expert – a genius in fact. Or so I'm told."

"Oh, I don't know about that," said de Clerk.

"Come on man, don't be bashful," snapped Heston. "Going ahead with this operation is the biggest call of my career. Believe you me, stealing documents from MI6 is not a day-to-day occurrence on Fleet Street. Whether or not you are a genius is a pertinent question. What's your IQ, for a start?"

"It's 161," said Jenny.

De Clerk coloured and sipped his coffee.

"Right, higher than Einstein's IQ," said Heston. "So you are a genius. And it pains me to admit this, but Jake here's probably not that far off either."

"I'd say Jenny's brighter than me," Jake hastened.

"This is my point," said Heston. "We've got four highly intelligent people in this room. And Edwin knows the system inside out, he's got his fingers on the buttons. There *must* be a way to get this codeword."

Jake had never seen him like this: he realised what the story meant to his boss too.

And Heston didn't know the half of it.

The room swayed as the enormity of what they were doing hit home. The risks, the rewards, the philosophical ramifications. For the knowledge was always with Jake: the outcome of this operation was already foretold, and by some nebulous cognizance that was watching them even now.

Nesta's electromagnetic network; Eusebius's All-Seeing Eye.

"So all of you, think!" said Heston, wrenching Jake back into the room. "We can work out how to do this!"

They sat with heads bowed, as if in prayer. Heston bought more coffee; ideas were discussed and discarded. Then Jake cleared his throat, a curious twist to his mouth.

"Only two people in the world know this codename, correct?"

"Correct," said Jenny. "Not even the PM is briefed on this. Not even The Queen."

"Then there's only one thing we *can* do."

Suddenly Jenny saw it too. "He's right," she said. "Thinking about it laterally there is only one way."

Heston leaned in. "Which is?"

"We will need to get *them* to discuss it."

*

"Good thought that man," shouted Heston, clapping his hands. "And once they're discussing it we record them – a classic tabloid sting. Why didn't I think of that? Easy! I used to be chief investigative reporter on the *Sun*."

"Easy?" De Clerk looked pained. "Easier said than done, my friend, even if we were somehow able to socially engineer a conversation between two of MI6's smoothest operators."

"You could hack their email accounts?" suggested Jake. "Impersonate Charlie, try to wheedle it out of Evelyn?"

"Oh don't be soft," said Heston. "This is MI6 for fuck's sake."

"Actually, I'm pretty confident I could hack the accounts," said de Clerk.

"How?" Heston was incredulous. "MI6 must have the most formidable firewalls on the planet."

"I helped design them," he replied. "But unfortunately that's no use to us."

"Why not?" asked Jake.

"Because neither of them would ever mention the codeword by email."

"They'd only say it verbally," said Jenny. "And inside an SSR."

"Just for today might we try and steer away from the jargon?" said Heston. "For the sake of those of us who aren't professional spies?"

"Ok, ok," said Jenny. "They would only discuss it in a secure speech room."

He winced. "Secure speech room? I don't like the sound of that."

"You book them to discuss something top secret," explained de Clerk. "They're deep underground – thick walls, completely soundproofed. And each room is equipped with a Nace machine."

"What's a Nace machine?" asked Jake, a child again.

"It detects electronic circuits," replied Jenny. "You bring your mobile in and it beeps. Bring your car keys in and it beeps. Bring a bloody torch in and it beeps – you can't secrete any kind of recording device in the vicinity."

"Is this 'Nace' a physical object?" asked Heston.

De Clerk nodded. "Yeah, it's a sort of black column and at the bottom is a strip with LED lights which blink to show it's functioning. Even the frequency these things work on is top secret. They're made by Q Branch – you know, James Bond and all that?" He looked bashful. "Q Branch actually exists."

Heston produced an irritable noise. "Jesus."

"Look, secrets are MI6's game," said de Clerk. "If secrets were easy to lose, what would be the point in the organization?"

"There's one other thing on our side though," said Jenny.

"What's that?" said Heston.

"It's that people are fallible," she replied. "Even Charlie. That's the basis of espionage, it's why we bother. People lose concentration, people have affairs. They have drug habits, they like to show off. Every MI6 officer thinks they've got the coolest job in the world – there are some monster egos in Vauxhall

Cross, believe me. But they can't boast about their work to anyone except each other. That's why there are so many bars in the building. So staff can let off steam and talk about the day-to-day stuff."

Jenny recalled Waits's face in Istanbul when she'd drawn attention to his obesity.

For a start he was very overweight ...

"If Charlie's got an Achilles heel it's his pride," she finished. "Get them communicating and he'll boast to her. I'm certain of it."

The challenge was formidable, but they had righteousness on their side. They were energized now, convinced it could be done. And by the end of the day they had their plan.

80

Sent: 14.06
From: evelyn.parr@mi6.gsi.gov.uk
To: charles.waits@mi6.gsi.gov.uk

Dear Charlie,
Just a thought – what with this inquiry the opposition want I thought we should go over the security of you know what file. Are you available at 11am tomorrow to discuss securely?
Best,
Evelyn.

Sent: 14.13
From: charles.waits@mi6.gsi.gov.uk
To: evelyn.parr@mi6.gsi.gov.uk
whatever wrong with my security old girl?
C

Sent: 14.20
From: evelyn.parr@mi6.gsi.gov.uk
To: charles.waits@mi6.gsi.gov.uk
There's no-one I'd rather trust with it. But this does strike me: it's had the same name, as far as I know, since the war. I wonder whether that's wise. I have booked SSR B19, assuming you can make.
Best,
Evelyn.

Sent: 14.22
From: charles.waits@mi6.gsi.gov.uk
To: evelyn.parr@mi6.gsi.gov.uk
oh ye of little faith! i have renamed every two years. pain in arse to sort but suppose prudent to change again. yes 11 fine.
C

*

Sent: 14.23
From: charles.waits@mi6.gsi.gov.uk
To: evelyn.parr@mi6.gsi.gov.uk
evelyn
want to talk re: you know what file. think we need to rename. whats your diary like tomorrow.
C

Sent: 14.45
From: evelyn.parr@mi6.gsi.gov.uk
To: charles.waits@mi6.gsi.gov.uk
Dear Charlie,
Happy to meet of course. Won't there be a lot of hoops to jump through? Why necessary?

Best,
Evelyn.

Sent: 14.00
From: charles.waits@mi6.gsi.gov.uk
To: evelyn.parr@mi6.gsi.gov.uk
bit hot upstairs & no10 sniffing about. feels like sensible precaution. have booked SSR B19 for 11.
C

81

Queen Elizabeth II's foremost computer expert bit deep into his knuckle. It was nerve-racking enough hacking the email accounts of his bosses, but already it was 11.05 a.m., with no sign of them. That meant Waits was late. And Charlie Waits was never late.

De Clerk readjusted his earpiece, nudging up the volume. Nothing but the hiss of recorded silence. Perhaps he hadn't mimicked his boss's voice well enough in the emails. Or – worse – someone else had booked B19 between his early-morning slot and Charlie's session. For all his brains de Clerk knew then that he was a fool. If Jake and Jenny fled he had no evidence of his own. They would do him for breaching the Official Secrets Act and prison was a certainty. De Clerk shoved the backpack further under his desk; the feel of the toolbox inside it did nothing to calm him. His pulse was soaring and his shirt clung to the shoulder blades with the sweat. An unsent email from Waits to the head archivist filled his screen. Serial number, date, belt3 – and a gap for the codeword. Chickening out was still an option. Just.

Keep calm, Edwin, keep calm.

A door opened in his ear and he scrabbled to readjust the

volume. He heard chairs being moved, the rustle of coats. And finally: a voice.

*

Charlie Waits blew the steam off his tea. "So, how the devil are we?"

"How the devil are we?" Parr repeated. "Rather stressed, I'd say. And you?"

A few strands of hair had fallen over her eyes and she tossed them away, fixing him with the stare of an iguana.

"I'm enjoying myself," said Waits. "This is what it's all about, remember? This is the sharp end, the buzz. Once everything's done and dusted I'm going to take a trip with the wife, leave the kids with the in-laws. The Amalfi Coast perhaps. Been too long."

"Lovely. But if we could move on from your holiday plans for just a moment ..."

"But of course," said Waits.

He held up his hand and turned on his mobile, the three chimes of the start-up process loud in the soundproofed room. At once the Nace began beeping and a red light twinkled at them, like a Vulcan eye, monitoring proceedings.

"Bloody thing reminds me of *2001 A Space Odyssey*," said Waits. "Let's hope it's not reading our lips, eh?"

He turned off his phone, which emitted a 'plonk' as it powered down; the Nace ceased its racket and the agents relaxed.

"Well then," said Waits. "Goodbye Elvis. Hello – what? Go on my dear, you choose."

*

Yes! De Clerk slapped his knee, mimicking, though he didn't know it, the characteristic response of Adolf Hitler to news of a triumph. He tugged out his earpiece and drilled the word into the keyboard like a woodpecker. Then he paused, cursor hovering over the 'send' button. Once this email was gone there really was no way back. He closed his eyes and sent the bastard.

A response came within the minute. Elvis was not in Gosport. Elvis was in the building. De Clerk half-walked, half-ran through Vauxhall Cross – an observer would have guessed at an upset stomach. A lift whisked him to the third floor below ground level and he stepped into a corridor. Signs warned that it was a restricted area, ordering him to display identification at all times. At the end of the corridor was another lift, this one guarded by security guards with MP5 machine pistols; they carried ID passes, but their uniforms bore no insignia. Beside them a young woman with horn-rimmed glasses and a Shoreditch-type haircut sat at a computer. She would be a graduate and smart, but not brainy enough for the fast track. De Clerk showed her his identity card and authorization code.

"Thank you very much, Mr de Clerk. And if you'd like to look into the camera?"

Click!

The machine studied de Clerk's bone structure and retina and it liked what it saw. The blast-proof elevator doors rolled open, beckoning him down to MI6's archive.

He was almost in.

The lift took an age to descend. It was made of foot-thick steel panels – the most powerful IED yet encountered by the British Army could have gone off inside and it would have contained the blast like popcorn in a saucepan. With each floor the level of restrictedness increased. De Clerk was going right to the bottom.

Keep calm, Edwin, keep calm.

The elevator stopped. The doors opened. And de Clerk stepped into what resembled an aircraft hangar, divided into corridors by steel cabinets. Stepladders set on rails could be slid along each row; his mind swam to think what secrets this room must hold.

"Mr de Clerk?" A ginger-haired archivist with handlebar eyebrows looked up from his classic car magazine and beckoned him forward, a twinkle in his eyes. "Look into the camera please. I'll need your identification, and you'll have to sign here, here and here."

Seven floors up Parr suggested a new codeword.

The archivist began perusing the labels, walking to the far end of the corridor. "No, wait, that can't be right." His eyebrows twitched. "We must have gone right past it. Back the way we came then."

De Clerk wanted to scream and drag him down the aisle.

"Ah," said the archivist, coming to a halt. He unlocked a cabinet, sliding out the drawer to reveal a large metal box. When he opened the lid there was the hiss of escaping gas, and de Clerk caught the whiff of decaying paper. Two dozen files were stacked inside.

"Dum de dum," the archivist hummed as his fingers skipped through the paperwork. "Dum de dum de dum."

De Clerk realized he was opening and closing his fists. He forced himself to be still. *This was taking too long.*

Eighty feet above them the two spies reached agreement.

"Here we are," said the archivist. "You'll find the inspection table at the end of the corridor."

Four pages were in his hands. Brittle; yellowed; sporting an array of 'top secret' stamps. De Clerk reached out to take them ...

82

Charlie Waits held court to an audience of one.

"The good news," he began, "is that GCHQ's managed to get a trace on Chung's line of communication to Beijing. A routine fishing expedition picked it up this morning. She's still in Italy for now, but funnily enough she's just requested a private jet to ... guess where?"

Parr hated being toyed with like this. "Where?"

"London!" cried Waits. "If Chung is anything like you or me, and I fancy that she is, she'll keep the inscriptions close by. We know from experience that their lot are no match for our Frank. And it'll only be a matter of time until we pick up Wolsey and Frobisher, what with de Clerk on the case."

"He is good," admitted Parr.

"No man I'd rather have on side," said Waits. "There's nowhere to hide from a computer genius in this day and age. So you see, my dear, we'll get out of this yet."

"I never doubted you, Charlie. And good idea to rename the file too."

The tranquillity cleaved from Waits's face.

"That was your idea," he said.

"No it wasn't."

"Yes it was."

Waits's lips formed a pink circle. "Oh glory," he said.

The spymaster switched on his mobile. This time the Nace remained silent. His chair was sent skittering across the floor as he dashed for the device. He saw it at once: the panel above the LED display was not flush with the casing. Waits tore the section away to reveal a bundle of foreign electronics soldered inside. A power source, a listening device, the beeper de Clerk had installed to impersonate the disabled machine. A wire led from a battery to the flashing LEDs. With growing horror Waits saw how it had been done. Whoever had pulled off this outrage knew his ritual of turning on his mobile to test the Nace. At the start-up tone the beeper had been activated remotely.

"No." Waits spoke calmly, as if someone had handed him the wrong change in a shop. "Oh dear me, oh dear me no."

Parr looked on; there was nothing to be said. Their most precious secret had been whisked from right under their noses.

*

De Clerk stepped out of the lift at ground level. Beyond the X-ray machines and the olive-green glass he could see sunshine; he was almost out. Five security guards manned the exit, machine pistols slung under arms, and another wave of sweat broke over the traitor's chest. His brow glistened, his skin was pale. A muscle in his cheek wouldn't stop twitching and he felt a weight pressing down on his lung, as if an invisible stone was crushing the air out of it.

Oh Jesus. Not this again. Not now.

At the age of twenty-one de Clerk had been talked into a lad's holiday in Magaluf. After a week of drinking and attempts to chat up girls – neither an activity he excelled at – he had suffered a panic attack and been rushed to hospital. And the attacks had continued throughout his entire twenties. He hadn't suffered one for years, but now the old feeling came back stronger than ever. The racing heart, the shrinking lungs, the constriction of his windpipe by a malevolent inner hand.

A guard scrutinized him. "You all right there, sir?"

"Fine," de Clerk croaked.

The room was spinning.

"Are you sure, sir?" The guard was a liver-spotted gent in his sixties with whom de Clerk usually had a good rapport. He oozed suspicion.

"Feeling a bit fluey," the spy managed, fighting to control his breathing.

Keep calm, Edwin, keep calm.

Two armed officers appeared, footsteps echoing in the space. A drop of sweat detached itself from de Clerk's nose, splashing on the floor.

"You do look at bit peaky," said the guard. "There's a lot of it about this time of year. You go and have a good lie down."

The sentries clicked off in the opposite direction.

"Thank you," gasped de Clerk.

The guard nodded. "Mind how you go, sir."

As de Clerk staggered into the fresh air the alarms went off, a multitudinous shriek that erupted from the building in a wall of sound. He stumbled into a black cab, slamming the door as the first guards rushed from the building.

"Just drive," he uttered. "Get me out of here."

As the taxi shot over Vauxhall Bridge, de Clerk surrendered to the panic attack – bent double on the back seat, eyes rolling in his head like those of a drowning man. The towers of Battersea Power Station were an upturned table juddering across the Thames and a pillar of cloud rose above the chimneys, as though the generators had kicked into life. The thunderhead climbed hundreds of feet, billowing with wrath until it connected with the stratosphere: like a wormhole linking central London to outer space.

83

Jake jumped at the fusillade of frantic knocks. It had been a morning of mental crucifixion in the Islington flat, the minutes dragging out until they were convinced de Clerk had been taken. But there were three fast raps, two slow: the sign that all was well. Jake ran to the door, yelping as he bashed into a table in the hallway.

"It's him," he shouted to Jenny as he peered through the spyhole. "He's alone."

De Clerk stumbled through the door. "I did it," he breathed. "I actually did it."

He collapsed onto a sofa and lay there panting, hairs plastered across his forehead. Jenny pressed a glass of milk on him – it was what de Clerk had fetched himself after the fight at The Oval. Only then did she ask to see the report.

"Oh, I don't actually *have* the pages," said de Clerk.

There was a moment of stunned silence.

"It's a top secret archive, not a bloody lending library. They don't even let you make notes there."

Jake recovered first. "Well, what was the sodding point in that then?"

"It's all in here." De Clerk tapped his cranium. "I'm a genius, remember?"

She laughed. "Of course, I knew this. He's only got a photographic memory. As do I, as it happens."

Jake pinched the bridge of his nose between thumb and index finger, glancing between the faces of the two spies. They were a different breed of human.

She fetched some paper and de Clerk transcribed the missing pages of the Dicks Report. Fifteen minutes later he passed them his handiwork.

And this is what they read:

Such was his psychological state that we were all prepared for some major deterioration. The one thing I had in my mind was that Hess would become homicidal or suicidal. I had considerable concerns he might turn on me, like many paranoiacs do when they are feeling cornered. It was on the 15th that this climax was reached. I had already given extra instructions for the guards on duty to be especially watchful. What I did not reckon with was that at four in the morning or thereabouts, Hess demanded to see me. The door of the cage behind which was his room on the landing had to be thrown open. Hess, fully dressed in his air force uniform including his flying boots, rushed towards me and hurled himself over the banisters. There was a thud on the floor below and groans from Hess. We rushed downstairs where Hess was lying fully conscious at the bottom of the oak staircase with an obviously broken leg. I tended to his injuries. It was then that, crisis reached, he began talking freely. It was as though some final barrier of reserve had been broached. The delusions he went on to outline were so extraordinary not only in their imagination, but in the vividness of detail, that I am bound to recount them at length. I feel sure they may be of use, not only in expanding upon our understanding of the patient, but also for what they might reveal about the Nazi psyche at large – and indeed for the wider discipline of psychiatry.

Hess began by outlining at length what he claimed were his 'true' reasons for fleeing the Reich. He first described how he had felt increasingly an outcast at what we might call the 'court' surrounding Hitler. Hess felt he had fallen down the 'pecking order'. He no longer enjoyed the special favour of Hitler and he had relinquished the role of 'gatekeeper' to his Fuhrer. All this he couched in the kind of catastrophic language that might be employed by, for instance, an obsessive and spurned lover.

From our earlier conversations, it is easy to see why Hitler may have dispensed with the services of so limited an individual. It is also clear what psychological damage this must have caused, for Hess regarded – and I believes still regards – Hitler with a kind of fawning hero-worship for which there is no obvious equivalent among the British to their politicians.

Hess says he had also begun to have second thoughts about the general approach of the Nazi regime, particularly with regard to the Jews and other persecuted minorities. While his hatred – it is not too strong a word – for the Jews remains undimmed, he claims to have become disturbed by pronouncements made by Heinrich Himmler of the SS and his deputy, a man named Reinhard Heydrich, on the plan for dealing with what he describes as the 'Jewish problem'. Hess intimates this may go far beyond their forcible resettlement in Palestine or Madagascar, though he remained vague on the specifics.

This may seem surprising, for Hess has been assumed as radical as Hitler himself on the subject. And yet we should perhaps not be wholly surprised by this apparent contradiction. Hess is, as I have already detailed, a conflicted individual – the sort of man who might within the duration of a single conversation swing between one conviction and its diametric opposite, between amiability and sullenness, between pride and a sense of crippling inadequacy. Moreover I sense there is a grain of good in the man, unlike some other members of that blasted coterie with which Hitler has surrounded himself. Hess said it was the combination of these two factors that brought about a nervous crisis which must have resembled closely that which we have observed here in Mytchett Place.

He then began to unfold a delusion quite unlike any I have yet encountered in paranoiacs, in both scope of ambition and richness of its tapestry. Indeed I began to wonder whether this man might not after all possess the capacity of intelligence in some distorted form. Hess described how senior members of Hitler's inner circle had become secret adherents of a pagan religion first practised in ancient Italy, by the Etruscan civilization. Of course, rumours that Hitler and Himmler practise Satanism and the occult are nothing new (I take the evidence for this claim to be patchy). Nonetheless, I pressed him to continue and asked him to explain how this religion had come to their attention. Hess claimed Himmler had inducted many of Germany's top scholars and archaeologists into a division of his organization named the 'SS Ahnenerbe'. Its goal was to find archaeological evidence for the shadowy mixture of Teutonic myth and folklore on which the Nazi world outlook is founded (and in which Himmler is a fervent believer). Hess said that Himmler hoped to prove the Germans are in some way a 'chosen people' with a 'divine destiny'. To this end, though it might seem fantastical, Hess says he has launched hunts for Atlantis and the Holy Grail. Himmler, Hess claims, believes he is living through the end of Christianity and ordered these archaeologists to prove the pagan origins of the German 'Volk'. It must be said that in this at least, Hess's account chimes with our own analysis of this exceedingly odd character and his foibles. The patient said that Himmler commandeered Wewelsburg Castle as his headquarters – his 'Camelot', Hess described it. This is the seat of the order of Teutonic Knights which Himmler is striving to found in the SS. There, if the patient can be believed, he hopes to collect under one roof the Grail, the artefacts of Atlantis, et cetera. I pressed Hess again: why was it the Etruscan religion that so enraptured the senior Nazis? Here the most astonishing element of his schizophrenic imaginings unfolded. At this point he became very highly agitated, and I became once again concerned at the possibility of further attempts to do himself harm.

The patient claimed that in 1933 the 'SS Ahnenerbe' were excavating a site in Italy when they came upon a most remarkable tomb. It belonged, Hess said, to a small child, and the archaeologists became extremely excited, convincing themselves they had found the resting place of the prophet of the Etruscan faith. Hess said that contained within the tomb, alongside evidence of human sacrifice and other ritual offerings, they uncovered the holy text of the Etruscan people inscribed on scrolls and sealed with beeswax into alabaster jugs. It had been believed lost, and after a few brief investigations of my own I can confirm the text is not currently known to historiography. Hess became quite wild by this point – like an animal, foaming at the mouth. I was worried for myself and my patient. However the revelations pouring forth were so extraordinary I let him continue in the hope they might allow me such an insight into the man's mind that I may be better placed to help him recover his sanity. He went on to claim this text detailed the various means by which Etruscan soothsayers interpreted the will of their gods and thus predicted the future – namely: examining the flight of birds; studying the livers of sacrificial animals; interpreting celestial phenomena such as comets; and studying the shape and form of bolts of lightning. Hess went on to claim that each of these disciplines was studied with utmost scientific rigour by the 'SS Ahnenerbe'. The first three methods were found to be quite useless. However Hess asserts that the final method proved effective and with it the SS were able to prophesise future events with astonishing accuracy. Hess insists Hitler, Himmler and the few senior figures privy to the discovery have since become reliant on the technique for decision making.

By the patient's account, the tomb of this 'wunderkind' was respectfully sealed and the scrolls borne to Wewelsburg Castle. There they have purportedly been guarded these last seven years. Heinrich Himmler, so Hess says, had by this point convinced himself that the 'mysterious Etruscans' described by DH Lawrence in his recent work were none other than the long-lost ancestors of the German people, a claim he backs with the observation that their script bears a resemblance to Germanic runes. It should be said at this point that there is not the slightest evidence that the Etruscans are Germanic in origin or visa versa; reputable scholars agree they originated either from northern Turkey, which is the classical tradition, or northern Italy itself, an area preferred by modern anthropology.

It does indeed seem remarkable that the leaders of a highly-developed Western society might place their faith in superstition. Yet so detailed were Hess's descriptions that I did not dismiss it out of hand, and indeed began to wonder whether there might not be an element of truth in some of what he was saying. Perchance, some of these senior figures think they have stumbled upon something of genuine efficacy. It is agreed that there is a tendency towards mysticism amongst some of its leading figures. Hitler himself is convinced he was been chosen by providence to lead the German people to greatness. I shall alert MI6 to these conclusions through the appropriate channels in case they can take advantage of this curious state of affairs.

Convinced the discussion may be instructive on the issue of how to 'de-Nazify' the German people in the event of British victory, I urged the patient to continue, even though many of his proclamations were the ravings of a lunatic. Hess went on to claim each of the German successes in foreign policy over the last seven years, and indeed they have been numerous, was enabled by the prior consultation of this Etruscan text. Hitler's foreign policy has been characterized by brinkmanship. Yet in the reality constructed by the patient, it was not brinkmanship at all but foreknowledge. Hitler, he claims, knew he could remilitarize the Rhineland unopposed. He knew the western powers would not stand in the way of Germany's unification with Austria, and he knew that Britain would not go to war to save Czechoslovakia. Each of Germany's successes on the battlefield – the invasion of Poland, Norway, the Low Countries, France and the Balkans – was in Hess's fantasy achieved not by Hitler's brilliance but his reliance on augurs. It was even possible, Hess said, to summon down lightning bolts at will, and he claims personally to know how this could be done. He offered there and then to conjure up such a display so I would know him to be speaking the truth. Mindful of the potential psychological damage of his failure to achieve this feat and of my Hippocratic duty as a doctor, I declined this offer. What more proof then, Hess went on, than to compare the creation of the German Empire in Europe, conquered against such huge odds, with that of ancient Rome, the only people in history to have accumulated such a mass of European territory with comparable speed. For Hess believes Rome also manipulated this power to build its thousand-year Reich.

I asked the patient to return to the purpose of his flight. What then, in light of this new background, had he hoped to achieve by coming to Britain? This Hess was happy to relate, and he did so in great detail. It reminded me of the pride of small boys who have prepared something carefully and then done it. He told me he had determined to teach Hitler a lesson for rejecting him and 'get one over' on his rivals in the SS whom he saw as plotting 'uncivilized' and 'un-German' acts. He claimed that Hitler had forbidden a single copy of the scrolls to be made, because he was very paranoid about others laying their hands on it. Only the original scrolls could be inspected and these were stored at Wewelsburg Castle with access permitted only to very highest echelons of the Nazi regime, a group he listed as himself, Hitler, Goring, Goebbels, Himmler and his deputy Heydrich. So it was, at the height of what I take to be one of Hess's periodic psychotic and nervous episodes, that he claims to have taken it upon himself to steal these scrolls and fly with them to Britain in the hope of bringing about a reverse in the war, a measure of revenge on his former comrades, and perhaps of securing for himself a leading position in British society. Where then, I asked him, were these scrolls? Again he had the answer: upon landing in Scotland he was seized by the conviction that they would be better off destroyed and that 'no good may come of them'. Therefore upon landing he claims to have burned the text, hoping its mischief be ended once and for all. It is another example of the depth and intricacy of the delusion. Each query is met with an answer and without hesitation and I am certain the patient believes every word he says.

Hess claims to have resolved never to breathe another word of this matter, hoping to forestall a British attempt to locate other copies of the text. But now he has reached, so he says, so desperate a strait – shunned and condemned to death in absentia by his former comrades, held prisoner by the country he fancied would welcome him – that he no longer cares what happens to the world and the people within it, nor indeed whether he lives or dies, and this explains last night's suicide attempt. Having finished his tale the patient suddenly began to weep and he did so most grievously. He has since become catatonic and resists all subsequent attempts to be engaged on the ancient Etruscan matter once more.

84

Jake stared at the four pages. "This is it then. This is how the Secret Service knew, all those decades ago. This is how the paths converge – Rome, Nazism, MI6. Churchill and the 'ancient Etruscan matter'. God only knows what Winnie made of it all."

Jenny produced her smart phone and Googled: 'Hitler + lightning'.

At once the search engine summoned up thousands of pages. Her eyes flitted from left to right as she read. Occasionally it seemed she would say something, but words never formed themselves. Her complexion had turned the colour of bad mackerel.

Finally she voiced a single word. "Blitzkrieg."

"Lightning war," Jake translated. "It was the name they gave to their battle tactics. Rapid motorized advances, encircling entire armies at a time."

"And there's this," said Jenny, swivelling the tablet.

On the screen was the symbol of Himmler's SS; the crooked letters formed two bolts of lightning.

"The badge was designed in 1933," said Jenny. "About six months after Hess claimed they found Tages's tomb."

"My God," said Jake, who was also on Google. "Look at this entry from the war diary kept by Goebbels, Hitler's propaganda guru. It's dated 26th September 1938, at the height of appeasement – when Hitler bluffed Chamberlain into throwing Czechoslovakia to the wolves."

> *Things have turned out just as the Fuhrer predicted. He is a divinatory genius. But first, our mobilization. This will proceed so lightning-fast that the world will experience a miracle.*

"So the Nazis did buy into it too," she said, her breathing shallow.

"And here's a speech Hitler gave threatening the Jews in June 1941," said Jake. "Jesus, just read this one."

> *They can laugh about it, just as they used to laugh at my prophecies. The coming months will prove that here too I've seen things correctly.*

Jake recalled the dream he'd had in Rome: how the beat of the drum had transmogrified into the sound of jackboots.

"There's more," said Jenny. "Much more, in fact. Lightning and storm imagery is shot through almost every pronouncement Hitler makes in the build-up to war. Early in 1938 he says the attack on the Czechs must be carried out '*blitzartig-schnell*' – 'lightning fast'. And this quote's from the same year – when Hitler is threatening to invade Austria."

> *I have a historic mission and I will fulfil this because providence has destined me to do so. I'll appear in Vienna like a spring storm. Then you'll see something.*

"Feat after coup after bluff." Jake's voice was husky. "And lightning was never far from Hitler's mind."

"How did Hess's flight go down with him?"

"Hold on." Jake pulled up a page from the historian Ian Kershaw's biography of the dictator.

The first Hitler knew of Hess's disappearance was in the morning of 11 May. One of the Deputy Fuhrer's adjutants turned up at the Berghof. He was carrying a letter which Hess had given him before taking off, entrusting him to give it personally to the Fuhrer. When Hitler read Hess's letter the colour drained from his face. Albert Speer heard an 'almost animal-like scream'. 'Goring, get here immediately!' he barked into the telephone. 'Something dreadful has happened'.

'The Fuhrer is completely crushed,' the Propaganda Minister noted in his diary. The letters, he claimed, were full of 'half baked occultism'.

According to one account, Hitler was 'in tears and looked ten years older'. He told General Udent, 'I hope Hess falls into the sea'.

'I have never seen the Fuhrer so deeply shocked,' Hans Frank told subordinates a few days later.

"Then the job of discrediting Hess began," said Jake, pointing to another paragraph. "Straight away the Nazi propaganda machine began trying to paint him as a lunatic."

The German communiqué of 13 May acknowledged Hess's flight to Scotland and capture. It emphasized his physical illness stretching back years, which had put him in the hands of mesmerists, astrologists, and the like, bringing about a 'mental confusion' that had led to the action. It also held open the possibility that he had been entrapped by the British Secret Service.

"And read this," said Jenny. "It's an excerpt from a Nazi Party newspaper dated 13th May, 1941."

As is well known in party circles, Hess had undergone severe physical suffering for some years. Recently he had sought relief in methods practised by astrologers. An attempt is being made to determine to what extent these persons are responsible for bringing about the condition of mental distraction which led him to take this step.

"It's as if the German leadership were trying to get in a pre-emptive publicity strike," she said. "In case he started singing like a canary."

"And yet the British didn't try to turn Hess's flight into a propaganda coup," mused Jake. "It's always been seen as one of the odd things about the affair. You'd expect them to make hay having captured the Deputy Führer. But they were strangely quiet."

Suddenly a bit of Churchill came to Jake. His Finest Hour speech, 1940; the penultimate line.

But if we fail, then the whole world, including the United States, including all that we have known and cared for, will sink into the abyss of a new Dark Age made more sinister, and perhaps more protracted, by the lights of perverted science.

That word again: science. 'The lights of perverted science.'

The journalist's frown deepened.

But that's what it is, Jake. Don't you see?

"After the news broke the Nazis arrested dozens of people connected to Hess," said Jenny. "Hitler ordered Hess shot on sight if he ever returned."

"Yet as it happened Hess was the most high-ranking Nazi to escape the death penalty at the Nuremberg Trials," he muttered. "He lived out the rest of his days in solitary isolation and died of old age in 1987. Why?"

Jenny had turned even whiter. "The Cold War was on," she whispered. "He was kept alive."

She pushed the report across the table, as if it was unclean. And then came something totally unexpected.

"I believe him," she said. "I believe every word of it."

*

"Believe who?" said Jake.

"Rudolf Hess." Jenny faltered – she looked reduced somehow. "I ... I think he was telling the truth."

"Telling the truth?" De Clerk scoffed. "About what?"

"The *Disciplina Etrusca*," Jenny said, shrinking further into herself. "When he said that it ... that it helped them."

"You can't be serious. You're not saying ..."

Jenny's shoulders juddered, and Jake saw how he must have looked at his own awakening in the Monastery of Debre Damo.

"I don't understand how," she said. "*But it works*."

"You're mad," said de Clerk. He stalked out of the room.

"You're not mad," said Jake. "I believe it too."

He told Jenny about his own epiphany. How he had seen a bolt of lightning guide Florence to the monastery; how she'd *sensed* danger, foretold by thunder every time; how lightning from the north-west always augured ill, just as Tages said it would. Most of all, how Roman history ebbed and flowed with the appearance of lightning.

"Then we met Dr Nesta and I saw how this phenomenon could have a scientific basis after all," Jake continued. "And now this. Half the Nazi state was modelled on Rome. The salutes, the architecture. The eagles and banners."

"And that run of victories," said Jenny. "From 1933 to 1941 it was triumph after triumph – Hitler conquered Europe in eighteen months flat."

"But immediately after Hess's flight the victories end," Jake replied. "The miscalculations set in. A month later Germany invades Russia – the Fuhrer's most catastrophic mistake. By the end of the year they're at war with the USA too. Hitler bit off more than he could chew. Germany lost the war."

"Every major decision the Nazis took after Hess's flight they got wrong," said Jenny. "All of them. And Roger Britton's death – it wasn't coincidence, was it? Dr Dicks tells us here that Hess boasted he could conjure up a lightning bolt. He offered to prove it. I think after Dicks finished his interviews Hess taught what he knew to MI6. Why else would Churchill be called to study the ravings of a madman?" She drew a long breath. "MI6 put Hess to the test and Hess delivered."

"Which means ..."

"Which means Roger Britton was killed by Charlie Waits with a bolt of lightning."

"And ever since then MI6 has been hunting for the rest of the text," Jake finished.

"But it still makes no sense," said Jenny. "Surely conjuring up a lightning bolt takes more power than reading the future? How could Charlie do one and not the other?"

"Quite the opposite," said Jake. "What would use up more energy – making electricity jump a few hundred feet through the air, or calculating the movement of quadrillions of atoms? Without the *Disciplina Etrusca* to hand that was beyond Hess. It remained beyond Charlie – and his predecessors too." He shook his head, half-laughed, breathing out through his nose. "Let us therefore brace ourselves to our duties ..."

Jenny frowned. "But if you've known it was real since Ethiopia, why on earth didn't you tell me?"

"You'd have thought I was mad," said Jake. "And I ..."

"And you what?"

"Jenny, I ..."

A drawer banged in the kitchen and the words "like you" died on his lips.

85

Fendi Selleria looked out of place in Heathrow Terminal Two, Florence decided as the designer bag swivelled to meet her. She had bought it on a whim in Rome with her latest stipend from Beijing; with each success her retainer had increased and she was now a wealthy young lady. Earning more than her father, in fact. She watched without emotion as one of her team rushed to the carousel to pick it up. It was nice to have nice things. But money was no longer her motivation.

Beijing didn't know Florence had kept back part of each inscription. The most vital verses – they acted as a spark, igniting the rest of the incantation – these she had hoarded like Croesus. Florence didn't want some nobody back in Beijing piggybacking off her work, setting themselves up as a rival *fulguriator*.

That was her destiny, hers alone.

Again she felt that curious prickle of energy at the thought of what she was becoming. It branched out through her nervous system like ... Florence frowned. The feeling was like forked lightning itself: fingers of energy crackling from her core to the extremities of her body.

She wanted more.

After the breakthrough in Ethiopia, Florence had felt herself on the cusp of greatness. Then the heavens called her to Italy. And there was no doubt that the Pian di Civita once held something of great power: Florence felt that same energy thrumming from the hilltops. But there had been a hitch. The tomb had been empty, and since then her powers were rolling back, like a tide drawing out to sea. Without the incantation to *dii superiores* she knew the All-Seeing Eye would remain occluded, as if suffering from glaucoma.

After the failure at Pian di Civita she had camped for a week on the hills of Lazio, much of it spent in a trance. Jake's route – historical detective work – was not for her. Instead each night she sent perverted litanies up to the stars, while her agents huddled together and whispered about spirits and ghosts. But the skies remained sullen.

Just when Florence feared it had forsaken her, the sign came.

They were at breakfast in a hotel restaurant, CNN blaring in the background. A glance was enough. Strange that it hadn't revealed itself to her naked eye – yet she knew it was the calling. By then Florence had learned to let the crackle of her second soul guide her, as a migrating bird is pulled across continents by a call it cannot understand. The finger was pointing the way once more.

And there was a circuitous feel to this journey, pleasingly so. She was summoned to London.

*

"Quickly," Florence snapped, glancing at her watch. It was gone 2p.m. and she was in no mood to wait – not now she was so close to that thing which had occupied her every waking moment these last three years. The agents were burdened with luggage, but they quickened their pace. Florence's star was rising in Beijing; her displeasure at the calibre of her previous team had been acted upon and their replacements were hot stuff, subordinate to her every whim.

They were good, but not good enough to register the smartly-dressed man lingering at arrivals with a copy of the *Telegraph*, one brogue tapping on the pavement. He looked too pampered to be a threat, too obviously soft.

That man had murder on his mind.

*

Charlie Waits watched Florence's team head for the motorway in two Mercedes saloons. Moments later the gunmetal BMW swept up with Davis at the wheel; Parr sat alongside him. Nobody spoke as the car purred down the M4. Davis left half a dozen cars between them and their quarry, changing lanes often while Waits ensured they didn't have a tail of their own. He was rather enjoying all this. Soon the spires of west London's business district came into view: GlaxoSmithKline, Sega, an office of glass that resembled Noah's Ark. They skirted Kensington and hit the Paddington flyover, soaring over the West End.

"They're aiming for the Chinese Embassy," observed Parr. "Must be – we're heading straight to Portland Place."

"Shall I bring them to a halt?" said Davis, whose hands gripped and released the steering wheel repeatedly.

"Not yet," said Waits. "We'll make our move once they turn off the main road. Brace yourselves – I fancy this might get a bit hairy, ladies and gentlemen."

But the Chinese delegation weren't heading for the embassy. Instead the Mercedes cut through the City of London before nosing onto the Embankment, where Britton had been struck dead a few weeks previously. The car only slowed when Tower Bridge poked into view – that, and the Norman fort in its shadow. Once the very name could chill the bones of a Londoner, for tragedy seeped through every murder hole.

The Tower.

86

There it was again, ringing in his head: the tramp-tramp-tramp of leather on cobbles, and below it a baritone of thunder. When he closed his eyes he saw millions of points of light, swirling and flowing and rising into peaks; a few lines of poetry came to him and he murmured them under his breath.

With domineering hand she moves the turning wheel,
Like currents in a treacherous bay swept to and fro.

The poem was ancient, but for the life of him Jake couldn't place it – the verse must have seeped into his mind during his research.

"What's that?" asked Jenny.

"Oh, some poem," he said. "It's about fate. I forget the author."

"Don't think about it, Jake. There's no point."

It was those two dreams. He couldn't shake them, and for the first time Jake wondered if he was going mad after all. He pressed the palms of his hands into his eyelids until his vision bloomed with primrose and when he opened his eyes – they were bloodshot – his gaze fell on the Dicks Report.

"Will a hand-written copy be enough for us?" asked Jenny with a glance at the pages. "Can you publish?"

Jake considered it. "With the sworn affidavit of two ex-MI6 officers it might be usable, along with everything else we've got. The footage you shot in Ethiopia is crucial. But ..."

"But what? Tell me."

"If we slam all this in tomorrow's edition, and if people actually believe it – what do you think will happen next?"

Jenny understood. Every nation in the world would begin the scramble, every fortune-seeker too.

"I don't like it," said Jake. "Whatever *it* is. It feels unwholesome. It brings glory to one nation and death to the next on nothing more than a whim. And so far all I've achieved is placing passages of the work into the hands of the last person on earth I'd want to have them."

"She doesn't have it all, though," said Jenny. "And Eusebius's trail ended in Italy, remember? The job's done, Jake. Hess did it for us."

When Jenny looked up Jake was staring at her with such intensity she flinched.

"Did he though?"

"What do you mean?"

"Did Hess finish it for us?"

Jenny narrowed her eyes. "Well, he *says* he did ..."

"Exactly." Jake massaged his sinuses. "He *says* he did."

"Is there evidence to the contrary?"

"Hess was the most senior Nazi not to be executed after the Second World War, and he lived until a ripe old age. What does that suggest to you?"

"I don't know, Jake. Spell it out for me."

"Put yourself in Hess's boots," he said. "You've betrayed your country. You hope to make a new life in Britain, but you're not sure what reception you'll get. You have in your possession a document that could change history. Do you burn it? Or do you keep it? As an insurance policy ..."

Jenny's eyes flared. "It's what I'd do."

It was then that Jake Wolsey made a last leap of intuition. The human brain, the might of reason: a match for any ancient lore.

"I'll tell you what I'd have done," he said. "I'd have buried it. Or stashed it somewhere, so I had a chip to bargain with. Wasn't Hess taken to a local farmhouse when he landed?"

Jenny was nodding.

"Listen to this," she said, reading from her smart phone. "Churchill ordered the prisoner be treated with relative dignity. As befitted a foreign statesman he was *permitted to keep his personal effects*."

Jake's mouth had become a thin white line. "Before we publish anything I want to go to Scotland," he said. "I want to find this farmhouse and check out the crash site with a resistance meter, satisfy myself there's nothing unpleasant there."

Jenny shuddered again, and he knew she too felt the fear that had reduced Hess to the rudderless nothing encountered by Dr Dicks.

The face is bestial, ape or wolf.

"I know it's a lot to take in," said Jake.

"I can cope," she said.

Jenny smiled at him, defiant again, and Jake knew he was developing feelings for this person stronger than anything he'd known; stronger than whatever presence Dr Nesta had detected in the darkness of space; stronger than the bonds of predestination that tied every human to their path.

"Let's get to Scotland then," he said.

"We may as well visit Mytchett Place first, it's only in Surrey. And didn't we read that Hess was held prisoner in the Tower of London too?"

Jake said nothing.

The Tower.

Thunderstruck.

"The Tower," said Jenny when she saw it too. "It was struck by lighting two days ago."

"The reason Niall was late for our meeting."

For thirty seconds all Jake and Jenny did was breathe. They heard the noise of a bus pulling up sink through the walls, the heavy groan of its departure; a child playing in the flat above and thudding floorboards as a parent gave pursuit.

Jenny's phone began ringing and they both jumped.

"Then there's no time to lose," she said. "Hold on, let me get rid of this."

But when she listened to what the caller had to say her face collapsed downward as if the muscles beneath had been torn away.

"No, Daddy," she whispered.

*

Jenny wept at last: it was silence, stillness, the salt water painting translucent stripes down her face. Her father did the talking, words of sadness, words of beauty, words human beings hear once or twice in a lifetime and are meant for them alone. Her knees pointed inward, like those of a child starting school. She had lost her mum.

And Margaret never did return to her kitchen.

Neither of them knew how long Jake held her; minutes became hours and passed in a blur. De Clerk poked his head around the door and, seeing something significant was happening, darted away.

More of that poem had come to Jake; it was Roman, he was certain now.

No cries of misery she hears, no tears she heeds,

But, steely hearted, laughs at groans her deeds have wrung.

He held Jenny tighter: trying to channel strength into her, afraid for them both, but there was nowhere to escape from it.

This was the fabric of reality.

On nothing more than a whim ...

It was late afternoon when Jenny thought about the future, the fifty-fifty chance she would share her mother's fate. She had to know.

Abruptly she turned to face Jake. Their faces were inches apart, and for an instant he feared she might try to kiss him. Letting her do so now would be wrong and he would resist her if she tried. But Jenny was in a different place; her eyes crackled with some new determination.

"The Tower," she said. "*Let's go and get it.*"

87

In its time the Tower of London has played many parts – prison, palace, mint and zoo – and staring at the citadel Jake saw how its tangled history had been converted into stone. Medieval walls were overlaid with Tudor and Georgian additions and a terraced street protruded over the walls; the cube-shaped White Tower rose above the hotchpotch. When it was built this was one of the tallest buildings in Europe. Now the keep was dwarfed by Gherkin, Shard and Tower Bridge alike, yet still it held its own, drawing the eye back.

The queue to get in was six abreast and foreign tongues commingled in the spring air; there were interested glances at the blonde with the expensive camera as Jenny and Jake strolled to the entrance.

A Beefeater stopped the pair with an open hand. "There is a queue, you know."

"Jake Wolsey, reporter. And this is my photographer."

The Beefeater was unimpressed.

"I'm here to interview the Constable of the Tower."

"He's expecting you, is he?"

"We've got an appointment."

There was a cursory bag search and they were in.

Rudolph Hess had been imprisoned in a building known as the Queen's House, a wattle-and-daub lodge in the central courtyard. It was the finest surviving pre-Tudor house in London, protected by moat and wall from the Great Fire of 1666. But there was a complication. The Queen's House was now the private residence of the Constable of the Tower, and this was no lowly guardsman. Only a General or Field Marshal could take the role, personally appointed by the Queen. The incumbent, General Sir Richard Mayflower, had been commander of the British Forces in Afghanistan; he'd briefly run the whole shebang, during the interregnum between two American commanders.

But there was always a way of getting in to these places.

Wearing his journalist's hat Jake had cooked up some feature about interviewing residents of historic houses. And the Tower's press office jumped at the chance for free publicity, strong-arming the general into giving up an hour of his time. The plan was for Jenny to ask Sir Richard to show her the most photogenic rooms, leaving Jake to scour the chamber in which Hess was held prisoner.

The Beefeater led them past Traitors' Gate, where Anne Boleyn had arrived by boat, lifting her dress over effluvial waters before her appointment with the block. Then came the Bloody Tower, where two princes had met their end.

Jake caught Jenny's eye as they threaded through the complex. She smiled sadly and, with an effort, looked ahead. Finally they penetrated the inner wall. To the east of the courtyard stood the keep, sucking the tourists in, and to the west was what might have passed for a village green; ravens trotted about with clipped wings. Beyond that stood the Queen's House, busby-wearing Fusiliers standing guard. The Beefeater led them to the door and knocked three times. It was opened by a red-faced man with a shock of white hair. His back was very straight and his jaw looked as if it had been hewn from iron and bolted to his head as an afterthought.

"Wolsey, is it?" He crushed Jake's hand. "Richard Mayflower. And this is ...?" The general's eyes darted to the left.

*

Sir Richard led them through the house, stopping at rooms of interest. At one point he announced they were in the room where Guy Fawkes was interrogated; Jake could feel history seeping from the floorboards.

"We're particularly interested in seeing the room where Rudolf Hess was held," said Jenny.

"Ah! Well, you're in luck." Sir Richard seemed able only to grin or frown, face segueing between the two states on order. "That happens to be my sitting room. I was thinking we'd take tea in there while your colleague gets this wretched interview out of the way ..."

The room was built for the medieval stature and Jake ducked to avoid the beams. Antique rugs were cast about and a red-brick fireplace dominated the far end of the room. Framed photographs were everywhere: Sir Richard meeting the Queen, Sir Richard shaking hands with President Obama, Sir Richard with his arm around General Colin Powell.

The interview began. The general wasn't a bad old boy when

he got going, with plentiful anecdote and a good line in self-deprecation. And all the while Jake was studying the room, wondering where he would stash a document of importance if he was a desperate man.

Presently Jenny announced she wanted to photograph the house – would Sir Richard accompany her?

"Charmed." Sir Richard ordered another grin. "You'll be all right amusing yourself here, I trust, Wolsey?"

The general escorted her out, chest thrust forward as if headed for the ballroom. Jenny looked back as they promenaded from the room – she was rolling her eyes.

First Jake checked the fireplace, exploring the brickwork with his fingers.

A brick was loose.

Jake clawed it out to reveal an empty space and a few crumbs of desiccated mortar. The rest of the brickwork was solid; so were the flagstones. Next he inspected the floorboards, but there no nail out of place, no suggestion of a compartment. Jake strained his ears for the general's return. Nothing could be heard but the collage of creaks and tics as the timber-framed lodge breathed, shifting itself minutely. Jenny was doing well; Jake hoped the old goat wasn't being too lecherous. But he was ten minutes into the search and he'd got nowhere.

Jake paused, forcing himself to think. The windows consisted of diamond-shaped panes held in place with strips of lead, the White Tower distorted by imperfect glass. Aged planks formed a box beneath the window to sit on – Jake pictured Hess rocking there for hours as his predicament hit home. He knocked on the window box. It was hollow. And the cracks between the planks were wide enough to slip sheets of paper through.

Jake snatched up a poker – its end tapered like a crowbar – and listened for the general's return. He dreaded to imagine what Sir Richard would do if he caught him tearing up the period features. But there was no sign of the general and

Jake smiled at the thought of Jenny leading him on, endlessly retaking the same photograph.

He squeezed the poker into a crack between the beams and pulled. There was no give at all; the oak was centuries old and hard as steel. Jake heaved again, putting his back into it this time, but still the wood held. He clambered onto the window seat, bent double to avoid the ceiling. A group of Chinese tourists peered up at him from the green, but there was little light in the room and the warped glass would hide his vandalism. Jake stamped on the poker; the plank snapped with a sound like a gunshot.

There was a bundle of papers inside.

Old papers.

88

Jake fished out the pages. Printed text was arranged in columns and Queen Victoria warded off a Russian bear in caricature; the year was 1848. He was holding several pages of *Punch* magazine, illicit reading for a former Constable of the Tower.

The sound of Jenny laughing loudly at some wisecrack tore Jake back to the present and he tried to replace the plank. But the damn thing wouldn't fit. He stamped on the board – it snapped into position – and his shoulders slumped with relief.

Then he realized *Punch* was lying on the floor.

Jake fiddled the pages through the cracks and replaced the poker as Sir Richard strode into the room. The general ambled to the window and gazed out at his fiefdom. The broken plank was right under his nose; it looked horribly conspicuous to Jake. But Sir Richard was studying his minions, on the lookout for shirkers, and the intruders used the hiatus in his attention to carry out a silent conversation.

Jenny raised her eyebrows, head jutting forward. *Well?*

Jake smiled, with a half-shake of his head. *Nada.*

She pivoted both hands. *What now?*

He shrugged. *Search me.*

"Chap down there taking an awful lot of interest in Queen's House," observed Sir Richard. "Funny little fat man."

Jake ignored him; Jenny had gone oddly still.

"Still, he's got a cracker of a wife," Sir Richard went on. "Quite the filly. Lovely silvery hair. Amazing how some chaps do it. I suppose he's an enormously wealthy stockbroker or something." The general laughed in disgust at the thought. "Are we done then? I've got a tower to be running."

Jenny didn't seem to have heard him – she was looking straight up.

"I said, my dear, are we almost done?"

"No," said Jenny. "No, I'd say not. You've probably got a few more questions to ask, right Jake?"

The journalist sighed, a man defeated. "I think I've got enough material to be honest."

"Right, excellent," said Sir Richard, slapping his thighs. "I'll see you out then. When do you plan on publication?"

But Jenny ignored the question. "Jake – *are you sure* you don't have more questions?"

"Completely sure."

She glared at him. "But you normally ask *a few more questions.*"

"Do I?" he said. "Do I?"

Then he noticed: Jenny was staring him in the face and rolling her eyes towards the ceiling, Sir Richard oblivious to the gesture. When Jake followed her gaze he physically jolted.

Carved into one of the planks were the initials *R.W.R.H.*

"Actually I wouldn't mind a few more snaps," Jenny told the general. "Just to be on the safe side. If you'd be good enough to escort me again?"

Her mouth twitched flirtatiously.

"Well, if you insist ..."

As the general departed he shot Jake the look of the conqueror-to-be. Jake snatched up the poker and dragged an armchair under the initialled spot. The plank was held in place by two blackened nails – they protruded from the wood, as if they had been removed and pushed back by hand. He plucked them out and squeezed the poker through the cracks, levering a two-inch gap between the planks, then pushed his hand through to feel splintery wood. The poker slipped, clattering to the floor, and the beam snapped down on his hand. The vandal emitted a silent scream.

Jake was trapped: one hand in the ceiling, the blood cut off from his fingers, the poker out of reach. Without it he wasn't strong enough to prize up the plank, so he wrenched out his hand, skinning his fingers. The plank snapped shut.

There was no time to consider the pain. Jake grabbed the loose brick from the fireplace and repeated the process, slammed the brick into the gap this time. It held. Jake thrust his forearm into the compartment between the ceiling and the floor above until the flesh was squeezed white. His fingers brushed against something dry and brittle, something that crinkled to the touch.

Jake felt his bladder go weak: it was paper.

Now he had two fingers on the bundle and he paddled it towards the gap, clods of black swept in its wake, spilling into the room. Jake coughed as the detritus fell, swaying on the armchair. A corner of yellow protruded from the ceiling and he snatched it into daylight.

The papyri in his hands dated indisputably from antiquity; they were the colour of over-stewed tea and crumbled to the touch. The letters were Roman and at once Jake saw the name of the scribe.

EUSEBIUS.

Below it he recognized another name.

TAGES.

Imprinted alongside the ancient text were a series of pink

stamps: a swastika, an Eagle, the words *'Streng Geheim'*. Jake felt the room constrict around him. His throat felt raw and there was a throbbing in his ears. He was holding in his arms a full and unabridged copy of the *Disciplina Etrusca*.

89

Lack of an amorous encounter had left Sir Richard in petulant mood and he swept them from the house, too worked up to notice the bundle under the reporter's arm. As Jake descended the staircase one question confounded him. Why would Hess mark the beam with his initials? It drew attention to the very place he intended to keep secret. Suddenly the answer came, and Jake saw the Deputy Führer must have had a degree of cunning after all. The nearby Beauchamp Tower was renowned for the graffiti famous inmates had added during their incarceration – the inscriptions were now protected by Perspex screens. Hess must have calculated that as a person of historical significance, his initials would ensure the planks remained untouched. Sir Richard opened the front door with a bark of farewell. Jake stepped onto the green – and walked right into Charlie Waits.

"Wolsey, my dear old thing," said Waits. "Fancy seeing you here."

The spymaster was flanked by Davis and Parr, and when he saw the papyrus bundle his eyes seemed to retract into his head.

"Give it to me," he said in a voice that quivered with want.

"You can't have it," said Jenny. "It's not for you, Charlie."

There was silence as the spymaster digested this impudence.

"How did you three get past the sentries?" snapped Sir Richard. He glared at the scarlet-clad guardsman. "What the hell are you playing at, man?"

"They're MI6, sir," shouted the soldier. "Had to let them through, sir."

"MI6?" repeated Sir Richard in a voice of wonder.

Jake punched Charlie Waits in the face.

The journalist couldn't say where the impulse had come from – he had never hit a man in his life. But his powerful shoulders lent the blow force and Waits sprawled on his back like an upended turtle.

Surprise bought them a three-second head start.

*

Jake and Jenny were sprinting across open space: it was a killing ground. Now Davis would execute them, right here, in front of hundreds of tourists. He reached for his pistol with an automatic movement – and withdrew thin air.

The assassin had been forced to leave his weapon outside due to the search. Waits had thought it best to go incognito, for if force was needed they could commandeer the troops. Davis stood stupefied as the pair dashed across the courtyard, flightless ravens bounding from their way.

Jake sensed Jenny falling behind and grabbed her by the hand, hauling her along as soldiers fanned across the citadel. *They were being penned in.*

Only one option was left open: the White Tower. They fled up the steps and into the keep.

A potbellied knight reared up in front of them on his armoured horse: this was the battle armour of Henry VIII, and they were inside the Royal Armoury. Display cabinets bristled with weaponry. There were cutlasses and rapiers, muskets and pistols, every device of murder that could be dreamt up by man and inlaid with jewels. Davis and Waits pursued the pair inside, leaving Parr at the entrance to make clear that what transpired within was MI6 business. Sir Richard was compelled to obey, remaining with the troops and furious at this emasculation.

Alarms had sounded and the public streamed past Jake and Jenny in the opposite direction as they were forced ever-upwards. They sprinted through a Norman chapel to emerge into a hall that glittered with axes and daggers; a curator stood by an open cabinet.

"There's a fire alarm," said the curator. "You can't be here."

"Get out of my way," Jake shouted.

Footsteps were closing in, but the curator folded his arms, feet wide apart. "You. Out. Now."

Davis and Waits appeared in the hall behind them. From the display case Jake snatched the cutlass of Oliver Cromwell – there was a dent where a Royalist musket ball had struck the blade – and he ran the tip between the curator's throat and navel.

"I said, out of my way!"

The curator raised his hands and flattened himself against the wall. "Ok, ok, take it easy mate ..."

They rushed past, Jake still grasping the cutlass. Waits grabbed the sword of the Mad King George, inlaid with a golden coat of arms; Davis took an executioner's axe.

Jake and Jenny fled deeper into the Tower, through chambers which have forgotten more stories than most rooms possess. They arrived at a spiral staircase where sightseers were sent back to ground level by process of convection.

Four squaddies blocked the exit.

The soldiers had been loitering in the keep when the alarm sounded, and at the sight of Jake with his cutlass they gave a cry of glee at having something to do during a tedious deployment. So the hunted pair found themselves charging up instead of down, ascending a staircase closed to the public. Even as he fled Jake knew they must confront the hydra, for the staircase could only lead to one destination. And suddenly they were staggering onto the roof of the White Tower, the sensation of space overwhelming.

"What now?" panted Jenny.

"This," said Jake, fumbling in his pocket for a lighter.

Before he could ignite the papyri two figures emerged from the keep.

90

Davis closed on Jenny at once, swinging his axe through a figure of eight. The iron blade emitted a thrumming noise as it cleaved the air and she retreated, raising her hands.

"Put it down," she pleaded. "I can't fight you."

Davis continued to advance, grinning like a bully; the axe-head was a blur and Jenny found herself pinned against the battlements. She shrank against the masonry, but there was nowhere to go except down. The blade hummed closer, preparing to bite into her neck, severing her spinal column, and Jenny flinched and screwed up her eyes ...

The humming stopped. Strong hands grabbed Jenny by the wrists, spinning her around, forcing her into a prone position. A knee pressed down on her neck, making her prisoner. So she had a sideways view as Jake Wolsey and Charlie Waits locked horns at last.

Waits moved with grace when armed, swishing the blade before him, languid and playful. The weapon seemed to have unleashed his inner ballerina; he was light on his feet and he advanced side on. Jake knew there was only one way to survive this: he had to kill Waits and then Davis, one after the other. He jettisoned the papyri and faced his foe, waggling the sword.

In a few seconds I'm going to be actually fighting this guy.

Jake swung at Waits then – a lover's blow, crude and lunging. The spy parried the swipe and laughed, as though Jake had revealed himself a trifle *gauche* at the club bridge night. He'd used no strength whatsoever to render the blow impotent; it was all in the technique.

He's only a trained fencer.

The realization crashed over Jake like fractured ice.

Must have learned it at Eton or somewhere.

Now Waits assumed the classic fencer's stance: side on, knees bent, fist behind back. His blade was extended and slightly lowered and he advanced on Jake with a series of half-skips, like a bouncing crab.

"Huzzah!"

The blade fizzed out of nowhere, knocking Jake's own sword aside, jarring his wrist.

"Huzzah!" cried Waits again, sword shivering forward once more. The journalist's defence was blown open with a clang.

"Huzzah!" An elegant swipe this time, placed on Jake's shoulder.

The flexibility of the blade introduced an element of whiplash to the strike and it spun Jake around. The cut was a half-inch deep, clean as a surgeon's incision. The journalist felt a wave of panic. *I'm fighting for my life here.*

Tourists gathered in the courtyard below – the fire alarm must have been a ploy to move them outside so they could admire the performance theatre. But Jake wasn't conscious of the audience. The blade grew heavier by the second and already he had a dead arm. Waits could have run him through with ease, but he was playing to the crowd. The spymaster's swings had built to a rhythm, a grand slam tennis player with an opponent on the ropes. Each stroke was met with an 'ooh' and an 'aah' from the crowd and Jake's blade bounced from left to right. He gripped the sword two-handed now – he no longer had the strength to wield it with one arm. The smile fell from Waits's face, as though the stance outraged his sense of fair play, and he flicked out with the sword of King George III.

"Huzzah!"

The blades met in a shower of sparks and Jake found he was holding the sword one-handed again.

"Huzzah!"

Another clash, and Jake stumbled backward, bumped against stone. Below them the crowd roared, sensing blood.

"Huzzah!"

Waits's sword nuzzled Jake's, as if docking with it; then in a twirling motion the royal blade seemed to wrap itself around that of Oliver Cromwell, causing it to turn with force. Jake was forced to let go: his sabre sang through the air before crashing onto the battlements. The applause from below was spontaneous and prolonged.

91

The spymaster's forehead glistened with perspiration and he blew a chestnut-brown forelock from his glasses: the executive letting loose on the squash court.

"My dear boy, you've really given me the run-around these last few weeks," said Waits. "Not bad for an amateur, I must admit."

Jake sank to the floor. "Why are you doing this, Charlie?" he panted, leaning on his thighs. "How many will you kill to get at it? Is this being a patriot? Is this the British way?"

"Why?" Waits cried to Davis. "He asks us, *why*?"

One of Waits's hands was in the pocket of his chinos and with the other he raised his blade until the tip brushed the hollow of Jake's throat.

"Before I put out your life," he said – Davis looked on, transfixed at the prospect of bloodletting – "let me give you a lesson in geopolitics. Nations never stand still. They rise or they fall. It is an inalienable fact of history. Now, what do you think is happening in the world today? What is the broad historical theme of the age we live in?"

Jake didn't reply.

"I submit that it is this," said Waits. "The end of the

ascendancy of the West. The transfer of power to the East. Oh, it's a scary time to be a westerner. We face the very real prospect that the world will be run by the Orient in three decades' time. Of course, that may turn out for the good. But it may not. The Chinese are a cruel race, as anyone familiar with the East will tell you. And I rather fancy that once in the driving seat our Oriental cousins will not be as magnanimous with wealth and debt as the West has been. It's a great unknown, Jake, and a world run by the Orient is not a world I want my daughters to grow up in. Thus, we must defend our position." He smiled, revealing pointed incisors. "And sometimes that means defending ourselves *very* aggressively."

"By murdering everyone in our way?" said Jake. "That doesn't sound much like the West I know."

"Oh, you are a silly sausage," said Waits. "Do you think the West is an omelette made without breaking the occasional egg? Do you think *Rome* was built without brute force and repression?" He laughed. "Ask Carthage about that one, ask Corinth! Ask any of the other cities our predecessors razed to the ground so Western society might triumph over the barbarous East."

Waits was too engrossed in his theme to notice the slight figure who had emerged onto the roof, stealing toward the discarded papyri. And Davis only had eyes for the blade which hovered at Jake's windpipe.

"*Rome*," Waits said again, rolling the R with great reverence. "Western Civilization mark one, if you will. Ask yourself this, Jake. What happened when Constantine brought about the empire's downfall. Was it for the good? Or for the bad?"

Jake bowed his head.

"I think we both know the answer," said Waits. "Why, it was *bad*, Jake, very bad indeed, a scarcely imaginable cataclysm. It ushered in nothing less than a new Dark Age. Great works of science and literature were lost for all time. We find skeletons an inch shorter due to malnutrition. Trade routes that had lasted two thousand years fell out of use. In some places money was abandoned for barter and exchange. And art? It regressed from naturalism to distended heads and pointy feet." Waits shook his head. "Why, we even forgot the world was round."

He gestured to the skyline of London with a sweep of blade. "Look around you. The West, mark two. This is what's at stake, boy. We *are* Rome. China *is* the rising Persian Empire. Russia awakes again, and the Arab Spring has left a billion Muslims in a state of ferment. And lots of them are spoiling for a fight with us. Goths and Vandals, barbarians at the gates. Don't you see it? History doesn't repeat itself, as Mark Twain put it. But it does rhyme."

Unwavering fanaticism was in Waits's eyes. "This is a war of civilizations, Wolsey, it always has been. Europe's a busted flush. So we have a choice. Do we play Augustus? Do we breathe another five hundred years into our civilization? Or do we repeat the mistake of Constantine and condemn ourselves to oblivion? Now consider what would happen if the power to predict the future fell into the hands of our enemies. I confess that I tremble at the prospect."

When the journalist spoke it was with the calmness of someone who knows he is about to die and is resolved to say his piece.

"Britain's enemies have had this power before, Charlie," he began. "Or have you forgotten how this science came to your attention in the first place? Hitler, Himmler, Goebbels and Heydrich – they are your predecessors. And mark my words, corpse after broken corpse, you people have got a long way to go to catch up with the Nazis. So consider instead the blood on the hands of the last men to wield this power as I put your question back to you. Is it for the good? Or for the bad?"

Waits had no answer and it enraged him. "You are a political *child*," he spat. "Now, enough of this nonsense."

He drew back the sword, ready for the capital stroke.

A new voice interrupted him, a female voice. "Hello, chuck."

Waits wheeled around to see Florence Chung. The priestess had been inside the armoury when the alarm sounded, but rather than rushing for the exit she had hidden. Now the *Disciplina Etrusca* was clasped before her like an instruction manual and her cheeks were flushed with triumph.

Waits raised his blade. "You."

Florence sniggered. "Do you really think a sliver of steel is any match for a fully blown *fulguriator*? A worthy opponent of the legacy of Tages and Rome? Really, Charles, I expected more. Let's do this the old fashioned way. If you think you can handle me."

"Very well. So be it."

Waits dropped his sword and raised one arm to the sky, murmuring and closing his eyes.

His hand was trembling.

Florence placed on her head a scarlet cap that finished in a tube pointing skyward, as if funnelling the contents of her brain toward the clouds. Jake had seen one of these in Britton's office; at the time he had laughed. But there was nothing funny about it now. There was nothing to laugh about as Florence also began murmuring, one hand raised in a rival supplication. The voices rose in intensity, chanting that tongue which bore no resemblance to any Indo-European language. Immediately the wind picked up, stirring this way and that, undecided which way to blow.

Jake noticed how cloudy it had become.

The sky was darkening, casting the world into half-light. Waits's voice had become shrill, and to Jake's dismay he realized he could understand snatches of what the spymaster was saying.

And then everything seemed to *slow down.*

*

The edge of Jake's vision was deteriorating like a badly-tuned television picture. He viewed the world in three colours: black, white and purple. His neck was stiff and his head felt leaden. With an effort he turned to face Waits, whose face folded and flapped like a sail; his mouth was a jet-black hole. Florence stood with one arm raised: the pose of a rock star after a thunderous last chord. Her eyeballs flickered with violet and Jake could see right through to the capillaries inside her head, where lights danced. The leaves on the roof spiralled in dust devils and clouds were sucked towards the duelling *fulguriators*, as if there was a vacuum over the Tower.

He heard the first stirring of thunder.

The chanting turned manic, the beat of the drum, the beat that had begun so very long ago. Now a twinkle of purple-blue danced in Waits's eyes too, as if a plug was short-circuiting in his frontal lobes. The cloud had gathered itself into two knots, one above Waits, one above Florence, the inverse peaks of the network's wrath.

And then everything slowed down *even more.*

92

A seagull was frozen in mid-air, wings pushing downward like the hour hand of a clock, the space around them a solid. Florence's face was halfway through saying something; her lips were thrust left as if she'd been slapped by an invisible hand and her eyelids were shut, though violet seared through them.

The clouds glowed ice-blue, electricity seeping into the twin protrusions. Jake remembered enough of his GCSE science to know what was happening. The clouds were becoming loaded with negative charges from the ionosphere, which were being pushed to the base of the cloud. When the electric potential hit ten thousand volts per square centimetre, ionization of the air would occur. Then the step leaders would trace their way from sky to earth, fingers of plasma seeking the quickest way down.

He could see it happening.

A purplish tendril snaked towards Waits; Jake knew a step leader took a few thousands of a second to reach the ground, and now he understood why the seagull was frozen in mid-beat. A second step leader began to burn its path towards Florence, superheated ions clearing a way for the negative charge to follow in a bolt of lightning. And here were the positive streamers. A lambent flame tapered from Waits's head as positive ions strained upward, trying to make a connection; another sprouted from the funnel of Florence's cap.

It was a race.

But the streamer flapping from the head of Charlie Waits was longer, already it was a metre high, and the step leader reaching for it was way ahead of Florence's. Waits remained frozen; Jake wondered if knew what was about to happen.

Step leader and positive streamer connected.

The spell was broken. The air exploded. A billion volts of electricity surged through Waits's body, which became hotter than the surface of the sun. In the resulting detonation his head, arms and most of his upper torso vanished. What remained – two blackened legs, a hunk of cauterized abdomen – wobbled on the spot and capsized. His chinos puffed into flame. Jenny and Davis were slammed into the west battlement by the shockwave and Jake was cast in the other direction, winding himself. Displaced air bypassed Florence like a razor in a wind tunnel; the seagull flew away.

The priestess glanced around the rooftop, seeking another victim, and her gaze settled on Davis.

"You," she said, in a voice that sounded metallic and distorted. "I've got a bone to pick with you."

Davis calculated the odds and threw himself off the battlements; the splintering of bone when he landed carried up to the rooftop.

"Suit yourself," said Florence, turning to face Jake.

Her eyes were matt red.

"You did this to me, Jake," she said with that same awful slowness. "Thank you."

He was too petrified to speak.

"Did you have a thing for me once, Jake? You can tell me."

Jake shook his head.

"Yes, yes you did. It's ok, plenty of men do. Poor Jake. Poor, unloved Jake."

She readjusted the cap, raising her arm once more, and Jake listened as for a final time Florence Chung invoked all the dark power of the void.

This time he understood every word.

The placation of *dii consentes*, the pitiless advisers of Tin. The seduction of *dii novensiles*, casters of lightning. The appeasement of *dii superiores,* the most potent of all the numinous powers that surrounded the All-Seeing Eye. And then the most dread incantation of them all: the appeal to Tin himself.

The sky darkened. The cloud above Jake had become an anvil, gathering itself up, ready to smash him. Time ground to a halt. The sense of gravity was overwhelming and the weight of atmosphere crushed the air from his lungs.

It began at the tip of his nose. A purple flame flickering upward like a glow-worm, wiggling out of his body. And here came the step leader, beautiful and bizarre. Negative and positive, yin and yang, just as Dr Nesta had hypothesized. Jake's world had turned the colour of a photographic negative; he could make out the silhouette of Florence, but it was like staring through peaty water. The fingers of plasma strained to touch a few feet above him and Jake knew this was the ever-anointed date of his end. Foretold by thunder, like all things.

A flicker of movement.

A swipe in the gloom.

A dazzling shock of blonde.

And suddenly it was over.

93

Jake came round to see the priestess's head topple off her shoulders and her body keel over backwards. Behind the decapitated *fulguriator* stood Jenny, blade clasped horizontally in the manner of a samurai. The severed appendage rolled once, twice, three times, coming to a rest at Jake's feet. Florence's left eyelid twitched, steam rising from her corneas. The pupils of those blood-red eyeballs contracted to pinheads.

Sightless.

Anne Boleyn, Catherine Howard, Lady Jane Grey; Florence Chung. The last person to be decapitated at the Tower, as Hess was its last prisoner. For the second time the sword of Oliver Cromwell had put an end to they who would rule absolutely.

History doesn't repeat itself, but it does rhyme.

The clouds fizzled with unspent energy, lightning shimmering along their undersides, and again Jake was reminded of a cerebral mass: angry but impotent, thoughts seething through it.

Jenny dropped the blade and gasped. Then she fell to her knees, staring at Florence's head.

"I killed her," she said. "I killed someone."

Jake placed a hand on Jenny's shoulder. "You killed it," he said. "She had become an it."

They became aware of two things: first, the smell of burning oak, and second, the crowd. In an attempt to seal in the intruders Sir Richard had ordered the outer gates closed. But the storm was unlike anything the tourists had seen before and it had reduced them to panic. Now smoke rose from the roof, the beams ignited by the lightning; the general had no choice but to open the gates so the crowd to escape. They watched Evelyn Parr join the throng.

"Quickly," said Jake, gathering up the *Disciplina Etrusca*. "We've got a window of opportunity to get out of here."

The soldiers were taken up with the evacuation and they fled the White Tower unimpeded. As Jake joined the stampede he glanced at the keep and felt a stab of sorrow. A building that was evil and beautiful, English and French, a repository of history itself; it was being consumed. He took Jenny by the arm and steered her through the outer walls without looking back.

*

The City of London was a ghost town on a Saturday, its glass anthills dormant. The noise of sirens carried from Tower Hill as they ran and a helicopter skimmed overhead. They stopped underneath the Gherkin – a statement of power to rival Vespasian's Colosseum – and Jake placed the bundle of papyri on the ground.

"Right," he said, sparking his lighter. "Here goes."

"Wait."

Jake extinguished the flame. "What is it?"

"Before you destroy it ... there's something I need to do. One thing."

"What the hell are you talking about?"

"Whatever killed Mum. I need to know if I'm a carrier."

She picked up the bundle and flicked through the pages from beginning to end.

"You're not serious," he said.

"Is it a laughing matter?"

He sparked the lighter and took the papyri from her. "No way. It burns."

"Why not?" she said. "What harm would it do to find out this one thing? You don't know what it's like, living under a death sentence."

The flame neared the papyri, but Jenny grasped him by wrist, pulling it back.

"Wait," she hissed. "Let's think about this. With this document we could do whatever we wanted. We could clean out Monte Carlo, go into politics. We could be rich – Jesus, Jake, we could be powerful beyond our wildest dreams."

For an insane moment he considered it. But then he recalled the beat of the drum, the tramp of boots, the blood-red gaze of the lightning priestess at her most terrible.

She was proposing a deal with the devil.

"Jenny ..." He stared at her, willing her back. "Let it go, Jenny."

She blinked, and she was her old self again. She wept for a second time then, kneeling on the pavement and burying her face in her elbow.

"I almost gave in," she whispered.

"But you didn't give in."

A breeze turned the pages of the manuscript, each of them stamped with a swastika.

"Burn it," she said.

The flame danced in Jake's hands before leaping to the bundle.

Energy.

Almost two thousand years ago it had fallen to earth in sunlight to be sucked up by the papyrus plants of the Nile Delta and converted to matter. Then it had been harvested, beaten wafer-thin, written upon and stored. For centuries it had lain underground, waiting to be disturbed. Waiting to end the lives of sixty million people. Now that energy was released at last in a flare of heat and light. Flame raced inward from all sides, like the Red Army encircling Hitler's bunker.

The last scrap to be destroyed carried a name: *TAGES.*

And then it was gone.

*

Overhead the cloud had broken up to reveal a chink of blue.

"What now?" said Jenny.

"Now?" repeated Jake, as he crushed the ashes into dust. "Now we have a choice. We can publish everything we have. We can drag down Evelyn Parr and half of MI6. We can rewrite history. Christ, I might become the most famous journalist of all time. Watergate is a minor traffic accident by comparison."

"Or?"

"Or we flee. We flee from Evelyn Parr and whoever she recruits. We go abroad and we never breathe another word of this to anyone who lives. We destroy what evidence we've gathered so Niall Heston's got nothing to back up his story and the paper can't run it."

"Why would we do that?"

"To stop word of this science spreading to every government and treasure hunter and would-be despot in the world. The genie goes back in the bottle."

"Where would we go?"

"I don't know," Jake admitted.

"What would we do?"

"I don't know that either. But ..."

His heart was pounding.

She looked up at him. "But what, Jake?"

Her eyes were clear.

"But ..."

This was it. This was what it all came down to. Still his heartbeat raced, yet when he spoke it was with certainty.

"But we'd have each other."

The air around them was charged. Jake held out his hand; his fingers did not tremble. She offered hers in return, the positive streamer to his step leader. There was the briefest hesitation. Then their fingers touched, and a spark seemed to dart between them – a spark that was wholesome and pure.

Jenny laughed. "Fate," she said. "Do you believe in it, Jake?"

He looked at the ashes of the Book of Thunder. The wind was spreading them across the concourse with its invisible fingers, pushing them into the cracks of the pavement; taking them up into the air. And he couldn't help wondering if what they had found together was the point in it all.

Epilogue

What is love? It is this: being so connected to someone you cannot bear to be apart from them, even for a moment. It is the sensation of possessing a bond to another person, and if you wander far from your beloved that bond is stretched and cries out in pain. But it never snaps, no matter how far you might travel. It is magical. And when you have it, that bond is the strongest power on earth.

Jake felt the might of it as he looked at Jenny sleeping in the aeroplane seat. He studied her perfect ear, the sprig of sunlight-coloured hair that erupted above it. He kissed her cheek, drawing in the aroma.

When one short hour, sees happiness from utter desolation grow.

The Boeing 737 was over Turkmenistan and in a few hours they would land in Bangkok. What then? He had absolutely no idea. But it was exciting – not knowing what path they would take, where their futures lay. Jake was happy.

He couldn't sleep, so he decided to have another drink. But when the hostess poured him a glass of red wine Jake drew his hand away, staring at the blood-red liquid in its transparent cup. He didn't want it, but he did want it. His contentment was thrown into disarray.

It was the stillness of the alcohol that was the irony. While Jake's soul raged the wine was motionless, the membrane of its surface perfectly defined.

Waiting.

Such is a game she plays, and so she tests her strength.

He hated it then, just as he hated Tages and all the power of the void. But he also realized he had a choice. To drink, or not to drink? Whether or not the decision was preordained, it was his to make.

"I've changed my mind," he said. "I'll have a soft drink. And a newspaper, if you've got one."

"Certainly, sir." She handed him a tomato juice. "Will the *Telegraph* do?"

Jake unfolded the broadsheet, careful not to disturb Jenny with its inky sails. The main article on page five caught his eye: an important portrait of Napoleon had just gone under the hammer at Sotheby's, *The Peace of Amiens* by Devosge. The artist had portrayed the French Empire as a new Rome and the little corporal was depicted as Augustus. Jake admired the work as the cup went to his lips.

He let go.

The vessel pirouetted through the air, as another drink had done four weeks previously in a pub in King's Cross. Napoleon stood before a stormy sky. In his hand was a scroll, and on that scroll were characters.

Etruscan characters.

Another copy was out there. History itself was a lie.

Dawn was breaking over central Asia, and at that altitude Jake could see how the world was truly a disc, rotating beneath the void. As he stared at the featureless landmass he fancied he heard laughter – it was grating, guttural, slightly amused. On the horizon storm-clouds were gathering.

Timeline of Etruscan and Roman History

Ninth century BC: The Etruscan civilization rises on the Italian peninsula.

Eighth century BC: Life and death of Tages, prophet of the Etruscan religion.

753 BC: The small town of Rome is founded, ruled at first by Etruscan kings.

600 BC: Etruscan civilization reaches the height of its power. It is based on independent city-states and gains its wealth through trade and iron ore.

509 BC: The Roman Republic is founded after a dynasty of Etruscan kings is overthrown by Rome's inhabitants.

390 BC: Rome is destroyed by Gauls – the last time it will be sacked for nine centuries.

343 BC: Rome's conquest of Italy begins with defeat of local tribes.

265 BC: The final defeat of the Etruscan city-states by the Roman Republic. The whole Italian peninsula is now under Roman control.

264–146 BC: The Punic Wars, in which Rome defeats the rival empire of Carthage – despite Carthaginian general Hannibal crossing the Alps into Italy with his elephants. The defeat of Hannibal coincides with an increase in pagan piety among Romans. Rome starts to build its Mediterranean empire, invading Spain, Sicily, Sardinia and North Africa.

146–101 BC: Rome continues to expand across the Mediterranean. By the end of the period it also controls Greece, Turkey and Romania.

91 BC: A century of unrest begins, with seven civil wars including Spartacus's slave revolt. This coincides with

widespread neglect of pagan religion in parts of Roman society. Palestine, Syria and Egypt fall under Roman control.

44 BC: Julius Caesar assassinated after ignoring an Etruscan soothsayer's warning.

31 BC: Caesar's nephew Octavian defeats Mark Antony and Cleopatra to become ruler of Rome. Shortly afterwards Octavian is renamed Augustus, the first emperor. The Roman Republic comes to an end and democracy is abandoned. Augustus presides over a great increase in pagan piety.

50 AD: By now Etruscan is no longer spoken in Roman society, Etruscan writing has vanished, and Etruscan culture has ceased to exist.

70 AD: Construction of the Colosseum begins under the Emperor Vespasian, using treasure from the sack of Jerusalem.

98–161 AD: The period of 'High Empire'. Under the emperors Trajan and Hadrian, Rome reaches its maximum size, the zenith of its power and the height of its cultural achievement.

Second century AD: Christianity spreads throughout the Roman Empire.

235–284 AD: The Third-Century Crisis, a chaotic period of civil war, plague, hyperinflation and barbarian invasions. The empire briefly splits into three independent states. The Emperor Valerian is captured and killed by the Persians; the Emperor Carus is killed by lightning.

284 AD: Emperor Diocletian takes power and restores order and prosperity to the reunified empire. His reign is marked by an increase in pagan fervour.

312 AD: Following a battlefield vision, the Emperor Constantine converts to Christianity, which becomes the dominant religion of the empire. He moves the capital to Constantinople (modern-day Istanbul).

337 AD: The scholar Eusebius begins writing *Life of Constantine*, following the emperor's death.

376–476 AD: Decline and fall of the Roman Empire.

395: The rise of the Byzantine Empire begins in modern-day Turkey, a Christian society and the successor to Roman civilization.

Historical Note and Acknowledgments

All of the history cited in the novel is real. So too are the quotes, although I have edited some without using ellipses for reasons of brevity, pace and impact. I used an 1845 translation of *Life of Constantine* published by Samuel Bagster and Sons of London and a more recent translation by Averil Cameron and Stuart G. Hall. Chapter 19 quotes an 1880 biography of Eusebius published by Little, Brown. Ian Kershaw's *Hitler 1936-1945: Nemesis* was published by Allen Lane. The quote opening the book is from *The Consolation of Philosophy*, translated by V.E. Watts, published by Penguin in 1999. The Brontoscopic Calendar exists; a grave some speculate may be that of Tages really was discovered in 1982. Good luck finding it, though. The Dicks Report also exists, and excerpts from Henry Dicks's clinical diary (held by the Wellcome Trust) are used with the permission of the Dicks family, to whom I am very grateful. The original journal is reproduced accurately up to Hess's suicide attempt; the 'missing pages' and their contents are, of course, my invention. The Dicks family have also asked me to make clear that Henry Dicks saw Hess as a patient; his role in the case was a medical one and was not, as far as we know, directed or influenced by the intelligence agencies. After that I'm afraid it is fiction. There is not really an Etruscan inscription on the ceiling of the Monastery of Debre Damo, nor is there one in the Istanbul cistern. *The Peace of Amiens* by Devosge is as described, *sans* the Etruscan characters on his scroll. Sadly, to the best of my knowledge it is not actually possible to predict the future by studying bolts of lightning.

I am hugely indebted to the Etruscan historian Jean MacIntosh Turfa – not only for her help and support throughout the project, but also for her amazing work on the Brontoscopic

Calendar, which sparked the idea for the tale. She even gave me the title of the novel! Dr Ronald Pearson kindly allowed me to draw heavily on his own theories and explanations for my depiction of the scientific reality behind 'the network', many of which I use verbatim. I am a history geek, not a scientist, and I couldn't have done it without him. Needless to say, any mistakes are my own. I owe another huge debt of gratitude to my agent, Robin Wade, and my editor, Andrew Lockett. Big thanks to all my friends and family who helped with proofing and criticism along the way, especially Bec. And of course to my friends and brothers who ventured into the badlands of Ethiopia with me. The same intrepid/foolhardy gang has since taken part in expeditions to Sierra Leone, Burundi and the Congo to research the sequel and a third title, and they were not uneventful.